Summer Rain

By Jamie Jo Skeen

To Rachel – Who encouraged me to finally make this dream a
reality

Contents

Prologue

She was relieved the summer rain was a light drizzle. Ever since hydroplaning during her first pregnancy on the I-15, Hannah had been nervous driving at high speeds when there was water on the roadway. She had the wipers set to intermittent, and that was enough to keep her vision clear. The radio played in the background, and she sang along occasionally, but mostly, she was lost in her own thoughts.

Her mind drifted to the summer of 1991. She and her best friends were turning twenty and had decided to celebrate with a two-week road trip. They were on the cusp of their adult lives, and naïve enough to think everything would turn out roses. She took a deep breath, feeling the familiar bitterness start to constrict her chest. Wishes had come true for one of them, and close for the others. Her? Not so much.

She flashed back to their last night in Portland, hiking into Forest Park at night to bury their time capsule. They had spent the morning at Pioneer Place scouring stores for something they thought best represented them. That afternoon, they wrote out their hopes and dreams for their future to read to each other by flashlight before tucking them away in a box they planned to return to twenty years later.

Rain like this one had started ten minutes into their hike. Hannah scoffed, thinking of each young and hopeful face, caught in the glaring beams of light, casting a wish into the night each of them sincerely thought would come true. What fools they had been! They had written out their dreams of Happily Ever After as though they stood a chance. Instead, life had knocked the shit out of them. Some more than others.

Almost thirty years had come and gone. For one reason or another, they hadn't made the trek back to the Pacific

Northwest as promised. Now, it was the month before their forty-seventh birthdays, and for some reason, her friends had been able to get them to commit to searching out the long-buried time capsule. Hannah still couldn't believe she'd agreed to it. She wasn't in a good place and reading her ridiculous rainbow and unicorn rantings from thirty years ago wasn't going to help. She took a swig of her coffee, now cold, and looked at the time on her dashboard. Twenty more miles or so, and she would be reunited with the women she had loved, hated, supported, and resented over the last thirty years.

She turned the music up, singing along to distract herself from her thoughts. She knew she was in a dark place the last few months and frankly got on her own nerves with her self-pitying moroseness. She crossed the Broadway Bridge, spotting the Waterfront Pearl condos on the west side of the Willamette River.

As she turned into the parking lot off of Naito Drive, she rolled her shoulders and popped her neck. Maybe this could be a new beginning. Maybe being reunited with her friends and going through this damn time capsule would be the jumpstart she needed to get her life back on track. Maybe it wasn't too late for her to have Happily Ever After.

"Who the hell are you kidding, Han. Your shot is over," she said to herself.

Part One

July 13, 1991

"Do you see her yet?" Sally Johnson lifted her hands to block the morning sun from her eyes. The park was full of spectators waiting to watch as the runners finished the half marathon. Some had already come across the finish line, and if Hannah ran as fast as she usually did, she would be crossing the finish line any moment. Sally stood on tiptoes, her light brown ponytail swaying as she hopped up and down to try to see over the tall man who had just walked in front of her.

Jentry Davenport gave a lazy smile from beneath her oversized dark sunglasses. As usual, Jentry was dressed in black and grey, her long, shiny black hair falling in perfect waves down her back. "You feeling anxious to get going with our adventure, Sal? Worried Hannah is going to take too long?" Jentry said, looking at Sally sideways.

"Oh, Jentry. You know that's not it. I just want Hannah to get here by her goal time. She's only got two and a half more minutes." Sally smiled but didn't take her eyes off the canyon. Quiet and shy beyond measure when they first met, it had taken Sally some time to get used to Jentry's droll sense of humor and sarcasm. She was a little afraid of Jentry at first, and tried to steer clear of her, until Hannah had assured her Jentry's flippant attitude was really a façade to hide how insecure and vulnerable she really felt. Knowing that helped Sally to look past the brashness and see the heart inside of Jentry. Sally understood what it meant to feel insecure and out of place. Once she could relate to her on that level, she extended the hand of friendship. They soon realized, despite completely different upbringings, the two girls had more in common than they first thought. They loved each other like sisters now.

"I see her. She's right behind the guy in the green shirt," Paige McLean called to Sally and Jentry as she fumbled for her camera. Paige was the resident photographer, and seldom went anywhere without her trusted Nikon in tow. "Go, Hannah! You've got this!" Paige shouted at her cousin as she furiously clicked away with the camera.

Hannah was quickly approaching the finish line and shot a tired grin at her cheering section as she passed. Sally glanced at the large digital clock next to the finish line and saw Hannah was going to beat her goal time by twenty seconds. "You've done it, Han!!" she screamed, jumping up and down. She shook her head as Hannah broke into a sprint, passing two people in the final stretch.

Sally was still amazed at Hannah's endless amount of energy. Paige had nicknamed her the Energizer Bunny in fourth grade because she was always on the go, and the other girls had picked up on the name, frequently calling her EB when they were wiped out for the day and Hannah still had energy reserves.

On the sidelines, Jentry, Paige, and Sally exploded in cheers, catcalls, and clapping as Hannah crossed the finish line. They snaked their way through the crowd until they spotted Hannah near the water table. She flashed them a dimpled smile before taking a big bite of apple. Her dark blonde braids were plastered to her head with sweat, and her face was red and flushed. Sally had learned the look was fairly typical for Hannah, who was often chasing one adventure or another.

"You did it, Hannah! You beat your goal! I'm so proud of you!" Sally threw her arms around her friend.

"Sally, you're going to need another shower now. Hannah's a sweaty mess. Sorry, Love," Jentry said to Hannah. "You'll understand if I don't hug you right this second?"

"Aww, c'mon Jen. You know how much I love when you go all PDA on me." Hannah winked at Sally as she jokingly slapped Jentry on the butt.

"Okay, girls, come stand over by the race banner for a picture. Hannah, get in the middle." Paige directed the girls away from the congestion at the drink table and over to the entrance to Riverview Park. They obediently followed, knowing you didn't put up a fight when Paige had her camera out.

Sally was uncomfortable with all the photos Paige wanted to take in the beginning. With her quiet personality and her slightly larger dress size, Sally felt out of place compared to her roommates when they first met. She was reminded of the song from Sesame Street, 'One of these things doesn't belong here, one of these things isn't the same.' One look at Paige, with her platinum blonde hair and big cornflower blue eyes, Sally had thought she should be in front of a camera instead of behind one all the time. At 5'7", Jentry seemed to tower over Sally's 5'2" frame. Sally also couldn't help comparing her thin, fine, mouse-brown hair to Hannah's thick, naturally curly dark blonde mane. She coveted hair that could look that good first thing in the morning.

While Paige and Hannah had athletic builds, Jentry looked like a 1940s movie star: a stunning olive complexion from her mother's Brazilian heritage, shiny dark hair that hung to her waist, and an hourglass figure Sally noticed boys staring at quite frequently. Jentry's wardrobe came from stores and designers Sally had never heard of, while hers consisted mainly of denim and flannel.

She had been pleasantly surprised at how friendly and welcoming Hannah and Paige had been. She had expected girls who looked like them to not want to be seen with plain-looking girls like her. She soon realized her insecurities could cause her to judge people too quickly. Her friendship with these three had taught her never to judge a book by its cover.

Growing up on a goat farm and spending her time helping her mother make goat milk soaps, lotions, and lip balms hadn't left Sally a lot of time to spend on haircare routines and fashion. She dreamed of the day someone would see past her shy demeanor, her size fourteen jeans, and her Idaho farm girl upbringing. She hoped to find someone who would view her strong testimony, many talents, and kind character as just the right combination for an eternal wife.

"Okay, say cheese, Chicas," Paige instructed, climbing on a boulder to get the perfect angle.

"Cheese Chicas!" the girls said, smiling at Paige.

"Let me get one with you now," Sally offered. Paige willingly handed the camera over to her and threw one arm around her cousin's shoulder and the other around Jentry's waist. After a few more shots, the girls headed for Jentry's silver Jetta.

"Okay, Loves," Jentry said as she turned the key in the ignition, "Let's get Hannah hosed off so we can get this show on the road."

***

While Hannah hopped in a quick shower, Jentry supervised the loading up of the Limbrey's red and grey Suburban, making sure suitcases, camping gear, and coolers were all accounted for. She had been planning this trip for over a month and wanted to make sure it went off without a hitch. They had realized luggage for two weeks, along with camping supplies, was never going to fit into Jentry's Jetta. Hannah had talked her parents into loaning them their old Suburban for the trip.

Jentry had first met Hannah, Paige, and Sally almost two years ago, in August of 1989, when she first arrived at Deseret Towers to start her freshman year at Brigham Young University. Their applications for dorm rooms had been turned in late, so rather than ending up in a two-person room, they had been put in the Commons Room, a windowless space in the center of the floor with four murphy beds, desks, and closets.

7

Jentry felt like an outsider from the beginning. Cousins Hannah and Paige had grown up as next-door neighbors and were best friends. Although neither of them had met Sally before that first day, she was brought up in the same culture and spoke a common language of Mormon slang and terminology that Jentry, as a new convert to the church, was only starting to learn.

On their first night in the dorms Paige, ever the diplomat, suggested some questions to put everyone at ease.

"So first, when is everyone's birthday? Mine is July first," Paige had started.

"And I was born a few days after Paige in the same hospital. July fourth. It's literally the worst birthday. No one cares. I got so gipped," Hannah laughed.

"That's crazy you both have July birthdays," Sally said, still a little timidly. "I'm also a July baby, but I'm at the other end of the month. July thirtieth."

The group turned to Jentry. "What are the odds? July eighteenth."

"What are the odds indeed?" Paige questioned. "Hmm. Okay. Birth order. What number are you, and how many siblings? I'm the oldest in my family. I have a younger brother, Lane, and spoiled twin sisters, Blake & Blythe."

"What interesting names. Mine is so plain Jane," Sally said, then started laughing. "Actually, that's my middle name. Sally Jane. I have four older brothers. Then, mom had one more girl and boy. Carrie and I are pretty outnumbered."

"I'm the one and only in my family," Jentry offered. "I wish I could say it was because they stopped at perfection, but it was really because my mother didn't care much for mothering."

Sally looked at Jentry aghast. "Oh, Jentry, I'm sure that's not true," she said, consolingly patting her leg.

Jentry, uncomfortable with the gesture, shrugged. "If you ever meet Fernanda, it will be evident within minutes."

"Well, I have more of a middle-sized family," said Hannah. "I have my amazing older brother, Sam, who recently left on a mission to the super exotic, world-renowned state of Montana, and a younger sister, Esther, who is probably redecorating our bedroom with posters of Kirk Cameron as we speak."

The girls laughed and segued into a brief debate on television and movie heartthrobs before Paige changed the subject back.

"Hey! Wait! I just realized something. Not only do we all have July birthdays, but we're also the first girls born into our families."

Jentry relaxed, thinking maybe she would have more in common with these girls than she originally thought.

Over the next few months, she learned the similarities came in twos or threes. Though Jentry and Sally had completely different upbringings and temperaments, they both shared a love of reading and enjoyed the classic works of writers like Bronte and Austin, as well as Mary Higgins Clark mysteries.

Hannah, Paige, and Sally enjoyed the outdoors and loved being active. Jentry also liked being out in the sun, as long as it meant she could lounge in her swimsuit with a diet coke and book in hand. She had explored some of the trails near her house growing up, but never at a pace that would break a sweat.

Sally was raised on country music and had a collection of cassettes by artists Jentry had never heard of. The other girls were more into pop and metal. When it came to movies, Hannah and Jentry loved the ones which elicited goosebumps and screams, while Paige and Sally were suckers for romantic comedies.

Before long, the four girls were inseparable, with the guys in their student ward nicknaming them 'The Companions' because you never saw one without one of the others. They had to explain to Jentry the term was a missionary joke, as missionaries for the Mormon church went out in twos and referred to themselves as companions. The girls played along and even made themselves black nametags they would wear to church on Sunday.

The second semester, they were able to get regular dorm rooms, with cousins Hannah and Paige sharing room U-305 while Jentry and Sally shared U-320. Jentry talked her parents into purchasing a townhouse south of campus when they became sophomores. They kept the same roommates and used the third bedroom for crafts and homework.

They had shared so much over the last two years. They had been there for each other through first dates and first kisses. They had shared hugs of support over break-ups and make-ups. They'd shared notes from class, housework duties, and clothes. They had double, triple, and quadruple dated, and they'd spent Saturday nights with just the four of them snuggled under a blanket in front of a video and a bowl of popcorn. Though she had felt like an outsider in the beginning and had only known Hannah, Paige, and Sally for barely two years, Jentry was certain of one thing. They would be best friends forever.

"Alright, Loves, I think we have everything," Jentry said, pushing the cooler into the backseat once she saw Hannah come down the stairs, hair in French braids again.

"You still want to do this trip, Jen? I thought you liked your break from us last summer?" Hannah smiled at Jentry while hefting her duffle bag into the back of her parent's suburban.

Jentry rolled her eyes. "Yes, I loved being stuck all alone in Portland all summer while you and Paige were at home together, and only two hours from Sally."

"Poor Jentry," joked Hannah, "Stuck in a mansion all summer with her own maid, while the rest of us have to work to pay for our next semester."

"Well, this summer, I have my own place in Provo, and a job like you blue-collar girls do," Jentry joked back, grateful for their townhouse and her summer internship at the Springville Art Museum.

The summer between her freshman and sophomore year had been miserable for Jentry. Hannah and Paige were next-door neighbors back home in Providence, Utah, and Sally lived on a farm only two hours away from them in Rupert, Idaho. She felt so left out and lonely in Oregon. The friends she had once been close to in high school now seemed so foreign to her. Their life philosophy was still the eat, drink, and be merry lifestyle she had once embraced as well. But since joining the Mormon church and living a year among members at BYU, she felt a stark difference between her and her childhood friends.

She talked on the phone to Sally almost daily and got letters from Hannah and Paige at least once a week, but she still found the time away from them almost unbearable. She finally enrolled in two summer art classes at the Cascade Campus of Portland Community College to have something to do. This summer, she determined would be different.

Under the guise of a big twentieth birthday celebration, she had suggested the girls take a long road trip together. If she had her way, it would last all summer. But Sally was obligated to attend a few family reunions, as well as needed on the farm. Hannah and Paige needed to work in order to replenish their school funds. Plus, Paige had married her returned missionary, Evan Lindburg, in April. He was happy to let her have one last hurrah with her best friends but couldn't part with his bride for a whole summer.

Eventually, she got them to agree to a two-week road trip, which she would fund. She tried hard not to seem too eager, but she was sure they could see right through her.

While Jentry was the money behind the trip, Sally was the brains. She had taken polls on destinations, planned a gas and food budget, and assigned activities. After considering trips to never-before-visited locations, they had decided to spend time at each girl's favorite place to go on summer vacation when they were growing up. The semester ended in late April. Everyone worked for a few months before meeting back in Provo for Hannah's half-marathon before starting out on their road trip. Now, they gathered around the car, ready to start their adventure.

***

After a quick stop for gas and Junior Mints, they turned north on I-15 and headed for Bear Lake. Even though it wasn't quite noon, the July temperature was up to one hundred degrees. Hannah turned the dial all the way up on the air conditioning and put a mixed tape in the cassette player. She cranked the volume as the girls started singing along.

"Put it on Paige's song!" Sally said, reaching forward and grabbing the Junior Mints.

Paige laughed and forwarded the mixed tape to the third song. The girls started doing their car dance moves and singing along with Freddy Mercury to *Another One Bites the Dust*. It had been the standing joke at the beginning of their freshman year that this was Paige's theme song, in relation to the guys whose hearts she broke each week. Paige was beautiful. Not just cute, or pretty, but genuinely beautiful. She had been a beautiful baby and had even done some modeling for local department stores through high school.

In school, she was always popular with the boys, but so down to earth and kind that the girls wanted to be her friend as well. Outgoing and bright, it was no surprise to anyone when she was elected Student Body President and Homecoming Queen her senior year at Mountain Crest High School.

She hadn't been interested in dating seriously her freshman year and would entertain the girls with stories of the boys' advances she would put a stop to. All of that changed when Paige met returned missionary Evan Lindberg in October.

As the other girls sang along to Queen, Paige smiled, remembering their third date.

The morning had dawned with a clear blue sky over Provo, though some low grey clouds were hanging over the mountains across Utah Lake. Paige hadn't given them a second thought as she got ready for a hiking date with Evan. She had only known him a month, and this was to be their third date. Paige had dated a lot in high school and went on a few dates the first few months of college before meeting Evan, but no one had given her butterflies the way he did. She thought he was absolutely perfect. She loved his curly brown hair, and she felt she could stare into his toffee-brown eyes forever. Even though it was late October, he still had a nice tan from his last summer in Mesa, Arizona. Evan waited in the U-Hall lobby while Paige finished getting ready. Hannah had braided her hair while she quickly put on a little bit of makeup. She grabbed her Mountain Crest high school sweatshirt, laced up her hiking boots, and gave Hannah a hug before heading downstairs. Evan was waiting in front of the elevator bank when she reached the lobby. He broke into a huge smile when he saw her.

"Good morning, Beautiful," he said and gave her a hug.

"Hey, Handsome," Paige replied.

They had met in their American Heritage evening class taught by Frank Fox. Paige had arrived early and chosen a seat near the front. She was getting out her notebook and pen when Evan sat down next to her. They had chatted before class, and he walked her back to the dorms afterward for the first week. It was when they bumped into each other dancing at The Ivy Tower he finally asked her on an official date. He took her to the Eyring Science Center to look at the stars through the observatory telescope and then to The Brick Oven for pizza. They talked and laughed for hours. Evan was not classically handsome. His eyes almost disappeared when he laughed, and he had a lopsided grin. He had a shorter, stockier build, perfect for wrestling, which he had done since second grade. He was on the BYU wrestling team and was starting to make a name for himself. He was confident, self-assured, and easy going. Yet, he frequently told her he sometimes found it hard to believe Paige McLean was interested in him.

"I haven't done this hike before, but I've heard good things," he said, placing his hand in Paige's and directing her to the doors.

"I've heard the same. I bet the fall colors will be awesome."

They sang along with the radio and talked as they drove up Provo Canyon. Turning at Sundance, they headed further up the mountain, past Aspen Grove, to the Summit Trailhead parking area. Evan grabbed a backpack from the backseat, filled with drinks and sandwiches, and they started up the mountain on the Horse Flat Trail.

Paige had been correct. The fall colors were breathtaking. Crimson reds, burnt oranges, and vibrant yellows covered the mountainside, interspersed with the deep greens of the pines. The trail was thick with trees and brush for the first mile and then opened up to a huge cirque. Instead of heading south to make the loop at the spring, they went west, heading for the short but steep, spur up to the Primrose Lookout. They stopped for a quick lunch beneath looming Mount Timpanogas.

"Have you ever hiked up to the Timpanogas cave?" Paige asked Evan, looking up behind them.

"This is my first time on this mountain. I've heard it's a good hike. Maybe we can do it sometime."

"We did it once as a family when I was in middle school. We'd come down to Provo for the 4th of July with one of my aunts. The dads all took the kids while the moms prepped a big picnic. When we got to the large stalactite in the cave called the Great Heart, my Uncle Paul told us the legend of Timpanogas. I was mesmerized!"

"I don't know the legend. What is it?"

"Well, there are so many versions, but the one I heard from my uncle is my favorite. Once, there was a beautiful Indian Princess named Utahna, who was chosen by her people to go up to the top of the mountain as a sacrifice to the gods to end a terrible drought. She climbed to the top all by herself. Right when she was about to jump from the cliffs, the handsome warrior Red Eagle appeared and begged her not to end her life. Utahna assumed Red Eagle was the great god of Timpanogas, so she obeyed and followed him to the caves, where they fell in love," Paige said, smiling at Evan. "One day, while hunting, Red Eagle was injured by a wild animal, proving he was human and not a god. Heartbroken, Utahna left him to finish her sacrifice to the gods for her people. After she jumped, Red Eagle brought her broken body back to the caves, where it is believed their two hearts became one, forming the stalactite now known as the Great Heart of Timpanogas."

They were so lost in each other, talking about the legends of Timpanogos, it took them awhile to notice the ominous clouds headed their way. By the time they did, it was too late to make it back to the car before the storm hit. Laughing, they headed down the steep trail, sliding in the instant mud as the rain came down in sheets. They stopped under a large limber pine near Horse Spring to take shelter for a minute. They were out of breath, soaked to the bone, and Paige's mascara was running down her face.

"Evan Lindberg," she smiled up at him, while trying to wipe the water off her face with the back of her soaked sleeve, "This is a date I will never forget!"

Evan stepped closer towards her, took her face in his hands, and kissed her. First gently, and then passionately. Paige pressed her body into his and wrapped her arms tightly around his waist. He tasted like salt, rain, and earth.

When they finally pulled away, they were both breathless. They ran in silence down the remaining two miles of the trail and once back in the safety of the car, cranked the heater and kissed some more.

A year later, he proposed to her on another trail, while visiting her for the weekend in Providence. They had been married at the end of April in the Logan Temple, as soon as the semester was finished, and honeymooned in Puerto Rico, where he had served his mission. She was grateful he understood the importance of her friendship with Hannah, Jentry, and Sally and had encouraged her to go on this road trip.

The three-and-a-half-hour drive to Bear Lake seemed to fly by. Between singing along with the radio, playing the alphabet game with billboards, and talking about all the fun activities they had planned while at the cabin, the girls reached the Logan exit in no time.

Straddling the Utah-Idaho border, Bear Lake was often referred to as the "Caribbean of the Rockies" for its unique turquoise water. Hannah and Paige's parents had purchased a cabin when the girls were seven, and the families had stayed there more times than they could count. They loved getting raspberry shakes in Garden City, jet skiing on the lake, and soaking up sun on the beach. Paige was looking forward to showing Jentry and Sally her happy place.

"Is anybody up for heading down to the beach once we've unpacked?" Paige asked as Hannah turned into Harbor Village. The Limbrey-McLean cabin was located halfway up the hill on Raspberry Patch Drive and had a spectacular view of the lake.

"I could go for suiting up and getting a little sun on my skin. We've got several more hours of light, right? Plus, it's hot today," Jentry said.

Hannah pulled into the driveway. "Okay, girls, we're here!"

Paige excitedly jumped from the car and ran up to the house, unlocked the front door, and disappeared. A moment later, the garage door opened, and Hannah pulled inside.

Harbor Village was located on the west side of Bear Lake above the marina. Condos, tennis courts, and a pool were located near the private entrance, with cabins covering the hillside. The Limbrey-McLean cabin was a two-story log structure with a steep, sloping green aluminum roof to keep the winter snows off. The logs were stained a deep red, and it was one of the few cabins with a small lawn area in front, big enough for a game of volleyball or badminton.

The girls piled out of the car and followed Paige inside.

"Welcome to our cabin!" Paige said excitedly, grabbing Jentry and Sally's hands. "How have we not been here before? It's not far from Provo. We've failed you," she said, then pulled them further inside. "So, the garage obviously comes straight into the kitchen and living room. Behind the fireplace is a hall leading to the master rooms."

"The fireplace is amazing," remarked Sally, craning her neck to follow the stone all the way up to the vaulted ceiling.

"It's nice to curl up in front of it in the winter, but I can guarantee we won't need it this week." Paige led Jentry and Sally to their bedrooms for the next week. "These each have their own bathroom, so you won't have to fight," she smiled. "Jen can take this first room, and Sal can have the second. You'll have excellent views of the sunrise over the lake. Han and I will take some of the bunks in the loft."

"Let's save the tour for after the beach," Hannah huffed, lifting a cooler onto the kitchen counter. "I say we unload the stuff for the fridge and get our bodies to the beach!"

"I second that idea, Love," said Jentry, heading out to the car to grab another cooler.

July 14, 1991

Sally woke up early Sunday morning in time to catch the sunrise and read her scriptures before starting breakfast for the girls. No one in the group loved cooking and baking as much as Sally did. Paige came close, and the two took turns making most of the meals while lecturing Hannah and Jentry on the importance of learning basic homemaking skills. While the others slept in, Sally had been in heaven whipping up waffles and buttermilk syrup while enjoying the views of the lake as the morning sun reflected off the surface.

After breakfast, they had a small Sunday devotional on the deck, discussing the importance of daily prayer, and then headed back into the canyon for a hike on Stump Hollow Trail. They had parked near Beaver Ski Resort and headed north on the trail for about four miles before turning around. It was lucky so much of the trail was shaded because the July temperature was already over eighty degrees by ten in the morning.

After the hike, the girls changed into their swimsuits and drove down to the beach, anxious to enjoy the sunshine and water while they could. The families kept an old truck at the cabin, which was always loaded and ready for the beach in the summer with chairs, floats, towels, and an awning.

Paige drove the truck down to the beach nearest the marina, which was still crowded with other vehicles and people. Bear Lake was a popular destination in the summer, whether for a stay at a cabin or a day trip to swim and picnic. The girls grabbed some chairs and towels and quickly applied sun block. Jentry popped open a Diet Coke while the other girls grabbed water.

"Who's up for some frisbee?" asked Hannah, running out to the water.

"I'm in!" Paige and Sally chimed at the same time.

"You coming, Jentry?" Sally asked over her shoulder.

"Nah, you girls go ahead. I'm going to relax and read for a bit," Jentry said as she delved back into *Weep No More, My Lady*.

After thirty minutes of frisbee, with each girl screaming as they fell into the chilly water, diving for the large yellow disc, they traipsed back up to the beach to lay out. Hannah pulled a beach chair up next to Jentry while Paige and Sally grabbed towels and laid them at the water's edge. They sat in silence for a moment, staring out at the crystal blue waters of the lake, each sipping from their water bottle.

"Can I ask you a question, Paige?"

"Well, that sounds strangely serious, Sal. Go ahead."

Sally smiled, still looking at the lake. "Would you say love at first sight is possible, like in all the books and movies?"

"I don't know, Sally." Paige paused, trying to think if she had felt love at first sight with Evan or just a major attraction. "I guess it could happen. But would it be love? Or just a crush? Just strong physical attraction? I think you have to know someone to love them, don't you?" she said, looking over at Sally.

"So, could you love someone you've never met? Like in person, but maybe, let's say, you've talked to them on the phone every day for a year?"

Paige gave a little chuckle, "I guess. Why do you ask? Should I be looking at our phone bills closer?"

Sally smiled and shook her head. "No reason. Sometimes, I wonder about love. Is it really like it is in the books, and movies, and fairy tales?"

Hannah and Jentry joined them, dragging their chairs to either side of the towels and catching Sally's last question.

"If you ask me," said Jentry, "I don't think I would want it to be. When I fall in love, I want it to be after I've known the person for years and years and know everything there is to know about them so they can't surprise me or disappoint me…or hurt me."

"That doesn't sound very romantic."

"Unlike you, Sally, I'm not a romantic. That can't come as a surprise."

Sally laughed out loud. "No, my dearest friend, it doesn't come as a surprise."

"Do you want the fairy tale, Sally?" Hannah asked.

"Fairy godmother, singing mice and all!" Sally said emphatically, and they all laughed.

The setting sun was their cue to call it a day. After loading everything into the truck, they headed back into Garden City for a burger and famous raspberry shakes and then headed back to the cabin to shower. Paige and Sally showered first, and while the other girls jumped in, they set up a mini spa night on the kitchen island. Paige had brought several colors of nail polish and a few face masks for the girls to try. Sally didn't like to wear a lot of makeup and was happy with some mascara and lip gloss. Hannah and Paige wore a little bit more, while Jentry had a massive amount of Este Lauder makeup and loved experimenting with new ways to wear it. While Sally didn't always remember to wash her face before bed, Paige took her skin care regimen seriously and was always trying out new masks and scrubs.

Finally dressed in their pajamas, their wet hair pulled back into ponytails or buns, they gathered around the island to paint their nails. They listened to the radio, talking and laughing while the paint dried, and then tried various masks to see which one they liked best. The later it got, the sillier they became.

"Guys! I love this song. Turn it up!" Sally said as Belinda Carlisle's *Summer Rain* came on the radio.

They all grabbed wooden spoons and began to sing and dance around the kitchen. Sally, covered in a green oatmeal mask, climbed on top of the bar stool and sang into her spoon like she was giving a concert. The girls were clapping and cheering as the front door opened, and three men walked into the kitchen.

"Now, this is a surprise," said one of the three, his blue eyes twinkling while a large grin spread across his face. The two behind him, one short with longer dark hair and one tall with red curls and freckles, laughed.

Hannah spun around, slugged the man in the arm, and then hugged him. "Sam! What are you doing here?"

"I got a few days off, so we thought we'd come to the cabin. We didn't expect it to be quite so full," Hannah's brother said, smiling at the girls. Sally had never met Hannah's brother, Sam, in person, but she knew who he was immediately from the photos of him Hannah had sitting on her dresser. Sally had been writing to Sam for most of his mission, and what had started as an act of service had turned into a crush. Possibly more.

"Hey, Paige."

"Hey, Sam."

"This must be Jentry," said Sam, walking up to Jentry, who had quickly removed the mask from her face.

"Yes. Nice to meet you," Jentry replied, reaching out to shake his hand.

"And the star performer has to be Sally!" Sam grinned from ear to ear and walked around the island.

"Umm, yes," Sally said shyly, ducking her head and not making eye contact. She carefully climbed down from the bar stool.

Sam went to shake her hand, but her arms were wrapped tight around herself.

"Seriously, Sam," said Hannah, regaining his attention. "We've had this booked for weeks. Mom knows we're here. Didn't she tell you?"

"I didn't ask. We were hanging out at Drake's and, on a whim, decided to come to the cabin."

The skinny red head stepped forward and waved at Jentry and Sally. "Hi, I'm Drake."

"Sorry, guys," said Sam. "Yeah, this ginger is Drake. We went to High School together, and both got back from The Mish in the last few months. And this hippie is Aaron. He's Drake's roommate this year."

"Sorry, guys, this is our cousin Paige and our friends, Jentry and Sally. Ladies, this is Aaron and Drake," said Hannah, pointing around the room, "Now beat it."

"Beat it? Where are we supposed to go?" Sam asked, reaching for a handful of the m&m's in a bowl on the island, almost knocking over a bottle of nail polish.

"Anywhere but here," Paige piped up. "Reservation only and you are not on the list, Samuel."

Sam tried to protest, but Paige cut him off. "Sam, Hannah's right. We've had this place booked for weeks; it's our girls' weekend. Hit the road."

"We're supposed to drive all the way back to Logan? It's ten o'clock at night. Man, you ladies are tough." Sam pulled on Paige's ponytail and laughed. "Alright, guys, you heard them. Home we go. We'll have to come up with plan B."

Sam good naturedly started to herd his friends out the door.

"Umm, couldn't they sleep upstairs this one night?" Sally almost whispered. They all turned to look at her. "There are lots of beds. That's sad for them to drive all the way back," she said, looking down at her feet. The oatmeal mask on her face was dried and cracking, but if you knew her well, as her friends did, you could see the red flush of embarrassment peeking through.

Sam smiled kindly at Sally. "That's really sweet of you to offer, Sally. Now I feel a little bad about barging in on you. I actually did know you were all up here and wanted to prank my sister. Drake's aunt has a cabin in Fish Haven, and we're headed there."

"Sam! Oh my gosh!" Hannah slugged Sam in the arm again. "You are so dumb."

"We're leaving. I really am sorry I interrupted your night. You girls get back to your girly stuff, and we'll get out of your way. But to make it up to you for interrupting your concert, we'll pick you up tomorrow after lunch and go boating."

✱✱✱

Hannah slipped downstairs and out onto the deck. She couldn't sleep, and it didn't help that the loft was stuffy and hot. Normally she slept with a bedside fan, but she had forgotten it in her rush to pack. She knew what was keeping her from a restful sleep and was annoyed it was still getting to her. Seeing Drake had brought up a lot of memories from high school that she had tried to forget.

As much as she loved Paige, it wasn't always easy having the most beautiful and popular girl in school for a cousin. Hannah felt cute enough and was told she was pretty, but she always felt inferior to Paige growing up, like she couldn't quite get out from under her shadow. She didn't blame her. How could she? Paige was her best friend and she loved her unconditionally, but the light didn't shine on Hannah

23

quite the same as it shone on her cousin. Her sophomore year of high school, she signed up for a drama class and auditioned for the Christmas play. It started as something to differentiate herself from Paige, but she ended up really liking it. She also liked the attention she got from the guys in class. It didn't feel secondhand, like it did when Paige was around. She wasn't old enough to date, but flirting wasn't against the rules.

However, one day during play practice, the flirting turned into something a little more, and Hannah found herself out of her depth and in a compromising situation.

"Wanna play chicken?" Greg Thomas smiled at her, placing his hand on her knee. She was in her Ghost of Christmas Past costume, which barely reached her mid-thigh. The drama instructor had a piece of blue fabric folded in half, stitched halfway up the sides, with a hole cut out of the top for her head. The neckline was wide, and she struggled to keep it on her shoulders. A thin white rope was tied around her waist, cinching the fabric, and causing it to show even more of her legs. This outfit wouldn't be allowed at a church dance, or even in school, but for some reason was okay for the play. Greg was a junior and had been flirting with her during rehearsals. She loved the attention and was hopeful he would ask her out eventually.

"What's chicken?" Hannah asked, much more naïve than she looked in her current attire.

"Well," Greg scooted closer to her on the couch. They were in a practice room behind the stage, shared by the drama and music department. He turned his body towards her and stared intently into her eyes. "I slide my hand slowly up your leg like this," he said, as his hand started moving up her thigh, "and you say chicken when you don't want me to go any further."

Hannah froze. She didn't know what to do or say. This wasn't just playful banter; this was him touching her, his hand quickly approaching the hem of her dress. Her body started to feel funny and scared at the same time. Before she knew it, Greg's fingertips brushed against her panties.

"Party scene to the stage. All actors in the party scene, please come to the stage," Mr. Burton's voice crackled over the intercom.

"Shit." Greg stood up and adjusted his pants before leaving the room without another word.

Hannah sat in stunned silence for a second and then began to cry. What had she done? This was against everything she had been taught about her body since she was a little girl. She knew letting a boy touch you before you were married was a grave sin, one that could chase the Holy Ghost away. She had been taught the importance of saving herself for marriage her entire life. Heavenly Father was serious about the Law of Chastity, and she had been taught to break it was a sin close to murder.

She tucked her legs up onto the couch, wrapped her arms around them, and started sobbing. That's when Drake walked into the room to grab the backpack he'd left behind after band practice.

"Hannah?" he faltered, "Are you okay?"

She couldn't speak; she was crying so hard.

"Do you want me to get someone?" he asked, stepping closer to her.

"No!" Hannah almost shouted, looking up. "I don't want anyone to know!"

Drake kneeled down in front of the couch. "Hannah, did someone hurt you?"

Hannah looked back down. "N...no...I'm not hurt."

"Did someone do something to you? Hannah, you can tell me. I want to help you. Sam's little sisters are like my little sisters."

Just then, Greg opened the door to the room, "Ready to keep…" he stopped midsentence when he saw Drake standing next to a crying Hannah.

"Did you hurt her, Thomas?" Drake asked, taking two giant steps toward the door.

"Back off, Pennington. Hannah and I were just having a little fun. Not sure what she's freaked out about."

Greg turned to leave the room, but Drake grabbed the back of his shirt and spun him around. "Hannah Limbrey is family to me, so I don't want you ever going near her again. Am I making myself clear?"

"Not a problem, dude," Greg said as he walked off.

Hannah was mortified and grateful at the same time. She took some deep breaths and got the crying under control. "Drake, please don't tell Sam. I don't want him to be mad at me."

"If Sam is going to be mad at anyone, it'll be that loser for taking advantage of you. I don't know what happened, and I don't need to, but I want you to let me know if he comes around again."

"We're in the play together. I'm going to see him every day until Christmas break. This is so embarrassing."

"Hey, come here," Drake reached down and pulled Hannah up into a hug. She leaned into his chest and started crying again. "This isn't going to get spread around. Greg isn't that stupid. He's not going to risk getting on Sam Limbrey's bad side. It's going to be okay. Just be careful, okay? You're too sweet of a kid to get mixed up with jerks like him."

Hannah smiled into the darkness, thinking of how kind Drake had been to her that day. He was right. No one ever learned about the incident from Greg. She, however, had broken down to her mother in the middle of the grocery store the next day, confessing she let a boy touch her privates. Her mother had quickly sent her to the car, so she didn't make a scene, while she finished the shopping. Hannah had screamed into the headrest of the car while she waited for her mother, so filled with shame and guilt.

Her mother had reported everything to her father, who took her for a drive to get an ice cream cone the next day while explaining the purpose of sexual purity. It was uncomfortable, to say the least. But nothing like having to share the details with her Bishop the following Sunday as part of the repentance process.

If only that had been her last confession to a parent or Bishop about messing up with a guy. She was so confident and self-assured in so many ways, and yet, at the same time, so desperate for love and attention from men. It didn't make any sense to her, and so she tried not to think about it. Push the pain, guilt, and shame down and put on a happy face. That was her mantra.

The eastern sky was starting to turn from a deep black to a rich indigo, indicating the sun would be rising before too long. Knowing a day on the boat with Sam and his friends required she be well rested, Hannah stretched for a few minutes before heading back upstairs and climbing into bed.

July 16, 1991

Sally was so distracted with her book that she didn't notice Sam coming in from the garage. Hannah and Paige had left shortly after sunrise for a fifty-mile bike ride around the lake. Jentry had shown an uncanny ability to sleep past nine each day, so Sally had enjoyed a quiet morning baking muffins and reading Jane Eyre for the third time. She sat at the picnic table on the deck, under the green and white striped umbrella, trying to protect her sunburned skin from the morning rays. She thought she had put on enough sunblock before the boat ride yesterday, but five hours on the lake had roasted her shoulders and knees. Next to her was a glass of orange juice and a plate with a half-eaten muffin.

Sally had been a voracious reader since fourth grade. The farm kept the entire Johnson family busy, so she read when she could during the day, a page here and there, but devoured chapters once the dinner dishes were done. Her parents frequently scolded her for reading when she should be sleeping yet praised her for finishing a book or two a week. Her fourth-grade teacher, Mrs. Jolley, had recommended a Nancy Drew mystery when Sally was falling behind in her reading level scores. That did the trick. Before the end of the school year, Sally was the best reader in the grade.

"Hey," Sam appeared next to her with a half-eaten blueberry muffin in his hand.

Sally gave a little scream and almost knocked over her juice.

"Oh, sorry. I didn't mean to startle you." Sam sat down next to her.

Blushing slightly and closing her book, Sally smiled at Sam. "I didn't hear you come in. Helen Burns just died, and I was engrossed."

"Condolences," Sam said with a wink, and nodded at the book. He took another bite of muffin. "Did you make these?" he asked, his mouth a little full.

"Yeah. I like to bake."

"This is really good. Betty Crocker or Jiffy?"

Sally smiled. "Neither. They're Sally Johnson. I made them from scratch."

"Wow. Impressive. Why so many flavors?"

"Well, Hannah likes banana, Jentry loves chocolate, Paige is a blueberry girl, and I'm partial to the oatmeal craisin. I make one batter and then add things to each batch."

"What a good friend. I'll have to try the oatmeal." Sam hopped up, ran into the kitchen, and returned with an oatmeal muffin. "You should market these. This is the best oatmeal muffin I've ever had. I mean, it's the only oatmeal muffin I've ever had, but it is definitely the best." He grinned as he took another bite.

"Thanks," Sally tucked her hair behind her ears. She wasn't sure what to say next. Her stomach was full of butterflies. "So, what brings you by? Are your friends with you?"

"They're out front. We were about to take the four-wheelers out. Drake is out of oil, so I was checking to see if we have any. They're getting everything loaded. Where's Hannah?"

"She and Paige are riding around the lake."

"And Jentry?"

"She's a bit of a late riser."

Sam smiled, "Well then, you better come with me, so you aren't too lonely here."

Sally felt her pulse quicken. "What? Oh no. I'm okay. I don't want to intrude on your guy stuff."

"You won't be intruding. Come on."

"Really, you don't have to worry about me. Jentry will wake up before too long, and they should be back from their ride in the next little while."

Sam stood up and held out his hand, "Sally, I insist. I want you to come with us."

Sally tentatively held out her hand. He grabbed it and pulled her up. She willed herself to let go of his hand and nervously tucked her hair behind her ear again. "Okay. Umm. I can be ready in five minutes."

"Great. I'll be poking around in the garage." Sam turned and headed in that direction. "Bring some of those muffins. Aaron and Drake will want some too," he called as the garage door shut behind him.

Sally stood in shocked stillness for a minute. Was she really about to go off with Sam by herself? She was half tempted to wake Jentry up to join her. But only half tempted. She ran to her bathroom, combed her hair back into a ponytail, and brushed her teeth. She studied her reflection in the mirror. Light brown hair pulled away from her face, light brown eyes with no makeup, fair skin with a hint of sunburn across her freckled nose from yesterday on the lake. She wished she had Jentry's exotic dark looks or Paige's blonde bombshell style.

Sally had felt so plain around her friends when they first met, but she got over it and usually didn't compare herself to them anymore.

She was a low-maintenance girl, to be sure, and was usually fine in jeans and a tee shirt. But right now, about to go off with Sam, she found herself wishing she were a little more glamorous. "Oh well," she said to herself, shrugging her shoulders. "I am what I am." She grabbed her chapstick and a hoodie and headed upstairs to the kitchen. She jotted down a quick note to her friends, put some muffins in a plastic bag, grabbed a water bottle out of the fridge, and headed out to the garage to find Sam.

Drake's truck was waiting in the driveway, and Sam was leaning on Aaron's window, talking to his friends. He waved as Sally came out the door.

"I've got muffins," she said, holding the bag up.

'I've got muffins?' she thought to herself. Lame. 'Don't talk, Sally,' she told herself.

"Great." Sam opened the back door to the truck, and Sally climbed in.

"Hey, Sally. Glad you can join us," Drake said, backing the truck and trailer up slowly.

"I hope I'm not crashing the party," Sally said as she put her seatbelt on and again reminded herself not to talk.

The guys had decided to ride up to the Paris Ice Cave. Even though the cave was small, they always had fun climbing around inside it. Drake was a bit of a lead foot, so the drive to Paris, Idaho, took less than twenty minutes. It was another fifteen minutes on dirt roads before they came to the Paris Spring campground and parked the truck. Sally watched in horror as only three four-wheelers were unloaded from inside the trailer. Her parents had a couple of old four-wheelers around the farm, and Sally had been riding them since she was ten. It had not occurred to her she would be riding with Sam. She wasn't sure she could trust herself not to pass out from being so close to him.

"So, Sally, you riding with me?" Aaron asked with a grin as he put his helmet on.

"Sorry, Bud, I've got dibs," Sam winked at Sally. "Okay, hop on, Sally," Sam said as he jumped onto a large yellow four-wheeler. He handed her a beat-up looking green helmet and put one on himself.

Sally did as she was told and climbed on behind Sam. She was sure he could hear her heart beating, even over the loud hum of the engine. Sally tried to steady herself by only lightly holding on to Sam's shoulders, but as he revved the engine and took off down the dirt road towards the turnoff for the caves, she instinctively grabbed him tightly around the waist to keep from falling off.

If there had been a posted speed limit, Sally was sure he was breaking it. Aaron, Drake, and Sam would leave Green Basin Road and take any offshoots they came across. Sally laughed, even as she hung on tighter when they jumped over a small creek bed. She watched the pines and aspens go by and searched within the trees to see if she could spot any mule deer or moose as they approached the Paris Ice Cave. Sally could see the wooden sign next to a small dirt parking area. Behind that, large outcroppings of limestone jutted out of the ground around the sinkhole that had formed the cave. The spring runoff from surrounding hills formed a small brook running down the doline into the cave entrance, sometimes making it inaccessible before July. By mid-summer, the water had dried out, and the small cave was ready to be explored. The three four-wheelers pulled into the makeshift parking lot.

Sam lifted the visor on his helmet and hollered to his friends over the sound of the engines, "You guys go on ahead. I want to show Sally the cave. We'll catch up with you."

"Dude, let's say meet back at this spot in three hours. That way, no one's getting lost looking for someone else," Drake said, checking his watch.

"Have fun, you two," Aaron winked at Sally, who hoped the blush she felt in her cheeks was hidden beneath her helmet.

Aaron and Drake continued up the road, kicking up dust behind them. Sam pulled up closer to the sign and killed the engine. He quickly removed his helmet and then turned around to help Sally with hers.

"Hope that's okay," he said, as he offered his hand to help her off the four-wheeler. "The caves aren't huge, but they're pretty cool. I didn't want you to miss it." He started steering Sally towards the trail to the southern entrance, still holding her hand. "Be careful; it gets a little slippery here."

Sally was trying to concentrate on putting one foot in front of the other to avoid thinking too much about the fact Sam was holding her hand. She was sure he could feel her palms getting sweaty. She knew the handholding didn't mean anything; he was only trying to keep her steady, but it gave her butterflies just the same. Sam led her around the corner and down into the mouth of the cave.

"Oh my gosh!" Sally exclaimed as she caught sight of the huge cavern. The drop in temperature as they neared the opening sent a shiver down her spine. Her eyes followed the cave walls in the chamber up about fifty feet. "This is so beautiful." The amateur geologist in her took over. She let go of Sam's hand and ran her hands over the cool limestone walls. A dark pool of standing water filled the bottom of the chamber. A worn-looking plank sat gingerly on top of it, daring visitors to cross the ominous water to reach the other cavern.

"Don't you think stalactites and stalagmites are so fascinating?" She asked Sam over her shoulder as she stepped carefully onto the rickety bridge. "Oh, and look at all the calcium carbonate deposits in these walls. That's some cool stuff. Do you have any idea how many things it's used for?"

Sam followed Sally across the wooden bridge to the opening between the two caverns with a bemused smile on his face. "I hate to admit I'm not the calcium carbonate expert. What are some of the things it's used for?"

Sally turned around and looked at him sheepishly. "You're teasing me. Am I boring you?"

"No, really," Sam laughed, "I'm not teasing, and I'm not bored. Enlighten me."

"Well," said Sally, walking up to the nearest cliff wall and tracing the delicate patterns with her finger, "The main use is in construction, as a building material, for example, marble or limestone like this. It's in cement. It's an extender in paints, filler in plastics, and is used in baby diapers. Isn't that funny?" She turned back to look at Sam. He was smiling at her. She momentarily lost her train of thought because she was so distracted by his dimples. She shook her head and walked over to the opposite rock wall. "It's used as a filler in medicines and as an antacid, which you probably already knew. And it's in toothpaste. Would you ever think toothpaste and cement have the same properties?"

"You know, it hadn't occurred to me." Sam walked up to Sally and grabbed her hand again. "Come over this way; you've got to see the other cavern." He led her into the rock field that sat in front of the northern cavern. "You've got to duck and watch your head in this part. I've been known to knock my head a few times." Bending in half, they picked their way over the rocks until they were far enough into the cavern to stand upright. "I wish I would have thought to bring my flashlight. It's pretty dark in here until your eyes adjust."

Sally tried to focus on the dark room. She could make out the shapes on the other side but dared not move straight across as this floor was also covered with water. She could see a small beam of light coming from the far end of the room that looked to be eighty feet high. She closed her eyes and took a deep breath. The smell of the wet rocks and the damp, trapped air was invigorating to her. "This is great Sam. Thanks for showing it to me."

"You are more than welcome, Ms. Johnson, geologist extraordinaire. I figured you'd like it, even though it's small. Come over here. There's a flat rock for sitting on a few steps to our left, if I remember correctly."

They found a rock large enough for the two of them to sit side by side in the near darkness.

"How'd you know I liked geology?" Sally asked as she wrapped her arms around her knees and pulled her hands into the arms of her hoodie.

"You mentioned it in your letters a few times. You want to study caves, right?"

"Yes, I love geology, but speleology is my passion."

"Speleology?"

"That would be the name for the scientific study of caves and karst features."

"Karsts?"

"That means an area where erosion has produced fissures, sinkholes, underground streams and caverns."

"You are a wealth of information, Sally."

Sally blushed, embarrassed her exuberance was painting her as a science geek. She was glad the darkness hid her red cheeks. She let out a big sigh, "I'm sorry. I'm sure you weren't expecting a lecture on the many uses of calcium carbonate and speleogenesis of the Paris Ice Cave. I can get carried away."

"Oh, no, Sally. I wasn't being sarcastic. I've always looked at this as a great place to explore and jump off cliffs into summer snowbanks. But I liked seeing it through your eyes. I'm no spello...person, and science wasn't ever my thing, but you make it sound interesting and fun. But half of that could be because you're so much cuter than any of my professors were." Sam nudged Sally with his elbow. She was sure her face was the same color as her red hoodie now, and thankful he couldn't really see it.

"I don't know what kind of professors you had at USU, but Bristow has a handlebar mustache that's pretty hot." Under most circumstances, Sally tended to be shy around guys and even around girls that she didn't know well. She could laugh and mess around with Hannah, Jentry, and Paige, but didn't usually let many others see that side of her.

Sitting in the dark with Sam inside the cold, damp cave, she felt so comfortable. It was almost like writing to him again. She had been able to be herself in her letters because there was no risk. He was her best friend's big brother a few states away, and she was just one of Hannah's roommates who was nice enough to write to him. With letters, she didn't feel self-conscious about her appearance. It didn't matter if she was sitting around in her flannel pajama bottoms with her hair in a ponytail. She felt so timid and awkward around Sam the first night at the cabin. Singing into a spoon in her pajamas with an oatmeal mask on her face was not how she had envisioned her first meeting with him. That surprise encounter had her retreating into her shell, and she hadn't really come out of it the next day on the boat. But not now. At this moment, she felt relaxed and comfortable, as if she could talk to him about anything. Even her insane love of all things geologic.

"You're funny, Sally Johnson. Smart and funny. A dangerous combination." Sam nudged her again. "So, are you ready to try some cliff jumping?"

"What? Here?" She looked around, trying to figure out what he could be referring to.

"Come on, I'll show you." Bent in half again, they carefully crawled out of the cave and into the open air. Sam pointed to the huge snow drifts that sat in the permanent shade of the eastern walls. "See that snow? It makes a pretty cushy landing. We climb up the wall there and then jump back in from those outcroppings. You have to watch you don't land on too icy of a spot and slide into any rocks, but other than it's pretty harmless. You up for it?"

Sally bit her lip as she tried to mentally calculate the drop. She had trouble going off the high dive at the pool, and this was definitely twice that height. "I don't think I can do it. I'm pretty wimpy."

"It'll be fun, come on." Sam started scrambling up the limestone wall, and Sally had no choice but to follow him. The climb up was easy enough as the holds were large.

She'd done a little rock climbing with her roommates, and going up wasn't the problem. It was the idea of jumping down that scared her. They reached the top, and Sam ran over to the edge above the highest drift of snow. "Okay, I'll go first. You follow right after me." Sam took a huge jump out into the air and fell fifteen feet down into the waiting snow.

Sally screamed in spite of herself and quickly covered her mouth with her hand. "I don't think I can do this."

"Sure, you can. I'm right here. I won't let you slide."

Sally hesitated; she hated to risk life and limb, but at the same time, if there was one thing she had learned from her friends, it was to try new things and conquer her fears. With a deep breath and a small prayer, she walked to the same spot Sam had jumped from. "Count for me, okay? If I count, I'll chicken out."

"One…Two…Three!" Sam shouted from below.

Mustering all her courage, Sally leaped from the safety of the rock. She couldn't help screaming as she fell through the air. Sam kept his promise and kept her from sliding down the snow into the rocks. She laughed as she picked herself out of the snow and dusted off her pants.

"Excellent job!" Sam said, slapping Sally a high five. "What did ya think?"

"Scary, but fun."

After a few more jumps, they climbed out and headed back to the four-wheeler. Sam checked his watch. "We've got almost two hours left before Aaron and Drake come back this way. Let's ride some more."

They put on their helmets, and Sam headed back the way they had come, then quickly turned left off of Green Basin Road, headed up towards Midnight Mountain. Sam didn't drive as fast without his friends around, and Sally was able to keep her balance with her hands on his shoulders. The views were spectacular. Sam stopped to point out Paris

Peak and Bloomington Peak to their South. Sally thought these mountains were some of the prettiest she'd ever seen.

By the time they met back up with Aaron and Drake at the ice cave parking lot, dark grey clouds were beginning to move in from the West, and they worried they might not make it back to the truck before the summer rainstorm reached them. Thunder reverberated off the mountainsides, and a hard rain hit before they made the turn towards Paris Spring. All four of them were soaked through in minutes, and the mud from the road seemed to have somehow made its way underneath their helmets and inside their clothes. Sally started the heater in the truck while the guys loaded the four-wheelers onto the trailer. She was glad she had brought the bag of muffins, as she was starving. They'd missed lunch by a few hours and would probably be getting back closer to dinner time.

On the drive back to Garden City, the guys devoured Sally's muffins and talked about sports. Sally stared out the window at Bear Lake and wondered at the turn her day had taken. This was definitely not what she had envisioned herself doing when she woke up this morning. She pressed her forehead to the window and smiled to herself. No, this was better than anything she could have imagined.

It was almost five o'clock when Aaron's truck stopped at the driveway to let Sally out. She could see Paige on the deck in front of the grill. When Paige saw Sally get out of the truck, she waved. "She's back!" Sally heard Paige shout to the girls in the cabin.

"Thanks for letting me tag along today, you guys," Sally said as she hopped down from the truck. The old awkwardness welled back up as she glanced at Sam before shyly looking away. "See ya." Sally shut the door and started down the driveway.

Sam rolled the window down and hollered after her. "Hey, Sally, how much longer are you guys going to be here?"

"We're heading off on leg two Friday morning."

"Oh. Okay, well, uh, see ya around then," he waved.

She waved back and then hurriedly ran down the driveway to the deck, where Paige was waiting with her hands on her hips.

"Where have you been all day, girlfriend?" Paige nodded absently at the guys as the truck pulled away, while grabbing Sally's hands.

"You got my note, right? Sam wanted me to go four-wheeling with them. It wasn't rude of me to leave you guys, was it?"

"No, Turtle, it wasn't rude. Did you have fun? Where'd you go?"

"Yeah, it was fun." Sally picked up one of the sliced tomatoes on the plate next to the grill. Paige had all the fixings for burgers ready and was about to put a few patties on the grill. "We went up to Paris."

"Looks like you went rolling in mud. We heard some thunder, but the storm missed us," Paige said as she appraised Sally.

"We got hit with a storm on the way back to the truck. I couldn't believe how quickly the road turned to mud. Do you think I have time to shower before dinner is ready?"

"I insist you shower before dinner is ready," Paige said. "I'll start Hannah and Jentry's burgers, and I'll wait for you to get dressed before I put ours on."

"You don't have to wait. Eat."

"No, I don't mind. You go take a nice hot shower and come back out here ready for a cheeseburger and tell me all about your day."

Sally grabbed another tomato and headed off towards the shower.

The hot water felt so good, and she didn't want to rush, but she knew Paige was waiting for her to eat. The drain was running with dark water due to the mud caked on the back of her legs. She grabbed the loofah and the vanilla-scented body wash and scrubbed the dirt and grime off of her arms and legs. She quickly lathered her hair with shampoo and ran some conditioner through it before washing her face. As the hot water rinsed the suds off of her body, Sally let her mind replay the day.

She thought about Sam's perfect face, his smile, the sound of his laugh. And she thought about what it felt like when he had held her hand. She held her hands up in front of her face and sighed. Would she ever feel his hands in hers again? Probably not. She forced herself to turn off the water and dry off. She wrapped one of the yellow towels around her head and the other around her body. She rubbed some moisturizer on her face and some baby lotion on her arms and legs.

Turning the light and the fan off, she stepped out into the bedroom and froze. Standing in the bedroom doorway was Sam. Sally let out a little scream at the surprise of seeing someone there. Then she screamed again as she realized she had only a small bath towel around her and quickly backed into the bathroom and shut the door. What was he doing here?

"Sally?" Sam's voice called gently from the other side of the door.

She was so embarrassed she didn't know what to do. She felt like a fool for screaming. Not only once, but twice. And to be caught in her bath towel was mortifying. Where some girls might have used getting caught in a towel as an opportunity to act coy or flirtatious, Sally, with her sense of propriety and dedication to LDS standards, only found it incredibly uncomfortable. "Yeah?" she finally managed.

"I didn't mean to scare you. You left your hoodie in the truck."

"Oh...um...thanks," Sally said from behind the door. She still hadn't turned the light back on and stood there in the dark, listening to see if Sam had left yet.

After a few moments, she heard Sam start to retreat. "I'll leave it by the back door. I hope the mud comes out. Well, I'll be seeing you, Sally. Again, sorry I scared you."

Sally pressed her forehead to the door and tried not to cry from humiliation. "Yeah, thanks, Sam. I'll see you around."

July 18, 1991

Ahh! I'm a few days (several!) behind because we are having SO MUCH FUN and I'm exhausted at the end of each day. This was the best idea ever! I wish I could take credit for it. We're on a two-week road trip and I'm having the time of my life with my besties – Jentry, Paige and Sally.

We're at the tail end of the week at Bear Lake. It was so cool to show Jen & Sal our beloved Garden City. They loved getting raspberry shakes almost every day, as they should.

I was annoyed when Sam and his bozo friends showed up one night at first, but it ended up being awesome because they took us out on the boat. No one skied, but we did tube off the back and that was the best. Sally looked terrified. Haha.

Yesterday we went to Minnetonka Cave. Sally was in heaven! It's one of the biggest limestone caves in Idaho and her little geology heart was so happy. Jentry, on the other hand, was constantly ducking thinking she'd seen a bat. That girl cracks me up.

Have I mentioned before how much I love my friends? A hundred times, I know. We've had some great discussions this trip about the Gospel, future goals, and who we want to be in this life. They challenge me to be better.

The dynamic is a little different with Paige as a married woman. Evan calls her every night. I guess that's what love looks like. But even with her married and living in Orem, we're still The Companions. Forever!

July 19, 1991

Sally had spent much of the three-hour drive to the City of Rocks National Reserve educating her friends on the history, geology, and significance of The City, as locals and climbers called it. The area had been a stop along the California Trail, and Sally excitedly showed them the names written on Register Rock in axle grease when they entered the park from the east. The granite outcroppings, some as high as six hundred feet, were as beautiful as Sally had remembered. After setting up their tent on the backside of Bath Rock, they explored and climbed on the nearby formations as the sun started to set.

Sally got the fire going while the others prepared their dinner. Hot dogs, chips, and s'mores were on the menu tonight, and Sally enjoyed teaching her friends how to roast the dogs perfectly.

"Why do hot dogs taste so much better when camping?" Hannah asked as she took another bite.

"Is this not how they normally taste?" Jentry asked, slightly confused.

"What do you mean?" asked Sally as she squirted mustard onto her dog.

"You do remember this is my first camping trip, loves?"

"Right." The other girls said in unison.

"And that would make this my first..." Jentry let her sentence hang in the air.

"Your first hot dog?" Sally asked incredulously. "How is that even possible?"

"Well, I guess if you have a personal chef, you don't need to live on pig guts like commoners," Hannah laughed while doing a British accent.

"Oh, please don't tell me what's in them. I've heard horror stories. Let me just enjoy the moment."

They finished dinner and visited around the fire until it was embers. Sally had left the rain guard off their four-man tent so they could watch the stars until they fell asleep. After heading inside, Sally excitedly told them about one of her favorite camping traditions.

"So, we have this game we play at night when we camp. I don't know why, but we only play it when we're sleeping under the stars. We call it "Last night I dreamt," and you describe a dream you actually had before or you make one up. Then we have to guess if it was a real dream or fake."

"That sounds fun," Hannah said while rubbing lotion on her feet and then climbing into her sleeping bag.

"My brothers, George Jr and Stephen were so much better at it than the rest of us kids," Sally said. "Stephen's dreams were actually a bit disturbing. So, I'll go first to show you how it's done." Sally cleared her throat and began. "Last night I dreamt I went to the mall, and Mrs. Knapp, the math teacher, was there, inside Dillard's, cutting people's hair by the perfume samples." She laid back on her pillow. "Ok, real or fake."

"Hmm," mused Paige, "That dream is kind of lame, so I'll vote fake."

"Lame? What do you dream about then?"

"A lady never tells," Paige laughed and swatted Sally on the arm.

"Well, it was real, so one point for me."

"You never said points were involved. Do I need to grab paper and a pen? What are we playing for?" Hannah asked, as competitive as always.

"Oh, sorry. First one to five wins, and then we hit the hay. That's farmer talk, Jen, for going to sleep."

"I have heard of the expression, Sal. I mean, we've been roommates for two years now."

"I'll go next," said Paige, staring up at the stars through the roof of the tent. "Let's see. Last night I dreamt I was going along a steep, steep cliff, and someone wanted to push me off. Chad, an old boyfriend, was there trying to pull me up, but I kept sliding, and when I fell, I kept falling and never stopped."

"Geez. That's dark," piped up Hannah. "I'll go with true. You have to have a dark and twisted brain under your bubbly exterior. Though I doubt Evan will appreciate you dreaming about Chad."

"Ha! Dang, you're correct. Zero points for me. Bummer."

"My turn then, hmm," Hannah said, thinking. "Last night I dreamt I became a famous movie star, and I dated all these hot babes: River Phoenix, Johnny Depp, Tom Cruise, Kirk Cameron, Val Kilmer, and Dennis Quaid. I had a little romance with each of them."

"Please say I heard you wrong, and you didn't say Dennis Quaid. Or put Kirk Cameron in the same category as Tom Cruise," Jentry scolded.

"Hey, to each his own."

"I think it's a lovely list, Hannah," Sally said consolingly. "I vote true."

"Sadly, those fine specimens are only in my daydreams. Maybe I'll get lucky tonight, though. Okay, Judgey Jentry, let's hear yours."

"Alright, loves. Remember that movie where they shrink Martin Short, and he ends up in Dennis Quaid?"

"Innerspace, right? With Meg Ryan, too?" Paige asked.

"That's the one. Last night I dreamt I was twins with Meg Ryan, and Dennis Quaid had a twin brother named Dennis the Menace. We were all in the Innerspace pod in Martin Short playing Rook. We traveled through Martin until we hit his kneecap and got a hole in the pod. Fluid started coming in, and we were all screaming, then I woke up."

They were all giggling quite hard. "Jentry! That was so creative and funny," Sally said, "I mean, Dennis Quaid has to mean you made that one up, since you mocked Hannah, but it was fun."

"I will have you know, my dear Sally, it's one hundred percent a real dream. I had it after watching Innerspace on a date at the campus theater last year. One point for Moi!"

"That's not the kind of stuff I would think you dream about." Hannah sat up and pinched herself. "Did those words come out of our Jen's mouth? Did I fall asleep already and dream this?"

"Hardy Har," Jentry smiled, as she threw her pillow at Hannah.

They played another round before settling down to sleep. Sally couldn't wipe the grin off her face, so happy to have her friends camping in her beloved City of Rocks. The second leg of the road trip was off to a great start.

July 20, 1991

Sally was an early riser. From the age of ten, she had responsibilities on the farm that required an early start to the day. When she left home for college, the habit had stuck. Try as she might, she could not stay in bed past six o'clock. The other habit she had developed years ago was starting the day with scripture reading.

For her twelfth birthday she had been given her very own set of scriptures by her Grandma Johnson. She had picked Sally up, and the two had driven into Burley, where they enjoyed a special lunch before Grandma Johnson took Sally to the Deseret Book store, where she let her pick out a new set of scriptures. On their way home, Sally held the precious new books in her lap. She had chosen the large Triple Combination with the large Bible in bright blue leather. She had traced over the silver embossed name in the bottom corner: Sally Jane Johnson. After running her fingers along the silver edged pages, she finally lifted the books to her chest and gave them a squeeze. She made a promise to her grandmother that afternoon that she would read her scriptures every day.

Sally had kept her promise and had not let one day start without spending time in her scriptures since her twelfth birthday. But today when she opened them, she was surprised to find an envelope with her name on the outside, tucked inside the pages of Mosiah. She recognized the handwriting at once, and her heart skipped a beat. Sam. It was with great restraint she set the letter aside and read the last chapter of Mosiah. After changing out of her pajamas and throwing on some sweats and her favorite BYU hoodie, Sally tucked the letter in her pocket, quietly unzipped the tent, and headed for Bath Rock.

As a child, the monolithic Bath Rock had been a favorite of Sally's. She enjoyed the quick climb up the back side and the 360-degree views of City of Rocks from the top. It only took Sally a few minutes to make it to the north peak. She sat for a moment, watching the early morning sun rays spread light on the towering rock formations before taking a deep breath and pulling the letter out of her pocket. It was written in purple ink on lined paper torn from a five-by-seven notepad. Sally smiled, feeling certain Sam was making do with whatever he could find when he decided to write to her.

"Dear Sally,"

Sally bit her lip, noting that in all of the letters Sam had written her as Elder Limbrey, he had only addressed her as 'Sally.' Surely, he didn't mean anything by the 'Dear,' did he?

"Forgive me for writing rather than speaking to you in person, but I thought this way would put less pressure on you. Plus, I wasn't sure if you were sufficiently recovered from our last encounter."

Sally cringed as she remembered coming out of the bathroom in her towel only to run smack into Sam.

"This might seem strange, but I find I very much miss hearing from you each week. An Elder loves to get mail and stay connected with everybody back home, and it was fun the day I got the care package from Hannah with letters from all her roommates. You were great to keep writing to me, but I must admit at first, I viewed your letters as ones from Hannah's roommate. However, as time passed, I came to view them as letters from my friend, Sally. It was fun to hear about Hannah and Paige from someone else's perspective, but more than that, I very much enjoyed your insights on the gospel and your thoughts on life at the Y and

"Earth School" in general. You are incredibly wise, Sally, and I actually learned a lot from your letters.

"Don't tell Hannah, but I'm not really sorry I crashed your girls' getaway. It was nice to finally meet you in person. Hannah says you're the sweetest person she knows, and I agree.

"I'm wondering if, by chance, we could continue our conversations, only this time in person rather than on paper, every so often. BYU is only a little over two hours from USU and I'd be happy to make the trip if it meant getting to spend more time with my friend, Sally. Enjoy the rest of your trip.

Sincerely, Sam"

Sally read the letter again. And again. She didn't know what to think. First, she was perplexed as to how he had slipped a letter into her scriptures without her knowing. But more than that, this letter was so different from the ones they exchanged while Sam was in the mission field. Those had covered deep topics, and they had shared personal and spiritual experiences with each other, but the letters weren't so, so...formal. Sally was so caught up in thinking about Sam and the letter she didn't notice Hannah making her way across the rock. Before she knew it, Hannah was sitting down next to her.

"Geesh, Sal, you're going to make the rest of us look bad by getting up so early."

Sally jumped at the sound of Hannah's voice.

"Whoa. I didn't mean to scare you," Hannah looked at Sally suspiciously, "What are you reading that has you so oblivious to the world around you?"

"Oh, nothing," Sally blushed as she tried to tuck the letter back into the pocket of her hoodie, fumbling from her nervousness.

"Sally Jane Johnson, are you keeping something from me? Best friends are supposed to share everything, remember?"

Sally stared at Hannah, unsure of what to say. She hadn't told Hannah how often she had written to Sam, and she certainly hadn't let her know how strong her feelings for him were. She was afraid Hannah would tease her, and in spite of knowing how much Hannah loved her, she wasn't so sure she would like Sally to be in love with Sam.

"Oh, Hannah!" Suddenly, Sally began to cry.

Hannah's eyes widened. "Sal, Sal, I'm sorry. I didn't mean to pry." Hannah put her arm around Sally and patted her back.

"This is so embarrassing. I feel like such a dork. I don't know why I'm crying. Well, yes, I do." Sally wiped her tears with her sleeve and tried to smile. "It's just this letter. Ahh! I don't understand it, and it caught me off guard, and you caught me off guard. Oh, man. This is too weird." Sally's words almost ran together as she nervously tucked her hair behind her ears.

"You're losing me, Sal. Start at the beginning."

"Well, remember when you had us send that care package to your brother?"

"Yeah."

"Remember how he sent us each a letter the next week?"

"Yeah."

"Well, I wrote him again." Sally looked sideways at Hannah to try to gauge her reaction.

"Okay, Sally, I don't see what's so embarrassing about that."

"Well," Sally took a deep breath, "I didn't tell you. I didn't try to purposely keep it from you, but I didn't actually broadcast it either. I know how close you two are and how picky you said you were about the girls he would date. Not that a letter is dating, of course!"

Sally could tell Hannah was trying not to laugh. Sally's shy and reserved nature was so different from Hannah's extroverted, gregarious personality. She was an open book and the first one to strike up a conversation with strangers anywhere she went, while Sally was the opposite. She had come out of her shell with her roommates but had still earned the nickname Turtle for how shy she was around others, especially the opposite sex.

"Well, actually," Hannah said, "In earlier times, some gentleman courted the ladies purely by correspondence." It worked. Sally laughed and visibly relaxed. "So, you wrote to my brother a few times. No big deal. Did you really think that would bother me?"

"I guess I didn't think it would bother you, but I thought it might be weird. I mean, you only asked me to send him the one letter, and I ended up writing him the whole mission."

"Wait a minute? You wrote him the whole mission?" Hannah slugged Sally in the arm. "How often?"

"Just once a week."

"Really? How did I miss that?"

"Because I made sure I grabbed the mail each day." Sally smiled shyly.

"So, umm…what's this letter you were trying to stuff in your hoodie?"

Sally looked down at the letter poking out of her pocket and blushed again. Should she dare show it to Hannah? Would Sam want his sister to read it? Perhaps Hannah could offer insight into what made Sam sound so formal all of a sudden.

"I found it this morning in my scriptures. I don't know how it got there. I came up here to read it. Actually, it's so different sounding from his other letters and I didn't know what to make of it."

"Well, you're lucky I came along then. I'm an expert on Samuel Theodore Limbrey, and I can assist you in your quest to decipher the meaning of said letter. Hand it over."

"Don't tell him I let you read it, though, okay?"

"Cross my heart." Hannah took the letter from Sally and quickly read it. Sally watched her face intently. It changed from nonchalant to surprised to extremely amused. Sally was starting to regret sharing it.

"Well, I'll be hog-tied!" Hannah laughed in a fake Texan drawl. She handed the letter back to Sally with a huge grin on her face. "So, you're who he was referring to. It seems you weren't the only one being all secretive about the letters."

"What do you mean? I mean, I figured he didn't tell you we were writing either, because you never mentioned it, but what do you mean I was who he was talking about?"

"No way!" Hannah smiled. "That information is worth too much. What will you give me for it?"

"Hannah!" Sally almost begged, "You can't say he talked about me and then not tell me what he said."

Hannah looked at her friend with one eyebrow raised. "Sally Jane Johnson, I think you've been keeping more than a secret pen pal from me. I think there is much more to this letter writing business than you're letting on."

Sally closed her eyes and covered her face with her hands. "This is so embarrassing." She peeked out at Hannah from between her fingers.

"I think you might have a crush. A crush on my brother! Sally Jane, you little tart."

"Tart?" Sally laughed and smacked Hannah on the knee. "Han, I can't believe I'm saying this out loud...but it is way more than a crush." She sighed and turned to stare off at the valley before them. "The first letter was just in fun, with Jentry and Paige. The second letter, I was thinking of my brothers and how much they liked getting mail on their missions. Same with the next couple. But a few months down the road, it became more than that. For me, anyway. I'm sure it was the anonymity of not really knowing Sam, but I could tell him anything. And we would play these fun question-and-answer games."

"Like what?"

"Well, there were two. The first one was serious. You know how the Ensign magazine has a Question-and-Answer section, with doctrinal stuff? I'd ask him a question one week, and he'd answer the next. Then he'd ask me one, and I'd research it and answer him back. Then, some weeks, neither of us could think of a serious question, so we'd ask silly ones, like the kind you make fun of in magazines." Sally laughed, remembering some of them, "He's so funny. Anyway, over time, I started to feel..." she broke off, unsure of how to describe it. "It's silly, I know. I mean, it's so one-sided. I'm his kid sister's roommate. The goat girl from Rupert. I'm sure the letters didn't mean half as much to him as they did to me."

"I am going to hurt you one of these days. Quit being so hard on yourself. Sally, why don't you see yourself like the rest of us do? You may be a goat girl, and you may be from Rupert. But what is wrong with that?"

"Hannah. I'm a realist. You and Paige are beautiful, bubbly blondes with muscles from head to toe. Jentry is a dark and mysterious beauty guys find a challenge. I'm just... just...I'm just Sally. I'm ordinary. I've got ordinary brown hair, and ordinary looks, and a very ordinary body. I'm the kind of girl guys want to help tutor them in math, not the kind they want to date."

"You are so crazy. You've had tons of dates."

"That you've arranged!"

"Only because you are too much of a turtle to arrange them yourself. Sally, there is nothing ordinary about you. You are brilliant, for starters. You have a freaking academic scholarship to BYU. Those aren't a dime a dozen. You have a 4.0 GPA, and you are one of a handful of girls who aren't majoring in elementary education. You are a super duper scriptorian. You know so much about the gospel because you live it. It's not lip service to you; it's real. You are willing to try every new thing that we've thrown at you. I mean, you rock climb now, and road bike. You kayak. All these things you had never done before. Your baking skills are next level. And, Sally, you really truly are the sweetest, kindest person I know. And there is nothing ordinary about that."

"Okay, fine. I'm a genius. And I do make a delicious death-by-chocolate cake. But I want to be beautiful too. And I hate that I do! It seems so vain and petty. But I look at you girls, and I kind of covet the great genes." Sally started to cry again. She had never been this open with her friends about her insecurities.

Now Hannah started to cry. She threw her arms around her friend, "Oh Sally, do you really not know how beautiful you are? Your beauty shines from the inside out."

The girls hugged, cries turning to laughter; then Hannah pulled back, and a huge grin spread across her face. She cleared her throat, "As I was saying, you are..." but she was cut off.

"There you are!" Paige hollered.

Jentry and Paige had made their way to the top of the rock and were quickly scrambling over to them.

"How long have you been up?" Paige asked as she jumped from one ledge over to another,

"Hours!" Hannah said. She turned back to Sally, and grabbed her hand, "We'll finish this later. I assume you want this news kept undercover?"

"Yes, thanks," Sally said, relieved.

"I didn't say I'd keep it under cover. I just said I assumed you wanted me to." Hannah said with a wink as she started down the peak towards Jentry and Paige.

55

July 21, 1991

July 21, 1991

City of Rocks was so amazing! How have I never been here before? It's only two hours from home. We are having the best time with each other. I'm so glad Jentry had this idea. I love my friends SO MUCH!! Change is in the air. SHOCKER, Sally and Sam have something going on. I did NOT see that one coming! I'm not ready for the "real world" any time soon. I like being with my friends and having fun. I worry about the different directions we'll go in after school. Marriage. Jobs. Families. Ahh! Not ready. I wonder how much time we'll have together. Will we always be this close? Dumb question. We will ALWAYS be this close! Companions Forever!

Yesterday we explored the park after breakfast. There is so much to see and climb on. I loved watching the rock climbers around the park. They had some amazing skills. It was so hot though and there is not enough shade here. I don't think I'd ever come back in July. This morning, we took down the tent, grabbed breakfast at the McDonald's in Burley, and then dropped all the camping gear off at Sally's parent's house. Her mom was the sweetest! Sally looks exactly like her. I think it is a ten-hour drive from here, so we'll get to the Davenport's super late.

"How are you able to write in the car?" Paige asked, looking at Hannah in the rearview mirror.

"Well, I think about the words I want to say, and somehow my hand moves and makes letters on the paper with this weird tool in my hand," Hannah joked, though she didn't look up. She had been keeping a journal since seventh grade and tried very hard not to miss a day. President Kimball, the prophet when she was younger, had taught that Mormons should be a record-keeping people, and she had taken his counsel to heart. "I suppose next you are going to say it's weird to read in a car as well?"

"Heck, yes!" Sally interjected from the front seat. "I get so sick reading in the car, which is such a shame because imagine all the reading you could do on a long drive like this."

"I don't think there is a place I couldn't read," said Hannah, closing her journal.

"I bet you couldn't read on the back of a four-wheeler," Sally offered.

"It would depend on the speed," Hannah countered.

"I have a game we can play," suggested Paige. "I don't know its name, but one person starts the beginning of a story. They say a few sentences and then turn it over to someone else. The next person picks up the story and does the same."

"Sounds fun," Sally said. "Who's going to start?"

"I'll start, and we'll go clockwise. I'll point to you when it's your turn to pick up the story." Paige thought for a second and then began. "Once upon a time, there was a beautiful princess who lived in a forest surrounded by lakes and rivers. Her parents had named her Gladiola Louisa Esmerelda Amelia Renae, but everyone called her..."

"Madge!" Sally said, picking up the story. "Princess Madge had long red hair, the color of fire, and big emerald green eyes. Her skin was milky white, and her cheeks were always rosy. She had a dusting of freckles across her button nose. But Princess Madge was more than just beautiful. She also had a special power. She could..." Sally turned and pointed at Jentry.

"Whistle while doing a cartwheel?" Jentry shrugged. "Wait, that stinks. Do over. She could speak any language, including animal, elf, and troll. Because of this, her father, the King, had appointed her Special Linguistic Emissary of the Kingdom. Princess Madge was turning twenty soon, and so the King decided..."

"To host all the eligible Princes, Dukes, and Earls in the neighboring kingdoms to a tournament in order to win the hand of the fair Princess Madge," Hannah continued. "He was so determined to have her wed he even invited..."

"The first-born son of the Fairy King from the land of the Eastern Sun. The King had heard the heir to the Fairy Kingdom was smart, strong, and really good at Parcheesi," Paige laughed. "His name was..."

"Umm, umm..." Sally faltered. "Buddy. Buddy...Light..." She spotted a post in the distance. "Buddy Lightpole." The girls all laughed. "Buddy was very excited to be invited to the tournament for Princess Madge. He didn't go on many dates with the other fairies because they weren't attracted to his humpback and pegleg," Sally giggled. "But Buddy had a poet's heart and knew someday someone would see past his exterior and fall in love with the fairy that he was."

"The day of the tournament arrived," Jentry said seriously. "Fifty Princes, Dukes, and Earls, and one Fairy showed up to compete. The tournament consisted of five challenges. First, they would have to swim across the raging Sapphire River. Second, they would have to carve their own arrows and hit the bullseye of a target. Third, they would need to climb the tallest pine tree in the forest. Fourth, they would need to…" She passed the story back to Hannah.

"Hunt, skin, and cook a rabbit to be served to the King, perfectly seasoned. And fifth, they would have to dance the mashed potato."

The story continued for miles as their imaginations turned the love story of Princess Madge and Buddy Lightpole more and more preposterous. Hannah felt such love for her friends. Jentry and Sally felt like family now, too. She wished someday they could all live on the same street in Providence, like she and Paige did. With Sally and Sam liking each other now, she got her hopes up and thought perhaps that could happen. At least they could all be neighbors in Heaven, she thought. She was certain the maxim 'Families Are Forever' applied to friends as well.

"This rain is really coming down hard," Sally said from the backseat several hours later. They had all traded places when they stopped in Baker City for lunch, giving Paige a break from driving.

"We get a lot of rain in Portland," yawned Jentry, "But nothing like this."

"I totally adore thunder and lightning storms," said Hannah, straining to look past the steering wheel through the sheets of rain to scan the horizon for lightning.

"Sorry to break it to you, but I don't think there is any lightning. Just lots and lots of rain." Paige turned the defroster on to clear the windows, which were starting to fog over.

"When I was a little girl, if we got a massive storm in the middle of the night, my dad would grab Sam and bring him into mine and Esther's room, and we'd watch the storm from our window. Those nights are still some of my favorite memories with him."

"I had forgotten about that," said Paige. "I was sleeping over one night when Uncle Bruce gathered us for a storm. We were sleeping in your basement, and he came down with a bowl of popcorn and said to meet him on the deck with blankets. The echo of the thunder off the mountains was crazy loud."

As they came upon the rest stop at Deadman Pass, the rain started to let up, and Belinda Carlisle's song 'Summer Rain' started to play on their mixed tape.

"Turn it up!" called Sally from the back seat. The girls all started singing along as Paige cranked up the volume.

"Hannah, pull over and let's dance," Paige suggested.

Hannah pulled off 1-84 into the rest stop parking lot. She lifted the back hatch of the Suburban and turned the radio all the way up as the girls filed out of the car into the warm summer storm and began dancing and singing at the top of their lungs.

"Oh, my love it's you that I dream of. Oh, my love, since that day, somewhere in my heart I'm always dancing with you in the summer rain!"

They sang in unison.

They were soaked in minutes but didn't seem to notice or care. Sally laughed more than she sang and smiled at each of her friends. Paige dusted off her old drill team moves, which made Sally laugh even harder. Hannah grabbed Jentry's hands, and they spun in circles, singing.

A truck pulling back onto I-84 gave them a honk, and they waved back in return. When the song was over, they rummaged through the back of the car, digging out beach towels and drying off before piling back into the Suburban for the remainder of the drive.

July 22, 1991

"Happy Birthday to you! Happy Birthday to you!" Jentry sang as she opened each of her friend's bedroom doors while banging on a pot with a wooden spoon.

"Who are you, and what have you done with Jentry?" Hannah asked as she stumbled out of her bedroom, hair disheveled and curls matted. "What time is it?"

Paige and Sally came out of their rooms, rubbing their eyes and stretching. Jentry had waited as long as she could. "It's eight o'clock on the dot. I let you sleep in as late as I dared. I have an incredibly special birthday celebration planned for us. Today, we celebrate all of our birthdays with a day of pampering in downtown Portland, followed by a starlight adventure."

"I can't wait to see downtown," Sally said. "I was sound asleep when we drove through last night. Sally Jane Johnson reporting for birthday duty," Sally said, saluting Jentry. "What is our first assignment?"

"First, everyone take a shower and get dressed for a day in the city. Wear good walking shoes too. We're going to take the MAX into town, get manicures and pedicures, and then have lunch at The Melting Pot. After that, we'll walk around downtown and check out Pioneer Place Mall for some items I will explain over lunch."

The girls were out the door and headed to the nearest MAX station in time for the ten o'clock train. Jentry had grown up using public transportation and took the ability to get downtown without needing to worry about parking for granted. She tried not to laugh outright at Sally's wide-eyed enthusiasm over a twenty-minute light rail ride. Jentry was quite proud of Portland, and it made her feel good to see her friends fall in love with her city.

Built along the Willamette River, an offshoot of the mighty Columbia, Portland was a city that hummed with an eclectic, artistic energy Jentry felt sustained by. She didn't realize how much she missed her city until she was playing tour guide all along the riverfront to her friends. She took them from one fountain to another, pointing out various sculptures and statues along the way. Watching Hannah, Paige, and Sally crane their necks in awe as they looked up into the bronze face of Portlandia filled Jentry with pride. She was fourteen the October the statue floated into town on barges and was installed over the Portland Building entrance. She had already discovered she had a love for art, and a natural drawing ability, but it was gazing at Portlandia where she first realized art was meant to inspire and move people. She had spent hours sketching her on Saturday afternoons the following summer, trying to capture the depth of her expression.

The Melting Pot was two blocks south of Pioneer Square. After their spa appointment, Jentry treated the girls to a fondue lunch at the restaurant. It was there she explained the plan for the night.

"Alright, Loves," she said, while dipping her bread into the warm cheese sauce in front of her, "after this, we're going to walk off these calories by heading to Pioneer Place and split up to do a little secret shopping. Tonight, we're going to bury a time capsule in Forest Park."

"Is that allowed?" Sally asked.

"Sally, dear, what is my number one motto?"

"Ask forgiveness, not permission," Sally said, and the girls all laughed.

"The park is fifty-two hundred acres. We're going at night. We'll be in and out of there before anyone knows. And we're just burying a little box, not a body. I'm sure it's fine."

"Sounds like a rad adventure. I'm all for it. What are we putting in it?" Hannah asked.

"Glad you asked. We're going to the mall, and we'll split up so no one sees what we purchase. I want you to get a little something that represents you. Nothing too big. The box isn't huge. When we get back to the house, we'll write down our predictions for our life. We'll come back in twenty years and see how close we were."

"Ooh," Paige said, rubbing her hands together. "I love this plan. This sounds like a fantastic way to celebrate turning twenty."

***

The girls had left the house as soon as the sun set over the Cascade Mountains. They pulled off on the side of Skyline Boulevard and started grabbing their equipment.

"Paige, you carry the shovel. Hannah and Sally can wear the backpacks with our stuff and hold the flashlights, and I'll carry the box." Jentry passed the items out, and the girls started down the dirt lane and headed towards Wildwood Trail. They had barely left the main road when the raindrops started falling.

"Of course! What is with all the rain we're getting on this trip?" Hannah asked.

"Don't worry. I've got umbrellas in the car. Wait here." Jentry grabbed Sally's flashlight and jogged back to the Suburban. She returned quickly with four umbrellas, and they continued down the path.

"Is it weird if I think the rain adds to the ambiance?" Paige questioned from the back.

"Only if you think it's weird this makes me want to sing Eddie Rabbit," Hannah laughed and immediately started singing. *I love a rainy night. I love a rainy night.*

"I love to hear the thunder, watch the lightning when it lights up the skies," Jentry joined in.

"You know it makes me feel good!" Sally and Paige sang along loudly.

The girls continued down the lane, singing and laughing as they tried not to stumble on roots or slip in the mud. Before long, they came to the junction at Wildwood, and Jentry pointed out the pine tree she wanted to bury the box beneath.

"Are you sure you're going to remember this spot in twenty years?" Hannah asked, trying to make out the location in the dark.

"I know this trail well, I promise. And there is this little hollow under that biggest tree that makes it the perfect spot. Let's take turns digging. It shouldn't take too long. We don't need to go super deep."

"Are you kidding? Have you seen these biceps lately?" Paige joked, stepping forward. "I got this. Point to your spot."

Paige shoveled as Sally held an umbrella over her. The ground was soft enough that it was quick work. In ten minutes, she had a hole just the right size for their plastic bin. Hannah and Sally took their backpacks off and put them under the safety of the umbrellas so they could each get out their time capsule items and future predictions.

"Alright, Loves, hold up the item you chose to represent yourself, place it in the box on top of your letter, and tell us one thing you predict or hope for your future," Jentry instructed. "I'll go first. I picked two items. I couldn't help myself. The first, no surprise, is a can of Diet Coke. The second is a set of watercolors." Jentry placed her letter at the bottom of the box and set the soda can and paints on top of it. "And my hope for my future is to own an art gallery." Jentry smiled. "Who wants to go next?"

"I will!" Sally's hand shot up, and she stepped forward. She held up a tiny onesie with a pink giraffe on the front. "I know everyone jokes girls only go to BYU to get an MRS degree, and they're only looking for husbands. I really do want to get my Geology degree, but I also really want a husband and family. I've always wanted to be a mother, ever since I got my doll, Jenny, for my eighth Christmas." Sally placed her letter at the bottom of the box, then folded the onesie and placed it on top. "And my future prediction is I'm going to have seven children, just like my mom. I wrote down all the names I've picked out for them. Since I don't know how many I'll have of each, I wrote seven boy names and seven girl names, to be safe." Sally laughed and stepped back.

"Did you predict your future last name?" Hannah asked quietly, elbowing Sally conspiratorially, causing Sally's eyes to go wide as she shushed her friend.

"I bought a roll of film, because there is no way I am putting a nice camera in a box for twenty years," Paige said as she placed her items next to Sally's. "And I predict I will live happily ever after with my Evan and have the sweetest family. I'll be a photographer on the side for a little spending money."

"I really hope each of you have all your predictions come true," Hannah smiled at each of her friends as she stepped forward. "You're amazing, and I feel very confident when we dig this baby up in twenty years, we'll laugh at how spot-on we were. So, for my item, I got this snazzy hot pink sweatband and this keychain of a Nike swoosh to represent my current love of running, which I am sure I will do for the rest of my life. My letter was more goals than predictions. I may not have understood the assignment correctly," Hannah said, sheepishly looking at Jentry as her friends smiled back at her. "So far, I've only done half marathons. I have a goal to do a marathon by my twenty-second birthday. And another goal is to always make sure you fine ladies are part of my life, no matter what the future holds."

"Aww. I love you, Hannah." Sally reached out and gave Hannah's hand a squeeze. "I love all of you so much."

"Ditto," smiled Jentry.

"Back at you," said Paige.

"Love you more!" piped up Hannah.

They huddled together with the umbrellas while Jentry poured the dirt on top of the box and tramped it down. "Alright, Loves, I can't wait to come back here in twenty years and hear everyone's full letters. But for now, I'm kind of cold and ready for the hot tub."

Anxious to get out of the rain, the girls hurried back down Fireline Two as fast as they could.

July 22, 1991

Today has been BUSY! I can barely keep my eyes open. We arrived in Portland last night after a looonnng drive and went straight to bed. Today there was time to explore the Davenport estate. We've always teased Jentry about living in a mansion, but I had no idea her home was this big! It has wings! Like in Jane Austen books. It sits on top of a hill and overlooks all the peasants.

They have a gardener because there is no way her parents are mowing that lawn. It's got to be an acre. We finally got to meet sweet Lucia, who Jen has talked about for two years. She is so adorable. Five feet tall if that, and a head full of grey curls. Her accent is pretty thick.

Jen said she grew up in Columbia. You could tell she and Jen love each other. Would you believe we haven't met her parents yet? They were in bed when we got in and at work when we woke up. What kind of parents don't want to meet their only child's best friends? Guess Jen didn't exaggerate.

Jentry came up with THE COOLEST way for us to celebrate #20. We buried a time capsule in some forest. It was spooky, fun, and tender all at once. We're going to dig it up when we turn the big 4-0.

Tomorrow we're headed for Cannon Beach. I can't believe this will be the first time for Paige, Sally and me to see the ocean. What a bunch of hicks we are!

July 24, 1991

The weather in Cannon Beach is unpredictable and changes in a heartbeat. The sky can be black with rain that lasts only thirty minutes before clearing to reveal bright blue skies. There are days in the summer when the temperatures are so chilly beachcombers are bundled up in gloves and scarves, and likewise, days in the late fall where one can enjoy the beach in shorts and a tee shirt.

So, it came as no surprise to Jentry in spite of a spectacular day at the beach yesterday; this morning, they had awoken to a light rain and a drop in temperatures that kept them huddled around the fireplace while they played Parcheesi after breakfast. The rain eventually ceased and gave way to a low-hanging fog, which burned off around noon. They took their time getting showered and dressed and decided to walk into town to browse the shops and have lunch at Driftwood. They walked to town by way of the beach, cutting up at First Street. After walking through several art galleries and souvenir shops, they went into Ter Har's, where Jentry bought each of them matching Cannon Beach hoodies. By the time they made it to Driftwood, it was nearly two o'clock, and they were starving. They decided to all get a bowl of chowder and then split some fish and chips.

The server had brought them their receipt and Hannah was trying to convince them it wasn't too late in the day to hike Neahkahnie Mountain when a young man approached their table.

"Well, well, well," he said slowly as he came to a stop next to Jentry's chair, "What have we here? Ms. Jentry Davenport, aren't you a sight for sore eyes?"

Jentry's heart dropped in her chest, and for the first time in a long time, she wasn't exactly sure what to do. She saw her friends were smiling politely at the stranger that had interrupted their lunch, not knowing he was responsible for Jentry's darkest moments in life. Her stomach flip-flopped at the realization her two worlds were about to collide. Her past was something she tried to forget and never talked about. She wasn't sure her friends would still love her if they knew how wild her high school years had been. She took a deep breath and squared her shoulders, willing her voice to sound steady before speaking.

"Am I? Interesting," she finally looked up at him and said nothing more. She kept her face impassive while he looked at her with a smirk playing across his lips.

It had been over three years since she'd last seen him, and she was disappointed to see he'd only gotten better looking with age. He was taller than she remembered, probably six feet. And he'd definitely been working out. A lot. She hadn't remembered his muscles straining at his shirt sleeves before. He was wearing his dark hair a little longer. She had always liked running her fingers through his thick hair. His hazel eyes were still proud and rebellious.

"Jentry, where are your manners? Aren't you going to introduce me to your lovely friends?" he finally asked, turning to smile at each of them.

Jentry seethed at the insult, "Buckley Van Wagoner, these are my lovely friends," she said, trying not to clench her teeth. Jentry noticed Paige looking at her intently and slightly nodded her head, knowing her friend had noticed how uncomfortable she was.

"Nice to meet you, Buckley. Please excuse us though; we were just leaving," Paige said as she stood and pushed in her chair. Hannah and Sally followed her lead.

Jentry gave her a grateful smile as she stood as well, ignoring Buckley as she stepped around him and tried to follow her friends to the door. He grabbed her arm as she passed. Jentry turned, looked at her arm, and then up at him with a raised eyebrow.

"I didn't mean to upset you, Doll. I was surprised to see you and wanted to catch up."

"Let go of my arm, Buckley," Jentry said calmly, "And don't call me Doll. There's nothing we have to catch up on. Our lives went in quite different directions. By your choice if you remember. Now, if you'll excuse me, my friends are waiting."

Buckley let go of her arm but quickly grabbed her hand instead. "We have a lot to catch up on, and I think you know exactly what, or who, I should say, I mean. I know you've changed since high school, Jentry. So have I. Please, I just want to talk. Give me thirty minutes of your precious time to find out what happened."

Jentry looked over her shoulder at her friends. They were waiting at the door with curious looks on their faces.

Paige mouthed, "Do you need help?"

Jentry shook her head no and held up a finger to say she'd be a minute. Turning back to Buckley, she pulled her hand free. She didn't want to have this conversation with him. She didn't want to relive a past she couldn't change and wanted to forget. But maybe she did owe it to him to discuss it one last time so they could both have closure. Maybe he regretted how things had turned out before.

"I'm only here a few more days, and I'm trying to have a nice vacation with my friends, but I'll give you your thirty minutes. Tonight. Come by the house at eight." Jentry quickly hurried back to her friends, wondering if she was making another big mistake.

"Let's go get some Tillamook ice cream, Loves," Jentry said as she headed out of the restaurant, trying to act like her usual self but catching the curious looks her friends were giving each other.

"Jen, are you okay?" Sally asked, putting her arm around her friend.

Jentry smiled at Sally. She was so tenderhearted and always so attuned to everyone's feelings. "I will be after a double scoop of ice cream," Jentry smiled.

***

Jentry had been persuaded by Hannah to take the girls on a late hike to Saddle Mountain after their strange lunch encounter. Worn out from the 1640-foot elevation gain in two and a half miles, the girls decided to call it a night earlier than usual. Hannah and Sally were asleep as soon as their heads hit the pillow. Paige fell asleep with a book in her hand about fifteen minutes after crawling into bed. However, a few hours later, Jentry still couldn't sleep in spite of how tired she felt. She decided a cup of hot chocolate might help and quietly slipped out of the bedroom she was sharing with Paige.

She sprinkled a little cinnamon into her mug and wrapping her robe more tightly around her, slipped out the back doors onto the deck overlooking the water. The sky was cloudless tonight, and the moon shone bright over the Pacific Ocean. She leaned on the railing and slowly sipped her hot chocolate. Lost in her thoughts, she didn't notice the figure approaching from the sand below. As he set foot on the stairs leading from the beach up to the deck, a motion sensor light switched on. Jentry jumped, almost spilling her drink, before realizing it was Buckley coming up her steps.

"Perfect!" Buckley said, a little too loudly, "You're still up."

"Buckley, it's almost midnight. What are you doing?"

"You said you wanted to talk to me," he said as he reached Jentry.

"I said I was willing to talk to you. There's a difference. And I said eight."

71

"Don't be mad, Doll," Buckley said as he leaned in closer to Jentry. "I got lost."

The smell of alcohol on his breath was unmistakable. "You're drunk, Buckley," Jentry said disgustedly. "Some things never change."

"I'm not drunk. I've had a drink."

"A drink? I doubt that. You know, Buckley, I can't believe you'd show up here this late and in this condition and think we can have any kind of a conversation. I knew this was a mistake. Go home."

"Playing hard to get, again, Doll? You always did like to lead me on. Invite me over, let me get close, push me away. It was all part of your game." He stepped closer and grabbed her around the waist. "But if I remember right, it was a game where there were two winners, because you always gave in in the end."

"Let go of me, Buckley," she said through clenched teeth as she put her mug on the railing so she could use both hands to push him away.

"Jentry, Jentry, Jentry," he whispered, "We both know why you had me come here. You want me. Don't fight it." He pulled her tighter, trapping her arms in the embrace, and started kissing her neck.

"Stop it, Buckley," she said, her voice catching. She turned her head, trying to block his mouth.

"You don't want me to stop, any more than you did when we were in high school. I know you like it rough." He grabbed her by the front of the robe and pushed her up against the railing, kissing her hard on the mouth as he did.

Jentry pushed against him but was no match. She tried to keep her lips closed to his and cringed as she felt his tongue pushing against her mouth. She tried beating on his chest, but he only grabbed her wrists and held them above her head as he continued to press his body into hers. Tears streamed down her cheeks as she tried to scream, but any noise she made was muffled by his mouth over hers. He shifted his body slightly, allowing her enough room to bring her knee up as hard as she could between his legs. He let go of her, cursing as he doubled over in pain. She tried to run to the door, but he reached out and grabbed the back of her robe. She let out a scream as he pulled her down to the balcony. He quickly climbed on top of her, pinning her arms at her sides with his legs.

"You're going to pay for that, you stupid little bitch." He brought his arm back, ready to strike Jentry.

She squeezed her eyes shut and braced for an impact that didn't come. She opened her eyes and found Hannah holding his arm with both of hers to keep him from hitting her, while Paige was at her side with a can of pepper spray aimed at his face. Sally stood in the doorway with the phone in her hand.

"You've got two seconds to get out of here before we call the police," Paige said, holding the spray steady.

Buckley yanked his arm out of Hannah's grip and stood up. "Settle down, ladies," he laughed. "Jentry and I were having a little fun, weren't we, Doll?"

"You're a pig!" Jentry said through tears.

"And you're a slut. But that's what I always liked about you."

"Your two seconds are up," Paige said as she stepped closer to Buckley, spraying the pepper directly into his face. "No one talks to my friend like that."

Buckley screamed as his hands came up to his face.

"I suggest you get your sorry ass back to your place so you can rinse that off," Hannah said calmly as she helped Jentry stand up. "We'll call the police if you're not off this property in thirty seconds. Come on, girls," she said as she ushered them into the house and locked the French doors behind them. They stood side by side, watching Buckley stumble down the steps to the beach, screaming in agony, clutching at his face.

Moments later, they were seated around the living room; the lights were off, and the room glowed from a few candles Paige had lit. Jentry sat next to Sally on the couch with a blanket wrapped around her. No words had been spoken since they had come inside from the deck. She wasn't sure she was ready to break the silence but knew it was time to tell her story. She took a deep breath, catching the cinnamon vanilla scent in the air.

"You probably have a million questions. I'm not sure if I can answer all of them, but I can try."

"You don't owe us any answers or explanations, Jen. We just want to sit with you and make sure you're ok," Hannah offered.

Jentry smiled, "I know I don't owe you anything, but I want to tell you my story. I need to, really. I've kept a part of my life from you, and it doesn't feel healthy anymore to keep it inside." Jentry looked at each of her friends and then back down at her hands. "My parents weren't super involved, as I've mentioned. They were very career-focused, and they're both really exceptional lawyers. They aren't exceptional parents, so it's a good thing they only had one child.

"I feel like our housekeeper, Lucia, did more to bring me up than anyone else. She wasn't around all of the time, though, so too often, I was left to my own devices. I don't know if I was looking for attention from my parents, if I was being stupid, or just trying to have fun. But around tenth grade, I started acting out and breaking a lot of their rules. I'd been a great student all through elementary and junior high. Stayed out of trouble, got straight A's, and spent my spare time drawing.

"Something changed once I went to high school, and I started being a little more rebellious. My grades slipped a bit, and I started going to more parties and messing around. Nothing crazy. Not for Portland teens, anyway. I'd have a few beers at parties, and I'd make out with a lot of different guys. Tame stuff, really, for around here." She stopped talking for a minute, her eyes wandering over to the window, though only blackness and the dancing flames from the candles around the room were reflected back at her.

"My junior year of high school, I started dating Buckley. He was a senior, and we met in an economics class. He came on real strong right off the bat. Lots of flirting and attention, and I ate it up. He had a couple of annoying younger brothers, so we'd hang out at my house most of the time. We got into my dad's liquor cabinet the second time he was over. Lucia had gone, and my parents weren't ever home before eight. It was the first time I tried vodka. It burned so hard going down. I didn't love the way it tasted, but I liked how it made me feel a little dizzy and happy at the same time." Jentry closed her eyes and could picture everything about that afternoon.

The sun was starting to set, and the trees in the ravine were throwing long shadows onto the deck. The patio doors were opened wide, and she stood in the doorway with the bottle of vodka in her hand. The radio was playing, and as Need You Tonight by INXS came on, Buckley turned the radio up a little louder. His arms reached around her from behind. He took the bottle from her hand and had another swig.

"Come over here," he whispered into her ear, singing along with Michael Hutchence.

Jentry giggled and turned around, wrapping her arms around his neck. "I love this song. It makes me feel tingly inside," she whispered before pulling him into a kiss.

Buckley picked her up and sat her down on top of the patio table. "Tingly, huh? More tingly than I make you?" he asked, bending down and kissing her on the neck.

Her head was swimming, and she couldn't tell if she felt dizzy from the liquor, from the lyrics of the song, or from Buckley's lips on her skin. She only knew she was feeling a new kind of energy pulsing through her body. It scared and excited her at the same time. She grabbed Buckley's hair and moved his head from her neck to her breasts. His hands slipped under the back of her shirt, releasing her bra clasp. He slipped her shirt over her head and then led her back into the house and up to her bedroom.

"We had sex for the first time that day. It became a game to me then. How quickly could I make him want me, and then how long would I tease and toy with him until I gave in." She looked around the room at her friends and smiled ruefully. "A few months later, my period was late."

"Oh, Jentry," Sally whispered, grabbing her hand.

"I was too young to really be aware of my cycle, but when I started throwing up my breakfast every morning, I was able to put two and two together. I actually told Lucia first. Isn't that strange? I trusted my housekeeper more than my parents. With good cause. My mother immediately suggested I get an abortion. I went to Buckley after that, foolish enough to think we'd start a family or something. I thought I loved him, and I thought he loved me. Turns out he just loved screwing me. He told me to get rid of it and come back when I was ready to ride him again."

Sally audibly gasped, and Jentry patted her hand. "See? There's a reason I keep this stuff buried. I'm not that girl anymore, but I worry I'll always be thought of as some teenage slut now."

"Don't say that," Hannah said emphatically. "Don't you ever say that or think that again. You made some mistakes. They don't matter now. All that went away when you were baptized," she said. "We love you just as much, Jentry. I promise."

Jentry smiled softly at Hannah and leaned into Sally's hug. She had been the most worried about Sally's reaction.

"What happened with the pregnancy?" prodded Hannah.

"Lucia caught me crying in my room after telling Buckley. I explained I didn't think I could get an abortion. She told me about a niece of hers who had been married for several years and had been unable to have children. They had started talking about adoption. David and Sofia Mulder. Though Lucia was Catholic, Sofia had joined the Mormon church when she met David. Lucia introduced us, and immediately, I felt they were meant to be my baby's parents. My parents were furious at Lucia and threatened to fire her, but eventually backed down. They didn't really care enough about me and my choices to put up too big of a fight.

"When my senior year started the next month, they hired a tutor. Most of my friends stopped coming around because it was too awkward. Sofia became my new friend, even though she was six years older than me. We would go for a walk a few evenings a week, and that's when she would talk to me about the Gospel. I was baptized before the baby was born. I loved David and Sofia, and part of me wanted to always be in their life, but I worried I would get too attached to the baby and things would be complicated. I never held my child. They were in the room with me as I gave birth, and the doctors put her directly in Sophia's arms the second the cord was cut. The nurses had been instructed to usher them into another room immediately."

"Her?" asked Paige.

"Elodie Elizabeth Mulder."

"Elizabeth," Paige said softly, "your middle name."

"I thought we'd keep in touch in the beginning, but they were busy with a new baby, and I was trying to figure out the next stage of my life. I finished my senior year at home with my tutor, took an art class at PCC, and then enrolled at BYU. I think my essay on adoption and baptism made up for my drop in grades. My test scores didn't hurt," Jentry paused, and the girls let her take the time she needed to continue.

"They wrote me a few letters during the first few months, giving me updates about Elodie. They sent me a photo of the three of them on her first birthday. She's so beautiful. But I couldn't handle it. I wrote back, telling them how much I loved them and little Elodie and how grateful I am for them, but I had to move on. That's how I ended up in Provo and met the most amazing friends a girl could ask for."

"Did you ever hear from Buckley again?" asked Paige.

Jentry laughed dejectedly, "Not once. I never even saw him again after the day I told him I was pregnant. My parents had someone in their firm draw up the paperwork for him to sign over his parental rights. He didn't hesitate. His dad contacted mine once to make sure no one had a legal claim on Buckley for child support." Jentry took a sip of the herbal tea Sally had made her and got lost in her thoughts for a moment. "I heard from some friends at school he was dating someone else pretty seriously within a week. So, until today in town, no, I hadn't heard from Buckley Van Wagoner, father of my child."

July 25, 1991

At nine o'clock, while Jentry, Paige, and Sally slept in after the late night of talking, Hannah drove over to Ecola State Park for a run on the Clatsop Loop Trail, which wound through the lush Sitka spruce forest. Hannah wasn't used to the strange weather on the coast. This morning, a thick fog hung over the beach again, completely masking the ocean into something that could be heard but not seen. Hannah doubted this fog would burn off at all. The air was getting wetter, and before long, a light drizzle soaked her clothes. She was glad she had put on a long-sleeved shirt and pants for the run but still felt a chill in spite of the sweat she had worked up.

She knew this would be a shorter run and had set a faster pace than she did when she was training for a half-marathon. From the Indian Beach parking lot, she had headed north on the Cannon Beach Trail and then cut over to the Clatsop Loop Trail to head back to the car. As she rounded a curve, she looked through a break in the trees to see if she could spot the ocean through the rain. She took her eyes off the unfamiliar trail for a moment and, in so doing, did not see the exposed tree root that crossed her path.

Her left toe caught on the root, twisting her ankle as she went down. The sharp, shooting pain in her foot was intense enough to cause her to cry out. She was worried her ankle was sprained. As she sat in the middle of the muddy trail, with the rain coming down harder, she wondered how long before her friends came to look for her. It was then she realized she had their only vehicle. The hopelessness of her situation struck her as quite comical, and she started to laugh through her tears of pain. Another runner came around the bend and stopped in his tracks.

"Uh oh. This doesn't look good. You okay?" he asked.

"Define okay," Hannah said, wincing a little as she tried to move her left foot. "I think I sprained my ankle."

"You know, there are some shelters close by. Why don't I get you out of the rain and take a look at it?"

"Umm," Hannah hesitated, appraising the stranger. She figured a serial killer wouldn't be out on this trail in this weather and was in enough pain to accept help where it was offered. "Okay," she finally agreed.

The man quickly slipped his arms under her and picked her up. She guessed he was a few inches taller than her. He had the slender build of a runner. Most of his hair was underneath a 49ers baseball cap, but a few tight black curls escaped. His nose was slightly crooked, suggesting it had been broken, and he had a few days' worth of stubble on his chin. He smiled down at her as she put one of her arms around his neck, revealing straight white teeth with the tiniest gap between the front two. His skin was a rich brown, and despite her pain, Hannah felt butterflies appear in her stomach.

"This is a little awkward," she said, smiling.

"What? Having your arms around a handsome stranger or being a clumsy runner?" He winked at her as he effortlessly jogged back in the direction he had come.

Hannah noticed his almond-shaped eyes were the color of dark chocolate and danced with mischievousness. "Actually, I meant my getting you all muddy. Sorry about that."

"What's a little mud when rescuing a damsel in distress?"

Hannah laughed again, "I'm Hannah."

"Morgan. Nice to meet you."

They arrived at the clearing known as Hiker's Camp. Several small log cabins were nestled in the woods, as well as a few covered picnic tables. The cabins had wooden bunk bed frames in them, where hikers doing the 382-mile Oregon Coast Trail often slept for the night. Hannah had noticed them earlier and remembered Jentry talking about them on the drive from Portland. Morgan went inside the first one and sat Hannah down on one of the wooden bunks. Sitting beside her he gingerly slid off her shoe and took her ankle in his hands. Hannah winced again as he examined her foot.

"On a scale of one to ten, what level of pain would you say you're at?"

"You sound like my doctor when I got appendicitis. I guess if that was a nine or ten, then this is a five or six."

Morgan smiled down at her. "I should mention I'm a doctor. We're all trained to sound alike. It's soothing to the patient." He winked at her again. "So, a five or six?" he said, looking back down at her foot and carefully twisting it from side to side to check the range of motion. "It's slightly swollen, but my guess is it's a minor sprain. Get some ice on it and stay down for a day or two."

"Well, I guess if I'm going to be a clumsy runner, you're the right man to have come along. Thanks for helping me."

"You're welcome. And I was kidding when I called you that."

Hannah glanced out at the opening of the shelter to see if the rain had let up at all. No such luck. She figured they were at least a mile from the parking lot, and she didn't know how she'd make it back to the car.

As though he could read her mind, Morgan said, "Let's wait another ten minutes and see if the rain lets up. Then I'll take you back to your car. Can you wait that long?"

"Yeah. I'm pretty tough," she replied with a grin.

"You did drive here, right?"

"Yeah. Did you?"

"I'm staying in Seaside and took the Tillamook Head Trail here."

"Well, if you can drive me back to my friend's place, I'll have someone get you back to Seaside."

"Deal. Until then, how about a game of twenty questions? Make's the small talk easier."

"Okay," Hannah agreed, finding Morgan oddly to the point but quite friendly. She had decided he was not a serial killer or ax murderer. "I get to go first."

"Okay."

"What's your full name and where are you from?"

"So, we're doing two questions at once, huh? Okay. Full name is Morgan Dewayne West, and I'm from Beaverton, Oregon. Same questions to you."

"Hannah Limbrey. Providence, Utah."

"I haven't heard of Providence. Where's that?"

"It's in Cache Valley. By Logan. About an hour or so northeast of Salt Lake City. Have you ever been to Utah?"

"Absolutely. My buddies and I have been to Moab and Canyonlands a few times."

"Where do you go to school?"

"I'm about to start my first intern year at OHSU. I got my BA in Anthropology from Colorado State, did my first two years of med school at Gonzaga in Spokane, and finished out at UW in Seattle."

"You must like rain," Hannah teased.

Morgan laughed. "I do like rain. But I like being close to mountains and the ocean more."

"That's understandable."

"Are you in school?"

"I'll be starting my junior year at BYU next month."

"Okay, the next logical question would be, what's your major, but that's too easy. So, I'm going to go with what's your sign?"

"Seriously?"

"Astrology is serious business, young lady."

"I'm a Cancer, actually."

"Interesting. Do you fit all the characteristics? Loyal? Emotional? Manipulative?

"I'm all the good traits, none of the bad. I can't believe you even know that stuff. Is that part of medical training nowadays?"

Morgan smiled at her, and Hannah was surprised to find her pulse quickened a little. In spite of the pain in her ankle, she found she was quite enjoying her time with this stranger.

"We spend an entire year on it. Actually, I had a crazy aunt who fancied herself a bit of an astrologist and psychic. Her readings used to be the entertainment at family reunions."

"I bet that would be fun. What was the wackiest prediction she ever gave you?"

"Hmm." Morgan stroked his chin as though deep in thought. "Oh, well, there was the one she gave me a few years back. She said one day I would meet a pretty girl on a run in Oregon."

"Really?"

"Yeah, but she said the girl would be clumsy. In fact, I think she even said when I first saw her, she would be covered in mud, sitting in the middle of a trail, laughing hysterically."

"I was hardly hysterical," Hannah insisted.

"Why were you laughing, if you don't mind my asking?"

"I have our only car, I didn't tell my friends when to expect me back, and I realized they couldn't come looking for me very easily. The direness of the situation just struck me as funny."

"That's actually pretty impressive. To be in pain but see the humor. Best way to get through life."

"Okay, next question," Hannah smiled. "Favorite comfort food."

"Easy, it would be my Aunt Corrine's fried okra."

"What?!" Hannah made a face. "Of all the foods in the world, you choose okra?"

"Don't knock it until you try it. She uses a delicious batter that gives them a little kick and then makes a remoulade sauce for dipping. Wish I had some right now."

"I've never heard of that. Now I feel bad about my favorite."

"We can't all have highbrow taste. What's your favorite comfort food?"

"Cook and serve chocolate pudding."

Morgan laughed. "From a box?"

"Yes, and you have to eat it while it's still warm and just starting to develop the little skin on top," Hannah laughed as well.

"Sounds like a delicacy."

"I don't know why it isn't served at more five-star restaurants," Hannah smiled up at him. "What kind of medicine are you going into?"

"I'm debating between general surgery and orthopedics. I won't need to officially decide for at least a year. This year, I'll be rotating through different specialties, which will help me make my decision."

"I hope your future is everything you envision. And some day, when you're a world-famous doctor, I can say, 'I knew him when.'"

"When what?" Morgan asked mischievously.

Hannah laughed. "When you were lost on a trail at the coast, and I helped you find your way in a rainstorm, of course. Seriously though, do you come over to the coast often?"

"I love the ocean and come over when I can. This trip is because I'm out here with friends. Some high school buddies and I try to knock out a mountain bike trek every summer. This year, we're biking from San Francisco to Seattle. We try to bike about fifty miles a day. We stay at campgrounds or cheap motels at night. There are seven of us, and we take turns driving a support car as close to the route as possible in case there are any problems."

"Have there been problems?"

"Eddie got a bad flat in the middle of the Mendocino National Forest. That ended up slowing us down a day."

"That sounds like so much fun. How cool you guys have stayed close."

"Yeah, we all grew up in Beaverton and met in kindergarten. It's a good group of guys. I'm lucky."

Hannah nodded in agreement. She thought of Jentry, Paige, and Sally and how lucky she felt to have them in her life. "Oh dear!" Hannah looked down at her purple Swatch. "My friends are going to wonder why I'm taking so long. I think we've talked a little longer than ten minutes."

"Time did seem to slip away. I apologize if I've held you up."

"Don't apologize, Morgan; I've enjoyed every minute, and it's taken my mind off my pain."

"Well, it looks like the rain isn't going anywhere, so let's get you back home and get your ankle elevated and iced." He picked her up and headed back out into the rain. Rather than taking Clatsop Loop Trail, where he had found Hannah, he opted for the wider Cannon Beach Trail on which she had started. It was a wide dirt road and posed less risk of another fall.

Hannah pressed her face into Morgan's chest to try to keep it as dry as possible as they headed down the trail. This had been such a strange and exciting morning. Her ankle still hurt, she was drenched, and yet her stomach still felt full of butterflies.

She hadn't felt like this for quite some time. Hannah dated occasionally, but not seriously. She'd fallen for the charms of a much older man her freshman year and ended up in another compromising situation. After one more humiliating confession to the Bishop, she decided she needed to erect a pretty big wall in order to keep herself safe and guard what was left of her virtue. She put up a valiant fight against falling in love, afraid she would lose all willpower when she met her soul mate. Despite her best efforts, it seemed that whenever she had the opportunity to be cautious and careful, she would instead run full force into her next mistake.

After too many trips to second base, she had spent the last six months not dating at all, trying instead to focus on school and exercise. She had forgotten what it felt like to be attracted to someone. As they made their way back to the car, she couldn't help but imagine kissing Morgan's incredibly full lips.

Within twenty minutes, he had Hannah returned to Jentry's beach house.

"Knock. Knock," Morgan called as he opened the door and stepped inside. "Hope everyone's dressed," he whispered to Hannah, smiling.

Jentry came around the corner from the great room. "Hannah. What on Earth?" she said upon finding a soaking wet and mud-covered Hannah in the arms of an equally soaked stranger.

"Hey, Jen," Hannah said. "I biffed it on the trail, and my new friend, Dr. West, here, found me. He thinks my ankle is sprained."

"Here, bring her in here by the fire," Jentry said, turning back down the hallway. Paige and Sally stuck their heads out of the kitchen to see what was going on. Jentry led Morgan to the great room and started to clear a spot on the leather couch for him to lay Hannah down.

Paige and Sally gathered around Hannah and started fussing over her. "Hannah, Love, you are a mess," Jentry said, shaking her head while covering Hannah with a fleece blanket.

"Thanks, Jentry."

"Do you have a first aid kit here? I want to get her foot wrapped," Morgan asked Jentry.

"I might have something in the bathroom. Let me go check."

"Hannah, you must be freezing. Can I make you some hot chocolate? Can she take a hot shower, doctor?" Sally asked, slipping into the maternal role which suited her so well.

Morgan smiled. "You don't have to call me doctor. Morgan is fine."

"Oh, sorry. Yeah, Paige, Sally," Hannah interrupted, pointing at the two of them, "This is Morgan."

"Why don't you help her take a quick hot shower? I'll get an ice pack ready," Morgan said.

"Morgan, really, you've done enough. I'm okay," Hannah said, though she was in no hurry for him to leave.

"I insist. I've got to see this through. You get cleaned up. As Jentry said, you're a mess."

On cue, Jentry came back into the room. "All I could find were a couple of band aides and some Neosporin."

"Oh, where is my brain? There's a first aid kit out in the car," Sally said. "There should be a bandage in there, as well as an ice pack. I'll get it."

"Come on, Han, I'll get you into the shower while she gets the kit." Paige let Hannah lean on her while she limped down the hall to the bathroom.

"Can I get you a towel or anything, Morgan? You look cold too," Jentry asked.

"That'd be great, Jentry. And do you have a phone I could use to let my buddies know where I am?"

"Sure. There's one in the kitchen," said Jentry, pointing behind him. "I'll go grab you a towel." She disappeared back down the hall.

Twenty minutes later, Hannah was showered and dressed in pajamas, settled under a warm quilt on the couch. Morgan had her foot wrapped and propped on a pillow. Jentry had found some ibuprofen in the cupboard and given it to Hannah along with a big glass of ice water.

"Morgan, can you stay for breakfast? These waffles will be done soon," Paige called to him.

"That is genuinely nice of you to ask, but I better not. We're supposed to make it to Long Beach, Washington today. Thanks, though."

"Oh, Jentry, I told Morgan someone would give him a ride back to Seaside. Can you do that?"

"No problem. I can wait to eat."

"Thank you, Jentry. I'm sorry to wreck your morning."

"It's no problem at all. You saved our Hannah. It's the least I can do."

"Thank you." Morgan turned back to Hannah. "Well, I think I've done about all I can do for you, Miss. Keep your foot iced and elevated through tomorrow, and then see how it's doing. You strike me as the type who might try to push through an injury more than you should," he said.

"I might be guilty of having done that before. But I promise to be a good girl. Thanks again, Morgan, for all you've done to help me. I'd probably still be in the middle of that trail if it weren't for you."

"Glad I could help. You take care, Hannah."

"Are the keys in the car, Han?" she asked as she put on a jacket.

"Yeah. Thanks, Jen."   Hannah watched Morgan walk down the hall and was surprised at how much disappointment she felt.

As he got to the front door, Morgan paused. "Excuse me, Jentry, one sec," he turned back and quickly walked back to Hannah. "Could I call you in a few weeks to check on your healing and finish our twenty questions?" He smiled sheepishly.

Hannah couldn't help but smile from ear to ear as she said, "You can call me anytime. Somebody, grab me a paper and pencil."

July 25, 1992

Oh my gosh! The craziest thing happened today, and I met the cutest guy when I biffed it on a trail. I've never dated a black guy before. There aren't a lot of them in Cache Valley or at BYU. Not that this was a date. His name is Morgan. Like Morgan Freeman, from Driving Miss Daisy. And he's going to be a doctor. And he asked for my number. Ahhh! But honestly, he lives in Oregon, and I live in Utah, and so the odds are not great.

And let's not forget how I'm nervous about dating now because I keep letting guys go too far. Not all the way of course! But I'm still sinning. Why am I so weak? So easily tempted? I want to be good, like my mother. And my friends. And the Savior, of course. Duh.

I sprained my foot today which put a damper on things. I also got a strange phone call today from my favorite brother. (Only brother.) We'd left the beach house phone number with our folks, and he tracked us down. The plot has thickened! That is all I'll say for now, because I'm in desperate need of more ibuprofen.

July 27, 1991

Hug Point was so named because of the way the old stagecoaches had to 'hug' the point of the land when they rounded the outcropping of rock that went right to the ocean's edge before the highway was put in. Deep grooves were imprinted into the bed of the rock from the wagon wheels that had passed that way. Hug Point Beach was always one of Jentry's favorites. On the south side of the point were two small caves perfect for shielding oneself from the cool Pacific winds. A narrow stream cascaded down the small cliff where the trees met the sand. Its waters made a pool for children to play in before meandering down to the ocean. For the last night of the trip, before heading back to reality, Jentry had taken over the planning from Sally. She had always loved picnicking at Hug Point and thought it a fitting place to have their last beach fire and marshmallow roast.

"Okay, Loves!" Jentry hollered from her bedroom as she finished securing her hair in a ponytail. "Paige and Sally, I'm going to drop y'all off at Arcadia Point. You'll have about a thirty-minute walk and time for Sally to enjoy her Paige Alison McLean one-of-a-kind professional photo shoot. We'll drive back to town to pick up our pizza and then meet you at Hug Point. You almost ready?"

"Give us five more minutes," Paige replied as she finished curling the last section of Sally's hair.

"Is there any chance we'll walk past it before you get there to flag us down?" Sally asked.

"I think you've got over a mile walk in front of you, and Paige will be stopping you every five minutes for a photo, so I'm hoping we don't eat all the pizza before you get there."

Jentry stood in the doorway and gave a conspiratorial wink to Hannah.

Sally turned around and looked in the mirror as Paige sat the curling iron down. "Paige, can I hire you to be my full-time make-up and hair assistant? You actually make me forget I'm a farm girl sometimes."

"Sally Jane, you look pretty spectacular." Paige had curled Sally's hair into spirals and put a little more make-up on her than she usually wore. "You don't need me. I was just working with the gorgeous looks the Good Lord already gave you. Your spectacularness has extraordinarily little to do with some curls and Cover Girl. Okay, Sal, I got to do hair and make-up, so Hannah insisted on being your clothing stylist."

Hannah, lying on the bed with her foot propped, motioned to the clothes on the chair in the room. "For your casual beach wear tonight," she continued, "I have chosen to pair these red and pink plaid capris with a white tee and a pink cardigan in case of a cool Pacific breeze. Completing the ensemble are white Keds and silver hoop earrings."

"Cute, though I'll feel a little overdressed for a beach fire. Are you sure my jeans and a sweatshirt won't work?"

"Silly Turtle," said Paige, throwing Sally the pants, "Remember, I'm doing a photo shoot. You have to look the part."

"I love you in pink, Sal. Not my color, but definitely yours," Jentry said.

Sally sighed and grabbed the pants. "I've been victim to your photo shoots for two years now, Paige, and I still never felt quite comfortable being gussed up."

"Come on, Gimpy, let's get you in the car," said Jentry, helping Hannah up off the bed.

She dropped Paige and Sally at Arcadia Beach and watched them make their way down to the sand.

Backtracking into town, she picked up pizza from Pizza a Feta and then made her way to Hug Point. It took several trips to get their picnic and Hannah to the caves.

It was nearing six-thirty when Paige and Sally came around the bend of Hug Point Beach.

"Well, it's about time. I was starting to think Hannah and I were going to have to eat a whole pizza by ourselves," Jentry said, feigning indignation while motioning them over to the blanket.

"My fault," Paige said, raising her hand. "I went camera crazy."

"I figured as much. The fire is going, and the food is still warm." Jentry had their picnic blanket laid out at the edge of the large cave and had a small fire going a few feet from it. The cooler was next to the pizza, and Jentry had already put the paper plates, cups, and napkins on top of it. Hannah was on the edge of the blanket with her foot propped up on a pillow.

"Look at your rad beach fire skills, Jen," Paige said as she plopped down on the blanket. "Pretty impressive."

"I'm not just a pretty face, Love," Jentry replied, stoking the fire with one of the roasting sticks. "Let's eat," she said, turning back to her friends.

"You don't have to ask me twice," Sally said as she placed a slice of pizza on a plate.

"Wow," Paige said, looking towards the waterfall on her left. "This is really pretty. I can see why it's your favorite."

"Yeah, I always loved this place. Cannon Beach is beautiful, too, but there is something special about how secluded this beach is. When I was younger, I'd grab a blanket and a book and walk down here to escape the parents."

"They'd let you come here alone?" Sally asked, shocked.

Jentry gave a rueful smile. "Sal, I doubt they noticed. They never said anything if they did. I'd be back in time for dinner, we'd eat, and then pretty much go back to our separate lives. Remember, my childhood wasn't all warm and fuzzy like yours."

After eating, Jentry, Paige and Sally walked around the beach, with Paige stopping and posing them for pictures more times than they could count. Sometimes, Sally would take over duties, so there was a record of Paige being on the trip as well. The sun was now low on the horizon, and it wouldn't be long before it set over the Pacific Ocean. Jentry and Paige had rejoined Hannah back at the fire while Sally walked down to the water's edge.

***

An unusually warm breeze had picked up and was lifting Sally's hair off her shoulders. She stood with her bare feet in the wet sand as the tide brought the cold ocean waters up to her ankles and then pulled it back into the ocean. The majesty of the ocean thrilled her. The sound of the waves crashing over each other, spraying against the rocks, spoke to something deep inside her. She didn't want to take her eyes off the mighty Pacific, not knowing when she would see it again.

She could hear the faint sound of her friends talking and laughing, carried on the breeze, and smiled. What an adventure the last two weeks had been. She felt more connected to these girls than ever. She thought of the quote she had recently read by English writer John Evelyn. *Friendship is the golden thread that ties the heart of all the world.* The image delighted her, and she closed her eyes and pictured a golden thread connecting her heart to those of her friends.

At the sound of a guitar, she opened her eyes and cocked her head, trying to place the tune. She instantly recognized Jim Croce, one of her mother's favorite artists. A voice started singing, and Sally brought her hand to her mouth in shock. She had heard that voice sing once before. In a truck headed for Paris Springs.

"Yeah I know it's kind of late. I hope I didn't wake you.

But what I gotta say can't wait. I hope you understand."

She turned slowly, daring to hope he was there for her. He was walking down the beach, playing a beat-up guitar, his eyes locked with hers. She watched him, motionless. He smiled at her and continued singing, walking towards her.

"Every time I tried to tell you the words just came out wrong.

So, I'll have to say I love you in a song.

Yeah I know it's kinda strange. Every time I'm near you

I just run out of things to say. I know you'd understand."

Thirty feet. Twenty feet. Ten. Five. Now, he was right in front of her. She was looking up at him, tears in her eyes, a smile on her face.

"Every time I tried to tell you the words just came out wrong.

So, I'll have to say I love you in a song."

Sally felt the tears spill out of her eyes and run down her cheeks, but she made no move to wipe them away. She seemed frozen in place, transfixed in a dream she never thought would really come true.

"Every time the time was right the words just came out wrong.

So, I have to say I love you in a song."

Sam stopped playing and slipped the guitar strap off of his shoulder. He held it in one hand as he took Sally's face in the other. Without the accompaniment of his instrument, he continued to sing to her.

"So, I have to say I love you in a song."

He smiled as he wiped her tears with the back of his hand. Then slowly, he leaned down and tenderly kissed her. Sally melted into his arms. At the same time, she heard an eruption of cheers and clapping.

"I've always loved that song."

"Just the song?" Sam asked, with a twinkle in his eyes.

Sally blushed but smiled at him. "No, Samuel Limbrey. Not just the song."

He leaned down and kissed her again, and she caught the standing ovation they received from the corner of her eye. Sally pulled away with a giggle and looked over at her friends. "Part of my time-capsule wish just came true!" she shouted over to them.

July 30, 1991

Happy official birthday to the lovely Sally Jane Johnson, who was dropped off in Rupert earlier today.

We made it back to the townhouse. I'm going to stay the night with Jen and then head home for two weeks to work before school starts.

This trip ended up being so much more meaningful than I anticipated. It started out fun, and the fun continued of course, but I feel like our friendships reached new levels. It's hard to explain exactly. There were so many moments where I would just look over at my friends and think these girls are gifts from my Heavenly Father and I just admire and respect them so much.

I want to be more like them in so many ways. I want Jentry's courage. She has faced some hard challenges in life, but she has pushed through them with grace, and works hard to make her dreams a reality. It took courage for Jentry to open her heart to us and let us love her. She hadn't known real love and acceptance with her dumb-dumb parents and her stupid ex-boyfriend. I'm so glad she was brave enough to let us in.

I want Sally's humility. She is one of the most spiritual, kind, loyal, loving people I know. She's so smart and beautiful too. She doesn't see herself the way we see her. And that's not the humbleness I'm talking about. She has a spirit about her which radiates love. She follows the Savior and loves Him unabashedly, and I wish I had a fraction of her doctrinal knowledge.

I want Paige's confidence. She knows who she is, and she doesn't have to try to prove herself to anyone. She knows what she wants in this life, and she makes it happen. I feel like she could handle anything life throws her way and not be shaken. I worry WAY too much about what others think about me and I don't think feelings of inferiority ever cross her mind, but not in a bad way. She's not conceited or stuck up. She just knows her worth.

We'll all be back in school in a few weeks. It's just Jentry, Sally and I in the townhouse now. We've made plans to meet up with Paige every day we can. I can't wait to see where our lives go in the next twenty years before we dig up our time capsule. I know one thing though. We will always be best friends and support each other through this life.

PART TWO

September 7, 1991

They had a ward party up the canyon last Saturday. Hot Dogs and visiting. I met a new guy from church named Lucas Russell. He has the best head of hair. I ended up talking to him for half of the night. There was some witty banter back and forth, but overall, I think he comes off conceited.

I wish Morgan would call. I thought I would have heard from him by now. It felt like we really hit it off and he was interested. He was just so fun to talk to and so good looking.

It's been strange being back in the townhouse without Paige. I'm glad she's still on campus with us. We all try to meet at the Wilkenson Center at the end of the day to visit before heading home.

September 19, 1991

Luke (Lucas) is growing on me. It helps that I still haven't heard from Morgan. He asked me out and we went to his place and watched Star Trek, which was kind of lame, but it was something to do. Sam and Sally are madly in love. They talk on the phone almost every night. He can't come down each weekend, because of school and work, but comes down a lot.

I have a religion class with Paige on Tuesdays and Thursdays. Our teacher is Brother Top. He's great. Also, he loves my writing and frequently reads my papers in class, which is pretty cool. He explains the Gospel so well. I feel my testimony growing so much stronger than it used to be. Before it was because my parents told me everything was true. Now I know it is. And I just want to

LIVE it! I am so grateful to belong to the <u>one true church!</u> And to know what I need to do to make it back to Heavenly Father. I'm so grateful for the Atonement. I don't know what I would do without the repentance process.

Jentry has started trail running with me. Can you believe such a miracle? Who is she?? Haha. We don't go far, but she says she's enjoying it. We've been starting at the Rock Canyon trailhead and going up to the first bridge and back. I've found so much joy in running and hiking and being outdoors. I would love it if Jen could too.

October 1, 1991

I kissed Luke last night. I don't know if I've ever been kissed like that.

November 29, 1991

Sally opened the door to her parent's house and threw her arms around Sam. She had hitched a ride with some friends a few days before to spend Thanksgiving with her family. Sam had braved the snow and winds of I-84 to spend the weekend with her.

Sally had told her parents about him in August, and she and Sam had come up to Rupert over fall break so he could meet her family. The Limbrey and Johnson households were quite different, but Sam seemed to fit in and genuinely like those he had met so far.

Tonight, Sally would be taking Sam to see the Christmas lighting on the Town Square, a Rupert tradition she looked forward to every year.

"Hi, beautiful girl," Sam said, giving Sally a quick kiss as her mother came around the corner.

"Sam, I'm so glad you made it safely," Ellen Johnson said warmly. "I was about to herd this crew into the van, so we aren't late for the lights. Do you have a scarf and gloves? It's a cold one tonight. Sally Jane, grab Sam something from the closet," Ellen ordered without waiting for Sam to reply.

George and Ellen ushered everyone out to their passenger van. They drove into town and parked at the church on Eighth Street. They walked two blocks south toward the square, staying close to each other to fight off the cold night air.

"This is amazing," Sam said as he and Sally strolled around the block, bundled up against the weather.

Rupert's town square was like stepping back in time. A large greenspace with trees, a gazebo, and a fountain was surrounded by quaint shops on each side. People crowded the square and the streets surrounding it, which were closed to traffic. Cocoa and doughnuts were being sold from a food truck, and the line was long with people hoping to warm up with the hot beverage.

Sally's family was gathered on the street outside of the Ropers, waiting for the firetruck to come by. Carrie and Graham had run off with friends, but Sally's older brothers were there, along with their wives.

"Is this crowd only people from Rupert?" Sam asked, wrapping his arms around Sally to keep her warm.

"Oh no, people come from all over the area. It's more magical than the Fourth of July. Rupert is designated as a Christmas City USA, you know."

"I did not know," Sam said with a grin.

The blare of the old siren could be heard before the firetruck came around the corner, decorated with wreaths and lights. Hanging off the side of it and shouting into a megaphone was Santa. The crowd went wild.

"Ho Ho Ho! Who is ready for some Christmas magic?" the man dressed in red asked the crowd. "Count down with me."

With one voice, the crowd chanted, "Ten, nine, eight, seven, six, five, four, three, two, one!"

Suddenly, lights shone all over the square. They were wrapped around trees, covered the gazebo, and hung on the storefronts. The crowd roared with cheering. A loud boom echoed off the buildings as fireworks exploded overhead.

Sally arched her head back and clapped with delight. She loved the holidays and was excited to be sharing this favorite tradition with Sam. "Isn't this wonderful?" she asked, turning around to look at him. She let out a gasp as her hand flew to her mouth.

Sam was kneeling in the street, a ring box in his outstretched hands. "Sally Jane Johnson," he yelled over the crowds, "Would you do me the honor of becoming my wife?"

"Yes. Yes!" Sally shouted back while her family whooped and hollered behind her. She pulled off her glove and stretched out her left hand. Sam took the ring from its box and slipped the round-cut solitaire on her finger.

Sally threw her arms around him, as he spun her.

"This is amazing, Sammy. I love you so much. I can't wait to be your wife."

"I love you, Sal. We're going to have the most wonderful life together."

Sally's family forgot the fireworks and crowded around the newly engaged couple to admire the ring and offer congratulations.

December 26, 1991

Merry Christmas! I had such a magical holiday season. Jentry and Sally came home with me for the holidays. Paige went to Mesa with Evan. She gets to escape the cold and snow, and I'm jealous. I wish Luke was from somewhere warm, instead of Colorado, where it still snows. He's gone home for Christmas as well, which is kind of a relief. He's putting a big push on me to get married, and I just don't know.

I want what Paige and Sally have with Evan and Sam, and that is NOT Luke and me. Jentry tells me he's not right for me all the time. I've tried to break up a few times, but he says it's Satan trying to keep us apart. Jen says that's garbage, but what if he's right? What if he and I really are going to be great together? I don't know. He's coming to Logan on the thirtieth to meet my family. I love him enough, but it lacks deep emotion. Sometimes I wonder if he didn't have such great hair and wasn't such a good kisser if we would still be going out. Is it weird that I have dreams about Morgan and the trail still? Not daydreams. Real nighttime dreams.

February 1, 1992

I'm crying as I write this. I found out today that I'm pregnant. I haven't told anyone yet. Not even Luke. How am I going to tell my parents? Everyone is going to know we had sex. And it was <u>one time</u>! What are the odds of pregnancy? Heavenly Father must be so disappointed in me.

I'm disappointed in myself. I'm better than this. Why was I so weak? Honestly, I didn't consider Luke marriage material, and now I'm having his baby??? This is like something from General Hospital or Days of Our Lives. Ahhhhhhhhhh!!!!!! I feel like I just blew up my life. I'm going to be the talk of the family.

And what will my friends say? Sally does baptisms at the temple every week and is so good and pure. How do I tell them this?

What is to become of me? And my life? And this baby's life? I'm not ready to be a wife or mother. But I chose to sin, so I've got to suffer the consequences.

February 3, 1991

Hannah answered the door wearing the same pajama pants and sweatshirt she had been in for two days. She had skipped class and barely left her bedroom. She told everyone she was sick with a cold. She knew she needed to tell Luke about the baby, so she finally called him and told him to come over. She opened the door and motioned for him to come in.

"You look terrible," he said, as he sat down on the couch.

"Nice to see you too," Hannah mumbled as she shut the door.

"You sounded serious when you called," Luke said, "Like you're having doubts about us again."

"Luke," Hannah tried interrupting.

"Let me finish. You're probably having doubts after, you know, we had sex. I think Satan got a hold of us, and we gave in, but it's fine. We'll talk to the Bishop and straighten things out. I don't think anything bad is going to come of it. Probation at best. We aren't the first students to have sex before marriage. We aren't getting kicked out of school. Seriously, what's the worst that can happen?"

"I'm pregnant," Hannah blurted. Luke stared at her without a word, so she said it again. "I'm pregnant, Luke. Barely. A couple of weeks. But I am." She waited for him to respond. She wasn't sure what she expected him to do. Cry? Laugh? Propose? He sat there, almost in shock.

"I don't know what to say, Hannah. This is very unexpected."

107

Hannah laughed sarcastically. "Well, we knew it was a risk. Now what?"

"What do you mean? Now we get married."

"Luke, I don't know if I'm ready for marriage."

Luke stood up, agitated. "That's not what it felt like the night you seduced me."

"What?" Hannah choked out.

"Look, Hannah, one of us has never broken the Law of Chastity in any way, and the other has had issues. I was willing to look past your sins because I think we'll be great together. Forgiveness and the Atonement and all that. But you wore me down. You're the one who took me back to your room to make out and let it go too far. I never pressured you. You were putting the moves on me. So, if you loved me enough for sex, certainly you love me enough for marriage."

Hannah sat in stunned silence. She had been so careful and hadn't put herself in a compromising position for a year or more. She was doing so well at sticking to her dating boundaries. Then, one night, they got carried away. Her friends were out, and she had the house to herself. It went from kissing, to necking, to her removing her shirt.

"I didn't put a gun to your head, Luke. If I remember correctly, you're the one who happily took off my bra. And you clearly were up for what came next," she said, stressing the word up. "This isn't just on me. Geez, Luke. You're making something difficult even harder. Do you know how nervous I was to tell you? How scared I am about my future? How ashamed I am for my sins?" Hannah said, starting to cry.

Luke put his arms around her. "Sorry. I was caught off guard. We'll be okay. We'll get married right away. Before you're showing. No one has to know."

"Some people have to know," Hannah said through tears, "Like our parents and our closest friends. The Bishop."

"We'll figure it out. This isn't how I wanted us to start our life together, but we'll make the most of it. We're not going to let Satan win. We're meant to be together. I know it. I love you, Hannah. I know you love me and fight it for some reason."

Hannah wasn't so sure. She wanted to be madly in love and knew she was settling with Luke. He was Mr. *Right Now*, not Mr. *Right*, and she knew it deep down in her heart. She also knew she couldn't give up her baby. She knew how hard that had been for Jentry and didn't want the same kind of heartbreak. So, when Luke got down on one knee, with no ring in his pocket, in what had to be the least romantic proposal ever, she said yes.

February 8, 1992

Hannah was sitting in the living room a week later. She had told her friends she had something to tell them, and they'd made plans to meet early Saturday morning after breakfast. Paige had driven over from Orem, and now she, Jentry, and Sally sat across from her with smiles on their faces. Hannah was sure they had no idea what her news was.

Hannah took a deep breath. "There's no way to say this that isn't awkward and uncomfortable, so I'm just..." Her voice caught, and she had to pause for what felt like a full minute. "I don't even know how to say this."

Sally moved across the room, sat next to her, and took her hand. "Hannah, whatever it is, we're here for you." Concern was written all over her face.

Hannah cleared her throat. "I'm pregnant." She heard a small gasp of surprise from Sally but kept going, staring at the carpet. "Luke and I messed up on New Year's Day, and now I'm pregnant, and we're getting married. I'm trying to be happy about it. About the wedding and the baby, but really, I'm afraid of both. And I'm so embarrassed. I think I'm smarter than this, and now I'm just in over my head, and my life changed on a dime. I feel like I'm on some train that is shooting down the tracks so fast, and I just want to get off and catch my breath."

Jentry, in an unusual show of emotion, leaped across the room and threw her arms around Hannah, crying. "I know exactly how you feel, Han. Exactly. It's going to be okay."

"That's a really hard situation, Han," Paige said. "I feel awful you're so sad. But we love you no matter what, you know that, right?"

"I know it," Hannah said, chin quivering. "I know you'll love me no matter what, but I don't want to disappoint you or make you ashamed of me."

"I'm going to hurt you if you ever say that again," Paige said, trying to laugh to ease the tension. "You're human. We all make mistakes."

"Sally doesn't," Hannah said, seriously.

"What? Yes, I do. I mean, they're different than yours, but I make them."

"Name one."

"I haven't been to the temple in over a month."

"Not even close to a mistake, Sal!" Hannah rolled her eyes.

"Well, the point isn't about mistakes," Sally said. "Yours, mine, or anyone else's. The point is we love you, and we're going to support you and help you with this."

"Exactly. What can we do, Hannah?" Jentry asked, arms still around her.

"We sat down with Dad and Mom a few days ago. We've decided to get married on March seventh. It's soon, but I'm due in October, so no point waiting. Mom wanted to give me a wedding and reception still, but I'm just not feeling it."

"That's so sad, Hannah. Don't treat your wedding like something to be ashamed of and hide. You're doing what you feel is best for a child, and that is very, very brave. Please let us help you make it special," Sally offered.

"A month doesn't give us a lot of time, but we can pull something off. Maybe we could plan a shower or cater a reception or something?" Paige offered.

"We're in the middle of the semester. I don't want to put you guys out."

"If it wasn't this situation and you were getting married under different circumstances, what would you have wanted, Hannah?" Sally asked, grabbing a notebook and pen.

"A summer wedding," Hannah deadpanned.

"We'll have to do our best with March, Love. You never know with weather, so you'll want an indoor ceremony, most likely."

"No reception! And nothing in a church gym. Something small. Uncle Thomas is the Bishop now, so I guess I'll ask him to do it."

"I bet my dad would love that."

"Love is a strong word to use for marrying your knocked-up niece to a man she has misgivings about. Maybe a wedding and small meal with our families and very closest friends?"

"I know," Sally said excitedly. "There's that beautiful hotel in Sardine Canyon. Next to the golf course. Sam took me to dinner at the restaurant there once. Sherwood Forest or something?"

"Sherwood Hills," corrected Paige.

"That's it. We could rent a conference room for the ceremony and have a small luncheon after. Paige and I can help with baking, and Jen can use her artistic flair to decorate, you name it. Then you guys could stay there for your honeymoon night."

Hannah considered it. She might regret doing nothing, and it would send a terrible message to Luke and his family if she didn't want to celebrate their wedding. She owed it to him to give her all. He was the father of her child, and he loved her. She could try.

"I like that idea, Sally. I'll run it past my mom tonight. You guys are the absolute best. I was so afraid to tell you." Hannah started to cry again.

"Never be afraid to tell us anything, Han. Ever. We're family. We're best friends, Love." Jentry squeezed her again.

"This is when we circle the wagons and take care of each other. You're not alone with this. Heavenly Father loves you. The Atonement is for you. We love you. We're going to go crazy for your child. And we'll welcome Luke into our family with open arms," Paige said as the girls stood and hugged.

"I couldn't do life without you guys," Hannah said, feeling hope for the first time in two weeks.

Luke and I have been married for two whole days. We got married in the morning at Sherwood Hills. In attendance were my parents and siblings, his parents and siblings, and of course Jentry, Paige and Sally. Oh, and Uncle Thomas and Aunt Jenny. It was small, but it was lovely. The room was decorated with lots of pink flowers and white Christmas lights. Uncle Thomas, aka Bishop McLean, talked to us about the importance of a Gospel centered home before officially marrying us. We had a luncheon afterward with soups and bread bowls. Simple. Sally made us a pink wedding cake. It was delicious and beautiful. We stayed the night in the hotel. It was strange to be able to have sex without guilt. It wasn't as romantic and passionate as I had hoped. Maybe disappointing sex is a punishment for not waiting. I am determined to make the most of my marriage. I owe it to Luke and this baby. I'm going to be a loving wife and do my part to bring the Savior into our home.

Luke thought we would save money living in Salt Lake Valley, instead of Provo, so we're in West Valley City right now, which is kind of the armpit of Utah, but whatever. We live in the SunBurst Apartments in a little one bedroom our families helped us furnish with cast offs.

April 15, 1992

On April 7th, armed with a tape recorder, Luke and I headed over to Dr. Bodily's office to hear the heartbeat. It was pretty amazing to hear the fast swish of our baby's heart when it was still too small to even be felt.

I have morning sickness. I throw up my breakfast most days, but then feel fine.

We're so poor, it's embarrassing. We're on food stamps and Medicaid. I had a little bit of savings for the next semester when we got married, and that helped us get our apartment. Luke had nothing saved and didn't even have a job when we got married. I am living a life 100% different than what I'm used to.

The semester ends on the 18th. I've had a few finals already, but what's the point? I won't be going to school in the fall. Luke thought it was best if I took a break from school and work to help support us so he can get his degree faster. He's going to do a double major in Political Science and Economics. He has big plans to be the President of The United States someday. He'll work this summer to try to save for a few classes, but we won't be able to afford a full load of credits with a baby.

I've been selling the Illustrated Stories from the Book of Mormon door to door while I keep looking for something else. It sucks.

April 29, 1992

I finally got a real job!!!! I went in to pay our rent and overheard they were hiring, and asked if I could apply. I was hired as a leasing consultant and will work Monday through Friday from 9 to 5. They knew I was expecting and didn't care! How lucky is that? Plus, now Luke and I get half-off our rent!!! This was a really big break for us. Today was my first day and it was so fun. The people in the office are so nice. This feels like such a weight has been lifted off of us.

May 23, 1992

Cache Valley in May was awash with wildflowers, the hillsides a vibrant green, with snowcapped mountain tops towering on all sides. Unless it was snowing. The temperature could be seventy degrees one day and forty degrees a few days later. Winter weather reared its ugly head on occasion into early June. Planning an outdoor reception in the middle of May was a risk, but one Sally had been willing to take. A small storm had covered the valley floor with an inch of snow the previous weekend, but today, the temperature was a perfect seventy-three degrees, with an ever so slight breeze blowing in from the south.

Sam and Sally had been sealed in the Logan Temple in the morning and now were hosting their reception on the lawn at the historic Old Rock Church in Providence. Sally had been standing in the receiving line for two hours, and her feet were killing her. She was grateful for all of the support from friends and family, but at this point, she was tired and hungry enough to envy Hannah, Jentry, and Paige, who sat talking at a table in the corner while enjoying the food her mother had catered by Juniper Inn.

When there was a break in the line, she kissed her mother on the cheek, grabbed her new husband by the hand, and headed for her friends.

"Make way! Make way! Tired and hungry bride approaching!" Sam joked as they sat down.

"What can I grab you guys?" Evan asked, rising.

"All of it," Sally said, pouring a glass of water. "I can't believe how hungry hugging a bunch of people has made me."

"I felt the same at my reception," said Paige.

"You may feel tired, Sal, but you don't look it. You look absolutely stunning. Both you and Paige have made the loveliest brides," Hannah smiled at Sally. "I'm starving as well because I'm eating for two, and this peanut developed an appetite early." Hannah wasn't showing yet, but she rubbed her belly as if she were.

Evan returned with food for Sally and Sam and sat back down. "So, you're headed to Cannon Beach for the honeymoon?" he asked.

"Yeah," Sam said between mouthfuls of fruit tart. "Jentry was nice enough to arrange for us to stay at her family's place for a week. We have some fond memories there, and I look forward to making more," he said, kissing Sally on the cheek.

"When we get back, we're moving into the cutest little farmhouse in Millville. I'm lucky I was able to transfer so many of my credits over to USU. New husband. New school. New address."

"I'm actually changing addresses soon, myself," said Jentry before taking a sip of water.

"What's this?" Sally asked, eyes wide.

"This is news to me, too," Hannah said, looking aghast.

"Well, with all of you married now, it's not going to be the same living in the townhouse. I've applied to Portland State University. They have a great art history program, and the Portland art scene is a little more advanced than Provo."

"I had no idea you wanted to do this, Jentry. I'm kind of speechless," Hannah said, eyes starting to water.

"I started thinking about it at your wedding, actually. I tried picturing myself at BYU without all of you guys and couldn't."

"When will you move?" Sally asked.

"First week of June. I've got to pack and figure out what I'm going to do with the townhouse. In fact," Jentry turned to Evan and Paige, "I know you're happy in your grandparents' place, but the townhouse is paid for. I'd rather have you guys live in it than rent it out."

"Seriously?" Evan asked. "We were just saying how nice it would be to live closer to campus and our jobs."

"Let's talk later, then, for sure," Jentry said.

"I can't believe you leave so soon. We'll have to make every second count before you go." Hannah turned to her friends and smiled sadly. "Seriously, though. This is it. This is where our paths really start going in different directions. Sam and Sally are moving to Millville. Evan and Paige are in Orem now, maybe Provo soon. Luke and I are in West Valley, and Jentry will be in freaking Portland. I'm not ready." Hannah's voice caught.

"Evan, will you grab my camera and get a picture of me and my friends? Let's go over here by the willow tree," Paige said, pulling them behind her. They stood in a row, arms around each other. "I love you girls with all my heart," Paige said, trying not to cry.

"I'm going to mess up my makeup if I start crying," Sally said, wiping her own tears with the back of her hand. "This is why I don't wear it. I can be such a bawl baby."

"Companions forever. Promise," Hannah said emphatically.

"Promise!" Her friends said in unison.

Evan returned with Paige's Nikon. "Okay, say cheese, Chicas!" Paige instructed, with a catch in her throat.

"Cheese Chicas!" they laughed.

<u>June 1, 1992</u>

I miss living in the townhouse with my friends. Jentry left for Portland today. Paige and I met her for lunch at The Brick Oven on Saturday. Sally didn't get back from the honeymoon until late last night, so she couldn't join us. Paige and Evan are moving into the townhouse tomorrow.

Luke and I only have one car, so I can't go see anybody whenever I want. He has a job in the shoe department at the mall, and so he has the car during the day, since we live in the same place I work.

I'm very lonely.

June 14, 1992

Deciding to leave Utah behind and move back to Oregon was one of the harder decisions Jentry had made in the last few years. She had been so happy in Provo with her friends, but with all of them married now and living in different towns, it didn't make sense for her to stay. She had let her parents know her plans to move back home in March and was informed they were already planning a move to Brazil to manage a new division of the law firm they worked at. When they told her their plans, she was saddened but not surprised to hear how this would affect their only child hadn't been on their radar.

True to form, they threw money at the situation. They sold their house on Skyline Drive and bought Jentry a three-bedroom condo at Harrison Towers downtown, near the waterfront. They continued to pay for her education and turned the title of the Cannon Beach house and Provo townhouse over to her to do with what she would. A contract was created detailing a generous monthly stipend until she turned thirty or married.

With little fanfare, they dismissed Lucia, said goodbye to Jentry, and moved to Brazil the week after she returned.

She stayed another week in the Skyline house before the new owners took possession while she waited for her new apartment to become available, as well as updated. Her mornings were spent jogging in Forest Park, with a few trips past the time capsule to check that it remained covered. She never went more than three miles, and usually only one or two, but she was grateful Hannah had insisted on turning her into an amateur runner.

Her afternoons, she spent shopping for furniture and decor. The movers had arrived yesterday to load up the furniture she wanted from her parent's home, while the rest would be shipped to Rio de Janeiro.

She excitedly took the elevator up to the twentieth floor of Harrison Towers, new key in hand. Unlocking the door, she walked into the foyer and passed the entrance to a galley kitchen on her right. From the foyer was a hallway on the left leading to the three bedrooms. The living and dining rooms were straight ahead. She had three balconies thanks to a corner unit. The one off of the dining room looked down on the Lovejoy Fountain, while the ones off of the living room and master bedroom overlooked the Willamette River and Mt. Hood. Hardwood floors had replaced the old carpet, and the walls were painted crisp white before she took ownership.

She peeked into the first spare room and pictured a guest room for her friends. She hoped somehow Hannah, Paige and Sally would be able to visit her. The second spare room would be her art studio. She looked forward to filling it with canvases and paints.

She smiled as she walked into the large master suite and out onto her private balcony. She took a deep breath, closed her eyes, and listened to the sounds of her city. She loved Portland, and she was excited by the possibilities of the life she would make here.

The doorbell caught her attention. She let the movers in and directed the placement of the furniture in the various rooms after they laid down the large area rugs she had ordered. She may not have loving parents, but she was able to live much better than most twenty-one-year-olds because of their income. The movers were gone within an hour. Tomorrow, the new patio furniture and dishes would be delivered.

The Rose Festival was still going strong on the waterfront, so she decided to go in search of a funnel cake for dinner. Tomorrow, she would find a new jogging route in town.

August 8, 1992

Millville was a small farm community in Cache Valley, south of Providence. Sam and Sally had moved into a white frame home with a green metal roof on farmland his uncle owned when they had married. It was a simple house, built by Sam's great-grandfather. There were no hallways; the rooms opened into each other, most with a door leading to two different rooms. On the main floor was a living room, kitchen, two bedrooms, and a bathroom. The front bedroom had a door to a staircase, which led to an attic bedroom. A small space behind the kitchen qualified as a mudroom, which led to the unfished basement, with the washer and dryer. The back door of the mudroom opened onto a small slab of cement and a gravel driveway.

Sam's uncle had started renovations on the place a few weeks before they moved in. The carpet had been replaced in the living room and the bedrooms, and new linoleum flooring had been installed in the kitchen, bathroom, and mudroom. He let Sam and Sally take over the painting in exchange for a reduction in rent.

During the week, they were each busy with school and part-time jobs: Sam at a call center in town and Sally as a hostess at The Bluebird restaurant. On the weekends, they painted and made improvements to the little house. All of the walls had been painted buttercream yellow, while the trim and doors received a fresh coat of white paint. They had repainted the kitchen cabinets denim blue and bought new hardware for them.

They planted a salsa garden and did their best to keep the clover and dandelion-filled yard tidy. Money was tight for the two full-time students, but they had goals they were working toward as a couple, and each was willing to sacrifice for the other.

They had finished their yardwork and chores right as the sun was starting to set over the Wellsville Mountains. They decided to end the day with a walk over to the elementary school, where they could sit on the grass and watch the sunset.

"Do you have your lesson ready for tomorrow?" Sam asked as he took Sally's hand and started down the street.

"Yes. It's on the importance of fellowshipping, and I feel the spirit telling me this lesson was meant to teach me to have a heart for service."

"Sally Jane, you have the biggest heart I know."

"I try, Sam, truly. I know I can do better. It's easy to serve those you love and know well, like you, our family, and our friends. It's different to think about serving the people at church or, heck, even the people in your town. I'm going to do better."

"Well, if you put your mind to something, I know you'll accomplish it."

"Thanks, Sammy."

"I was thinking, Sal, now that we have the garden underway, what do you think about getting a goat and some chicks? Uncle Mike only uses the backfield. I bet he'd let us do something with the front quarter acre."

"Are you serious? Oh my gosh. Do you know how much I miss my goats and chickens?"

"I had no idea because you never talk about them or have pictures of them on the fridge," Sam said, nudging Sally playfully. "And truthfully, not that I would want to admit it to anyone, your family's goat cheese and milk has really grown on me."

"We would need enclosures for both. Sheep can be pastured, but goats need shelter from the elements. Do you think your uncle would really let us do it?"

"I don't see why not. It's Millville. You're expected to have farm animals."

"Let's do it. Fresh eggs and milk would save us a lot of money. I'll call my folks tonight and see if they can get us set up with something."

They walked behind the school to the swings and watched the sunset, holding hands. Sally was head over heels in love with Sam. He told her she was beautiful every day, which she appreciated. More than that, he told her she was wise and kind, which meant more to her than beauty, which would someday fade. She was so blissfully happy with her marriage and life.

August 22, 1992

Two weeks later, Sally's parents, George and Ellen, along with her sister, Carrie, and youngest brother, Graham, came over in a truck and trailer with two nine-week-old Nubian female goats, four baby chicks, and material for building enclosures and fences.

George, Graham, and Sam first assembled the goat structure in the field to the east of the house. Sam's Uncle Mike had agreed to let them use the front pasture, and it already had a sturdy woven wire fence around it. They put upon another to cut the space in half, making room for goats on one side and chicks on the other.

Sally was instantly smitten with the baby goats, one marbled tan, one cream. They were friendly and cuddly, and she and Carrie had fun playing with them while their enclosure was built. Ellen sat next to her daughters with the chicks in a box. Between the chirping and the bleating, Sally and Carrie were in constant giggles.

"Now those are cute," Sam said, wiping sweat off his face as he knelt down to pet the goats after stopping for a drink. "Those ears. How did I not know goats had ears that hung down like bunnies?"

"Not all of them. Nubians do, which is why they are so precious," Carrie said, nuzzling the cream-colored goat in her lap.

"What are we going to name these ladies, Sal?" Sam asked.

"That little one is Goldie," she said, nodding at the marbled goat, which had wandered over to lick Sam's boots. "And this one is Opal."

"Wow. You didn't even hesitate," Sam said. "Goldie and Opal. I like it. Especially because that means I get to name the chicks."

"What?" Sally said, laughing. "There are four chicks. I'll name one, and you can name three. Then it's even."

"Alright. I'm going to get their coop ready, and then we'll give them their new monikers."

It was after dark before everything was complete. Ellen had left typed instructions for the care of the animals on the fridge before the Johnsons headed back to Rupert.

"Okay," Sally said, a little nervous. "What are you naming yours?" They stood outside, with a large summer moon illuminating the enclosures.

The golden-colored Buff Orpington chicks all looked the same, so Sam pointed randomly, "Scrambled, Fried, and Deviled."

Sally looked at him aghast. "Say you're kidding."

When he started laughing, she did, too.

"You can name them all, Sal."

"Phew. Since they are such little girls, I thought their names could be after Little Women. Say hello to Meg, Jo, Beth, and Amy."

"You are my actual favorite," Sam said, taking Sally in his arms and kissing her. "I hope you like your mini farm, Sally Jane."

"I do, sweetheart. It will be a fair amount of work to manage school, my job, my church calling, the garden, animals, and you, but I think I'm up for the task."

"Me? How hard am I to manage?"

"Not hard at all. You're putty in my hands. Kiss me."

"Ooo. Yes, please."

<u>October 12, 1992</u>

<u>On October 9th Luke and I went to see For Love or Money. Around</u> three in the morning I awoke for my hourly potty break. I got back in bed and two minutes later felt a little drip...drip. At first, I thought I had lost control of my bladder! Then it hit me that my water had just broken! I leaped out of bed exclaiming "Oh shit!" as I ran to the bathroom. Up until I got to the hospital, I hadn't felt any contractions, but when they hit, boy did they hit! The nurses got tired of me begging for an epidural and finally gave me one around 6:00. What a wonderful drug!!!

Luke went home to sleep as he was nursing a sore throat and cold, and I settled into my bed, oblivious to the hell my body was going through. Paige and Sally made me promise to call them when I went into labor, so I did that next. Paige made it to the hospital within the hour, and Sally arrived about an hour after her. They would step out into the hall and call Jentry with updates every so often.

By 11:00 it was time to push, and Luke showed back up just in time. Can we talk about pain? I tried so hard to be brave and strong. Luke made it easier. He stood by my side, rubbing my arm, stroking my forehead, calming me down. He was wonderful, truly.

At 12:08 PM on October 10th, with the help of forceps, Heather Catherine Russell came into this world. Tears streamed down my face as I held our beautiful little daughter. I have always believed in a Heavenly Father who loves us, and who has an eternal plan for us, but nothing has ever testified of those truths more strongly than the birth of my child. I have never experienced anything as spiritual as bringing life into this world and look forward to doing it again, and again, and again. There aren't words to describe my feelings as I held Heather. I was filled with such overwhelming love, peace, happiness, and hope. It was also so amazing Paige and Sally got to watch her come into the world as well. Luke has been the best father since the second that little girl was born. He strutted around the nursery like he was king of the castle. I've never seen him so proud, and with good cause. Heather was more beautiful than any other baby born that day. Luke would push Heather's cart down to my room with the biggest gleam in his eye. It's so wonderful what children bring out in adults. We knew Heather had been born with a ton of black hair, but it wasn't until the nurses gave her a bath we realized it stuck straight up! We have had many laughs at her expense.

Having Heather has helped Luke and I grow closer. Maybe this marriage will end up being the best decision I ever made.

May 21, 1993

"I can't believe you girls have graduated. I'm so jealous!" Hannah said as she pushed Heather's stroller up the gravel walkway to Sam and Sally's house.

The graduation ceremonies for BYU and USU were in April. Paige had graduated from BYU, while Sally had transferred to Utah State University when she married Sam. Although they had seen each other then, they decided to get together at the end of May for a graduation party with just the three of them. Jentry had graduated from Portland State and wanted to join them but had recently started a job at the Portland Art Museum and couldn't get away. Hannah always felt like they were cheating on Jentry when they got together without her.

"Let me at my niece!" said Sally, picking up seven-month-old Heather and squeezing her. "She's such a little butterball! Come in, come in. I have lunch ready for all of us so we can catch up." Sally ushered the girls into her small farmhouse. "I'm so glad we decided to have our own little celebration together."

"Look at your homemaking skills, Sal. They have gone through the roof." Hannah marveled, looking at the table Sally had set. There were slices of ham, creamy mustard for dipping, a caprese pasta salad, and a strawberry cheesecake.

"You know I always loved baking. Now I'm trying to do more cooking as well. We planted a salsa garden last year, and I'm looking forward to canning again this fall. Sam loves salsa," Sally said.

"Very impressive," Paige said.

Sally laid Heather back in her stroller, and they all sat down at the table in the kitchen and dished up their plates.

"I can't believe it's been almost four years since we were little freshmen in the Commons Room. I'm so proud of you guys for getting your degrees. I know that took a lot of work."

"Do you think you'll go back, Hannah?" Paige asked.

Hannah sighed. "I don't see it happening anytime soon. Originally, Luke had me quit so I could support us while he got his degree, but then he never went back to school." Hannah had found herself crying in her closet the first week of marriage, feeling like she'd made the biggest mistake of her life. She was trying to do the right thing for her baby and didn't feel like she could give up on a brand-new marriage. She ignored her gut and rushed into an engagement with Luke. What choice did she have? After Heather was born, it was really good for a couple of months. Luke was more attentive and helpful. Before long, things were upside down again. She was too embarrassed to tell her friends how unhappy she was. Their lives were going so well, and she didn't want to be pitied or judged. Married life was a big disappointment on so many levels, but she tried hard to be positive and look for the silver lining.

"He lost his job in January and said it saved money to not pay for daycare for Heather. I made enough for us to scrape by on, and that was good enough for him. Well, I got tired of working while he stayed home with her, so last month, I went to the Army offices and brought a recruiter home."

"You did not," Paige said, surprised. "What did he do?"

"He joined the Army," Hannah laughed. "I told him I wasn't supporting him anymore. That was his role. He had talked about joining before. I just gave him a nudge. He leaves for basic training in a month."

"Oh my gosh! This is such crazy news," Sally said, tucking a stray strand of hair behind her ear.

"I've given notice at my work for the job and the apartment. Heather and I are going to move in with my family for the eight weeks of training and then we're moving to Monterey, California. He'll be stationed at Fort Ord while he goes to the Defense Language Institute."

"I can't even process all of that. It's so much change for you. How do you feel about it?" Paige asked.

Hannah shrugged. "I'm sad to leave Utah and not be close to my family and you guys, but I'm really happy I'll get to be a stay-at-home mom. Going back to work when Heather was six weeks old was the worst thing ever."

"On the bright side, now we can come visit you and go to the beach," Paige offered.

"What about you two?" Hannah asked while putting Heather's binky back in her mouth. "What's next for the graduates?"

"Sam still has a year of school. So, we'll be in Millville until he graduates, maybe longer. We really like the rural life with chickens and goats," Sally said. "He's talking about opening up a CPA firm with Drake Pennington here in the valley. I have an interview with the Logan School District next week to see about getting on at Logan High as a science teacher."

"Our rival?" Paige joked. "How dare you, Sally Jane."

"I tried Mountain Crest first, but they didn't have any open positions," Sally said, raising her hands in surrender.

"You're forgiven then," said Paige.

"What's your plan, Paige?" Hannah asked.

"Evan really likes his IT job at Ancestry. He's thinking about going for his Masters. He hasn't decided yet. I'm glad I changed to a Secondary Ed degree with a minor in History. If I need to work full-time, teaching will be more useful. I'm keeping my part-time job at Wells Fargo for now. But for the most part, Evan makes enough to feed all of us." Paige looked pointedly at her friends, then added, "All three of us."

"Ahhh!" Hannah and Sally screamed, startling the baby and causing her to cry. Hannah picked her up, rocking her until she settled down. "How far along are you?"

"Oh, barely. I'll be six weeks on Monday, I think."

"Have you felt sick at all? I threw up my breakfast every morning for three months with Heather."

"Don't jinx me. I haven't thrown up yet, but I'm starting to get heartburn."

"I'm so happy for you guys," Sally said, squeezing Paige's hand. "Do you have names picked out?"

Hannah and Paige laughed, knowing Sally was obsessed with baby names. She'd made a list of one hundred names she liked when she was fifteen. It included first, middle, and nicknames. She told them all the time how heartbroken she was she had lost it.

"We've talked about maybe doing Book of Mormon names."

"I vote Abinadi," Hannah said.

"What about Nephi?" Sally said with a smile.

"Not that outlandish. There are some names in there that aren't too weird. We were thinking Jacob, Jared, or Benjamin at first, but those sound like regular names. So now we're trying to find something else. Of course, if it's a girl, we're in trouble. We can't think of any girl names."

"Oh please, please don't take Sariah," Sally begged. "You have dibs, of course, because you're preggers and I'm not, but Sam and I have already decided all our children will have names that start with an S. Isn't that going to be so sweet? I want my first daughter to be named Sariah. I always thought it was such a beautiful name, even if she was a bit of a complainer."

"Pinky promise," Paige said, linking pinkies with Sally.

"How crazy that not too long ago, we all lived together, and now we'll be in three different states," Hannah said, sadly.

"Does anyone have plans to visit Jentry anytime soon?" Paige asked.

"I don't see that happening for us. Money is too tight," Hannah said sadly.

"I'm going to visit her in July. I'll go out for a week. I can't wait to see her apartment downtown and go to her museum," Sally said. "I wish you both could come. It's so strange we haven't all been together in over a year. I thought for sure she was going to come see us last Christmas, but then they had the weird ice storm."

"Thank goodness for letters and phone calls to keep us connected," said Hannah. "Don't forget about me when I move. Hopefully, we'll all be together before long."

Sally's phone rang, and they were excited to find Jentry on the other line. Sally put the phone on speaker, so Jentry could catch up on all the news they had just shared with each other.

August 9, 1993

"I know we have several months, but I feel like we need to pin down some names. Sally has fourteen names picked out for some future child, and we haven't landed on anything yet," Paige said from the passenger seat as she and Evan drove to another doctor's appointment.

"No one can measure up to Sally's baby name obsession, babe. Don't even try," Evan said with a smile. "Maybe we leave the Book of Mormon thing behind and do a combination of our parents' names. Douglas Thomas? Thomas Douglas for a boy?"

"Nope."

"Jenny Kristi for a little girl. We can call her JK."

"Oh yes, she'd never be teased for having the same initials as just kidding."

"Okay. How about L names to go with Lindburg? Lance or Laura? Leanard or Laney?"

"You're hilarious today, Evan," Paige smiled. "Seriously, honey, I do like the Book of Mormon names idea, I just can't decide on one."

"I have a plan. Tonight, we write them all down and draw from a bowl."

"Right. And then we get a daughter named Coriantumr."

"Oh. I like that. We can call her Cori for short."

Paige punched Evan in the arm and laughed.

"Paige, you pick whatever you want for this baby. I just want you to be happy," he said, squeezing her knee.

"I'll be happier if I can pee soon."

"Almost there."

They pulled into the medical complex and checked in for their appointment with Dr. Richards. After a twenty-minute wait, Paige was weighed and taken back to an exam room.

"Good morning, Paige, Evan," Dr. Richards said, closing the door behind him. "How are you feeling, Paige? You're in your second trimester, correct?"

"Yes, Sir. Anxious to get to the halfway point," Paige said as she climbed onto the exam table.

"How are you feeling? Any reflux or heartburn?" Dr. Richards asked as he listened to Paige's heart.

"Mild, maybe? I haven't thrown up since the first trimester. I'm super tired and kind of itchy. My back hurts a lot, too, but otherwise, I'm not bad, except for the start of stretch marks. I'm much bigger than my cousin was at this point."

"Those are pretty common symptoms. I'm not too worried. Lay back here, and let's listen to the heartbeat."

Dr. Richards moved the small doppler over Paige's protruding belly. He moved it from left to right and back again. "Well, Evan and Paige, we are going to have to move this party down the hall to my ultrasound room. I'm hearing two heartbeats."

In a daze, they followed Dr. Richards to the next room, where Paige climbed onto another exam table. Evan held Paige's hand while looking at the screen in front of Dr. Richards.

Dr. Richards lifted Paige's shirt slightly over her belly. "This is going to be a little cold," he warned before squeezing gel onto her stomach. He dragged the tool over her belly, moving it around as images came in and out of focus on the screen. "Congratulations, you're going to be the parents of twins."

Evan leaned down to kiss Paige on the cheek, "You're the most wonderful wife in the world to give me two kids at once."

***

"Hello?" Hannah answered.

"You are not going to believe my news!" Paige almost shouted into the phone.

"How funny. You won't believe mine either."

"What's yours?"

"You go first."

"We just got back from our doctor's appointment, and we're having twins!"

Hannah screamed and whooped on the other line. "So many generations in a row. That's crazy. What are the odds?"

"I know. Mom is so excited, as are Blake and Blythe. They'll make good aunties."

"Does this change your due date? When is it again?"

"January third. And no, not really. He said twins usually come early, so they'll have a dreaded December birthday more than likely."

"I'm so excited for you. You'll be the cutest twin mom. I wish I could be there when they're born. I'll be in California by then. Sally is going to be so busy making baby blankets. Have you told her and Jentry yet?"

"You were first. After our mothers, of course."

"Of course."

"What's your news?"

"Oh, well, I'm expecting again. I must have gotten pregnant right before Luke left for basic."

137

"Oh my gosh. Our babies can be best friends, just like us."

"That would be amazing. Let's tell them they have no choice."

"When do you leave?"

"Not until the middle of September. Please say we'll get together before I go."

"Of course. We're coming up for Labor Day weekend."

"Perfect! Oh, shoot! Heather fell over. She's starting to scootch around the furniture, and she falls over all the time. I love you, Paige. I'm so excited for you. Congratulations again!"

"Love you, Han!"

October 1, 1993

I am finally in Monterrey! The last few months have been so crazy.

Heather and I lived in Providence from July through Mid-September. My family was so helpful with the baby. They each sacrificed so much for our family. Esther did so much babysitting so I could nap. Pregnancy is tiring! Mom and I developed a new layer to our relationship. Besides being mother/daughter, we are now women united by the joint task of trying to raise our husbands and children. I miss talking to her and doing things with her every day. She is so good at helping me find humor in what can seem like pretty tough times. Dad & I went on a few bike rides through the countryside. He was kind enough to ride tandem with me - and do most of the work. I will always cherish those months, the opportunity I had to grow closer to my family, and the chance they had to get to know Heather and come to love her as Luke and I do.

Luke spent two months at Ft. Leonard Wood for basic training. Then he went to Ft. Benning for airborne school. To graduate he had to complete five jumps from 25-5000 feet. Jumping out of moving airplanes is something I hope to never do. I'm so grateful to be a full-time mother to our children. He doesn't like the Army, but he perseveres for the sake of his little family. Of course, had he chosen to go back to school and not make me work to support us he may have had other options. Oh well. This is where we are now.

And, yes, I said children. I found out after he left for basic that I was expecting again. Not planned. Again. But I had gained so much weight from the pill and pregnancy and so I went off it. He refused to wear a condom and now we're expecting #2 in March.

On the 15th of September we loaded our very meager belongings into a U-Haul and took off for Monterey. Twelve hours with a baby, and pregnant! Not the best time. Actually, Heather was better than I expected. I was the one who was grouchy. We arrived at our new apartment at 8:00p.m. I was nervous as we drove across Fort Ord, passing worn down looking buildings. My spirits lifted when I saw our new apartment though. It's lovely, and on clear days you can see the ocean from my little back deck.

October 10, 1993

My baby girl is one!!! She is 100% the love of my life. I made her a cake decorated like a pumpkin which she mutilated and threw all over the kitchen. She also started crying when we sang her Happy Birthday. Funny baby. After a nap we took her swimming at the indoor pool on base. It was probably more fun for me than for the birthday girl. I can't believe how fast that year went by, and how much she grew. She is such a joy to have around. She's very inquisitive and smart. I had been beside myself when I got pregnant unexpectedly. Now I can't imagine any other path. I love being her mother with my whole heart. Her hair is dark like Luke's, but she has my curls and green eyes with the longest lashes. She's just beautiful! I love my Heather Cathrine so much.

December 12, 1993

I suspect Luke has a problem with the truth. I can't prove anything, but there are so many little stories he shares I don't believe. Like, last Sunday I went to church early for a meeting. He and Heather never showed up. When I got home, he said Heather had fallen and

December 11, 1993

Paige's back was killing her. She was glad it was a Saturday so she could sleep in and stay off her feet as much as possible. The bank had been so accommodating as she got bigger and bigger. She had a chair at the counter she could sit in during her shift, but moving around was difficult. She ended up quitting at the end of October, as Evan was making enough to pay all the bills.

They had put two bassinets in their room last week, as well as a rocking chair. Her mother, Blake, Blythe, and Sally had come down the first week of December to host a baby shower for her. Her sisters were so thrilled to have another set of twins joining the family. Julie and Jenny Hartvigsen were the third generation of twins in their family line. Aunt Julie used to joke with her sister, after watching her juggle the girls, that she was grateful the twin genes had skipped her. She was seven when her sisters were born and loved helping her mother take care of them. Paige used to pray she would have twins, making her the fifth generation to do so. When Dr. Richards heard two heartbeats at one of her earlier appointments, she was over the moon. Her due date of January third was a little over three weeks away, and she couldn't wait to find out if she was going to be the mother of boys, girls, or one of each.

"My belly is screaming for food," Paige said, nudging Evan with her foot.

"Is that true?" he asked, rolling over. "I don't hear anything."

"Listen harder."

Evan placed his ear on Paige's stomach. "Yep, I hear it now. All sorts of sounds, actually. A lot of gurgles in there."

Paige playfully hit him on the arm. "Would you pretty please bring us some frosted mini wheats?"

"As you wish," Evan said, quoting a line from their favorite movie. He got out of bed, threw on some clothes, and headed off to the kitchen.

Paige rubbed her belly and smiled. Life was so good. She was so in love with her husband, and they were so happy about their growing family. She was positive he would make the most amazing father and couldn't wait to raise the twins with him. Evan was her everything, and she knew she could handle anything life threw at her with him by her side.

"Little Ones," Paige said, talking to the twins as she had most of the pregnancy. "You two are going to have the best daddy in the entire world. We can't wait to meet you." Suddenly, she felt a cramp and then a gushing of water.

"Evan!" she screamed in panic.

Running down the hallway, he called to her, "Paige, what's wrong?"

"My water just broke," she said, starting to cry. "It's too early."

He was at her side now and stroking her face. "Ssh. It's okay. Dr. Richards said on your last visit they might come this early. It's going to be okay. Look how big you are! They probably weigh ten pounds each. They'll be fine."

She laughed through her tears and had him pull her up and help her to the bathroom while he gathered all the things they would need to take to the hospital.

Six hours later, Paige's hair was plastered to her face as she continued to push. Evan held her hand and cheered her on with each contraction.

"Ahhh!" Paige screamed, surprised at how much pain her body was in. Tears streamed down her face from the effort of childbirth.

Evan wiped the hair off of her forehead. "You are doing so amazing," he said, kissing the top of her head. "You're so close."

"He's right," Dr. Richards said. "One more big push should deliver the head of Baby A."

Stacey, the nurse in attendance, helped Paige lean forward with the next contraction. "Big push now, Paige. Let's get this first one out."

Paige pushed with all her might and felt the change in pressure as the baby's head came through the birth canal.

"One more for the shoulders," Dr. Richards said while holding the tiny head in his hands. Paige pushed again as Dr. Richards manipulated the shoulder blades and carefully pulled the baby out completely. "It's a boy," he said as their first-born son began to wail.

Tears streamed down Evan's face as he looked at his son and back at his wife. "Look what you just did! One more to go, Baby, you've got this."

Paige pushed again, and three pushes later, their second child came into the world.

"Another boy," Dr. Richards announced, finally placing both babies on Paige's chest.

Paige looked down at her newborn sons, so tiny and red. Her heart was filled with so much love for them, for her new little family, it felt like it would burst.

"Oh, Evan, look at them. They're so tiny and sweet," she said, through sobs.

"I love you so much, Paige. Thank you for making me a father."

Paige looked up at Evan and smiled. "I love you, Evan. I love you and the boys so much." She looked back at her boys, kissing each on the head.

"Will you take a picture of us?" Paige asked Stacey. "My camera is on the top of my bag."

Stacey took pictures of the happy family and then sat the camera down. "We need to get these fine gentlemen weighed, cleaned, and checked into the NICU for a bit," she said, getting back to business as she wheeled the carts for the boys over to Paige's bedside. "Do they have names yet? I've got a blue tag for Baby A and a green tag for Baby B until you learn to tell them apart."

"Which one is which?" asked Evan, "I've already forgotten which one was placed in Paige's arms first."

"The one on the right is A."

"Then this sweet boy is Ammon Thomas, named after my dad." Paige kissed the top of his head as Stacey placed him in the NICU cart.

"What a lovely name for a lovely little man," Stacey said, placing him under the heating lamp.

"His brother is Jarom Evan, named after the love of my life." Paige smiled up at her husband and then kissed little Jarom before handing him over to the nurse.

"You'll see them again soon. They look quite healthy. NICU is a precaution with all twins born at 37 weeks, which is much later than a lot of twins deliver. You grew them nice and strong," Dr. Richards said as he finished cleaning up Paige and moved to look at the boys. "Looks like Baby A weighs five pounds two ounces," he said over his shoulder to the nurse, who was writing the information down in their charts. "Apgar score of 8/9." He listened to Ammon's heart briefly before moving to the next cart to examine Jarom. "Baby B weighs four pounds eleven ounces. Apgar of 7/9." Two nurses wheeled the boys down the hall to the NICU while another came into the room to assist Stacey in taking care of Paige. "You'll get moved to a recovery room now," Dr. Richards said, removing his gloves. "Get some rest. I'll look in on you in about an hour."

"Thank you so much, Dr. Richards. Thanks for helping to get our boys here safely," Evan said, shaking his hand.

"Yes, thank you!" Paige agreed. "This has been the best day of our lives."

Once they had been moved to another room, Evan made phone calls to their parents while Paige tried to rest. She smiled at how excited he sounded on the phone as he described their sons.

"Hey, you," she said to Evan, smiling when he hung up the phone. "Get over here and kiss the mother of your children."

"With pleasure." Evan kissed Paige tenderly, then brushed her hair away from her forehead.

"Fatherhood looks good on you, Evan Lindburg." Paige took his hand and kissed it. "Take my camera and see if you can get pictures of them in the nursery.

"As you wish."

December 31, 1993

1993 was quite a year. I spent the first part of the year working and adjusting to motherhood. My sweet Heather made it so easy. She's such a good girl.

Jentry, Paige and Sally all graduated from college, and Jen and I moved to different states. Will I ever stop missing our time together at BYU? My awesome baby sister, Esther, started at the Y in the summer. I hope she makes the kind of friends I did.

Jentry got her dream job at the Portland Art Museum. Sally started teaching. Paige and I both got pregnant, me with #2, and her with two at once! I can't wait to meet her boys. She had them a few days ago. Ammon and Jarom. Aren't those names so sweet?

Luke and I had time together and time apart. There were a lot of resentments on my part at the beginning of the year when he wasn't working, and I was. The fact I didn't miss him when he was away had me concerned, but I ended up pregnant again. So, I'm trying so hard to focus on the positive and make a happy life with him. He's working hard so I can be a stay-at-home mom and that is huge to me! We have tried to have a date night once a week, even if it is just staying at home and watching a movie or playing cards. I think we're both trying to do our best here.

January 3, 1994

Paige finished burping Jarom and laid him in the bassinet next to his brother. They had purchased two but learned the first night home that the boys slept much more soundly next to each other. She patted their tiny backs and sang to them until she was sure they were fast asleep.

"You are precious and sweet, little Ammon and Jarom," she sang to the tune of Brahms's Lullaby. *"You're the babies mommy loves, oh, I love you I do. You are precious and sweet, little Ammon and Jarom. You're the babies mommy loves, oh I love you, I do."* She tiptoed out of the bedroom and shut the door behind her.

Heading to the kitchen, she started busying herself by rinsing bottles and loading the dishwasher. Evan had left after dinner to grab more formula and diapers. The weatherman was predicting a blizzard with whiteout conditions hitting the Wasatch Front tomorrow afternoon. It had been snowing off and on all day, but no more than any regular storm during a typical Utah winter. Evan wasn't used to driving in these conditions, being from Mesa, but after several winters in Utah, he was getting the hang of it.

Paige jumped when the phone rang. "Hello?" she answered, placing the phone in the crick of her neck so she could still do the dishes.

"Happy Due Date to you! Happy Due Date to you! Happy Due Date, dear Paige. Happy Due Date to you!" Hannah sang on the other end of the line.

"Can you believe it? How are the boys three weeks old already?"

"How are they doing? I can't wait to meet them. Those pictures you sent got here today, and they are so handsome, Paige. I love them already."

"Tell me about it. I'd heard stories about a mother's love, but nothing prepares you for that moment. I want to pinch myself every day that they're mine. I also want to take the world's longest nap," Paige laughed. "I'm so tired."

"I bet. I thought Heather was exhausting. I can't imagine twice the bottles and diapers. Are they doing well, though?"

"They're doing so good. Ammon was a little jaundiced while we were in the hospital, but he's lost his yellow tint. Evan was calling him Ammon Amarillo for a week."

"Amarillo? Oh, wait. Yellow in Spanish. Cute."

"Yeah. Evan is so sweet with them. It makes me crazier about him. Anyway, Jarom has a little heart murmur, but his doctor thinks he'll grow out of it by age two. So, for twins who were born only three weeks early, I got really lucky. We were in the hospital less than a week. I'm just so blessed."

"I'm so happy for you, Paige. You've wanted twins forever. Has Aunt Jenny been down to see them?"

"She stayed with me for a few nights when we first brought them home. Evan's mother was here for a week. She's a really fun lady. She taught me to play hand and foot. She left two days ago. Blake and Blythe have been pestering mom to let them skip school for a month to help out. They're good little aunties. Sally is sick with a cold, so she doesn't want to risk spreading anything. She says she'll be down as soon as she can."

"They're going to be so old before I get to see them. It probably won't be until this summer."

"How much longer until you're due again?"

"Two more months, exactly. I'm due on St. Patty's Day."

"And when do you find out where you'll be stationed next?"

"Oh gosh. That's way down the road. He won't graduate from DLI until the fall."

"I wish there was an Army base close by so you could come here."

"Yeah, too bad Hill is Air Force."

"Hey, Han, someone is at the door. Hold on, please." Paige sat the phone on the kitchen counter and dried her hands. She opened the door to find two Utah Highway Patrol Officers on the landing of the townhouse.

"Paige Lindberg?" the older-looking one asked.

"Yes, how can I help you?"

"Ma'am, I regret to inform you Evan Lindberg was in an automobile accident tonight. He was killed instantly. I'm so sorry."

Paige's knees buckled, and she fell to the ground, screaming.

"Ma'am is there someone we can call for you?" the officer asked, stepping into the room and assisting Paige to the couch.

"This can't be happening. This can't be true," Paige cried uncontrollably, her face in her hands.

The younger officer looked around the room. "Mrs. Lindberg, are you home alone?"

"No," Paige tried to catch her breath so she could speak. "The twins are here. They're in the bedroom. Oh, the twins. The babies," she sobbed, "Evan's babies."

"Ma'am, Officer Spellacy is going to sit here with you while I call your next of kin. Do you think you can give me a phone number?" the younger officer asked calmly.

Paige looked up and put her hand over her mouth. "Hannah."

"Hannah?" the officer questioned.

Paige stood up and ran to the kitchen. "Hannah? Hannah!" she almost yelled, as she fumbled with the phone.

"I'm here," Hannah said, "Paige, what's happening!? I can hear you screaming and crying."

"Hannah, it's Evan. Policemen are here." Paige could barely get out the words. She cried into the phone and heard Hannah start crying with her. "Hannah, Evan…Evan has been killed. I think I'm going to be sick. Please call my mother." Paige hung up the phone and ran to the bathroom to throw up.

January 21, 1994

Paige sat on her parents' living room couch, her legs crossed, arms folded, staring at the ground. She was dressed in black, her long blonde hair in a tight low bun. Her face was makeup-free, as she knew she would have cried it off all day. The past three weeks had been a blur. Phone calls with her and Evan's parents, planning for a funeral in Utah as well as a memorial in Mesa, moving out of the townhouse in Provo and in with her parents, giving notice at her job, all while caring for newborn twins.

Doug and Krisit Lindburg had agreed to have Evan buried in Providence, knowing Paige and the boys would be living there now. Paige was grateful for their support and heartsick for their loss.

In the room with her, also dressed in black and equally somber, were her three best friends. Hannah and Jentry had flown in a week ago. With Sally, they had helped organize a family meal after the service, as well as helped Lindburg family members find hotels. Now, they sat in silence with her.

January was a terrible time for a funeral. Two feet of snow covered the ground, and the temperature was in the twenties, making lingering at the graveside impossible. Paige had left the twins with Blake and Blythe at the church when the mourners headed to the cemetery. Now, they were in their bassinet in her old room.

She sighed, the most noise she'd made since laying them down and coming upstairs to sit with her friends. She was all cried out. No more tears fell. She felt only emptiness inside.

"You haven't eaten anything all day," Hannah finally offered. "We have the leftovers in the kitchen. Can I make you a sandwich? Bring you a roll? Anything?"

"I'm not hungry, Hannah, but thank you."

"Paige, you need to eat for the boys. You need your energy to take care of them," Sally said.

"My boys. My poor fatherless boys," Paige sighed again. "Will my heart ever not hurt like this?" She closed her eyes and pinched the bridge of her nose. "You're right, I need to eat. You can bring me something, Han."

Hannah went to the kitchen and returned with a plate of fruit, sliced ham, and a roll.

"Thank you. All of you. You've been so helpful these last few weeks. It was so nice of Hannah and Jentry to fly in. Especially with Hannah seven months pregnant. I couldn't have gotten through today without all of your help."

"That's what best friends are for, Love. You'd do the same for any of us."

"What are your plans now, Paige?" Hannah asked.

"Honestly, I don't know. I haven't thought past today. Truthfully, if I didn't have the boys to keep me going, I don't know if I would be getting out of bed each morning. My parents said I can live with them for a few months until I find my own place, but I can't think that far," Paige said, rubbing her temples. "Everyone said I would feel peace today, feel Evan close. I only feel heartbreak. I worry I'm passing my sadness on to the boys."

"I know it's not remotely the same, Paige, but when I found out I was pregnant with Heather, you know I was devastated. I wasn't ready to be a mother or a wife. I was sad and angry and all kinds of yucky things for a few weeks. And then, one day, I had the same thought. Can my baby feel how sad I am? So, I stood up and shook off my sadness. Literally. Just like this." Hannah stood up in the middle of the room, her belly straining at her dress, and began to shake her arms, swinging them at her sides. Then one leg, then another. She turned in circles, shaking fingertips and her head as well.

Jentry and Sally tried not to laugh, and then got up and joined her.

"Come on, Paige, shake that sadness right out. The boys need you to let that go," Hannah instructed.

Paige stared at her friends, shaking and spinning around the living room, and felt a smile start to lift the corner of her mouth. She slipped off her shoes and joined them. She shook her fingertips and hands, rolled her neck back and forth, and then started shaking her legs, walking around in a circle with her friends.

"Good job. The next part is to chant as you shake. Whatever feels right. I said, 'I love my baby, and we'll be okay,' when it was me."

Paige paused for a few seconds as she thought. "I can survive this," she said timidly.

Hannah took Paige's hands in hers, "You can survive this, Paige Alison. Now say it like you mean it."

"I can survive this."

"Louder. Mean it more. Mean it with everything you are for your boys."

"I can survive this!!!!" Paige shouted.

"Damn right you can, Love," Jentry said.

Paige smiled and beckoned her friends into a group hug. "What would I do without you three? I love each of you so much. Hannah, you're incredibly goofy, but I feel a little bit better."

"I promise you will survive this," Hannah said, kissing Paige on the cheek. "You are so strong, so loving, so faithful. You guys are going to be okay. It might hurt for a long time. Forever even, but on those days, it's hard; just shake that sadness out." She turned and started shaking her limbs in a circle around the room again.

The others followed Hannah around the room.

"I think I hear something," Sally said, stopping in her tracks. A faint cry was coming from downstairs. "I think they want to join us."

Paige and Sally went downstairs to grab the boys. Returning to the living room, the four friends continued to walk in a circle, Hannah and Jentry shaking their limbs, while Paige and Sally held the twins.

"We can survive this," Paige said with a tentative smile, then kissed Ammon and Jarom on the tops of their heads.

March 19, 1994

Paige followed Mamie McLean into the side door of the red brick house and down the stairs to the basement apartment.

"I feel like it's been years since I've been downstairs," Paige said, smiling at the familiar smell of the musty laundry room as they passed it before her grandma opened the door to the basement apartment.

"It has been years, dearie," Mamie said with a smile. "Your Aunt Cindy moved out a year ago when she got married. I've been letting different family stay here when they come to town, but I knew instantly I wanted you to live here when I heard about poor Evan." She pulled Paige close as Paige's chin began to quiver.

"This is so generous, Grandma. I'm so glad the boys and I will have a lovely little place to call home and that you'll get to know them."

"They are precious boys. I look forward to having you here."

Paige walked further into the small kitchen. The apartment wasn't large. Two bedrooms, a bathroom, a small living room, and an eating nook off of the kitchen. The home was older. Her great-grandmother had lived here for many years before she passed away. Mamie moved in after she was widowed. Maybe it's a good place for a widow to land, Paige thought to herself.

The kitchen cabinets had been painted a mint green, one of Mamie's favorite colors. The countertops looked like they had been replaced with basic white Formica. They had been orange the last time Paige had been here. The appliances were outdated and small, as well, but Paige didn't mind. She wouldn't be making much on a teacher's salary, and Mamie had said they could live here rent-free until they were back on their feet.

"I love it so much, Grandma." Paige threw her arms around her grandmother and squeezed her tight.

"The furniture is old and hodge podge, but it will do for now. Make this place your own, dearie. Whatever you want to do to make it feel like home makes no nevermind to me."

"I was hoping to paint the boys' room a pretty blue."

"Be my guest. Just don't get it on the carpet. I replaced all the flooring a few years ago."

"I'll be so careful with everything, Grandma. I love you so much. Thank you for this kindness."

"Widows look out for each other," Mamie said with a wink, "So you might need to make me some treats every once in a while."

"I promise."

March 22, 1994

"This blue is so pretty," Sally said, dipping her roller into the tray of blue paint.

"It's called Robin's Egg. I thought the name sounded pretty. Thanks for helping me paint, Sally. I want these fumes dried before I move the boys in."

"You've been busy this week. When did Mamie give you the keys?"

"Two days ago. I've wiped every surface, changed out the lights to a brighter bulb, shampooed the carpets, and set up my room. Mine and Evan's belongings were taken to storage right after the funeral until we could figure out what I was going to do. His parents were nice enough to pay for the fees while the boys and I were with my folks."

Paige paused, lost in thoughts of Evan and what she thought her life would be. She had buried her husband two months ago. It didn't seem real. She and the boys had moved into her parents' house, the three of them sharing her old room. She was barely functioning the first month. She took care of the boys at the expense of herself. Ammon and Jarom were such easy babies, and she knew that was a tender mercy from Heavenly Father. Her parents and her twin sisters helped with the boys each day and gave her time and space to mourn.

Her younger brother, Lane, was serving a mission in New York. He was unable to attend the funeral but wrote to Paige every week. They had not been close as children but were developing a better bond now.

One month ago, she had been sitting in a rocking chair with the boys in each arm, singing to them.

"I love Daddy, he loves me. We love Mommy yes siree. She loves us and so you see, we are a happy family. I love Ammon, he loves me. We love Jarom, yes siree. He loves us and so you see, we are a happy family."

It hit her then that they could still be a happy family. She needed to pull herself out of her grief and give the boys a life as close to what she and Evan had planned as possible.

"When do you start work?" Sally asked, interrupting her thoughts.

"I had my interview at Logan High last week, and I interview at Mountain Crest next Thursday. My teaching degree is coming in handy after all."

"I'll be praying you're hired at Logan so we can have lunch together every day," Sally said, smiling, and it warmed Paige's heart.

"Do you like teaching? I'm worried it's more than I'm ready for with the babies."

"Honestly?"

"Do you even know how to not be honest?" Paige laughed, climbing on a stool to reach the corners.

"Some of the kids are hard. Disrespectful. Don't really care about learning. But the ones who do want to learn make it worthwhile."

"I guess if we'd majored in Elementary Ed, we'd be working with darling eight-year-olds rather than smelly teenagers," Paige laughed.

***

Three days later, she officially moved into the little brick house on the corner of 200 East and 900 North. Sam and Sally had set up the cribs while her mother helped her put the kitchen together. She had traded out the two brown couches in the living room for one smaller sofa and two recliners, figuring that way, both babies could be rocked whenever she had company. Blake and Blythe sat in them now, each rocking a nephew. They had laid claim to one of the boys in the beginning. Blake choosing Ammon because they were both the firstborn, and Blythe happily claiming Jarom as her buddy, who, in truth, was more snuggly than his twin.

The phone rang, and Paige answered.

"Hello?... This is she...Thank you, I'm very excited."

The family was gathering around her, no doubt anxious to know who was on the other end of the phone.

"That will work for me...I'll put it on my calendar. Looking forward to it." Paige hung up the phone and looked at Sally. "Your prayers worked. I'll be teaching at Logan High when school starts up in August."

<u>March 26, 1994</u>

After the holidays and Evan's funeral I began concentrating on the arrival of #2. We found another crib and set up a little area in the corner of our large laundry room so the babies wouldn't wake each other. Since Heather was ten days early, I was positive this baby would be at least twenty days early. Every night I would make sure the house was spotless, and then lay in bed waiting for my water to break. I set myself up for a lot of disappointment. With every day that went by with no signs of labor, I got more and more discouraged. I felt like the baby would never be born.

On March 16th, one day before my due date, I went into labor. With Heather, I had an epidural, so I didn't really know what contractions were like. What a shock! When God told Eve she would bring forth her children in sorrow He wasn't kidding! I started having them around 4:30 PM, while at the commissary. When I got home, I told Luke to get ready because I'd probably have the baby that night. By 6:00 they were seven minutes apart. I called my family, my friends, and the babysitters, and then we headed for the hospital. We arrived at 7:00 with contractions five minutes apart. The nurse wouldn't let me have an epidural but did give me a shot of Demerol - which was about as effective as water. At 9:00 my body started pushing on its own. The nurse wouldn't let me push because they had to call the doctor from home. I didn't remotely experience any pain like this with Heather and I was really scared. There is nothing more infuriating than being told not to push while in heavy labor.

Thirty minutes later the doctor finally got there, and after about four pushes, at 9:45 Seth Lucas started his turn on Earth. He was 6 lbs. and 15 oz., 18 ½ inches long. I couldn't believe how tiny he was compared to Heather!! She seems so grown up now. He is such a handsome, sweet little boy. He has a head full of dark hair, like Heather. So far he is very mellow. He's so wonderful. Our daughter and son bless our lives in so many ways. Yes, parenthood can be difficult, and exasperating at times. But nothing compares to hearing your toddler say your name, as she wraps her arms around your legs. Nothing feels better than rocking your new baby boy to sleep and having him cuddle up to you. I'm so grateful our Father in Heaven trusted me with these wonderful spirits, and I vow to make sure they return to Him someday.

May 25, 1994

I'm struggling to keep up with my journal trying to juggle two small children.

My mom came out to help for a week after Seth was born. She cleaned and organized the house and bought me a nice recliner for rocking the children. It was so wonderful having her here. Heather loves Grammy so much.

I had two sick babies back-to-back. It was awful. Sethy got a touch of bronchiolitis at the beginning of the month. I had to take him in for X-Rays...quite scary. He was so little they had to place him in a plastic tube, with his arms stretched above his head. The technician expected and wanted him to cry, but instead he only did a pouty lip. It was hard not to laugh and cry at the same time. Poor Mr. Man.

It was Heather's turn to go to the emergency room two weeks later. She had a temp of 103 and was dehydrated. They strapped her to a board and strapped her arm to one too, so they could give her an IV. She was hysterical and it was all I could do not to become hysterical too. She had to go up for X-Rays, which didn't go over well either. Poor girl. There is nothing worse than having a sick child and not being able to do anything for them to make it better.

I'm so grateful for our medical benefits!

Jentry sent me a beautiful watercolor of Monterey Bay. I have it framed on my TV stand. She loves working at the PAM and taking art classes. She's so talented. I wish I had more hobbies and skills. One of these days I'm going to write my novel. And maybe I'll pick up quilting.

I talk to Paige most nights. My heart hurts for her. She misses Evan so much. She says the boys are doing well and she's loving on them as much as she can before she has to start work in August. I know how hard it was to leave Heather. I hope Paige will be okay.

Sam graduated last month. He and his best friend, Drake, are going to open their own accounting firm. He's so smart and likeable, I know they'll do great. He and Sally want to come out and see me next month. I hope it happens.

August 14, 1994

Sam and Sally did make it out in June! We went to the beach at Carmel almost every day. They went to San Fransisco one day and brought me back Ghirardelli chocolates. So yummy. Sam can see the difference in my marriage compared to his and Sally's. He pulled me aside to make sure I'm okay and see if Luke is treating me right. I started crying. He confronted Luke before leaving and told him he better start treating his sister better. That made Luke mad at me for days.

Esther and her roommate, Camdyn, flew in for a week vacation before school started again. Luke stayed home with the babies, and the three of us drove to San Jose and went to Paramount's Great America. It was so much fun, but so very expensive! They were a lot of help with the kids while Luke was at work. In the evenings we'd go into Monterey and down to the beach. I love living here. It's a real neat little town.

October 1, 1994

Luke and I got into another fight last night. That happens weekly at least. He claims to be sick almost every Sunday, so it's me trying to get two babies to church. He comes home from work and wants to spend the evening in front of the TV on his stupid Nintendo. The other day he gave blood at work and had to come home and play video games for three hours to recuperate. Are you kidding me? He's no help around the house, emotionally detached from me, and dropping the ball on guiding our family as a spiritual leader. It's so disappointing. He says I have unrealistic expectations, and nothing is good enough for me. I think I expect the bare minimum and I'm not getting that.

I will give him credit for watching the kids a lot so I can run errands or take a bath.

October 12, 1994

"Alright, everyone, on your break this weekend, I want you to be on the lookout for three things. Who can guess what they are? Yes, Caleb."

"Igneous, sedimentary, or metamorphic rocks?"

"Exactly. Bring a sample in on Monday, and we'll see if we can determine the type you found."

"Is this for credit, Mrs. Limbrey?"

"Thank you for asking, Alicia. This is for extra-credit," Sally explained as the bell rang. "See you next week, class. Have a great fall break."

The students hurried out of the classroom, excited for a four-day weekend. Sally straightened the room, even though she knew the janitors would give it a clean. She was gathering some papers to take home for grading when Paige popped her head in the door.

"Happy fall break, Mrs. Limbrey," Paige smiled from the doorway.

"You too, Mrs. Lindburg. I'm glad you'll get so much time with the twins this weekend."

"Me too. I plan on taking them on nice long walks every day. Do you need a ride?"

"No thanks. Sam wants me to meet him at the office. It's nice enough to walk. I'll see you Monday."

"Bye, Sal. Love you."

"Love you too, Paige." Sally grabbed her bag and headed out of the high school towards her husband's office, which was only a half mile from Logan High. They shared one car, with Sam dropping her off in the mornings. Some days, she'd let Paige take her home. Other days, she would walk over to the L and P offices in The Emporium. She'd grade papers or study while waiting for Sam to wrap up his day. They had made career and financial goals their first month of marriage they had stuck to, and having one vehicle as long as possible was one of them.

"Hey, Drake," she said, entering the office. It was small, with two desks on opposite sides of the room and chairs in between. Sam and Drake had big plans for growing their business. It was off to a good start, and Sally was sure it would be the best accounting firm in the valley in no time.

"Hey, Sally. How was school?"

"Great. We're discussing Geology this month, which is my passion, so I'm having a lot of fun. How's business today?"

"Amazing. Two new clients," Drake said, standing to stretch.

"That's wonderful. Where's Sam?"

"He's out back. Said to send you that way."

"Thanks, Drake. See ya." Sally waved as she walked back into The Emporium foyer. The building housed several offices and stores, as well as The Coppermill Restaurant on the top floor. There was an entrance off of Main Street, as well as on the west side of the building which led to a shared parking lot with other Main Street businesses. Sally walked outside and looked for her husband. She smiled when she saw him casually leaning on his red Ford Tempo.

"Hey, Handsome," she said as she wrapped her arms around him.

"Hey, Gorgeous," Sam said, placing a kiss on Sally's lips. "I have a surprise for you."

"You do? It's not even a special day."

"Every day is special with you, Sally Jane."

"Aww, Sammy. That's sweet to say." She hugged him again. Her life with Sam was a dream and something Sally thanked the Lord for every night in her prayers.

"Close your eyes and spin in a circle three times for luck."

"Okay," Sally laughed, spinning slowly so as not to lose her balance.

"Alright, open your eyes."

Sally opened her eyes to find Sam still leaning on his car, hands in his pockets. She looked at him perplexed.

"Oh, I did it wrong. Close your eyes and put out your hand, is what I meant to say."

Sally obeyed and felt something drop into her hands. She opened her eyes to find a key with a heart-shaped key chain. She looked at Sam, still slightly confused. He laughed and then gestured to the car parked next to him, a baby blue Ford Aspire.

"Is that for me?" Sally asked, wide-eyed.

"You better believe it. I've been saving up for a while. I figured as business continues to grow I might be working longer hours. I wanted you to be able to get home when it works for you."

"Oh, Sam! It's beautiful. I've never had a car all my own." Sally walked around the vehicle, taking in all the details. "You are the absolute best!" she said, throwing her arms around her husband.

"I'm glad you like it. Though I'll miss riding into town with you."

"Maybe we can still do it sometimes. Oh, Sam. Thank you."

"You deserve the world, Sal, and I hope I can give that to you. I've got someone coming in soon, so I'll be home after seven." Sam bent down and kissed her again.

"I'll have dinner waiting for you."

"Can't wait. Have fun driving that beauty home."

"Oh, I will!" Sally got in the car and ran her hand over the plush grey seats. She scooted the seat forward and adjusted the mirrors. She couldn't wait to show Paige her car. She decided to drop in on her before she headed home. She turned on the radio and laughed out loud when Belinda Carlisle's *Summer Rain* was playing. Singing along at the top of her lungs, she headed to Paige's house.

"That's it!" Sally said aloud. "I'll call this car Belinda."

November 22, 1994

Sally was waiting at the Southwest gate when Hannah and the kids got off the plane. She had volunteered to pick them up when she heard her mother-in-law had bought plane tickets so they could come home for Thanksgiving. Luke wasn't able to take time off, so Hannah and the kids were coming for a full two weeks without him. Sally was thrilled. The week would be busy with having Thanksgiving with the Limbrey's and running to Rupert for the Christmas tree lighting, but it would be worth it.

"Hannah!" Sally waved as she saw Hannah come out the gate, pushing a double stroller, but with a screaming Heather in her arms. "Oh dear, give this little lady to Auntie Sally." Sally took her in her arms, and the new face distracted two-year-old Heather into silence.

"Never fly with a baby and a toddler," Hannah said, looking and sounding exhausted. "I'm so glad to be here and so grateful for a short flight."

"Hugs for you, too, my dear." Sally squeezed Hannah as they walked towards baggage claim. "Look how big Seth is. Oh, my goodness. What a handsome man. I'm so happy you'll be with us for the holiday. Thanksgiving is my favorite."

They grabbed their bags and took the shuttle to Sally's car. Hannah's mother had purchased two car seats so she wouldn't have to check hers on the plane. After buckling Heather and Seth in the backseat, they headed for Providence.

"Here," said Sally, reaching around her seat and grabbing a baggie filled with muffins for Hannah. "I thought you might be hungry."

"Oh my gosh," squealed Hannah. "Your banana muffins. You know I'm crazy about these." Hannah took a bite and sighed. "I miss your cooking so much."

"I hardly have time to cook anymore. Grading papers at the end of the day leaves little time for playing in the kitchen."

"Do you like teaching?"

"It's fine for now, but I really wish I could get some sort of job out in the field. Can you imagine how fun it would be to explore caves and karsts all day?"

"Yes, I can. My days consist of bottles and diapers right now. I haven't had a good hike since Heather was born. I've hung onto weight with the pregnancies, so I'm sure I would huff and puff on the easiest trail."

"I don't believe that for a second."

"So, tell me the plan for the week."

"Tomorrow, we'll prep as much food as we can. Your mother is so nice and is letting me make all the pies."

"That's nice?"

Sally laughed, "For me, it is. I'm so happy to have three days off from school to play and bake. Thursday, we'll have Thanksgiving dinner at the church with all the Hartvigsen families in the valley. Your mom, Aunt Jenny, Uncle James, Grandma Susi, and all their kids. You'll get to see how big the twins are. Paige can't wait to see you. Then, on Friday, whoever wants to is welcome to come with Sam and me to Rupert for the night. We have the cutest town square and every year on the day after Thanksgiving, Santa drives around the square in a fire truck, hits a switch to turn on all the Christmas lights, and then starts the fireworks show. It's my favorite thing about Rupert."

"Oh, right. It's where Sam proposed. Sounds amazing. I wonder if Heather would be scared. Seth could sleep right through it. That child has slept through multiple earthquakes."

"You could always try." Sally paused to safely merge from I-80 onto I-15. A light flurry was starting, and she wanted to be extra cautious with her niece and nephew in the car. "Anyway, tomorrow night, Sam and I want to have you over for dinner and cards. Mom said she'd watch the kids."

"I would love a game night."

"Me too. Hey, Hannah, can I ask you about something?"

"Always."

Sally thought for a second, trying to determine the best way to bring up a possibly difficult subject. "Mom said something to me the other day, thinking I already knew, so don't be mad." Sally looked sideways at her sister-in-law. Hannah was looking straight ahead and biting her lip. "She said something about you looking forward to getting away from Luke for a bit." She waited, but Hannah didn't say anything. "Is everything okay, Hannah?"

A single tear fell down Hannah's cheek. "Well, I have two children with a man I don't really trust or enjoy," Hannah said with a sigh. "I don't know. I had concerns before we got married but had to overlook them once I was pregnant. I knew the first week of marriage I'd made a big mistake, but what was I supposed to do? I was embarrassed and disappointed. I was jealous of how in love you and Sam are, and Paige and Evan were. So, I pushed those feelings down and tried my best. I wanted my children to grow up in a home like mine, with parents who are crazy about each other."

"Oh, Hannah, I'm so sorry."

"I mean, it's not like he's beating me. I don't have the worst marriage on the planet. There's no compatibility or chemistry, but we make cute kids." Hannah laughed cheerlessly.

"What can I do to help?" Sally asked, grabbing Hannah's hand.

"Keep being the best Auntie to Heather and Seth. And don't tell the others. It's easier to put on a happy face and act like everything is fine than have everyone feeling sorry for me."

"I can do that." Sally smiled at her friend while silently sending up a prayer that Hannah would find peace on this small visit and happiness upon her return.

Sometimes, Sally felt guilty that her life was blissfully happy when her friends were facing struggles. She couldn't imagine losing Sam like Paige had lost Evan, and with small babies, no less. Then, to hear how sad Hannah was hurt her heart. Jentry seemed to be doing well in Portland, but Sally worried about her lack of a support system.

Sam was everything Sally had hoped for. Their life in Millville was so happy. They had goals they were working towards and plans for a future family they both looked forward to. Sally prayed that someday, all of her friends would be as happy as she was.

She glanced over at Hannah and found her eyes closed. A look in the rearview mirror showed Heather and Seth were out as well. Sally put in a Mormon Tabernacle Choir CD and turned the volume to low, hoping the sounds of the church choir would help them rest.

An hour later they were pulling into the driveway of Bruce and Jenny Limbrey's new home on Stewart Hill Drive in River Heights, a few miles from the home they had lived in when the children were growing up. With Sam and Hannah married, and Esther engaged, they had wanted a larger home for hosting holidays and entertaining grandchildren. Sally had helped Jenny set up one of the guest rooms for Hannah and the children and was excited to show her what they had put together.

"Wake up, sleepyheads," Sally said while gently patting Hannah on the leg. "We're here."

"I feel asleep on you? Oh, Sal, I'm so sorry." Hannah turned around to find Heather and Seth starting to open their eyes as well. "That's good, at least. They won't be terrors when they see Grammy and Pappy."

As they were getting the children out of their buckles, Julie Limbrey came running out the front door.

"Momma!" Hannah said, her voice catching as she threw her arms around her mother.

"We're so happy you're here safe and sound. Thank you, Sally, for picking them up. Let me see these precious children." Julie took Seth from Hannah's arms and grabbed onto Heather's tiny hand. "Let's get you two out of the cold. You're not used to this in California. Come inside and see what Grammy made you, Miss Heather."

Sally and Hannah watched them go inside and then grabbed the luggage.

"You have no idea how excited she has been to see those babies," Sally said.

"The worst part of living away is she isn't in their life every day. She came out in March when Sethy was born, but we haven't seen her since then."

They walked into the house, and Sally watched Hannah's face take in the large picture windows on the west wall of the living room with the view of the Logan Temple.

"Wow."

"I know. Mom says the view is what sold her on this house over the others they looked at."

Julie was sitting on the far couch holding Seth, with Heather snuggled up next to her. Heather held a new rag doll with brown curls, like her own. She was cuddling it the way Grammy cuddled Seth.

"Did Grammy make you a dolly?" Hannah sat the suitcases down and walked over to her daughter. Heather stuck the little doll up for her mother to see. "She's so pretty. Just like you." She kissed Heather on the forehead and then kissed her mom on the cheek. "I didn't know you were making dolls again. Thank you."

"Did you notice her dress?" Julie asked, nodding at the doll.

Hannah looked closely. "Oh my gosh. It's from her ladybugs onesie I loved so much."

"You had me keep some things in storage when you moved, and I found it as I was packing things up."

"You're the best, Mom."

"Sally, show Hannah her room, and then we'll get some dinner going. Dad should be home in about thirty minutes."

"What about Esther?" Hannah asked.

"She's spending Thanksgiving with Dustin's family in Reno. But she'll be here Saturday to see you and the kids."

Sally led Hannah down to the basement guest room and excitedly showed her the queen-size bed and two playpens.

"I'm so excited you're here, Hannah. I'm going to spend as much time with you as I can, but I have some errands to run tonight. I'll see you at breakfast. I've missed you so much."

"I've missed you too, Sal. You have no idea how much."

November 23, 1994

Hannah woke with a start. She had dreamt of Morgan again, something that happened every few months. The dreams were usually the same. They were sitting in the little cabin while it rained. She was feeling so happy, smiling and laughing. Then, Luke would appear in the doorway. She would have to choose between the two of them.

Never once did she choose her husband.

The dream concerned her and made her feel guilty every time. Why did she never choose Luke? Seth started to stir, so she picked him up and went upstairs with his bottle so Heather could get more sleep. She sat on the couch overlooking the view of the temple and noticed how relaxed and peaceful she felt being in her parents' home, even though it wasn't the one she grew up in. She turned when she heard her mother come down the hallway.

"That boy has grown so much in eight months. For someone so small at birth, he's turned into a little chunk." Julie came around the couch and sat next to them. "Let me feed him. You go take a shower and get ready for the day while Heather is still asleep."

"Deal." Hannah passed Seth over to her mother and went downstairs. She lingered in the shower, knowing Seth was in good hands, and was finishing putting mousse into her long curls when she heard Heather wake up.

"Hi, Mommy," Heather said in a squeaky little voice as Hannah came in the room.

"Hello Angel, are you hungry? I bet Grammy will have some yummy food upstairs. Let's get you dressed."

"I like Grammy."

"Me too." Hannah unzipped Heather's sleeper, changed her into a fresh diaper, and dressed her in warm clothes. She carefully brushed Heather's curls with some detangler and pulled them into two pigtails.

"Grammy, I have a hungry Heather with me," Hannah called as they walked up the stairs.

Julie had placed Seth in a swing in the dining room and was already busy in the kitchen. "I hope hungry Heather likes German pancakes."

"I do, Grammy," Heather said as Hannah helped her into a booster seat.

"You are so prepared for us, Mom. Car seats, playpens, swings, boosters. It's so great."

"Well," Julie said as she cut up a pancake for Heather, "I want you to see that coming to see us isn't difficult with the babies, so you'll hopefully do it more often."

The front door opened, and Sam and Sally walked into the kitchen.

"I thought I smelled your pancakes," Sam said, placing a kiss on Julie's cheek. "I hope you made a lot."

"They're easy enough to whip up if I didn't. Grab a plate."

"I've got to go into the office for a couple of hours this morning. I followed Sally over because I wanted to see the reunion."

"What reunion?" Hannah asked. "Are Paige and the boys here?"

"We are!" Paige said, coming into the kitchen, holding a twin on each hip.

Hannah jumped up from the table and hugged her cousin and the boys.

175

"Oh my gosh, Paige! Look at them. They're so big." Hannah kissed each boy on the cheek. "You weren't kidding when you said one looks like Evan and one looks like you."

"Aren't they so sweet?" Sally asked. "They love Aunt Sally too. Now I need to get Heather and Seth to feel the same."

Paige set the boys down, and they crawled over to look at Seth in the swing. The twins were three months older than Seth, and Hannah and Paige had great hopes they would be best friends.

"That was pretty fun," Sam said. "But let's see if we can make it better. Drumroll, please."

Sally started drumming on the table as Jentry came around the corner.

Hannah let out a scream, which was followed by tears. "We're all together. We're all together." The four friends wrapped their arms around each other, laughing and crying.

"How did you pull this off?" Hannah asked, turning to Sam.

"It was Sally. When she learned you were coming home for Thanksgiving, she contacted Jentry about surprising everyone. Sally and I picked Jentry up last night after she got you settled here. Worked great that you didn't fly in at the same time."

"We haven't been together since Evan's funeral, and that week was such a sad time. I wanted us to make another happy memory," Sally smiled. "Dad and Mom were generous enough to share some of their time with you."

"This is amazing. I can't believe you guys kept it a secret."

"I only found out this morning. Best Thanksgiving ever," Paige said, smiling.

"I'm off," Sam said, kissing Sally goodbye. "We'll see you guys at our house for dinner and games tonight. Mom and Aunt Jenny will watch the munchkins. Have fun making pies and catching up."

"Sally, grab the bucket of baby toys from the basement, and we'll get this group moved into the living room while we start on pies," Julie directed after hugging Jentry hello.

Hannah gave her mother another hug. "Thank you, Momma, for letting me have this. I love you."

December 1, 1994

I am having the best time in Utah and had the best Thanksgiving with all my family and my friends...who really are family.

Sally surprised us by getting Jentry to Utah secretly. She stayed with Sam and Sally. On Wednesday we hung out at my folks and let the kids play together. They're too young to really play, but they'll get there. Jentry told us all about life in downtown Portland and the museum. She seems really happy. I left the kids with my folks, and we all went to Sam and Sally's for games. So much fun! We were laughing so hard.

Thanksgiving was delicious and it was so fun to see my extended family. I'm sure glad I got such a great group of people to belong to. Heather loved the mashed potatoes but made the funniest face when I gave her a tiny bite of sauerkraut. She loves Grammy and follows her everywhere, which makes Mom happy.

On Friday we left the twins and Seth home with our moms and went to Rupert for the Christmas lights. Heather cried when the fireworks went off. Other than that, it was perfect.

Jentry flew back home on Sunday. It was a short trip for her, but we packed in so much fun. Maybe Luke will get orders to Fort Lewis next and I can live closer to her. Fingers crossed.

Pappy bought Heather a snow suit, and boots and whatnot, and then pulled her around the yard on a little sled. Her cheeks were so pink and cute! He's trying to win her affection over from Mom.

Luke has called a couple of times to talk to Heather. Mom and I have had some good talks about marriage and solving conflicts.

Hopefully, I can go back and do better. Seeing Sam and Sally has made me want to fight harder to make my marriage look like theirs. I wish Luke looked at me the way my brother looks at his wife.

January 3, 1995

Luke got his orders for Fort Lewis, Washington. I'll be 2.5 hours from Jentry!!! Yay! He's going to Airborne School in Ft. Huachuca first. He'll be gone for three weeks. I'll spend that time packing and getting us ready for the move. We'll be able to live on base again, which will be nice, but they assign it, so you don't know what you get until you get it. Two weeks after we get there he'll head to Thailand for two months to immerse in the language. His official army job is as a Thai Interrogator, but we're not at war, so who knows if he'll ever use it.

October 12, 1995

Heather turned three on the 10th. She is still a tiny little girl, (28 pounds, 34") and has so much energy. Paige said I should call her Energizer Bunny Junior. I can't remember the last time I felt energy. I need a nap most days. I'm sad to say she is no longer interested in napping every day and doesn't even seem to require rest. She loves all things girly, the color pink, Barbies, playing bride. She has a squeak of a voice and has everyone she knows wrapped around her finger. She stopped wearing diapers in September and is quite proud of her big girl status. She loves to sing and dance and loves attention. She's very goofy, very funny, and very sweet.

I almost don't have words for what has been going on, but I know I need to record this. Last week I discovered pornography on our computer. Pamela Anderson in all her glory. I was devastated. I knew my marriage was crappy, but this was like having the carpet pulled out from under me. We are taught porn is a grave sin and practically cheating. I called Luke at work, hysterical. Told him not to come home. I dropped the kids off at my neighbor Linny's, and checked into a hotel. I called my mom, his mom, and my Bishop. The Bishop came to the hotel room and basically said this was no different than if Luke had picked up a magazine from the drugstore. I'm sorry? That makes it ok? He's probably a porn addict too, based on his answer. Luke came to the room later that night and "confessed" he had a problem and has struggled since high school. I also asked him to come clean about Thailand.

He had gone to Thailand for a few months right after we moved here. His letters went on and on about his tutor, Jiap. When he got home, she was all he could talk about. He wanted to move her to America, help her get into college, and have her live with us. I asked him once if he loved her and he said yes, but just like a sister. Uh huh. There had been a story one night...I don't remember when or how it came up, but he told me he had gone to the bar with his friends and his Diet Coke had been spiked. He had woken up in his hotel room with a kindly prostitute sitting at the end of the bed, watching TV. She asked him if he wanted sex, and he said no. He said to me, "See how honorable I was." The story smelled like bullshit for so many reasons. So, we're in the hotel and I ask for the truth. I don't think I ever got the full story. I think he's holding back details.

I can't believe this is my life. I try so hard to do what is right. I try so hard to be a good wife, to be loving, to take care of the home, teach the children. He breaks my heart all the time. I don't know how much longer I can do this.

February 4, 1996

The Army transferred Luke from Special Forces into the 14th MI. The transfer means a $110 a month pay cut, and was based on his rank, not on the job he was doing.

Things are strained with us still, no surprise. He doesn't see why I'm so upset about the pornography and Thailand. I tell him it feels like adultery to me. He's jacking off to an image of another woman. How is that not infidelity? He's also mad I've told people about it. Like my mother and best friends. I told him I needed support to get through it, and he said, "This doesn't concern you." WHAT??

I don't think he's sorry. He sure doesn't act like it. We haven't had sex since November. We just go through the motions of trying to show up for the kids and be cordial with each other.

March 25, 1996

Mr. Seth is two years old! He is the sweetest boy. He loves his big sister and follows her everywhere. He loves yogurt, Barney, and swings at the playground. I am so in love with him. He likes me to rock him to sleep at night and sing to him. This family started off rocky, (and is still kind of rocky) but we've been blessed with such amazing little children.

April 13, 1996

"Thank you for coming in today. I hope you felt inspired by something you saw," Jentry said as she held open the front door of the museum to allow a group of students to exit after a tour.

She returned to the desk in the lobby, took a swig of Diet Coke, and absentmindedly smoothed her blouse. She was wearing what she wore every day to the Portland Art Museum. A black pencil skirt and a white button-up blouse. The only thing she ever changed were her high heels and jewelry. Her thick dark hair fell in waves down her back.

A room to the right of the desk was currently displaying a collection of local amateur artists. Each artist had submitted photographs of the work they wanted to have on exhibit, and the museum curator decided which items would be displayed. She noticed a man had entered the room and was standing with his hands behind his back, looking at a particular piece. She approached him and observed the fine cut of his navy suit and the silver just starting to show at his temples. He was tan and had a hint of a five o'clock shadow.

"Good afternoon," she said pleasantly, taking notice of his aqua eyes. "Welcome to the Portland Art Museum. Are there any questions I can answer for you?"

He looked away from the painting and saw her. She noticed he did a quick body check and felt confident he liked what he saw.

"This piece," he nodded at the watercolor in front of him. "What can you tell me about it?"

"This room is an exhibit of local amateur artists. For many of them, this is their first time having their artwork displayed in a museum, and it's quite exciting. This particular piece is a watercolor of Portlandia." She turned toward the painting, no longer making eye contact with him. "Are you familiar with the sculpture?"

"Is there a true Portlander who isn't?" he asked, friendliness in his voice. "I work right across from The Portland Building. I see her every morning."

"Lucky you," Jentry replied. "I remember watching her float down the river when she arrived here. She's my favorite sculpture in the city."

"This is watercolor, you say? I'm truthfully surprised watercolor can be this vivid and defined. I'm looking for a piece for my new office. I would love to have this over my desk in a much larger size."

"What size did you have in mind?" she asked, turning back towards him.

"This is what? Eleven by thirteen?"

"Yes, sir."

"Sir?" he smiled. "That makes me feel old. Donovan." He stuck out his hand.

"Jentry," she said, shaking it.

"Wait." He looked at her name tag and then back at the placard next to the piece. "This is by a Jentry Davenport."

"One and the same," Jentry beamed.

"Impressive talent."

"Thank you." She tried to maintain her composure. She'd been painting for over a decade and was happy doing it for her own enjoyment. It wasn't until recently she felt she might be able to start getting her name out into the art world as a serious artist. She had been surprised three years ago when she discovered watercolor was her favorite medium.

Now, to have this Donovan person complimenting her work made her want to shout with joy.

"What else have you painted?" he asked, scanning the room.

"Nothing else on display here. Each artist was allowed one piece. This piece inspired me to attempt painting different sculptures and art installations around the city. I'm working on a watercolor of the Salmon Street Springs with the Hawthorne Bridge in the background right now. Last week, I finished one of the Skidmore Fountain."

He stared at her intently, a smile playing at the corner of his lips. Jentry was surprised at how attractive she found him. He was clearly older than her. Much older than anyone she had dated.

"I would like to commission a piece of art from you. Portlandia. What is the largest size you can do?"

"Twenty-two by thirty."

"Could you have it completed for me by May twentieth?"

"I have painted Portlandia more times than I can count, Love. I'll have it ready for you by the twentieth, if not sooner."

Donovan reached into his wallet and handed a business card to Jentry. She read the name in bold italics across the front. **Andrews, Dixon, and Yonk.** *Global Wealth Advisors.* Donovan Dixon's phone number was in the bottom left corner.

"This is where you can reach me. We're in the Standard Plaza building. Thirteenth floor."

"Not superstitious, then?"

"Ha!" Donovan laughed. "Thirteen has brought me nothing but luck. Case in point, today is April thirteenth, and I've come across a beautiful new artist." He winked at Jentry. "Now, your fee. What does a watercolorist usually charge?"

"Well," Jentry said, looking up to the corner of the room and tapping her finger on her chin. "There's the cost of supplies. The board, the paints. That varies. Then there is the time involved." She looked back at Donovan and said, "Five hundred dollars should cover it."

"You're not a mass producer of this painting, correct? No one else in the city currently owns your work?"

"Not even my mother is interested in my work," Jentry said dryly. "My art covers my apartment, and a few pieces belong to my best friends, but live out of state."

"Portlandia is iconic. And I have a feeling I can get a wide audience to view your work. I'm a big believer in not underselling yourself. When you put value on your time or product, others will. One thousand dollars."

"Are you serious?" Jentry said, shaking her head in disbelief. "Thank you, Donovan. I appreciate your vote of confidence in my abilities, truly."

"I'd like to see some of your other Portland pieces. Perhaps they could find a home in the offices as well. Would you be willing to show them to me?"

"I can bring them in tomorrow. Salmon is half-finished, but you'll get an idea of what the finished painting will look like."

"I'll see you tomorrow then. When is your lunch break?"

"Noon."

"I'll see you then, Ms. Davenport. I look forward to doing business with you."

April 14, 1996

Jentry had worked on the Salmon painting until midnight, wanting to have more of it completed before showing it to Donovan. She found herself picturing the way his eyes creased when he smiled throughout the evening.

She had brought her leather portfolio case and stored it carefully under the front desk. Inside was the completed painting of the Skidmore Fountain, the partial painting of the Salmon Street Springs, and a sketch of the Elk Fountain she hoped to paint next. Today, her hair was pulled back into a high, tight ponytail. She wore red lipstick and several gold bangles on her left arm.

Donovan promptly arrived at noon. The suit jacket was gone, his shirt sleeves were rolled up, and his top button was undone. His hair seemed more unkempt than yesterday, but Jentry smiled, thinking it looked on purpose.

"Ms. Davenport," he said, nodding at her as he came towards the desk.

"Mr. Dixon, Sir," she said, grabbing her portfolio and turning to the older man behind the desk with her. "I'll be back in an hour, Frank. Thanks."

Donovan held the door open, placing his hand on Jentry's back as he guided her through. "I thought we could grab something at the café across the street, so you don't have to walk in those heels," he said with a grin.

"How thoughtful. The café is perfect. I love their scones." Without her heels, Jentry was 5'7, but her shoes added another two inches. Her collection would need its own closet soon.

Donovan picked a table in the back of the small café, and they ordered a light lunch.

"You don't look like an artist to me," he said after the waitress left their table.

"Do artists look a specific way?" Jentry asked, propping her elbow on the table and placing her chin in her hand.

"In Portland? I picture them as part of the grunge movement. Paint splattered overalls, glasses, braids. But you?" He smiled and shook his head.

"You haven't seen me on the weekends," she said. "And me what?" she raised an eyebrow.

"You aren't how I picture young artists in the big city."

The waitress returned with their order, interrupting Donovan. "Half BLT and raspberry scone," she said as she set the plate down in front of Jentry. "And Club sandwich with extra mayo." She set a plate in front of Donovan and left them in peace.

"When did you develop your love of art?"

"As a child. Our housekeeper would buy art supplies and do crafts with me. I took an art class in junior high and found I had a small amount of skill. Lucia encouraged me to pursue it, so I took more classes in high school, and eventually got my bachelor's in art history. Now, I work at the PAM by day and paint by night."

"It wasn't your mother encouraging you? You were closer to the housekeeper?"

"We don't have time to go into the nuances of my childhood, but yes."

"Did you go to school here?"

"I went to Brigham Young University in Utah for three years and finished at Portland State."

Donovan's eyebrows shot up. "And another misconception." He shook his head. "You're Mormon then?"

"I am. I joined the church as a teenager. Went to BYU to immerse myself in the culture and made the best friends a girl could ask for. I moved back to Portland after they got married."

"I have a few clients who are Mormon. Genuinely nice people."

"We try to be," Jentry said. "When did you develop your love of global wealth advising?"

Donovan smiled, the corners of his eyes crinkling in a way Jentry found incredibly sexy. "My grandfather and father were investment bankers. It was expected I build a career in the financial market, but I was able to make my own path."

"And an interest in art came next?"

"Art. Literature. Music. Architecture. My brain is wired for mathematics, but my soul? Ah, my soul appreciates the beautiful things of life." He stared at Jentry for a moment, his eyes seeming to take her in. "Speaking of beautiful things," he pushed his plate away. "Let's see these paintings you brought."

May 19, 1996

Saturday had been drizzly and grey, but the sun was shining Sunday morning, and as the locals said, the mountain was out, referring to the snowcapped Mount Hood. Jentry pulled on some jeans and a lightweight black sweater. She had finished Portlandia yesterday afternoon, and called Donovan to let him know it was complete. When they had parted after lunch, he had told her he would likely commission more paintings. She had been surprised and disappointed that she didn't see him again after that. They had talked on the phone a few days each week, and there was a hint of innuendo at times, making Jentry equal parts nervous and excited.

When she called him yesterday, he had asked her to meet him at Standard Plaza at noon with the painting. It was a fifteen-minute walk from Harrison Tower, and it would give her time to enjoy the city. She laced up her Skechers, carefully covered the painting with a protector, and placed it in her largest portfolio. She took the Pedestrian Trail past Pettygrove Park, deciding to add Dreamer to her list of iconic Portland sites to paint. She had always found the flowing abstract bronze sculpture appealing and wondered why she hadn't thought of it before. She cut through Keller Fountain Park and turned right on Fourth Avenue, walked another three blocks until she spotted the south side of The Portland Building. She crossed Madison and then turned right on Fifth, smiling as her beloved Portlandia came into view, her trident held high in her left hand, right arm extended, and beckoning to the people below.

Jentry stood underneath the hammered bronze sculpture and whispered the poem written by Ronald Talney for her dedication like a prayer. A habit she had formed every time she passed her since moving into the city.

"She kneels down and, from the quietness of copper, reaches out. We take that stillness into ourselves, and somewhere deep in the earth, our breath becomes her city. If she could speak, this is what she would say: Follow that breath. Home is the journey we make. This is how the world knows where we are."

She turned around to face Standard Plaza and saw Donovan leaning against a light post, smiling at her.

They stared at each other the entire ride up to the thirteenth floor. Donovan with a roguish grin across his face. He was in khakis today and a blue button-down shirt, sleeves rolled up again. His hair was combed back like it had been the first time she met him.

The offices of Andrews, Dixon, and Yonk were well-appointed. Donovan had told her at lunch they had moved into these offices several months ago and began a remodeling project. You could tell the firm made money. It was a perfect blend of masculine and modern. Donovan motioned to the second office on the left, and Jentry was impressed when he opened the door. Natural light filled the room from the floor-to-ceiling bay of windows on the east. A brown leather couch was centered under the window. The room was painted a dark navy blue but still felt large due to the natural light. A mahogany desk was on one wall, while the wall across from it held bookshelves surrounding a wet bar. Jentry carefully set her portfolio down on the desktop and walked to the window. She audibly gasped when she saw the view. Across the street, but below her now, was Portlandia.

"Oh, Donovan," she said, her voice reverent. "How different she looks from up here. You can see so many other angles, so many other details."

"I thought you would like that," he said, walking up behind her. "Now, let's see your version."

Jentry turned back to the desk and carefully opened the portfolio, extracting the board. She placed it on top of the desk and stepped back. Donovan studied the painting for a few minutes while she held her breath.

"I love it, truly. You used a different color palette for this one, didn't you? Just slightly. It creates a different mood than what I saw at the museum." He turned and smiled at her. "I'll be hanging her above my desk."

"If I may, I suggest a large, intricate gold-leafed frame and a three-inch white mat."

He looked back at the space and nodded.

"We're having an open house for our local clients in two weeks. Music, hors d'oeuvres, an open bar. Black tie. I'm looking forward to showing off my painting." He walked toward her, a look in his eyes Jentry welcomed. He stopped inches from her. "I'd like to show off something else. Come as my date."

"I bet you say that to all the young artists you pick up on in museums." Jentry smiled up at him coyly.

"I've got my eyes on one artist and one artist only." He lowered his face closer, his mouth almost touching hers. "Say you'll come as my date," he whispered.

"I'll have to check my calendar," she said and turned away from him to walk towards the door. "I hope you enjoy your watercolor and think of me every time you look at it."

July 23, 1996

Jentry came up and we took the kids to the zoo at Point Defiance. She has been a saving grace since moving here. Either coming to see us, or more often than not, bringing us down to see her and have a break. She loves the kids so much and is so sweet with them. Sethy grew into quite the little man this year. He is a real Mommy's Boy... and I'm not complaining! Seth learned the alphabet, and how to count to ten. He's talking earlier than Heather, probably because she is constantly talking to him. He is a delightful, super smart two-year-old, who is a joy to have around.

Heather is still the Princess of the family, and quite content in her role. She mimics everything I do. I've had fun teaching her silly dance moves. She is very funny and loving. She is delightful, super smart, and the sweetest big sister. She is a knock-out in the looks department and we dread when she turns 16. She's the apple of her Daddy's eye.

In June we were able to purchase our first home. It is an older home off Pacific Avenue, with three bedrooms and a basement. We LOVE it. Our neighborhood is filled with friendly older folk, and we are crazy about our ward. They have already put Luke to work as a youth Sunday School teacher and me as the Spiritual Living teacher with the women.

I try not to think about the hard things in my life, and focus on the good, like getting to stay home all day with the cutest kids in the world. Luke and I are doing okay. I'd rate our marriage a strong six or seven out of ten lately.

August 3, 1996

"God, you're beautiful," Donovan said, rolling off of Jentry and onto his side. He propped his head in his hands and stared at her with a smile she had come to know so well in the last few months.

Her relationship with him had been so unexpected. It had also caused her to evaluate where she actually stood in her faith. The first time she went through the temple to do baptisms, she had been shocked by what she witnessed and had the thought she was in a cult go through her mind. Then she thought of her friends, who she loved and respected so much, and shook it off.

It was easy to be a member of the church in Provo with Hannah, Paige, and Sally. But once back in Portland, the doctrines of the church became clearer, and she realized there was a lot she didn't believe anymore. It left her unsure of her testimony. Her love for her friends and her belief in their testimonies kept her going at first. She wanted to feel the spirit. She wanted to feel like she was a part of God's one true church, but she struggled to regain those feelings she had at baptism.

She went to church for several months and attended a few activities. She dated a returned missionary for a brief time but found him too patriarchal and pharisaical. Before long, she spent her Sundays painting rather than attending church. She soon found herself getting a cup of coffee a few times a month until it became a habit.

She couldn't say for sure she didn't believe in the Mormon church anymore. She just didn't think about it. Her doubts and questions were placed on the proverbial shelf, and while in Portland, she lived her life the way she wanted to. And that included coffee, wine, and occasional sex with various men she dated.

When she visited Utah, or her friends visited her, it was another story. No coffee. No tank tops. No skipping church. She felt guilty pretending to believe, but she justified it because the rest of the relationship with her friends was authentic and true. Besides, she still had a belief in God. She loved Hannah, Paige, and Sally fiercely. She helped them when she could. She called them every week. All of them had visited at least once. They had no idea she wasn't the perfect Mormon girl each of them was.

So, the night of the Andrews, Dixon, and Yonk open house, when Donovan asked if she wanted to come back to his house for a nightcap, she agreed. And when they stood on his penthouse balcony overlooking the river and city lights, and he pulled her to him and started kissing her passionately, she leaned into him letting him know she wanted him as much as he wanted her. When he started unzipping her dress, she let it fall to the floor, standing in front of him in black lace underclothes. And when he picked her up and carried her to his bedroom, she willingly made love to him.

Now they were at her beach house, escaping the city for the weekend. She reached up and ran a finger along his jaw. "You're not too bad to look at yourself, Love."

He bent down and kissed her. "Let's walk on the beach. Get dressed, and I'll make us some coffee."

She watched his toned, naked body walk out of the room and then threw off the covers. She grabbed the leggings and tee shirt she'd had on the day before and quickly put them on. She brushed her teeth, combed her hair up into a ponytail, grabbed her socks and shoes, and met him in the kitchen.

He handed her a cup of black coffee and kissed her again. She added creamer and they headed outside to walk up the beach to Haystack Rock while they had their favorite morning beverage.

"So, these friends you're always talking about. Do they know about us yet?" Donovan asked, taking a sip.

"Truthfully? I don't quite know what to tell them. 'Hey, so I'm seeing this man, and he's a lot older than me, and I'm crazy about him, and I sleep at his house as much as mine because I don't follow the teachings of the church anymore.' It feels daunting."

"Jen, you tell them when you're ready. Tell them what you're comfortable sharing. It's not lying to not tell them everything. It's being selective. And maybe these girls are no longer a fit for you."

"No!" Jentry said, alarmed. "They're my best friends. And it's not based on some shared religious beliefs. It's based on years of making memories and supporting each other. It's based on things we have in common and, funny enough, the things we don't. They're the truest friends I've ever had. I can't picture my life without them. Their lives are so different from mine right now, yes, but we're still best friends. I still talk to at least one of them a day. I'll never outgrow them or not fit with them anymore."

Donovan put an arm around her, pulled her into his chest, and kissed the top of her head. "I'm sorry I suggested it. I know you love your friends. Maybe I'll get to meet them someday. You're a smart woman. You'll figure out how to balance the friendships with them and your secret life with me as my sex goddess," he said, with a roguish grin on his face.

Jentry fake punched him in the chest. "Is that all I am to you? A fun romp in the sack?"

"What do you think you are to me, Jen?"

"I asked you a question first," she said stubbornly.

He leaned down and kissed her on the end of the nose. "Jentry Elizabeth Davenport, you are a minx who has me wrapped around her finger. You are the most intriguing woman I have ever met. You challenge me in a way no woman before you has ever done. I'm inspired by your talent, your intelligence, and your heart. These last few months with you have been an intoxicating ride I don't want to ever end."

Jentry looked adoringly up at him. She felt the same way. She had been afraid to fall in love, afraid to risk her heart. Because of Buckley's betrayal. Because of her parents' coldness. Yet, with Donovan, her heart felt safe. She knew he adored her, and she adored him in return.

"Move in with me, Jentry. I absolutely hate the nights we spend apart. I want to see your beautiful face first thing in the morning and last thing at night."

"I don't know, Love," she said playfully. "Where would we put your clothes once my shoes are organized in the closet?" She squeezed his hand and kept walking. "Seriously though, Donovan, Hannah, and the kids pop down a lot on the weekends. She needs an escape more than you know. It's so difficult to be torn between the man I love and my best friends. I can't give up my place. Not yet. Not with Hannah living so close."

"Playing hard to get?"

"Hardly. You got me a few times this morning already," Jentry said, playfully slapping Donovan on the butt. "I'm not ready yet, maybe someday. Don't give up on me."

August 15, 1996

"You're kidding, right?" Hannah asked Luke incredulously.

"No, I'm not kidding. You don't know what it's like being told what to do by people with less education and intelligence than me. I'm not using any of my training. I can't do this for the rest of my life. So yes, I plan to gain weight in order to fail physical training and be discharged. And yes, you'll need to pick up a job to help make ends meet."

"Let me get this straight," Hannah said, then lowered her voice so as not to wake the children. "Let me get this straight. You have the nerve to tell me I'm going to have to get a job when you're too lazy to make the military work and want to get fat as a coward's way out?"

"You're so judgmental. I'm not lazy, Hannah. I'm overqualified to be in the military and I want out to pursue other things."

"Overqualified? On what planet? You don't have a degree. You have no other job experience prior to this other than selling shoes at the mall for a few months."

"I read a lot. I know more than most of the people over me."

"About what topic? Greek mythology?"

"I knew you wouldn't be supportive. Nothing I give you is enough."

"Nothing you give me is...like how you gave me supporting you while you stayed home with Heather? Like how you gave me no car of my own for our entire marriage?

Like how you gave me infidelity with a porn addiction and cheating? You're right. That's not enough for me."

"I've told you I didn't let anything happen."

"You seriously think I believe when you were in Thailand, a kindly prostitute brought you back to your hotel after your soda was spiked and was naked and about to go down on you, but you stopped her?"

"Okay, okay. I didn't stop her. But I wasn't fully conscious. I think it was date rape."

Hannah put her hands over her face and started crying. "You are full of shit. You cheated on me, and you won't own it. I stayed with you for the kids and because you've said you'll kill yourself if I ever leave. And now you want to take away the only thing you've given me of value, my ability to be a stay-at-home mom, and expect me to help pay the bills. That isn't happening, Luke."

"I'm getting out. It's not going to happen immediately. It will take months to put on enough weight, which gives us time to figure out what jobs we can get to make ends meet. Now that we own a house and we're not on base, we won't have to worry about moving, but we will need to keep the mortgage paid. You have time to figure out what you're going to do to help out. That's the end of it."

"That's the end of it? You aren't the boss of me, Luke. I'm not working outside of this home. The children need me."

"Then start building a home daycare business, Hannah. I don't care what you decide. You need to do your share."

"You are unbelievable." Hannah stood up and headed for the front door.

"Where are you going?"

"I'm going on a walk, Luke, so I don't start screaming and scare the kids."

Hannah took off up Sixty-first Street, heading for Wapato Park. She angrily wiped away the tears that were coming one after the other. She didn't know how much more she could take of this marriage. She had brought up divorce to Luke on several occasions, and he always told her if she left him, he'd kill himself. How could she have his death on her conscience? So, she stayed and tried to make the best of things. She loved their children with all her heart and loved being able to stay home with them. She couldn't believe he wanted to take that away from her after all the ways he had let her down over the years. "I hate him," she whispered under her breath. It didn't help. She wasn't even sure she meant it. How could she hate the father of her children? But how could the father of her children be so selfish? She made it to the park and sat on a bench near the lake.

"Father in Heaven," she said softly, "My heart hurts. My life isn't what I wanted it to be. I feel so hopeless for my future with things how they are. I can't imagine if they get worse. Please help me. Forgive me for my anger. Help me if I really am judgmental to not be. I want to be a righteous daughter. I want the Spirit. And I want to be happy. Please, please make things turn out for me."

She sat on the bench for a few more minutes and then headed back home. She went into a dark house. Luke must have already retreated to the bedroom. Probably looking at porn. The phone started ringing as soon as she locked the front door behind her.

"Hello?"

"Hey, Love," Jentry said on the other line.

"Hey, Jentry," Hannah replied, trying not to sound as dejected as she felt.

"Sorry to call so late. I have some news I wanted to share."

"Do tell," Hannah said, laying down on the couch, the long cord reaching across the room.

"I wanted to make sure it was going to last before I said anything, but I'm seeing somebody."

"What? Oh my gosh, tell me everything," Hannah said, forgetting her own problems for a minute.

"His name is Donovan Dixon. He's much older than me. Eleven years older. He's so sexy, Hannah. Oh my gosh. I met him at the museum, and he had me paint something for him, and it picked up from there."

"That sounds so cool. Like something out of a movie. What does he look like?"

"He's tall. Six feet. He has brown hair with a little silver at the temples. He has the best smile. Really blue eyes. Like Caribbean ocean blue. I'm in love with him, Hannah. He treats me like a queen. Spoils me."

"You deserve it. Is he Mormon?" Hannah asked.

"No," Jentry sighed. "He was raised Christian. I think Lutheran."

"Are you okay with that? Not having the same faith?"

"I think we believe the same on the things that matter."

"I want you to be happy and find someone who appreciates you. That's what's important to me."

"Really? I've been afraid to tell you guys because I didn't want you to think less of him."

"Well, truthfully, I don't think Luke qualifies as Mormon anymore by most definitions. That doesn't stop me from living my faith. I'm sure it's the same with you."

"Yeah. For sure," Jentry said.

"I hope I get to meet him soon."

"Next time you come up."

"Wait, you said you've been seeing him for six months? We've been up since then. Secretive girl," Hannah laughed.

"Well, Love, I had to make sure it was a go."

"Understandable."

"How are you guys doing?"

"Awful."

"What's going on?"

"Luke told me tonight he's going to get fat on purpose to get out of the Army, and I need to find a job."

"Are you serious?"

"That's what I said! My exact words. Staying home with the kids is all I've got. We're barely making ends meet on the Army income. I can't imagine what it will be like when we don't have those paychecks."

"Do you need to come down for a getaway? I could grab you in the morning. Keep you until Numbnuts comes down and gets you himself."

Hannah laughed at the use of the nickname Jentry had given Luke.

"The kids would have fun playing in the Lovejoy Fountain. Say yes."

"Yes. Come and get me."

"I'll be there by ten. Pack for a week. Leave a note."

"I love you, Jen. What would I do without you?"

August 27, 1996

"Knock, Knock," Paige said as she stepped inside of Sally's hospital room. "Are you up for visitors yet?"

Sally smiled and beckoned her friend over to the bed, where she sat, holding a tiny bundle of pink.

"You just missed Sam. He left to get me a milkshake. Come meet my little girl."

Sally proudly pulled back the knitted blanket so Paige could get a better look at the baby inside. She had gone into labor early yesterday morning and was checked into the hospital by noon. She and Sam welcomed their first child into the world ten minutes after midnight.

"Oh, my goodness, what a pink bundle of beauty. Little Sariah, I love you already," Paige cooed. "Did you give her a middle name?"

"We decided on Jane. Sam said boys are named after their dads all the time, and more girls should be named after their mothers."

"Sariah Jane Limbrey. What a beautiful name for a beautiful baby. Can I hold her if I wash my hands?"

"Of course."

Paige washed at the sink in the room and then took the baby into her arms and sat in the rocking chair next to Sally.

"How was your labor?"

"It wasn't too bad. I was on the fence about an epidural until Hannah reminded me of her experience with Seth. I was more exhausted than I was in pain."

"That's impressive. You look amazing. Motherhood becomes you."

"It's nice to finally be part of the club. Sam and I waited four years to have a baby on purpose, which was hard at times, with our parents pressuring us for grandchildren and old ladies at church asking when we were going to start a family.

But Sam and I got to have a fair amount of fun first and save a good nest egg."

"Will you be teaching next term? They got a substitute for you for the first month, right?"

"Actually, L and P is doing well enough that I don't need to work anymore. I let the school know I wouldn't be back."

"Oh wow. I'm so happy for you and so sad for me. I'll miss seeing you every day."

"Well, now we can see each other for play dates."

"What do you think of my beautiful daughter?" Sam asked as he walked into the room, a hot fudge malt from Charlie's in his hand.

"She's perfect," Paige said, "But how could she not be with such great genes."

"You should have seen Sally, Paige. She was so tough."

Sally smiled tenderly at Sam. Her life with him was more than she could have ever hoped for. He was such a good man and treated her with such respect and love.

She couldn't wait to see how he would grow with fatherhood. He was already so smitten with Sariah.

There were times Sally had a stab of guilt for having a life so much easier than Hannah and Paige. She had voiced this to Jentry once and been reprimanded. Jentry had assured her no one begrudged her the life she had.

Today, however, as Paige handed Sariah back to her, she was too full of joy to feel any guilt. Marriage and motherhood were the best things to have ever happened to her.

January 1, 1997

Jentry sat with her feet in Donovan's lap. They had made a tradition of having brunch together every Sunday and walking along the riverfront. The weather had been too cold and wet for going out the last few weeks, even if they bundled up, so Jentry had made waffles with orange juice this morning. Donovan had insisted on bacon as well. They had been up late celebrating New Year's Eve, and it was almost noon before they sat down to eat. Now they were relaxing, each with a book in their hands.

When he saw she was serious about not moving in with him, Donovan made a grand gesture to let Jentry know how much he wanted to be with her. In December, he sold his condo at American Plaza and bought one of the penthouses on the twenty-fifth floor of Harrison Tower. She was now only five floors below him, and they were together as much as possible. She worked thirty hours a week at the museum as a tour guide and spent her afternoons painting in the studio she had set up in her apartment. She took a watercolor class twice a month through one of the galleries in town, wanting to perfect her technique. True to his word, Donovan had commissioned more art for the offices of Andrews, Dixon, and Yonk, as well as some small pieces for his home. Several of their clients had asked about her paintings and commissioned art as well.

"Okay," she said, setting her book down. "It's a new year. What is one serious goal you have and one fun goal?"

"I want to ravish you every single day. Twice. Does that count?" Donovan said with a wink.

"Depends. Is that the serious or the fun goal?"

"I hope you think it's as fun as I do. It sounds like you do each time."

Jentry threw a pillow at him.

"Serious goal, I want to grow our client base in three new countries. I've got a trip to Narita in two weeks to meet with some investors. Getting them to sign with us would be a fantastic way to set the momentum for the year."

"How long are you leaving me for?"

"Five days. Two of those are travel."

"And a fun goal?"

"I already said my fun goal. As my accountability partner, I need you to take me to the bedroom right now."

"After I've washed the smell of bacon grease out of my hair." She sniffed her nightshirt. "I love eating bacon, but it makes me stink."

Donovan pounced on her, pretending to gnaw on her neck. "Hot girlfriend that smells like bacon?" he said, still nibbling, "Perfect combination."

Jentry giggled and pushed him off.

"What are your goals, Jentry?"

"I've decided I want to apply to PSU and get my master's so I can become a curator at the museum," she said, beaming.

"Look at your grin. You're pretty pleased with that idea, aren't you? That's great, Sweet. Do it. You won't regret it."

"And for fun, I'd like to take a trip with you."

"You would? Where would you want to go?"

"Anywhere. As long as I'm with you, Love."

"I have an idea. Come with me to Japan. It's cold there this time of year, so we won't get to explore too much, and I'll be in meetings most of the day. Then, on the way home, instead of coming straight here, we go to Hawaii for a week. Will that do?"

Jentry squealed, jumped into his lap, and kissed him all over his face. "I'll ask for time off first thing tomorrow morning. Thank you, Donovan."

She stood and reached her hand out for Donovan to take. "Time to help me wash the smell of bacon off, hot stuff."

Donovan grabbed her, threw her over his shoulders, and let out a whoop as he ran for the bedroom.

February 4, 1997

I hope to someday be the mother my sweet children deserve. They really do mean the world to me, but I can be so impatient and easily agitated at times. Mind you, a 3- & 4-year-old as active, wild, loud, stubborn & independent as my two could make a person go grey. But I need to not take things so personal. Like when Seth says he doesn't like me whenever he doesn't get his own way. I hope someday my children will know how much I loved them, how I tried my best, and how I wanted nothing more than for us to be a forever family. I know I have to answer to God someday for the kind of parent I was & I pray I pass.

February 5, 1997

We had the funnest day today!! It was beautiful when we woke up... clear sky, bright sun. So, since it was Luke's day off too, we decided to make the most of it. We loaded some things up & headed for Ocean Shores. The kids were so happy & had so much fun. It was such a nice day we didn't even need jackets! I wish everyday was this nice. Heather entertained us on the drive home by singing along to the Ace of Base CD. She knows all the words!! She sings at the top of her lungs & just cracks us up. She is such a little pip. We are so crazy about her. She is such a funny little thing, and so beautiful. Got home from the beach at 7:00 & relaxed the rest of the evening.

April 15, 1997

We moved from my sweet little home into a 2 bedroom, 850 sq foot apartment. Luke hadn't been making enough at Domino's and wasn't paying our mortgage, so the house foreclosed. We needed to save money anyway, and this is cheaper than a mortgage, because it's low-income housing. I know the apartment is only temporary & best financially - still it is so hard!! The children seem to be adjusting well enough. They love the hot tub. The two of them are in one room and it's so small Heather & Seth don't have a bed. They sleep on sleeping bags & don't seem to mind.

November 11, 1997

My last two days have been pretty busy. Heather and I had doctors' appointments on Tuesday, and I had a candle party Tuesday night. It was a bit of a flop. Yesterday Seth went to his play group. He was so funny. Then after school Heather's Sunday school teacher had a tea party for the three little girls in her class. They were all dressed up and she bought these neat flower wreaths with ribbons for their hair. While they were doing that, I duct taped the windows to our car so they wouldn't leak anymore. We were getting rained on INSIDE the car! The moon roof and the back windows leaked. The water from the back windows dripped into the trunk and ruined everything in there. I had to throw away a stroller yesterday because it had molded. Luckily, I have a nice jogger stroller, so I didn't mind terribly. Then I replaced a broken headlight too. I was all greasy and everything! I'm the fixer in our family. Luke isn't good for any of that. I had a candle party last night too. The hostess earned four candles, which means it was a very good party. On the way home there was super thick fog, and it was then I discovered my new headlight pointed up and across my line of sight. That made for interesting driving.

Sam just got hired as an account controller for Logan Regional Hospital. I'm so proud of him. Baby #2 is on the way for them. They want to be surprised with what it is. Crazy that you can find out the gender ahead of time nowadays. What would the pioneers think??

<u>January 12, 1998</u>

Luke was FINALLY promoted to manager at Domino's in December. He had been told it would happen in October of last year, so we were slightly frustrated at how long it took. It meant a pay raise, but no change in schedule. The hours actually got a little worse if that is possible. After the Army, and then Domino's, I felt very much like a single mom who happened to have a male roommate. Free pizzas were a nice benefit whenever we wanted to have an impromptu party or pay a babysitter, which made date nights possible when he wasn't working. However, free pizzas didn't do much for our ever-expanding waistlines. I joined 24-Hour Fitness to try to reverse the pizza effect and shed close to 30 pounds in about two and half months. I'd work out for about two hours a day while the kiddos played in the daycare. It was great. But in order to save money I canceled the membership in October, fully intending to keep up the good work in my apartment weight room. As the saying goes, the road to hell is paved with good intentions. Not only did I not keep working out, I regained every last pound. I'm trying to come to terms with the fact I got stuck with the Limbrey fat gene and I'll be fighting it the rest of my life. Size two seventeen-year-old me never imagined her future would be weighing 155 and a size fourteen.

February 14, 1998

Donovan and Jentry sat close together in a booth at The Melting Pot, enjoying the cheese course and talking about Donovan's upcoming trip to Chicago. Jentry was used to him traveling a few times a year. When she wasn't busy with school and could get time off from the museum, she would join him.

She was in the early stages of researching her thesis and knew the break would give her some time to dive in. She had chosen for her title 'The relevance of the arts in shaping a city's cultural, social, and economic identity.' Donovan had been a great sounding board when she was trying to narrow down her topic. His love of culture and support of the arts was one of her favorite things about him.

They had enjoyed dates to the opera and ballet last year, as well as a long weekend in Seattle, where they visited several museums. Jentry's favorite had been the Seattle Asian Art Museum, located inside a gorgeous 1933 Art Deco building. They'd had dinner with Luke and Hannah as well. Donovan's thirty-eighth birthday was coming up, and they had talked about visiting Seattle again and exploring all three national parks.

"Have I told you how much I love cheese?" Jentry said, stabbing a piece of broccoli with the small spear and sinking it into the pot of gouda.

"The level to which this cheese is disappearing is a testimony to your love."

"Do I need to stop? Am I being a cheese hog?"

"If cheese makes you happy, then dip away."

"You make me happy, Donovan," Jentry said, wiping the corner of her mouth.

"Do I now?" he asked, leaning toward her with a mischievous smile on his face. He kissed her, first a simple peck, but as she leaned into it, he kissed her again, lingering, his forehead to hers.

"I love you, Donovan. This is a wonderful Valentine's date. Thank you."

"I love you, Jen. In fact, I love you so much I was wondering if you would do something for me."

"Anything, Love," Jentry replied, smiling.

"Anything? You don't know what I want you to do."

"True. I trust either I'll really want to, or you won't hold me to it," she said, as she smiled sheepishly.

"Let's put that to the test." Donovan reached into his pocket and pulled out a small, black velvet box. "Marry me, my Sweet."

Jentry sat wide-eyed and speechless. This was not the favor she assumed he'd be asking. Normally, Donovan was making some kind of sexual inuendo when he talked like that. She watched as he opened the box. Inside was a three-carat oval emerald surrounded by a halo of diamonds. She had never seen a more beautiful ring.

"Donovan..."

"We've been together almost two years. You are still the most intriguing woman I have ever met. You still challenge and inspire me every day. You love with your whole heart, in spite of the lack of real love from your parents growing up. You have turned into this fierce, compassionate, talented woman on your own, and it's a testament to your heart and soul. I know you're gun-shy. I know you like what we have going on now, but I'm hoping..."

"Donovan," Jentry placed a finger to his lips, stopping him mid-sentence. "I didn't know until you asked, but there is nothing I want more than to be your wife. Yes, my dearest love, I'll marry you." She wiped a tear from her cheek as Donovan placed the ring on her left hand.

"Woman, you have no idea how relieved I am. You said yes." He winked at her, melting her heart with the smile she loved so much.

Jentry held her hand up, admiring the ring. "This is exquisite. I've never seen anything more beautiful."

"I have," he said, giving her a kiss on the cheek.

Jentry turned to Donovan, her heart swelling with more love and emotion for a man than she would have thought possible before meeting him. She had been concerned by the age difference at first. Eleven years older was significant. The different religious beliefs, even though she didn't live hers explicitly, had also given her pause. Yet, they blended seamlessly into each other's lives from the start. She had loved every second of being Donovan Dixon's girlfriend, and she couldn't wait to be his wife.

"I don't want to wait," Jentry said, then paused as the dinner course was delivered to the table. "I don't want to wait. I don't need a big fancy wedding with all eyes on me, and a reception and all that nonsense. Let's elope."

"Are you sure you don't need more time to think about it? What about your friends? What about your parents?"

"When did I last talk to my parents? They set me up with the apartment and gave me the beach house, then moved to Brazil. I get a phone call on my birthday and Christmas and a deposit into my bank account each month to assuage their guilt," Jentry said, the bitterness leaking into her voice. "The girls, though? They would want to be there. Wherever there is," she laughed. "I'll think about it while you're in Chicago. But don't be surprised if I drag you off to a Justice of the Peace as soon as you get back."

March 1, 1998

I'm an Auntie again! Sam and Sally had another little girl on February 23rd. They named her Sabrina Jane. Such a pretty name. I love that Sally, Sariah and now Sabrina all have the same middle name. They're in the process of looking for a new house too. They want to stay in Millville and have land for their goats and chickens. I love that Sally has my brother living a small farm life.

And in other news, Jentry is engaged! I've never heard her as giddy and excited as she was the last time we talked. I'm so happy for her and Donovan.

I miss my family and friends so much. I'm glad I at least get to see Jentry every other month or so. I hope I can make it back home for a visit soon, but money is TIGHT, even with selling Salt City Candles for extra income.

March 22, 1998

My little boy is 4 years old. I can't believe it! It has flown by so fast. I want him to quit getting older. I want him to always be my little boy. I love him so much. I remember every detail of the day he was born. His birth was the second most amazing event in my life. I had such sincere intentions of being the best mother in the world...and now, I have so many regrets for all the times I've been impatient, neglectful, lazy, or just plain mean. I will always think my children deserve so much better of a mother than they got, but for some reason, Heavenly Father chose to send them to me. And for that I will always be eternally thankful. Nothing in my life gives me more pleasure than being a mother. And getting to be the mother of Heather and Seth is an honor. I love celebrating October 10 and

March 16 because those are the days two of Heaven's brightest, purest, most wonderful angels started their Earth Life. I pray someday I can pull it together enough to be the kind of mother they deserve. The kind of mother Heavenly Father believes I am capable of being.

April 7, 1998

Ahhhhh!!! I want to scream and shout and break something! In February Luke got a ticket for having expired plates on the Toyota. It would have only cost him $30 to register it. He didn't bother, got pulled over a second time and got a ticket that he "forgot about." Supposedly, we were sent notice that if he didn't pay the ticket by such and such date his license would be suspended. He says he never got any notice. On March 24th he ran a red light and was pulled over again. He was ticketed for that, plus for driving on a suspended license, PLUS the car was impounded on the spot. Well, of course, he didn't do anything to find out what it would take to get the car back. Had he bothered to check, he would have found out we could have had the car back in a couple of days for very little money. But no. He does nothing, until I finally call. As it turns out, all we would have needed would be to show the court proof of insurance and my driver's license, plus pay $50 for a release from the towing company. I called the towing company on Friday, and someone there told me that for $93 I could have the car. Today, however, they deny ever saying that, and say I would have to have the full $882 we owe for the time it has been in storage. They were so rude about it and practically called me a liar for claiming I had been told $93. Which I was!! They want the whole amount, which of course means we just lost our car. I had a bunch of stuff in it too, and they won't even let

215

you get it out. What a racket!! I am so angry right now, and so sad, and so disappointed, and so hopeless. I called my mom and started crying telling her we didn't need the $93 from her after all. When I was on the phone with her, Jeff Simpson called, and so I started

bawling to him. Jeff is the guy who brought Luke into NASE, selling life insurance. He is sure I need to be Luke's full-time secretary and put the kids in daycare.

I won't do it. Why should I have to give up everything because Luke can't make a decent living? We have been struggling and bouncing around from job to job for six years, and I can't take it anymore, I've given up dream after dream until I've lost all hope of ever having a life any better than the one we live now.

We do have some great blessings. I have a beautiful apartment. We have one car, we have food, we have clothes, we have health insurance, I have the best friends ever, and my family is wonderful. However - the beautiful apartment was furnished by my mom, the church pays the rent on it each month. The food is picked up at the Bishop's storehouse, the clothes are bought by my mother, the insurance is Apple Health, which is state welfare. Our bills are piling up and incurring more and more interest each day. We are $22,000 in debt. We have so many collection agencies after us, all wanting their money and wanting it yesterday. Our credit is shot. The only way we will ever own a home again is if we save 25% to put down. which would be $50,000, so it would never happen.

Now, if you ask Luke, the opposite is true. According to him our ship is about to come in, and we are only four or five months away from no debt and unbelievable wealth. Of course, he has been saying that for six years - but of course too, this time he means it.

How am I supposed to deal with this? I love him and resent him so much at the same time. I love him and want to hurt him! I love him and want to kill him right now! He just cost us a car! I liked it when my trials in life were trying not to kiss boys much more than I like my current trials. I never thought poverty would be something

I would have to deal with. Granted, thanks to my parents, we don't look like we are living below the poverty level which we are. But it is so hard to see everyone around you doing so much better. And I'm not even after worldly wealth. I want to be out of debt, be able to pay all our bills, drive a car that doesn't leak when it rains, and have a little money left over to play every once in a while. The sad thing is, I don't think any of that will ever happen. Every time I start to get my hopes up something like today always comes along to dash them. I hate when I do get my hopes up, because I seem to fall harder each time. It is easier to be content with nothing than to try to achieve anything and be forced to settle for less. Does that make sense? Probably not.

The worst part is I am horrible at hiding my feelings and our problems from the children. They wouldn't have a clue what our situation was if I wasn't telling them. I hate myself for doing it too. I get so sad when I look at them and think of all the things I won't be able to provide for them, like lessons, sports, vacations, etc. And now Jeff Simpson wants me to give up the only thing I have to offer...my time. My time as their teacher, mother, and friend. I don't want to send my kids to daycare.

Okay, I've stopped crying, and I'm feeling somewhat better. I need to go deep clean my kitchen and do some laundry and I just don't have it in me right now. I've been cleaning all day. It's all I ever do.

I hate that so much misery in my life is linked to money, especially since the church seems to teach you should be above wanting it. How

217

are you ever supposed to balance everything in life - being a wife, being a mother, being a teacher, being a cook, being a maid, being a taxi, being a Sunday school teacher, etc. and still have time left over to worry about how you are going to pay for electricity?

I better sign off today's journal. Too much gloom and doom.

May 15, 1998

Packing a small house, planning for a larger one, and taking care of a newborn and twenty-one-month-old baby had been no problem at all for Sally. She was organized and thorough and still found time each day to take her babies for a walk around the block after breakfast. She was grateful for a warm spring that had allowed them to prepare for this move as seamlessly as possible.

Before Sabrina was born, they knew they would need something bigger than their little white farmhouse. Sally wanted land for the goats and chickens, a large garden, and a big yard for the children. Sam wanted more than one bathroom. They had looked around the valley and, in the end, decided to stay in Millville. A 3000-square-foot, four-bedroom red brick rambler came on the market at the end of March. It was located on two acres of farmland on the southern end of town, on the way to the Coyote Research Center. They were already used to the sounds of the coyotes at feeding times and didn't think being a half-mile closer would make much of a difference.

The home had been built in 1995 and needed very little to make it meet their needs. Paige had insisted on helping Sally paint the girls' bedrooms. Sally had chosen a soft lilac for Sariah's room and a blush pink for Sabrina's nursery. Sam had started work on a sunroom on the north side of the home to let in more light and mountain views. An unfinished basement would be next year's project, which would add a second family room, more bedrooms, and another full bathroom. This was their forever home, and they were excited for the life they would build within its walls.

Sally was washing dishes by hand and thinking longingly of the brand-new dishwasher she would soon have when she heard someone come in the front door.

"Help has arrived," Paige said as she came into the kitchen. "Are you ready to get this kitchen moved over today?"

Sally hugged Paige hello after drying her hands. "You better believe it. I can't believe we'll be in the house officially tomorrow. We've had the keys for over a week. Sam wanted to make sure it was spotless for the girls, and I wanted their rooms painted, so it's a trade-off, I guess."

"Looks like you've got almost everything boxed up," Paige said, looking at the stacks of boxes on the dining table.

"There wasn't much to it," Sally said. "The girls are down for naps. Julie should be here any minute to sit with them while we run over to the house. I figured we'd load up our cars, give the new kitchen one more wipe down, and then unload real quick."

"If I ever move, will you be my project manager, Sal?" Paige said, lifting a box off the table and carrying it out to her car. "Aunt Julie just pulled in," she said over her shoulder.

Julie Limbrey came into the small home with a book in hand. "Sally, I feel like I'm getting off easy getting to sit with the girls while you do all the heavy lifting."

Sally smiled at her mother-in-law and grabbed a box. "I need the exercise so I can keep up with them."

She and Paige made a few more trips to get all the boxes. Then Sally hugged her mother-in-law. "The phone is on at the house. The new number is on the fridge. Call me if they wake up. Love you, Mom."

Sally led Paige down 500 East and turned left on 3700 South. There were only five homes on the small lane, and hers was the last one on the left. They pulled into the circular driveway and went inside. They passed the formal living room and walked through the family room at the back of the house to set their boxes down in the dining room off of the kitchen.

Sam and a small construction crew had completed the sunroom last night, and he was finishing cleaning up the project. "Hey gorgeous," he said when he saw Sally. "Come tell me what you think."

Sally and Paige walked through the French doors off of the dining room that had once led to the back patio but now was the entrance to a large sunroom. The outdoor brick was on one wall, while the west wall had been framed, sheet rocked, and painted. The north wall was framed three feet up, with large windows to the ceiling. There was a new French door that led to a patio slab on the east. The plush carpet had been laid late last night.

"This space is amazing, Sally," Paige said. "Much bigger than I expected."

"I love the house, but there aren't a lot of large windows, and you know how much I love to let the sunlight in. Thank you, Sam. It's everything I imagined." Sally threw her arms around her husband and kissed him. "We're going to get this kitchen ready. I've made muffins for our movers tomorrow morning. Last time baking in my little kitchen."

"You'll have to break this one in soon, Sweetie. I'm going to go home and shower. Dad and I will be back tonight to set up the girls' rooms."

"Perfect. Mom brought her playpens, and I'll set those up after their nap."

"See you soon, Sweetheart. Thanks for helping us, Paige." Sam headed off, leaving them to their work.

"Look at this contraption, Paige," Sally said, turning on the radio that was bolted to the underside of the cupboard to the local country station.

They wiped down the kitchen and unpacked the dishes while visiting Sally's plans for the house, their children, and Jentry's upcoming wedding.

"How have I not met someone Jentry's been dating for over two years?" Paige asked, putting a crockpot over the fridge. "He's been out of town each time I've visited."

"Hannah says he's amazing. She told me he reminds her of the guy from E.R., The big Hollywood heartthrob."

"George Clooney?" Paige laughed.

"Yes, that's the one. But with blue eyes. She says Jentry is so lovestruck around him. It makes my heart happy."

"I wish she could get him to take the missionary discussions so they could go to the temple," said Paige. "I think a mixed-faith marriage would be difficult."

"Jentry doesn't seem to mind. And from what Hannah says, he lets her be whatever and whoever she wants, so it doesn't seem to be an issue."

"I guess. Knowing I am sealed to Evan for all eternity brings me so much peace, so I can't help but want that for Jentry. However, I will love Donovan no matter where he sits on Sunday. Good hell. He sounds better than Luke, who is a returned missionary."

"Poor Hannah. Her spirit seems so broken at times, and yet she's so strong and full of love and laughter at the same time."

"I don't know how she does it. I can't wait to see her and the kids next month. I love that Aunt Julie brings them out twice a year."

"We'll have to plan another game night before the big wedding with all of us. See how Donovan does in a country setting. Maybe I'll make him feed the goats."

June 20, 1998

"Alright, my big boys, who's ready for another hike?" Paige asked, pulling up next to the Temple Sawmill Trailhead.

"Me. I am Mommy," Ammon said.

"Me too!" Jarom said, almost shouting. Paige was still working on teaching him what an indoor voice was.

Paige lived for summer vacation and had the ability to be with the twins full-time. Her mother had watched the twins the first few months after Paige started teaching at Logan High. Blake and Blythe were seniors in high school and needed more attention as they prepared for college, so Paige had found a family friend, Becky, willing to watch the twins. Once they turned three, she was able to put them in preschool two days a week and leave them with Becky, the other three. All of this was with assistance from Evan's parents, who sent her five hundred dollars a month to help with the costs of raising the boys. Doug and Kristi Lindburg lived in Mesa but came up to Cache Valley several times a year to see the boys. Paige was grateful for all of the help she received. She didn't know how she could have made ends meet without it.

She unbuckled the boys and helped them out of the car. "Alright, put on your hats so you don't get sunburned. Do you have your water?"

The boys held up their bottles, and they started down the trail. She couldn't take them far with their little legs, but she wanted to get them used to being in the mountains, so as they grew, it would be an activity they would do together. She let them walk ahead of her and set the pace. As they walked, she pointed out different trees, plants, or animals for them to take notice of. Her camera was always around her neck, and she was constantly taking pictures.

"Wook, Mommy!" Jarom hollered, crouching down on the ground and pointing at a fuzzy caterpillar.

"Great eyes, Jar Bear," Paige said, bending down next to him and taking a photo of the small creature. "That is a wooly bear caterpillar. Isn't he fun?"

"A woowy bear. Wike me!"

"Yes, sweetie. Bear. Like you." Paige smiled at Jarom, who was fixated on the caterpillar. He had a slight speech impediment Paige knew she would have to look into eventually, but secretly adored.

"Did you boys know one day that caterpillar will grow up to be a beautiful moth?

"What's a moth?" asked Ammon.

"They're like butterflies."

"I wike buttofwies," said Jarom.

"Me too. All right, boys, step carefully over Mr. Wolly Bear, and let's see how many steps it takes to get to the first bridge."

Paige started counting as the boys skipped down the trail. Her heart swelled with love and pride for her beautiful sons. She saw Evan in each of them. The boys were fraternal. Ammon was slightly taller than Jarom and had Evan's toffee-colored eyes and brown hair, though straight, like his mother's. Jarom had Paige's blue eyes and platinum blonde hair but had inherited his father's curls. She kept a photo of Evan in their room, smiling wide and wearing a BYU sweatshirt. Paige had taken it the day they found out they were having twins. They celebrated by heading up Little Cottonwood Canyon and hiking in the Albion Basin. She still missed Evan with all her heart. So many moments with the boys, like today, were bittersweet, thinking about him missing seeing his sons grow.

"Sixty-Six. Sixty-Seven. Sixty-Eight. We made it!" Paige pulled the twins into a bear hug and kissed the tops of their hat-covered heads. "Ooo. I just love you two handsome boys so much."

"I wove you too, Mommy," Jarom giggled.

"Me too," Ammon added, grabbing Paige's face in his little hands.

The moment almost hurt. A tear threatened to spill. "Your daddy used to hold my face like that, Am," she said and kissed his cheek.

"I miss daddy," Jarom said, wiping his nose with the back of his hand. The boys didn't fully understand what it meant to have lost their dad yet. They would feel the loss more as they grew, she was certain.

"Me too. But!" she said, forcing brightness into her voice. "He's always watching over us, isn't he?"

"Even when we go to the bathroom?" Ammon asked, concerned.

"Maybe not then. But right now, I bet he is. Daddy loved hiking. We used to go on hikes all the time. Whenever I'm in the mountains, I feel close to him."

"Me too!" Jarom shouted.

"We should always hike, Mommy," Ammon said with a serious expression. "So Daddy can hike with us."

"I love that idea, my brilliant boy."

June 27, 1998

When Jentry had called each of her friends in February with news of her engagement, they had been thrilled. Immediately, talk turned to how to have the simple wedding Jentry desired while also having her friends present. Sally had put forward an idea that Jentry had jumped on, and Donovan happily agreed to it.

As the sun was starting to make its descent over the mountains, a small group made their way up the Limber Pine trail to the large namesake Limber tree. Sally and Hannah, who had been visiting her family for a week, had gone up the trail ahead of the group to tie balloons around the split rail fence near the tree, as well as sprinkle rose petals and light lanterns in case they ran out of sunlight.

The others arrived fifteen minutes after them. The bridal party wore tan hiking pants or shorts and white sweatshirts as the mountain air still dropped to cooler temperatures in the evening in June. Jentry held a small bouquet of wildflowers tied with ribbon in her hands. Sally pulled a small veil out of Sam's backpack and placed it over Jentry's hair as they arrived at the tree. Paige had her trusty camera and took more than enough photos to document the event from the moment they left the parking lot.

"Alright," Sam said, grinning. "The moment has arrived to help these lovebirds tie the knot. Unofficially, as I have no power in the state of Utah, we know they ran into City Hall this morning to make it legal, but this is the ceremony that counts because it's with the people who love them. Donovan, come stand here with me."

Donovan squeezed Jentry's hand, then took the few steps up to Sam.

"Who gives..."

"Not yet, Sammy. She needs to walk down the aisle," Sally interrupted. Sally pulled Jentry fifteen feet from the tree, where the rose petals started. "There."

Hannah and Paige started humming the bridal march as Jentry and Sally made their way down the makeshift aisle.

"Who gives this woman to this man?" Sam asked solemnly.

"I do," Sally said, her voice catching. She let go of Jentry's hand and stepped back.

"In all seriousness," Sam began again, "When Sally told me about this idea for a mountain ceremony and asked me to say a few words, I was truly honored. Jentry is part of our family. She lives in the big city, and we don't get to see her as much as we'd like, but she is still a Limbrey. A McLean. A Johnson. The love these girls forged with each other at eighteen has grown and multiplied over the years. The support system they have created is a wonder. In the last few days, I have had the opportunity to spend some time with Donovan. He has spoken so lovingly of our Jentry and expressed a sincere desire to be a part of this group, becoming brother and uncle. You two seem so perfectly matched. We're so happy you found each other. And now, I believe Donovan and Jentry have prepared some words."

Donovan turned towards Jentry, taking both of her hands in his. "Never would I ever have predicted you would choose a trail in Utah for us to exchange vows. And the fact we are here, dressed in hiking shoes and sweatshirts, is one of the many reasons I love you. You are gloriously unpredictable. From the first time I met you, I had to readjust the lens through which I see the world. You have added an emotional balance to my life I didn't realize was lacking before you. I love taking you to new places and exploring them with you. I love our adventures and nights at the opera or ballet. But I also love sitting side by side and reading.

Being in your presence fills me. I found a poem by Australian poet Pam Brown, which encapsulates my thoughts.

"In you are flowers and firelight, stars and songbirds, the scent of summer, the stillness just before dawn.

I love you today, dressed in glory. I will love you always – dancing, singing, reading, making, planning, arguing.

I will love you cantankerous and tired, courageous and in terror, joyful, fearful, and triumphant.

I will love you through all weathers and all change.

For all you are is precious to me.

And every day I live with you and share your love is a gift to me."

Jentry wiped the tears off her cheeks and began. "My dearest Donovan, how can I put into words everything I feel for you? The day you walked into the museum was the day my once-shattered heart began to heal. I was determined to lead a happy life as a single woman, afraid to risk getting my heart broken or feeling the rejection I have from others in my life. My friends helped me first recognize my worth and lovability, and you took it to a whole other level. With you, I feel like the best version of myself because I am free to be my truest self. You make me feel safe. You make me feel valued. You make me feel seen. You make me feel beautiful, intelligent, and talented. I want to spend the rest of my life making you as happy as you have made me. I love you, Donovan. Enough to really be vulnerable," Jentry said with a shaky laugh. "I'm ready, Sam."

Sam turned and grabbed the guitar, leaning on the tree next to him. Jentry had called him a few weeks ago and told him she wanted to serenade Donovan as part of her vows. They had each been practicing separately and had time for one quick rehearsal together this morning. Sam started playing the Beatles version of *Till There Was You*. Jentry smiled at Donovan and began to sing.

"There were bells on a hill, but I never heard them ringing,

no, I never heard them at all 'til there was you.

There were birds in the sky, but I never saw them winging,

no, I never saw them at all 'til there was you.

Then there was music and wonderful roses,

they tell me in sweet fragrant meadows of dawn and dew.

There was love all around, but I never heard it singing,

no, I never heard it at all, 'til there was you.

'Til there was you."

As soon as she finished singing, Donovan swept her up in his arms. "You sing like an angel. How have you never sung for me before? Again, you surprise me." He shook his head and carefully set her back down.

The sun was completely behind the mountains, with its light fading fast. Sam sat the guitar down and spoke, "Donovan and Jentry, that was beautiful. You may now exchange rings."

Donovan pulled a thin gold band from his pocket and gently slid it on Jentry's finger next to the emerald. Jentry turned to Paige, who pulled a ring out of her pocket. Jentry had chosen a thick, hammered gold band for Donovan and put it on his finger.

"With no authority whatsoever, I now pronounce you already married. Donovan, you may kiss your bride."

As Donovan cupped Jentry's face in his hands and placed the gentlest kiss on her lips, Hannah, Paige, Sally, and Sam erupted into cheering and hollering. As dusk turned to dark, the group grabbed the balloons and lanterns and headed back down the trail.

Happy 27th Birthday to me. I'm thankful for this last year. It wasn't as tough as the year before, but still challenging enough to allow me to grow and develop lots more character!! Seriously though, I accomplished a lot, overcame a lot, suffered through a lot, and enjoyed a lot. I've hopefully made a few strides in the right direction towards my goal of returning to my Father in Heaven. I get caught up in the worldly routines sometimes, and don't always live the Gospel nearly as faithfully as I should. It would be easy to get discouraged and look at all my failings as proof I'll never make the cut on Judgement Day. The challenge is to acknowledge the things I do right, acknowledge my intent to be more like my older brother, whom I love so much. Then to try a little harder each day to conquer my bad habits and overcome the "natural man" tendencies. I'm so thankful to our Heavenly Father, who loves us in spite of us, and who is working with us each day until we get this Earth life right.

Luke likes to tell a story about Thomas Edison, who experimented with the light bulb 1000 times before getting it right. When questioned about how hard it must have been to have met with failure so many times, Edison replied something to this effect of "I never failed. I learned 999 ways it didn't work." That could describe my life. I'm not quiet to the point in life where my experiment is a raging success. But I haven't failed at life, in spite of mistakes and not so great paths, because I haven't given up trying to be obedient, trying to be righteous, and trying to just be a good person. I'm learning the things that don't work. Like, say, eating a pint of Ben and Jerry's at midnight doesn't work if you are trying to lose weight. Or sleeping in and playing on the computer all the time doesn't work if you want to have money to pay the bills. Yelling at a crying child to stop crying also does not work and tends to have the opposite effect. Thankfully, I have learned some things that do work. Having a weekly date night and taking the time to talk to each other about your dreams actually does work in making a marriage better. Counting on your children's fingers all the great things you love about them does work in building them up and strengthening your relationship with them. Getting up early and working hard actually does work to pay the bills. Turning off Spice Girls and turning on Yanni does work to get the children calmed down before bedtime. Best of all, sharing the pint of Ben and Jerry's with the whole family, rotating bites of delicious chocolate and caramel goo, does work to make you feel less guilty for eating it, and the children feel extra special for getting some of the "good" ice cream.

August 17, 1998

It's over. We made it almost six and a half years. The kids and I were already going to head to Cannon Beach to spend time with Jen while Donovan was on a work trip.

Right before we were going to leave Luke's boss called to ask me about his dental appointments. Apparently he's been lying to his work, saying he's at the dentist when he should be working.

He's lied to me about big and trivial things as long as I've known him, and it's a bigger problem than I realized if he is lying to others. In this marriage I've dealt with poverty, pornography, infidelity, pathological lying, physical and emotional neglect, and constant criticism. I can't do it any longer.

I left a note on the counter that said I'm done and headed to Oregon.

What is going to become of us?

Jentry says we can stay with her while we figure things out. Mom says to move back home. The kids don't know what is going on yet. I don't know what I need to do. I have no degree, and I've been a stay-at-home mom for the last five years, minus a part-time candle business. How am I going to support us?

How is this my life?

August 28, 1998

The four friends sat in the Adirondack chairs on the deck of Jentry's beach house, watching the sun start its descent over the Pacific Ocean.

Jentry had called Paige on her way to pick up Hannah and the kids and told her Hannah had finally left Luke, something her friends and family had been praying she would do for years.

Paige immediately called Sally and began planning a way to get to Oregon to see Hannah and offer support. Paige remembered all too well her grief at Evan's passing and how Hannah and Jentry had come to Utah in her time of need. She wanted to make sure she and Sally did the same.

Plane tickets had been purchased, and babysitting had been arranged. Sally brought six-month-old Sabrina, who was still breastfeeding. They had landed this afternoon and been picked up by Jentry and Hannah and driven straight to Cannon Beach.

Hannah and her children had been in Jentry's condo since the seventeenth. Jentry had wanted to keep it as a place for her friends to stay when they visited, so it worked out perfectly as a landing spot for Hannah. They had left Heather and Seth with Donovan's niece, Kennedy, for two nights. She had watched them on other visits to Portland and was a trusted sitter.

At Hannah's request, the drive to Cannon Beach was a divorce-free zone and spent catching up on each other's lives. After dinner at Mo's, they went to the house and sat in

232

silence, watching the sunset, with little Sabrina curled up in Auntie Hannah's lap.

"You guys have no idea what this means to me," Hannah said.

"This is what friends do. We circle the wagons. Just like you've done for each of us over the years," Paige said, reaching out and patting Hannah's arm.

"You're more than friends. You're my family. By blood, by marriage, and by choice. But more than that, you're my lifeline. You three, for the last nine years, have been my touchstone. Thank you for being here," Hannah said with a catch in her throat.

"What can we do to best support you through this, Hannah?" Sally asked.

"Help me make a plan. I've been in limbo land since we got to Portland, trying to have fun with the kids and make this transition easy. I think we've played in the Lovejoy every day. They don't really know what's happening, and I don't know how to tell them. Luke is coming to get them next week, and they need to know by then. How do you tell your children their lives will never be the same?"

"Heather and Seth are very smart, intuitive little people, Love. They likely already have suspicions, even if they don't know how to put a label on it. My advice is to sit them down tomorrow and tell them what's going on. You don't have to go into all the details, but you can let them know the basics. Mommy and Daddy aren't going to live together anymore, but they both still love you. That kind of thing."

"Jentry's right," Paige said. "I started explaining to the twins about Evan being in Heaven and watching over us when they were two. They'll grasp more than you realize."

"Okay, that's step one. I also need to file for divorce, find a job, figure out housing, and get Heather registered for Kindergarten. I have no money to my name. Everything was in Luke's name, and he put us in so much debt."

"What have Dad and Mom said about helping you?" Sally asked.

"They're giving me a little right now to help with gas and groceries, but they've said I need to have a viable plan by September before they decide what additional help they'll give."

"You're moving back, though, right?" Paige asked.

"Actually, Donovan and Jentry have offered us the condo for a while." Hannah smiled at Jentry. "I love the Pacific Northwest so much, you guys. You have no idea. The climate, the proximity to oceans and mountains. I loved the Tacoma area, and I love Portland. Right now, Luke plans on staying in Tacoma. So, if I stay here, the children are only a couple of hours from their dad."

"Jentry, you are so generous. Gosh. What a blessing you are," Sally said.

"You three are my family, like Hannah said. It's the least I could do. Well, I can do one more thing." Jentry paused for effect. "I called the museum this morning. They're looking for another front-desk receptionist. It's the job I had when I first started. Thirty hours a week. Benefits. They're pretty flexible. We'll need to figure out what to do with the kids when you're at work. But it's yours if you want it. You could start on the seventh."

"That sounds too good to be true. Thank you, Jentry."

"Okay, Han, housing and job taken care of," Paige said. "I'm sure you can find out what school Heather will be in by calling the district. I know you. You're scrappy and organized and great at to-do lists when you want to be. You've got this."

"Thanks, Paige."

"That's the mechanics," Paige said. "Now, what are your plans so that you stay the bubbly, adventure-loving, funny, nurturing woman we know and love? You're going to have a really full plate, and I want to make sure you're taking time for you."

"Aww, thank you for saying that. I try to still be all those things. I don't know the answer yet, but I'll think about it. I promise."

Paige looked at her friends and felt so much love in her heart for them. So much had happened in their lives since their first time at this beach together. Heartbreak and sorrow. Joy and success. She was grateful for their friendship and the ways they stayed connected, even though they lived in different states. The invention of email had been an amazing way to stay in touch. They had a chain where they gave weekly updates on their lives every Sunday, and she looked forward to reading them each week. Her heart hurt for Hannah, knowing what it was like to think your life was going to be one way and then having it take a different turn. At least her marriage had been full of love. She hated what Luke had done to Hannah over the years and seeing her light dim a little. While divorce and being a single mother would be hard, she was hopeful her cousin would find joy, happiness, and peace on this new path.

"This little angel baby is starting to wake up," Hannah said as Sabrina started stretching and opened her eyes. "Hello, Fancy Face," Hannah cooed. "I bet you want Mommy now. Promise you'll let me cuddle you again after you eat." Hannah passed Sabrina to her mother. "How crazy is it that once upon a time, my brother drove all the way here to confess his love to our Turtle, and now they're married with two adorable daughters?"

Sally grinned, "Paige did such a great job with my makeover, so I'd look presentable to him."

"Presentable? He would have loved you in a potato sack," Paige laughed.

<u>December 15, 1998</u>

Gosh, I love my children. We have had some really fun times these last few months. We are loving our new life in Portland. We've gone on hikes to lakes, oceans, pools, parks, and the zoo. We've read books, played games, and made lots of treats. One of my favorite outings was a hike up the gorge on. We left early enough for it to qualify as a "breakfast hike." I packed granola bars, water, and The Lion, Witch & Wardrobe for when we would undoubtedly stop to rest. The hike to the top is only a little more than a mile, but it had a good amount of elevation gain. It's steep. Let's put it that way. And it felt like 3 miles with such little hikers. But they were such troopers. Poor Heather had too small of shoes, and her feet were bleeding by the end. Seth made it all the way to the top and was so proud of himself. Too bad he insisted on my carrying him down the whole way. I ached for days! How did the pioneers trek across the country with little ones?

There has been a lot of laughter and good times, and there have been a lot of tears and sad times, too. They had an extremely tough time with the divorce in the beginning. Sometimes, I think everything is fine, and they have adjusted swimmingly, then they'll say or do something that gives me a glimpse into how much they are really hurting. I'm so sorry for the way my poor choices will affect them for the rest of their lives. I wanted their childhood to be as great as mine was, and it never will be. I miss them so much when they go to see their dad, which thankfully isn't often. They spent Thanksgiving in Colorado with Luke and his family, and that was the longest week of my life! We met Luke at McDonald's to exchange, and I was missing them and in tears before I even got home.

I have a few regrets from this year, as usual. But my biggest regret is I am still holding on to so much anger and bitterness. Luke tends to bring out the worst in me. Whether I am talking to him or about him, I feel like the ugliest parts of me come to the surface. I am ashamed after all my Father in Heaven has done for me, I am unable to afford Luke the forgiveness, understanding and love that I am shown by my Heavenly Father and Savior. I had such great plans at the beginning of all this to be the world's least bitter ex-wife. I was going to be the "bigger person." I wasn't going to ever speak ill of Luke. I was going to let bygones be bygones and move on. And I was NEVER going to say anything negative about him to the children. Well, I have failed miserably. And I mention all this so when my children read my journal someday, they will know my intentions were good. I'm sorry for my weaknesses, and I am sorry for my inability to be more forgiving and more full of charity. All I can do is promise to try harder. Granted, the marriage left a little to be desired, but I am left with two amazing little people who each and every day fill my life with love and laughter. And they deserve parents who are kind to each other.

We're going home for Christmas for a week. I'm excited to spend so much time with family and for the kids to get to see their cousins. Heather is oldest, at just barely six. The twins will turn five while we're there. Sethy will be five in March. Sariah is almost two and a half, and little Sabrina will be a year in February. Such little munchkins.

December 27, 1998

"Happy Birthday to you. Happy Birthday to you. Happy Birthday, Ammon and Jarom. Happy Birthday to you!"

The boys sat at the table in Paige's parents' home. Her mother had made them each a cake. Ammon's was decorated with Buzz Lightyear, while Jarom's was a cowboy theme with Woody from the Toy Story movies. Thomas and Jenny McLean sat next to each boy, while Doug and Kristi Lindburg stood next to Paige, who was madly snapping pictures of the whole event. Also in attendance were Paige's twin sisters, and Sam and Sally, with little Sariah and Sabrina. Hannah had arrived with the kids right as they started singing.

"I can't believe you handsome boys are five years old already," Paige cooed, running up to the boys and kissing them each on the cheek. "Are you sure you want to eat these cakes? They look too nice to destroy."

"Yes!" They shouted in unison.

While Jenny sliced up the cakes, Paige added a scoop of vanilla ice cream to each plate.

"Sorry we're late," Hannah said, giving Paige a side hug.

"No worries at all. You made it for the good stuff."

"You know, Seth is going to give me a hard time when he sees what the boys are getting," Hannah said as she scooped up some frosting with her finger. "Mamie is nice for saying yes."

"She's beyond nice. Mamie is a saint," Paige agreed.

After the cake and ice cream were cleaned up, everyone gathered in the living room. The boys sat on the floor next to a few gifts.

"Alright, you two. Take turns opening things because this year, everything is to be shared." Paige sat down beside them to help with the process.

Ammon grabbed a box and shook it. "Is this Legos?" he asked, listening to the sound of many small items tumbling inside the box.

"I don't know," smiled Paige.

Ammon tore into the paper and pulled out a box of milk bones. "What are these? Are these cookies?"

Jarom was already ripping into a gift and looked confused as he pulled out a canister of tennis balls.

"Hmm. What could all this be?" Paige smiled. She pushed another gift towards the boys. "Open this one next."

The boys both worked on the wrappings and pulled out two silver bowls.

"Is this for those cookies?" Ammon asked, looking more and more perplexed by the minute.

"Let's have Papa Doug and Nana Kristi give you their gift next. I think it will help. Close your eyes tight."

The boys covered their eyes with their hands and waited as Doug grabbed something from the garage and placed it in front of them.

"Okay. You can open them," he said, standing back so everyone could see the reaction.

The boys opened their eyes to find a tiny puppy in front of them.

"Oh my gosh!" Ammon said, his hand covering his mouth.

"Is this fow us?" Jarom asked, reaching for the small black puppy.

"Be so careful now," Paige instructed, helping Jarom hold the small dog.

The black Australian Shepherd had a white stripe down her snout and three white legs. She was plump and curly, already licking Jarom on the chin.

"My turn!" Ammon said.

"First, what do you say to Papa and Nana? And to everyone else who helped get things for the puppy?"

"Thank you," the boys said, as they went around the room giving hugs, while Paige held the little pup.

"Now it's my turn," said Ammon, sitting down next to her. He gently took the puppy and kissed it on her nose.

"Can I have a turn?" asked Seth as he, Heather, and Sariah came forward.

"Everyone can have a turn loving on her. Can't they boys?"

Ammon and Jarom hovered but still, willingly let their new pup be passed around the room. Someone on Sally's street raised mini and toy Australian Shepherds. She had told Paige about a new litter, and Paige had immediately talked to her grandma and in-laws about the possibility of getting the boys a puppy for their birthday.

"You've done such a good job, sweetie," Doug said as he put an arm around Paige.

She leaned her head on his shoulder and watched the boys with a teary smile. "They came out so good. Just like Evan. I've tried to do him proud and raise little men as polite, kind, and wonderful as he was."

"Does this sweet lady have a name?" Hannah asked as she took a turn nuzzling the puppy, who was all too happy to receive so much love.

"Juniper," Paige answered, not giving the boys a chance to pick something silly. "Named for the Jardine Juniper trail where Evan proposed."

Hannah passed the pup back to Jarom and came over to her cousin. "You're a great mom, Paige, and it has nothing to do with the dog. I'm always so impressed with how you manage things. Being a single mom is hard. I worry I get too impatient sometimes."

"Are you sure you don't want to move back to the valley? You'd have so much help with the kids and think how close the cousins would be."

"I think about it all the time. But I love Oregon. To be close to mountains and the ocean is amazing. Jentry letting us live in her old place has saved us, especially with Luke not making alimony and child support payments."

"Jentry's generosity is unmatched. She did the same for Evan and me with the townhouse. Made our first years easier."

"The children love Uncle Donovan and Auntie Jentry, but I do feel bad they don't see my parents more. Mom has been dropping hints big time to have us move back this trip. It's hard to know the right move. I don't exactly trust myself these days."

"It is. I know. You've got this. You're a good mom, too, Han," Paige said, giving her cousin a hug. Being a single mom was difficult. She was grateful for such a large support system here in the valley. She still missed Evan so much. Family and friends had tried to set her up on dates multiple times, but she wasn't ready. She couldn't imagine letting someone else in. "Have you thought about dating again?" she asked Hannah.

"I think about it a lot, actually. I want my chance to be madly in love. I'm a sucker, I guess. I've dated a little, but they're always more interested in me than the children. I need someone who loves my kids like their own."

"I hope your future is everything you hope for, Hannah, truly. You've had it hard. You deserve a break. When do you head back home?"

"I've got to be back to work on the second."

"Let's you, me, and Sally try to get a pedicure or something before you head back."

"Mommy, this puppy peed," Ammon interrupted.

"Oh dear, let's get her outside." Paige picked up the puppy and went out back into the snow with little Juniper.

December 30, 1998

Hannah had put the children to bed at eight o'clock and then stayed up playing cards with her parents, Esther and Dustin. At ten she went to bed and was asleep as soon as her head hit the pillow.

She stifled a scream when she opened her eyes to find Julie Limbrey tapping her leg in the middle of the night.

"Hannah, come upstairs. I've got to talk to you," her mother whispered.

Hannah rubbed her eyes and looked over to the foam mattresses on the floor to make sure the children hadn't stirred. "What time is it?"

"Just past five. This can't wait. Meet me in the living room," Julie said, then slipped out of the room. Hannah pulled an oversized tee shirt over her underwear and headed upstairs, still groggy and very confused.

"Is everything alright?" Hannah asked, coming into the room and sitting next to her mother on the sofa.

"I've had a dream, Hannah. You know I have certain dreams sometimes that feel more like messages and premonitions."

It had been years since she had heard about one of her mother's special dreams, but she knew her mother took them very seriously and considered them inspiration from Heavenly Father.

"Go on," Hannah said, tucking her legs underneath her shirt to keep warm.

"I dreamt I was on a very large, beautiful boat. It was off the shore from a beautiful island. The boat was lit up like a party was going on; there were tables covered with food, and people were mingling and laughing. Your father and I were there. Sam, Sally, and the girls. Esther, Dustin, and baby Jaken. All of my siblings, their children, everyone you can imagine who lives within the valley. Or even within two hours of it, like Esther. We were having a wonderful time, but I could sense something was missing. I started looking all over the boat. Everywhere I went, there was some family member, but I kept looking. I searched the whole ship, and the longer I searched, the more panicked I became. Finally, I came to the back of the ship, and I searched the horizon. There, in the distance, was a little rubber raft, and guess who was in it?"

"Who?"

"You, Heather, and Seth. You were all alone in the raft, and you were cold and scared, trying so hard to paddle to the ship, but you were going in circles. I could see sharks were starting to circle your raft."

"Geez, Momma, that's dark."

"Imagine dreaming it. It felt so real. I started screaming for help and pointing at you. Your father and Sam got onto jet skis and rescued you and the children. When you got back to the ship, you threw your arms around me and said, 'Momma, why did you let me drift so long?' I pulled you close and told you that you were safe now and I would take care of you. Then I woke up."

"That's a wild dream."

"Yes, but I think there is a message there. I think you're supposed to move back home immediately."

"We've talked about…"

Julie cut her off, "I know, I know. I worried you would feel like this was a scare tactic, but Hannah, it was real. As soon as I woke up, the Spirit told me to tell you it's time to move home. You need the support system that's here. Jentry and Donovan are wonderful, and I'm so grateful to them, but they aren't enough. Your children need to be around their grandparents and their cousins. Think of how much fun they have whenever you visit. It could be like that all the time. And truthfully, Hannah, you are a beautiful, wonderful young woman who could still meet someone. Twenty-eight is plenty young to remarry and have a wonderful life. This is where you will meet a returned missionary who honors his Priesthood. Not Oregon. Look at Jentry. She had to settle for a non-member, as wonderful as he is. I want more than that for you. The Lord does, too. That's why he gave me this dream. It's time to come home."

"I live rent-free in Portland, Momma. I have a good job I really like. Starting over again could be hard on the children. I don't know if Luke would even let us move further away."

"Luke," Julie said, rolling her eyes. "This isn't up to that deadbeat. He's not helping you with anything. He's too lazy and poor to put up a fight. Let's put out some feelers tomorrow and see what we can come up with for housing and employment. It may be a little tighter than Portland, but when we're obedient to the path the Lord wants us on, He'll open the way before us. I know that's true, dear girl."

Hannah took a deep breath and let it out slowly. Her mother had brought up moving home since August, but she had been so set on living near Jentry and being in a big city that maybe she was being too stubborn to listen to the spirit.

Did the Holy Ghost have to bypass her and speak to her mother in order to get her attention? She did want a chance at true love, that was for sure. She longed to have the kind of relationship Jentry and Sally had with their husbands, and Paige had known with Evan. She would have a much better chance of a temple wedding coming back to Utah. And it would be wonderful for Heather and Seth to grow up with cousins.

"Let me pray about it, okay? And let me get a few more hours of sleep. We can brainstorm after breakfast."

Julie pulled Hannah into a tight hug. "I knew you'd listen to me. You've always tried so hard to be a good and obedient girl. Your best life is in front of you. I just know it."

"It can't get any worse, can it?" Hannah laughed ruefully. "I love you, Momma. Thank you for caring about my life the way you do."

***

Hannah was buttering toast for Heather and Seth as her mother came into the kitchen.

"Dad called Uncle Mike first thing this morning. His rental house in Millville will be available February first. It's yours for the taking."

"The one Sam and Sally lived in?" Hannah asked, putting eggs and toast in front of the children and sitting down at the table.

"Yes. It's a precious little thing."

"Precious, yes, and also half the size of our Portland apartment."

"That's true, but think of how the children can play in the yard and have cousins close by."

"I'll die without a dishwasher."

"Don't be so dramatic. You're simply trading some nice amenities for a support system and the blessings of coming back to Zion."

"I guess. A month back in Portland will give me time to give notice and pack our meager belongings."

"Your dad and I are going to fly out the end of January. He'll drive a U-Haul for you, and I'll ride with you and the kids."

"I'll give Luke written notice right away, I guess. Jentry is going to be so sad. We have dinner with them twice a week. She's five floors up. I hate thinking of leaving her all alone."

"She's not alone. She has Donovan. And you have to think of what's best for you and the children. Dad and I have decided to give you some of your inheritance early. That will help pay for your move and get you situated while you find a job here. We'll cover three months' rent."

"That's so generous of you, Mom. Thank you." Hannah sighed and stole a bite of Seth's toast.

"What are you and Grammy talking about, Mommy?" Heather asked between bites.

"Well," said Hannah, forcing a smile she didn't quite feel yet, "Pappy and Grammy love you so much they want us to move back here and live by them. Would you like living here?"

"Yes!" Heather answered excitedly. "I would love to live with Grammy."

"I bet you would. We won't live with Grammy, though. We'll live in our own home close by."

"Can we get a cat now?" Heather asked. Heather had been obsessed with cats since she was four and asked for one every birthday and Christmas.

"We'll see about that, sweetie. What do you think, Sethy? Would you like to go to live by your cousins?"

"Yeah. Okay. I like that."

"See?" said Julie, "The children will do so well here. You're going to have the life you deserve, Hannah. It will make up for all you've been through."

"Let's hope," Hannah said. "I guess I have some phone calls to make and emails to send. Can I use Dad's computer?"

"Of course. OK, children, finish your breakfast and get dressed. We're going over to Auntie Sally's this morning for a playgroup with your cousins," Julie said as she stood to tidy the kitchen.

January 3, 2000

1999 was so full of adventure, fun, and triumphs. But it is also filled with many poor choices and regrets. As usual, I am pained and frustrated with what I can't undo, repair, or fix. But a new day and a new year offers a new hope. I always seem to start each year out with a mile long list of great intentions towards perfection. This year is no different. My loving mother told me my goals were too impractical and to "aim lower." I balk at such a suggestion! I aim high, and will continue to do so, for that is the essence of who I am. An emotional, faulted, flawed, imperfect woman – who knows she is capable of greatness. I aim for the stars with hope and faith one day I'll reach them. One day I'll tap into my potential and accomplish everything I was meant to. At the end of my life, I want to say "Yes, she made mistakes, suffered setbacks, and sorrowed over failures – but she never gave up – she never quit. She came back stronger and more determined after every setback. She believed in herself, aimed for the stars, and made it." I don't want to be remembered as average, or as a quitter. I don't want to be thought of as negative, pessimistic or someone with few goals and a low aim. I'm a fighter! I'm a survivor! And I will try and try until I get life right.

January 13, 2000

Last Tuesday Heather and Seth and I went with my parents to Bountiful for a concert called Saints on the Seas. It was so inspiring. I'm so grateful to my relatives who sacrificed so much so I could be born in this country and in this church. I so wish I could live the gospel better.

March 11, 2000

"Rise and shine, hot stuff. I've made us a celebratory breakfast," Jentry said, walking into the room with a tray of food. She set the tray down on the dresser and pulled the curtains open.

Donovan put a pillow over his face and rolled over. "Five more minutes."

"Your food will get cold, and this news will go flat, too. I've been hanging on to it for this very special morning."

"Lucky I love you so much, waking me early on a Saturday," Donovan said with a playful grin as he sat up in the bed.

"I don't think eight o'clock is that early, Love," Jentry teased as she handed Donovan a cup of coffee with hazelnut creamer. "Drink up." She kissed him on the forehead and sat next to him. After he'd taken two sips, she took the cup and set it on the nightstand. "Alright, that's enough. I don't want you to spill when you pull me into a congratulatory hug."

Donovan raised an eyebrow in anticipation, a smile forming at the corner of his mouth.

"I got the curator position."

"That's my girl!" he shouted as he pulled Jentry on top of him and kissed her. "I knew you'd do it. So proud of you, Jentry."

"I'm so excited. I start transitioning into the new role in two weeks. I've got to help train my replacement in the registrar department."

"We need to celebrate. This is huge."

"We do need to celebrate. There's more." Jentry walked to the dresser and returned with the tray of food. She sat it down in front of Donovan. "Surprise number two."

"Hmm," he said, examining the tray. "Eggs, sausage, croissant, orange juice. Nothing surprising here."

"Unroll the napkin."

Donovan picked up the napkin and unrolled it, revealing a home pregnancy test. He looked up at Jentry with wide but hopeful eyes. "Does this say what I think?"

"Two lines. I'm pregnant."

"You've buried me beneath this food, you minx," Donovan said, trying carefully to move the tray to the nightstand so he could get out of bed. He pulled Jentry into his arms, burying his head in her dark hair. "Jentry Elizabeth, carrier of my seed, how I love you."

"Is that my new title?" Jentry asked with a smile.

"How long have you known? Are you excited? How are you feeling?"

Jentry pulled Donovan back to the bed and snuggled up beside him. "My period is three weeks late. I figured it was the stress of the interview process. I took the pregnancy test yesterday evening. Yes, I'm excited. You know, I wasn't sure about children because my parents don't give a shit about me, and I worried that would be genetic somehow, but seeing my friends with all of their children and loving those babies as I do, made me want my own. How many

251

children now between the three of them? Six, with one of the way?"

"Your friends are rabbits," Donovan said.

"It's the Mormon culture, for sure. Anyway, after seeing how happy they were in motherhood, and feeling so much love for my nieces and nephews, it was easy to imagine a life like that for us. I knew we weren't planning on this. I forgot my pills when we went to Vegas last month and told you, but you still couldn't keep your hands off me," she teased, kissing him on the chest.

"Can you blame me, with a Goddess like you, for a wife. You get hotter and hotter each day. That ass, those breasts, are you kidding me?" Donovan rolled on top of Jentry and kissed her neck while sliding his hand beneath her nightshirt.

"Keep doing what you're doing, Love. I've heard pregnant sex is the best kind. Let's put it to the test."

After showering and cleaning up breakfast, they decided to drive over to the coast and spend the night at the beach house. She and Donovan loved spending weekends in Cannon Beach when work didn't keep them in the city. They would walk for hours along the coast. She and her friends had started a book club several years ago, and Donovan enjoyed hearing Jentry's descriptions of each book, as well as her thoughts on them. Sometimes, he even read them himself. Jentry kept paint supplies on hand, as well, and loved setting up an easel on the deck and painting the brooding Pacific Ocean.

Today, they talked of birthing plans and nurseries, motherhood and museums, baby names, and when to tell their friends.

After dinner at Local Grill and Scoop, they finished the night sitting on the deck in the dark, wrapped in blankets, and listening to the ocean waves crash on the beach.

"Nature calls," Jentry said, excusing herself. Donovan gave her a playful slap on the butt as she headed inside.

She pulled her pants down to sit on the toilet and didn't notice the blood in her underwear until she went to wipe.

"No, no, no, no," she whispered, as wiping revealed more blood. She stripped out of her clothes and ran the underwear under cold water. Her breaths were steady and deep, trying to calm the panic and disappointment forming in her chest. She grabbed a washcloth, ran it under hot water, and tried to clean herself thoroughly.

"Jen?" Donovan called, coming down the hall. "You've been gone a min…" His words were cut short when he saw Jentry in the bathroom, a blood-tinged cloth in her hand and tears in her eyes. "Oh, Sweetie, come here." He took her in his arms.

Jentry let the tears fall now, safe in Donovan's embrace. "I'm sorry, Donovan."

"Sorry? Jentry. Stop. This isn't your fault. It happens. Let's get you cleaned up, and I'll make you some tea."

Ten minutes later, they were back on the patio. This time, Jentry was on Donovan's lap, his arms tight around her, as she laid her head on his shoulder and silently cried.

"I didn't know how much I wanted to be a mother until I suddenly wasn't one." Donovan patted her consolingly on the back. "We can try again when you're ready."

"Really? Even though this wasn't planned, you would do that?"

"I would do anything for you, my little minx."

"Even though we have said no children for the last four years?"

"Even though."

"Even though you'll be forty this year?"

Donovan gave a slight chuckle. "I'm hardly ancient."

Jentry sat up, cupped Donovan's face in her hands, and kissed him gently. "I love you, Donovan Dixon. Even if you're an old man," she teased before kissing him again. "I think I do want to try again. Maybe not right away, but this year."

"Whenever you're ready, sweetheart."

March 31, 2000

"Who's ready for story time?" Sally asked as she lifted two-year-old Sabrina out of the high chair and washed the peanut butter off her face.

"I am! I am!" Sariah chanted, marching into the kitchen.

"Me too," Sally said, herding her daughters into Sariah's room, which was littered with toys and cheerios. "What should we read today?" she asked as they climbed onto the bed, Sally on the edge.

The question was rhetorical because, for the last three weeks, all Sariah wanted to read was *Oh, The Places You'll Go* by Dr. Suess. Sally didn't mind, as it was one of her favorites. Sabrina tried to get comfortable on her mother's lap, which was difficult for both of them, as Sally was expecting daughter number three in less than two months. She and Sam had been surprised by the gender of the first two but chose to find out this time around. She was still trying to decide if she should move Sabrina into Sariah's room or leave her with the baby, as they would both be in cribs.

Sariah snuggled up to her mother and turned the pages as Sally read. Before long, both girls were fast asleep. Sally had found if she tried to nap them right after lunch, they would fight her. But if she let them play for ten minutes and then read to them in a soft and soothing voice, they fell to sleep of their own accord.

She slowly stood up and went and laid Sabrina down, before coming back to cover up Sariah and turn on her bedside fan for white noise. She quietly picked up a few items and as many cheerios as possible before heading to the kitchen to clean up.

After the kitchen and living room were tidied, she laid down on the sofa, propped her feet up, and dialed Jentry.

"Hello?"

"Jentry, it's Sally. I literally did not think about it being in the middle of your workday until after it was ringing. Sorry."

"I have a few minutes. Is everything okay?

"That's what I'm calling about. I haven't heard from you in about three weeks. I should have checked in sooner. We never go that long without talking. Are you alright?"

Sally heard a heavy sigh on the other end of the phone.

"If I go into too much detail now, I'll start crying at work. I had a miscarriage on the eleventh."

"Oh, Jentry. I'm so sorry. I didn't realize you were trying."

"We weren't," Jentry said ruefully. "It was a surprise, and I didn't know how much I wanted to be a mother until it happened."

"I don't even have words, Jen. I'm so terribly sorry. What can I do?"

"There's nothing to be done. I got a promotion at work, and I'm putting my energy into my career."

"The curator position?

"Yes. I'm so excited," Jentry said, sounding anything but.

"That's amazing. You're going to be fantastic."

"Thanks, Sal. I better go. Can I call you later?"

"Always."

"Gotta go. Love you."

Sally hung up and got down on her knees.

"Dear Father in Heaven, poor Donovan and Jentry have lost one of your special spirits. Please comfort them at this time. Help her body heal and prepare for the next child you send them. Please let this be something that helps them grow closer to you. In the name of Jesus Christ, Amen."

Next, she texted Paige and Hannah and, within thirty minutes, was having a bouquet of flowers delivered to Jentry's penthouse.

Her phone rang at the same time Sabrina started crying, having woken from her nap. She saw it was her husband and answered with the phone propped between her shoulder and ear as she picked up the baby.

"Hello, my love," she answered, her typical greeting for Sam.

"I got it."

"You got the CFO position?"

"Yep. Logan Regional gave me a great recommendation and Cache Valley Specialty wanted to work with me from the start. This is such an awesome opportunity."

"I'm so proud of you, sweetheart. This is so exciting."

"We'll see if you still feel that way when I'm working longer hours the next few months."

"Of course. Just be there for the birth of this peanut."

"Promise. I'll be home by six. Let's go to Coppermill to celebrate."

"I'll get a babysitter. Love you, Sammy."

"Love you more, Sally Jane."

<u>We have five new kittens. Sassy had an all-white boy on the 21st. Star had four babies on the 27th. Two grey girls, and a grey boy, and a peach boy. The children want to keep all of them.</u>

<u>I'm coming home at 3:30, three days a week in lieu of a raise. It's so great to be home with my children. I'm so crazy about them!</u>

<u>Had breakfast with Paige and Sally at IHOP. I'm so thankful for my friends/family. We sure miss Jentry though. I think about our time at the Y and wish we could relive it every once in a while. Gosh, we had fun.</u>

May 30, 2000

"Hello?"

"Hannah, I'm so sorry to call this early. I'm in labor. I won't be able to get the kids after school," Sally said apologetically while trying to stay calm through a contraction.

"Oh, my goodness, Sal, that's wonderful. I'll work a half-day or something. Don't give it a second thought."

"Are you sure?"

"First of all, yes, The Old Rock is very flexible. Second of all, this is not the time when you need to worry about me. What's happening with Sariah and Sabrina?"

"We'd planned on Mom watching them, but when we called the house, her phone went to voicemail. Sam called

Dad and got the same thing. He thinks they're at the temple for an early session. They've been going the last week of the month lately."

"I'll be right over to watch the girls. Give me fifteen minutes to get us out the door, and call my assistant manager to come in early."

"You're the best, Hannah. Tell Marisol I say thank you."

Sally hung up and turned to Sam. "Hannah will be here in fifteen minutes. What do we need to do before she gets here?"

"We don't need to do anything," Sam said, hugging her quickly. "You need to sit and breathe while I grab everything. I got the girls out of the tub. How Sabrina gets syrup in her hair I will never understand. Hannah can help get them dressed. You've got your bag ready, right?"

"Yes. It's on the side of the bed. Please put some lotion in there for me. The diaper bag is in the nursery. It should be ready, too."

"Of course it is. Because I have the most amazing wife. I love you, Sal. I'm excited to get daughter number three here." Sam turned down the hall, and Sally sat on the couch and took long, slow breaths.

They had waited four years to have their first child but had decided to have their children close together once they started arriving. Sariah would turn four in August. Sabrina had turned two in February.

She was so grateful she was able to be a stay-at-home mother and be present in the girls' lives. Their daughters were a wonderful mix of her and Sam. Both had the same dark blonde fine hair, which she kept cut short at their shoulders. Sariah had Sam's big blue eyes, while Sabrina had her chocolate brown eyes. She was excited to see what this baby, who they had decided to name Sadie Jane, would look like.

Sally had started watching Heather and Seth when Hannah moved back to the valley. Hannah had been lucky enough to get a position managing The Old Rock Church Bed and Breakfast. She worked Monday through Friday and was able to be home with the children on most weekends. Hannah was able to drop Heather and Seth off at school on her way to work, and Sally made two trips to the school a day to get Seth from morning kindergarten and Heather at the end of the day when first grade got out.

In the afternoons, she did Joy School with all of the children, as well as field trips and activities to match their different ages and abilities. Heather and Seth loved playing with the goats and collecting eggs from the chickens. She loved her niece and nephew dearly.

Hannah tried to pay her in the beginning, but she and Sam didn't need the money. Besides, this was an act of service she could do for her dear friend and beloved sister-in-law who had faced such trials. She wasn't sure how she would balance everything once Sadie was born, but she was determined to be the best mother and aunt she could be.

She turned when she heard the front door open. Heather and Seth ran straight for the playroom and their cousins.

"I'm going to keep them home today. They can play and keep each other entertained. How are you doing? What do you need me to do before you leave?" Hannah asked, setting down a bag and coming into the living room.

"Keep trying to reach Mom and Dad. I've called my parents. They'll wait for her to be born before they head to Logan."

"You are the most relaxed laboring woman I've ever seen. You're born for this, Sal. I can't wait to see the princess you guys made this time."

"Thanks for coming, Sis," Sam said as he entered the room with the bags for the hospital. "We owe you one."

"My children practically live with you. You owe me nothing. Now get. I'll hold down the fort. I love you guys. Keep me posted."

Sally hugged all the children goodbye before she and Sam left for the hospital.

June 2, 2000

Hannah gave Marisol a rundown of the guests at the hotel and let her know Sara and Janell, the catering managers, would be in later to prepare for tomorrow's wedding reservation. She grabbed her book, purse, and keys and headed out back to her green Toyota Corolla.

She had been the manager at The Old Rock Church Bed and Breakfast for over a year now. Getting the position was a blessing to which she gave Heavenly Father full credit. With no degree and little job experience, she didn't think she had much of a chance. Luckily, her friendly and open manner made up for the sparse resume.

Hannah worked the day shift at the hotel and was in charge of hiring, scheduling, training, and payroll. Her staff included her assistant manager, Marisol, the catering managers, three part-time front desk clerks, two part-time housekeepers, a part-time cook who made the room service breakfasts, and two men who handled the maintenance and groundskeeping duties. She was a good manager, and her team enjoyed working for her. She held monthly meetings with everyone and always included a game of some type to build team morale.

The owner of The Old Rock Church, Silas Clark, had been incredibly understanding of her situation as a single mother. She was allowed flexibility and had even had Seth in the office with her when he was sick. She was so grateful for the opportunity and worked hard to be worthy of the blessing.

The staff alternated who stayed overnight when they had guests. They were allowed to sleep in one of the guest rooms, and Heather and Seth thought it was such an adventure to spend the night in the hotel when it was her turn.

Hannah went into the Hollywood Video on her way home to look for a movie for the kids. She was watching the twins overnight while Paige went to Salt Lake to visit Blythe for the night and thought a movie party would be fun.

She walked along the wall of the new releases, scanning for something appropriate for children, and didn't see the man crouched down in the aisle to reach a video on the bottom shelf. She knocked into him and heard her knee hit his head.

"Oh my gosh! I'm so sorry. Are you okay?"

He stood up, rubbing his head, and looked at her. She saw his expression change from annoyed to pleased when he saw who bumped into him.

"I don't think I'll need an ambulance." He stuck out his hand, "I'm Toby."

"Hannah," she said, shaking it. "I'm so sorry, Toby. I wasn't paying attention, and I can be clumsy." She saw Morgan's face flash in her mind, smiling at her in the rain. She shook it off and started to walk past the man she had bumped into.

"Have you found anything good to watch?" he asked after her.

"I'm looking for my children, so that limits my options."

"Ah, well, my nephews love Tarzan. And I saw Toy Story Two near that as well." Toby pointed in the opposite direction.

"Oh, thanks. Those might do the trick." Hannah smiled and noticed Toby had kind-looking brown eyes, though small and squinty behind his glasses. He had a roman nose, thin lips, and close-cut blonde hair, attempting to hide a growing bald spot. Luke had a head of thick, dark hair, which she had always liked, even when she didn't like him. Toby looked younger than her, but not by much.

"How many children do you have?"

"Two. What about you?"

"None yet. Hopefully someday. I've never been married."

What a strange man, Hannah thought. So unusually friendly. "I hear it works out for some people, so good luck on the hunt. Maybe The Bachelor is the movie you need to go with tonight."

"Do you watch a lot of movies?"

"I love movies," Hannah said. "I spend more money in this store than I should."

"If I didn't already have a date this weekend, I'd ask you to join me for one."

Hannah laughed out loud. "Who says I don't already have one?" Hannah had dated a lot since the divorce. There had been a few slightly serious boyfriends and a few casual flings. She didn't know exactly what she was looking for, but she knew she hadn't found it yet.

"Do you have a date next weekend?"

"Not yet," she admitted.

"What about doing something next Friday?"

"I work next Friday night. It's my turn to stay over at the hotel. I manage The Old Rock Church."

"My friend had their wedding reception there. Cool building. How about lunch on Saturday?"

"Sure. It's the least I could do after cold cocking you with my knee." Hannah gave her number to Toby and made her way over to the section with Tarzan and Toy Story Two. She grabbed some Red Vines and popcorn and then headed to Sally's to pick up the kids.

An hour later, she was cleaning up a dinner of chicken patty sandwiches and waiting for brownies to come out of the oven when Paige, the twins, and Juniper came through the door. Seth took the boys upstairs to play, leaving Heather alone with her Junie B Jones book, which she preferred over Legos.

"Thank you for taking the boys," Paige said as she hugged Hannah. "They're so excited. I don't know if they'll sleep tonight."

"We'll wear them out good. I told Seth we could build a fort in the living room so they can watch a movie from inside. I'm going to take them all on a little hike along the Deer Fence Trail tomorrow after breakfast."

Hannah had struggled with her weight during her marriage to Luke. She had gained forty pounds with Heather and hadn't lost all of it before getting pregnant with Seth. Luke's cheating and porn addiction had done a number on her self-esteem and given her massive body issues. Unfortunately, she turned to food as an emotional support, keeping her stuck in a cycle of weight gain and body shame. Paige had gotten down to her college weight after the twins and was fit and thin, something Hannah envied immensely. She had gotten her father's genes, while Paige had been blessed with Hartvigsen genetics like their trim mothers. Once an avid runner, Hannah struggled to find the energy to do more than hiking these days. She had lost fifty pounds after the divorce, and her confidence had soared. So had her sex drive and need for male approval. Within three months of returning to Utah, she had sex with someone she was dating and was disfellowshipped from the Church. It was disheartening to think she hadn't learned her lesson with Luke. Luckily, an IUD was in place, so at least she hadn't risked pregnancy.

"They'll love that. I've packed their hiking shoes and hats, and Juniper's leash and food. How was work?"

"Good. We've got a pretty full house this weekend, thanks to a wedding event. It's so hit-and-miss. Somedays, there's no one, and I can read for eight hours. How was not working all day because it's your summer vacation?"

"The best. I made some bread to take to Blythe and some freezer jam with Sally's raspberries."

"Her garden is the best. She must put fairy dust in her soil. Everything is so perfect. Hey, weird thing on my way home," Hannah dried her hands and sat down at the kitchen table across from her cousin. "I ran into Hollywood Video and tripped on some guy in the aisle."

"Of course you did," Paige laughed. "Was he mad?"

"Opposite of mad. He asked me out."

"Really? Did you say yes?"

"Yeah. He was kind of oddly forward but nice at the same time. We're grabbing lunch next Saturday. Toby. Sounds like a dog's name to me," Hannah laughed.

"You're brave to get out there. I couldn't. I can't picture myself with anyone other than Evan. I hope you find someone perfect for you, Han."

"I hope I find someone who wants to be a part of my children's lives. The other guys I've dated are only interested in me, and the kids are some sort of afterthought. Luke dropped the ball so bad. Doesn't pay child support, doesn't come see them. They need a dad in their lives who loves them and shows up for them."

"When did you last hear from him?"

"He called them on Easter. He met some woman online in January and moved to Grand Junction to date her. My parents offered to move him to Utah when we came back so he could be close to the kids, and he passed. But he's going to chase after her. He told the kids he's getting married in July and wants them to come, but I haven't heard anything from him about it."

"Sounds about right." Paige looked at her watch. "I better go. I think traffic will have slowed by now."

"Give Blythe my love," Hannah said, hugging Paige goodbye before she left.

She took the brownies out of the oven, changed into pajama pants, and pulled her long curls into a topknot. Grabbing several blankets out of the closet, she hollered to the children, "Who's ready to make a fort?"

The sound of little feet running down the stairs thundered above her, and she smiled. She absolutely loved living in the Pacific Northwest. Jentry and Donovan had looked after them well, and she missed them. However, seeing her children bond with their cousins and have them in their lives almost daily was a blessing she was most grateful for. Living next door to Paige had made her childhood extra magical, and she was glad Heather and Seth were having a similar experience.

Heather and the boys helped her attach blankets over the top of the TV and secure them on the back of the couch. The children brought blankets and pillows inside and got comfortable as she started Tarzan. She gave everyone their own small bowl of popcorn and then climbed inside to watch the movie with them. Heather immediately snuggled up against her mother, and Hannah kissed her on the top of her head. Life was good. Stressful. Financially tight. But so good.

June 6, 2000

The hotel is booked this month! We've got a wedding every weekend, and they must have a lot of out-of-town families, because we're pretty full all month.

I met this guy on Friday at Hollywood Video. Toby. I met him because I didn't see him and knocked into his poor head with my knee! Pretty embarrassing. He was really nice about it. Very forward, to the point of awkward, but he was nice and seemed harmless, so I accepted a date for lunch on Saturday. He came into the hotel today while I was at lunch and left some wildflowers for me with a note saying he looked forward to Saturday. That is so sweet.

Jentry called last night. She loves her job so much and is so happy with Donovan, but really wants a child. She's ready to try again and hopes to get pregnant this summer. She invited all of us to come to Cannon for the July 4th weekend. Sam and Sally can't with little Sadie, who is the cutest little thing! I just want to eat her up. Paige and I are going to see if we can swing it and drive up together.

June 10, 2000

Hannah pulled up in front of El Sol and saw Toby waiting for her by the front door. He waved eagerly, a big smile on his face, and pushed his glasses higher up on his nose.

"You made it," he said as he hugged her hello and then held the door for her. They walked into the dark Mexican restaurant and were quickly shown to a booth.

Hannah slid onto the bench and immediately placed her drink order. "Can I please get a Diet Coke with a squirt of raspberry syrup and water with lemon?"

"A Diet Coke for me, please. And we'll need a minute to order," Toby said to the waitress and then turned back to Hannah. "That's an interesting combination."

The waitress left to get their drinks, and Hannah smiled across the table at Toby. He was shorter than she remembered but still taller than her by two or three inches.

"This is the only place in town with raspberry syrup. I love it. So, tell me about yourself, Toby. Where do you work?"

"Nowhere right now. I'm between jobs, but I have enough to live on for a few more months. I'm still in school. One semester left, which I'll start in August."

"How old does that make you? Because you don't look twenty-two." Hannah smiled politely while probing, which was something she was known for.

"How old would you guess?"

"That's a dangerous game," Hannah said with a laugh. "I'll be twenty-nine next month, and I'm going to guess you're younger than me."

"I turned twenty-seven on June fourth."

"You're taking a little bit of time getting through school, then?"

"I've taken breaks to either replenish my funds or to adventure. In the back of my car, you'll find my camping gear, climbing gear, and mountain bike. I like to be ready to play at a moment's notice."

"That must be nice."

"Do you camp?"

"We didn't camp much growing up, but I went for a few nights with my best friends in 1991, and it was a lot of fun. I went once with my ex a few years ago."

"That was the last time you went camping?"

"I've been busy raising children, remember?"

"Tell me about them."

"Heather is my oldest. She's beautiful, smart, funny, creative, and a bit shy. She has long, dark curls and big green eyes. She'll start second grade in August. She loves to read and is obsessed with cats. Seth is six and will be in first grade. He's precocious, sneaky, funny, and wants to marry me when he grows up. He loves to build Legos and play with his Aunt Sally's goats."

"They sound great. Have you been divorced long?"

"Not long enough." Hannah took a sip of her drink. "It should have ended sooner, but that's the way of it usually, isn't it? I'm coming up on two years."

"Would you ever remarry?"

"Is this first date conversation, Toby? Don't you want to ask about my favorite movies or something instead?" Hannah said with a wink.

"Am I being too forward? I'm sorry. I think you're really interesting, and I'm curious about how someone as beautiful and funny as you is still single."

"Flattery will get you everywhere with me. You've been warned."

"Not flattery. I'm sincere."

"Well, Mr. Sincere, you're twenty-seven and never married. I see your garment line in your shirt, so I know you're Mormon. Are you divorced or a menace to society, as Brigham Young said about unmarried men around your age?"

Toby laughed. "I haven't found the right woman. And I've wanted to play before I settle down. Marriage and family are a big commitment and responsibility. I want to make sure I'm truly ready. All my high school friends are married, and all the guys I roomed with the last few years are either married or engaged. I'm starting to feel like an old man around campus."

"From someone who wasn't ready when she married and didn't wait for the perfect match, my advice is take your time. It's better to date forever and get it right than rush into the wrong relationship."

"Good advice. So, I take it you rushed the first time?"

"You could say that. We had to get married. Well, I guess we didn't have to. We chose to get married when I got pregnant. I tried to make it work and be a good wife, but it seemed like we were doomed from the start. There was a porn addiction and cheating on top of poverty. I lasted as long as I could."

"Wow. You're really up front."

"No other way to be. The math will show Heather was born seven months after we got married. And I'm very upfront about the porn and cheating because I want anyone I may choose to date to know that's a deal breaker for me. I won't go through that again."

"Does your ex live in the valley?"

"He's in Colorado. He doesn't see the children much. He stopped making an effort around the time the ink dried on the divorce decree. But that's alright. I've got a great support system, and they have a lot of really good men in their life. My dad and brother being top on the list."

"That's great. So, when you aren't working and parenting, what do you like to do for fun?"

"Reading, writing, hiking, baking. It's difficult to juggle it all, but I'm pretty good at taking me time."

"Would me time include going out with me again?"

"Ask me at the end of lunch," Hannah said with a smile.

"If you'll consider it, I'd love to take you and the kids rock climbing. Have you been before?"

"In college. That sounds fun. I bet Seth would love that. Heather is a bit timid, but it would be good for her to try."

"Name the date, and I'll make it happen. I think it would be super cool to take your kids. I think the sooner they start on stuff like this, the more confidence they gain."

Hannah smiled across the table and wondered at this strange man. He was awkwardly forward and a little goofy-looking, but he seemed earnest and fun. Her last boyfriends had been solely interested in her, and the fact that Toby wanted to include her children on an adventure warmed her to him. She decided to see where this went.

"Are you ready to order?" the waitress asked, returning to the table.

"Do you like burritos?" Toby asked.

"Yeah."

"One beef burrito with rice and beans and two plates, please," Toby said.

Hannah tried to conceal her shock that they were splitting lunch. She figured either money was tight or Toby was a cheapskate. She didn't make a lot at the hotel, but she could afford a full burrito. Oh well, she thought, there's leftover tuna casserole at home if I'm still hungry after this.

July 1, 2000

Toby and I have seen each other almost every night for the last three weeks. His name is Toby Keller, and he's from Franklin, Idaho. He's lived in this valley his entire life, with the exception of a mission to Puerto Rico! That's where Evan went too! It made me super nervous he didn't have a job when we first met, after Luke's crappy job history, but he has been hired by Gossner's and will start there next week.

He's so good with the kids, and they really like him. We've taken them rock climbing, hiking, and floating the Oneida Narrows in Idaho. He's so much fun and so different from Luke, who just sat there like a bump on a log. He's very flirtatious and romantic. He's brought me flowers a few times and written me a poem!!!

Paige and I drove to Portland on Thursday. We stayed the night in our old apartment. Jentry has hung on to it for guests. Meaning any of us, and the occasional client of Donovan's. It's a little fancier looking than when we lived in it. Less fruit snack wrappers lying about. Heather said it made her a little confused in her heart to be back because she loved both lives. Isn't that so sweet and mature? Gosh, I love her. Seth loved showing the Lovejoy fountain to Ammon and Jarom. We let the kids play in the water after breakfast while we visited. Paige and Jen had lots of questions about Toby.

We got to Cannon Beach around one and took the kids to Pig and Pancake for lunch. They played in the sand for the rest of the day right off the deck of the beach house. Donovan bought some kites and flew those with them once the wind picked up in the evening. Miss Heather really loves Uncle Donovan and is his little shadow whenever she can be. He's great with kids. I hope he and Jen can have their own someday.

We're going to stay through my birthday/Independence Day, and then head home. Jentry got us all a copy of the book The Rescue by Nicholas Sparks. We're reading it this weekend and doing a little book club on the last day. Haha. So fun!!! Gosh I love my friends and I love Cannon Beach.

Today has been a little rainy. What a surprise. It's great for reading, but the children are chomping at the bit to go play on the beach. Jen put a new hot tub in a few months ago, and the kids have been sitting out there since lunch. Hopefully the rain will clear in time for an evening walk to Hug Point.

My heart hurts a little being back too, so I know how my sweet Heather feels.

July 4, 2000

Paige had gotten out of bed early to do yoga on the beach before the rest of the house woke up. Afterward, she put some orange rolls in the oven for breakfast. They were Hannah's favorite, and it was her birthday today, so she wanted breakfast to be more than cold cereal.

After breakfast, the group headed outside. The sky was a beautiful blue, with no clouds in sight, and a warm breeze blew in from the south. The four adults settled into chairs with books while the twins, Seth and Heather, started a sandcastle contest off the deck.

An hour quickly went by, and Paige set her book down and inhaled the salty air, listening to the sounds of seagulls, waves crashing on the shore, and children talking and laughing. Life was good. She had a good job she enjoyed and made the most of her time with the boys in her off hours. They were growing like weeds and starting to lose teeth. Ammon was still slightly taller than Jarom and looked more and more like Evan every day. She had a picture of the two of them on the fridge, and if Ammon had curls, they would be mistaken for each other easily. Ammon was outgoing, boisterous, and fearless. Jarom favored his mother, from his blue eyes and blonde locks to his sweet and kind nature. He still had his speech impediment and would be working with a speech pathologist through the school this year. She felt a mix of joy and sadness in so many moments, like today. Joy that she got to experience this life with the boys, and sadness Evan wasn't by her side. She was so grateful for their temple sealing, and her knowledge she would be with him in the next life, though it left her lonely at times like this one.

"I need a Diet Coke," Jentry said, standing up and stretching. "Can I get anything for anyone else?"

"I'm good," Hannah mumbled, barely taking her eyes off of her book.

"I'll grab some juice boxes for the kids. It's getting warm." Paige followed Jentry into the beach house, grabbed four apple juice boxes out of the fridge, and walked down the stairs of the deck to take them to the children.

"Are you guys thirsty?" she asked as she tousled Ammon's hair.

"Yes, Auntie Paige. Thanks," said Heather, accepting the juice.

"Where's Jar Bear?" Paige asked, noticing he was missing from the group.

"He took his bucket to get more water from the ocean," Ammon said.

Paige looked down the beach towards the water, scanning for a towheaded boy in bright green shorts. Her heart started beating faster and faster as she started walking, then running towards the water's edge. She didn't see Jarom anywhere. She held her hand up to her eyes and looked south, then north, towards Haystack rock. That's when she spotted the bucket and shovel at the water's edge a few feet in front of her. She ran to it and saw J.L. in black sharpie on the handle.

"Jarom! Jarom!" she started shouting, turning in circles. By this time, her friends had noticed her distress and were running towards her. "Jarom's missing. His bucket is here, but I don't see him," she said in a panic.

"Hey, hey, it's okay. Take a breath. We'll find him," Donovan said. "I'll run south along the water. Jen, you run towards the rock. Paige, you and Hannah cover this area," Donovan said, motioning to the sand leading to the rows of beach houses. "Maybe he got lost getting back to the right house."

"What if he's in the water? He can't swim good enough to handle these waves."

"He hates cold water, Paige. Remember how much of a struggle it is to get him in Bear Lake? He won't have gone in the water. Come on, let's comb the beach for a block on either side of the house," Hannah said, hugging her cousin.

The group split up in search of Jarom, each calling his name as they looked for a small six-year-old boy. Paige was in tears, calling for him, imagining he had been taken or that, in spite of the temperature of the ocean, he had gone into the water. Ten minutes went by, then twenty, then thirty, with no trace of her son. She dropped to the sand and prayed, "Father, please, you know where my son is. Please help us find him," she paused and then whispered, "Evan, help me find our boy."

She got back up and looked to see if she could spot her friends. Hannah was a few houses down from her, walking along the property lines of homes and calling Jarom's name. She saw Jentry making her way back from Haystack, no child in tow. She couldn't see Donovan, so she continued to walk along the property line of the beach houses going north, repeating under her breath, "Please, please, Lord." She was about to turn around and walk back to the water when she heard a soft whimper.

"Jarom?" she called, running toward the sound. Behind a large patch of sea grass, next to a weather-worn short picket fence, sat her son, tears streaming down his face.

"Mommy!" he shouted when he saw her and flew into her arms. Paige cried harder now from relief and gratitude, kissing Jarom over and over. "Oh, my boy, I was so scared."

"I was scawod too, Mommy. I didn't wemembow wheow Auntie Jen wivved."

"Oh, sweetheart. You're okay. I've got you now." Paige scooped up her son and held him close as she walked back towards the house.

Hannah saw them and came running over, hugging them both. "You gave us quite the scare. I'm so glad you're safe." She kissed the boy on the cheek. "I'll go call off the search," she said as she headed towards Jentry.

"I'm sowwy, Mommy. I didn't mean to get wost."

"I know you didn't, baby. You're not in trouble. Don't go down to the water by yourself again, okay."

"I pwomise."

The other children saw Paige walking towards them and came running to greet them. She sat Jarom down as Ammon threw his arms around his twin.

"Jar Bear! I said a prayer you would be okay, and you were!"

Paige wiped a tear and smiled at her boys. They were such good and loving little men, just like their father. The children immediately went back to the sandcastle building, their nervous systems back in check, while Paige still felt remnants of anxiety. She took a deep breath to calm her heart rate, kissed her boys on the tops of the head, and instructed the children not to walk down to the water without an adult.

Donovan, Jentry and Hannah returned from the search, smiles on their faces.

"I'm glad that ended well," Donovan said. "Who's ready for lunch? I'm going to grill some burgers." Donovan headed into the house while Paige and her friends sat back down on the deck.

"Well, that is something I never want to go through again," Jentry said, shaking her head. "My heart was in my throat, so I can't imagine how worried you were, Paige."

"I wish I could say it was the first time one of the boys has wandered off or that it will be the last. All's well that ends well, right?"

"How close are you to finishing the book?" Jentry asked Paige and Hannah.

"Two paragraphs," Hannah said.

Paige flipped to the end. "I'm three pages away."

"I hope you've liked it, Loves. I'm excited to discuss tonight after the kids are in bed. I'll go help my Donovan with lunch. Keep reading." Jentry got up and headed for the back door, then paused and turned back. "I love you both so much. And your families. Sal, too, obviously. You three are one of the best parts of my life. I don't say it enough."

"We love you too, Jentry. Thank you for all you do for us," Paige said.

"Companions forever!" Hannah shouted, and they all laughed.

July 26, 2000

I am so in love and spending every spare second with Toby. He is so much fun! Oh my gosh. We are constantly going on adventures. Heather and Seth are crazy about him. About a week ago Heather asked me, "Are you going to marry Toby?" I told her I didn't know, and she said "Well, will you?" How sweet.

This is everything I've always wanted. He's kind, romantic, super fun, outgoing...everything Luke wasn't. He thinks I'm the most amazing woman he's ever met. He's so good to my dear children. This is what I have been hoping for.

He met my family and has come to game night a few times. Everyone loves him and thinks he fits right in with all of us. My mother can't believe he's willing to date someone with children. She said I must be his mom's worst nightmare for her son – a divorcee with children. Rude! I'm a helluva catch! This weekend we're going camping with his family in Idaho. Willow Flats campground. The kids are super excited. He has a brother with some children around their age. Should be fun.

July 31, 2000

I'm engaged! We are moving super-duper fast, I know. It's a little crazy. But we're so in love, and at this age, why wait? We had gone camping to this gorgeous place in Idaho and there was the most beautiful hike to this spring that went past all these waterfalls. We got to the campground before his family, and he took the children and I on this gorgeous hike while we were waiting. They loved it. He brought a camping mug so they could drink from the spring. They thought it was the coolest thing ever. The water was actually really tasty. We were playing by the creek and suddenly he pulled this paper out of his pocket and told us he had written a little poem for me. The kids giggled, but we all sat down on some big tree roots to listen.

Friday, the best day of the week, for most it's true,

but better than best it's the day I met you!

Looking to find some movies to buy

you caught me staring from the corner of my eye.

What started at Hollywood and happened so fast,

almost scared me away cuz of girls in the past.

You were so different I was happy to find,

that is why I'm here with you on my mind.

Whether up on the cliff or high on a swing,

you are tops in my book, you make my bell ring.

I may not be perfect, that you already knew,

but my life would be closest if I spent it with you.

I wish I could promise the road won't be bumpy,

or that I won't get older and ugly or lumpy.

The question remains, by now you should guess,

shall we put this love to the ultimate test?

You are a giant surprise, and this was not my life plan,

but your heart and your soul make me a better man.

You come as a package, you made that clear from day one,

and life with you three will be so much fun.

Your children are precious, so kind and so sweet.

Helping you raise them would be such a treat.

So here it goes, in a poem that rhymes,

I want you to know I'm not wasting your time.

I'm trying to make this as special as you,

and if you say YES, you can then say I DO

If we promise forever how happy we'll be,

Hannah Limbrey will you marry me?

Isn't he the absolute sweetest?! Heather and Seth went crazy and started clapping. Toby pulled the most beautiful ring out of his pocket. It's a square cut CZ with a simulated ruby baguette on each side. I love it so much! Some day we hope to have the money to put in real stones.

His family was at the campsite by the time we got back from our little hike, and they were very excited for us. They are really sweet people, and I'm excited to have them in my life.

I feel like my life has turned into a Fairy Tale. I'm so excited to spend the rest of my life as Toby's wife.

August 1, 2000

It had been a hot day, and Sally was grateful for her air conditioning. Summers had been brutal in the little farmhouse, and she often thought about Hannah and the children on hot days. She and the girls had just finished dinner. Sam was working late at the hospital, which worked out fine tonight because Hannah and Paige would be here shortly to plan the Bear Lake week.

Last August, Jentry had flown in, and the four of them had gone to the cabin for a week with all the children. They had such a great time and decided to make it a tradition. Jentry would be flying in on Friday night, and they would head to the cabin early Saturday morning. Sally was so excited to spend time with her best friends.

Sally started the dishwasher and wiped off the counter and table, then called to Sariah and Sabrina. Hannah teased her about producing clones. Sabrina looked identical to how Sariah had at two and a half, with the exception of Sally's brown eyes. Little Sadie was the spitting image of her big sisters as newborns. The fuzz on top of her head was dark, but Sally wouldn't be surprised to see it turn to Sam's golden blonde by her second birthday.

"Alright, little ladies, let's go feed the chickens and the goats their dinner treats." Sariah and Sabrina followed her out to the animal pens. She had Sadie on her chest in a pink baby wrap. She loved being able to go about her day without having to put her down very often. Sally was a big believer that babies couldn't be spoiled and loved on her girls as much as possible. They were the light of her life.

"Can I feed Goldie and Opal by myself today?" Sariah asked earnestly.

"Miss Sariah, I'm so pleased you asked. You certainly may. Remember to hold your hand out flat," Sally said while placing some pear slices in Sariah's outstretched hands.

"Yes, Momma. I remember." Sariah lifted the latch on the gate and walked into the pen with the eight-year-old goats. "Hey Miss Goldie, hey Miss Opal, it's treat time, my ladies." Sariah's squeaky voice repeated the phrase her mother said each evening as she called the goats to her. The goats came running as she held out her hands with a pear slice for each. She giggled as they ate the food from her hands.

Sally had the girls around the animals from a very young age and had shown them how to groom, feed, and milk the goats, as well as how to collect the eggs from Meg, Jo, Beth, and Amy. This was their second batch of chicks, as the first ones had passed over the years, but she named them the same to make it easier for the girls to remember.

"Wanna pet," Sabrina said, toddling into the pen.

"Help, Sissy," Sally instructed. Sariah took her sister's hand and helped her pet the docile Nubians.

"Let's go pick something from the garden for our little women." Sally and the girls walked to the garden beds in the back of the yard, and Sariah chose a few string beans off the vine. They walked back to the chicken pen, and again, Sariah asked to do it herself.

She broke the bean into small pieces and sat down on the ground in the pen. "Here chickie chicks. Here, little women." She held the beans out and let the chicks peck it from her fingers.

Sally smiled at her daughter. She loved that they could have the benefits of country living while also being in a large town. Not Millville, of course. That was tiny. But Logan and Cache Valley at large offered all the hustle and bustle Sally could handle. She couldn't imagine living in a real city like Jentry and did not for the life of her understand how Hannah pined for Portland.

As if on cue, Hannah pulled into the driveway, with Paige pulling up right behind her.

"Did we miss treat time?" Ammon called as he ran towards them.

"I'm so sorry, sweetie. We just fed them. But you can go give them some love."

Ammon, Jarom and Seth ran towards the pen and then stopped and took a breath, like she had taught them. The goats loved affection from the children, but they had to enter the pen calmly. Though very rambunctious and high-spirited in their other play, the boys obediently followed Aunt Sally's animal rules.

Sally never left children alone with animals, no matter how much she trusted the child or her pets. She let the boys hug Goldie and Opal for a few minutes and then called everyone in to wash their hands.

The older children ran outside to play, leaving Sabrina behind. She was scooped up by Paige and carried into the dining room. Sally had notebooks and pens on the table, as well as fresh chocolate chip cookies, and the friends sat down to plan the menu and activities.

"I can't remember what we did exactly last year for meal planning, but I thought it would be easier if we each were in charge of one type of meal. For example, Hannah could always make breakfast, Paige lunch, me dinner. Or whatever."

"I'm good with whatever you guys want, but you know mine won't be fancy. What do we have? Six children? Five and a half, with Sabrina? They aren't going to want gourmet food. Let's not kill ourselves over meals," Hannah said.

"Jentry will give us money towards the food budget since she isn't bringing groceries on the plane. I want it to be as fair as possible, so I thought we could shop together and then split the amount evenly. Would that be okay?"

"Sounds good to me," Paige said. "I'd rather take breakfast, if you don't mind, Hannah?"

"Lunch is easier. Are you sure?" Hannah asked.

"Yes. The boys love German pancakes and this breakfast casserole I make. I bet the other kids will like it."

"Perfect. Do we want to split who plans the daily activities?"

"Honestly, Sally, I think we can wing it once we're there," Hannah said. "Between the beach, the razor, some hikes, games, and movies, I think we'll be good."

"I have a problem with overplanning," Sally said sheepishly. "Keep me in check."

"Will do. Oh, you guys, I have something to show you." Hannah slipped her hand into her back pocket, pulled out her ring, and slipped it on her finger. She held her arm out towards Paige and Sally.

"Oh my gosh!!!" Sally screamed and jumped up from the table to hug her. "Congratulations, Hannah! I had no idea this was coming."

"Me either! But I'm really excited."

"You're very brave to try again, Hannah. I hope for only happiness and joy in your future," Paige said, coming around to hug Hannah.

"Have you set a date?" Sally asked.

"No, not yet. But we want to do it sooner rather than later. I'm still disfellowshipped, so this one won't be in the temple either, but now I'll get warm enough weather for a summer wedding."

"This is the most wonderful news. I hope we get to help you with planning this one, too."

"Of course. This will be Toby's first wedding, and I want it to be really special for him. Mom and Dad said they'd give me one thousand dollars towards it, which is nice. I'll do something simple but still lovely. I'm sure I'll want to talk wedding details once we're all together."

"Oh, Hannah, I'm so happy for you. This is night and day different from the first time you told us you were getting married, and I hope this marriage is night and day different, too. You deserve to be loved and doted on," Sally said, starting to tear up. Hannah was one of her best friends and her sister by marriage. It had been hard to watch Hannah's life cause her so much grief and pain over the years. She admired how positive and happy she was in spite of how hard things got. Sally said a quick prayer in her head everything would work out perfectly for Hannah and Toby.

Suddenly, a loud crack of thunder reverberated off the side of the mountains, causing the children to run screaming into the house.

"That's Cache Valley for you," said Paige. "Perfect weather one minute, storming the next."

"I love summer rainstorms, though," said Hannah. "Let's wrap the kids in blankets and watch it out on the porch like my dad used to do for us."

After quickly lying a sleeping Sadie down, Sally grabbed blankets, and they sat around her front porch with children in their laps, watching the storm and talking about nature.

"Ooh! I have a good song for this," Hannah said as the rain started coming down in sheets. "*Whispering our goodbye, waiting for the train, I was dancing with my baby in the summer rain,*" she sang.

"*I can hear him saying, nothing will change, come dance with me baby in the summer rain,*" Paige sang with Hannah.

"Sally, go get your wooden spoon," Hannah joked as the friends continued to sing their favorite Belinda Carlisle song, much to the confusion of the children.

August 10, 2000

Jentry sat on the weathered folding chair, her towel draped over the plastic, and watched her friends beneath her sunglasses. Hannah and Paige were in the shallows with Heather, Seth, and the twins playing frisbee. Or attempting to, anyway. The children had terrible aim. Juniper splashed in the water after them, getting the frisbee more often than the children. Sally was sitting in the sand with Sariah and Sabrina, playing with Barbies. Three-month-old Sadie was asleep on a blanket under the giant umbrella next to Jentry.

It looked exhausting. She marveled at how busy each mother was all week between meals, baths, diapers, feedings, entertaining, and refereeing. Hannah and Paige had some time to themselves as their children were older, and they could play cards at night uninterrupted once their children were asleep. But poor Sally was tethered to her youngest daughters.

Jentry thought back to her first time at this beach with her friends nine years ago. She remembered when talk would turn to marriage and children, not picturing a husband in her life, let alone a child. Now, she would give anything to join their ranks in spite of the chaos she had witnessed this last week. It had been five months since her miscarriage and three months since they had started trying to get pregnant again. Each time her period came, she felt like crying.

"Auntie Jen, come play dolls with us," Sariah hollered.

Jentry sat her Diet Coke down and headed for her little nieces. "You're going to let me play, Love? That's so nice of you, Sariah." Sariah handed her a Barbie, and she sat down and followed Sally's lead with how to play.

Jenrty had thought a lot about Elodie since her miscarriage. Much more than usual. She wondered if her daughter had played Barbies as a little girl. She turned eleven in February. Maybe she still played with dolls. "

"You look far away, my friend," Sally said.

"Sorry, Sal. I was thinking about Elodie for a second and wondering if she plays with Barbies."

Sally smiled consolingly, and Jentry went on. "I've been thinking about her a lot since my miscarriage. I didn't mean to be a downer."

"You're allowed to feel things, Jentry. It's natural. And I'm sure being around all of the children brings up a lot of feelings. It will happen when the time is right, and you'll be an amazing mother."

"Thanks, Sal."

"I love how pretty your Barbies are," Heather said, sitting down next to her cousins. "Those boys play too rough. Can I play with you?"

"Yes, you can have Aunt Jentry's Barbie. She doesn't know how to play."

"Sariah Jane!" Sally said, sounding appalled. "That isn't very kind."

Sariah looked at her mother with her head cocked to the side. "But you said we should always tell the truth?"

Jentry laughed, handed the Barbie to Heather, and left Sally to deal with parenting.

***

The older children were bathed and fed and enjoying popcorn in front of a movie. Juniper had been hosed off and was sitting at their feet, catching dropped pieces of popcorn. Sabrina and Sadie were in bed, and Hannah was shuffling cards for a game of Skip-Bo.

290

"How many times has Toby called you today, Love?" Jentry asked teasingly.

"Too many. I know. I'm so sorry. I want to be present with you guys."

"You're in love. You're fine. He's obviously obsessed with you, and we like witnessing someone treating you like you deserve," Paige said, laying a card down.

"Tell us what you like best about him?" Sally asked.

"I'd rather hear what she doesn't like. It's more interesting," Jentry said with a wink.

"I'm certainly too jaded to think everything is perfect. He's balding, short, on the nerdy side, and a little socially awkward. I can admit that," Hannah said with a laugh. "But those aren't the things that matter. He's kind, patient, fun as hell, amazing to my children, and he thinks I'm incredible, which is a big change for me. I'm nervous about him being single at this age and set in his ways, and after Luke's fail as a provider, I'm concerned about him not having a real job and still being in school. That said, I love him. It makes sense in so many ways and not in others. I get that. But he makes me want to take the risk of loving again."

Jentry had seen how miserable Hannah had been with Luke up close and personal. There had been so many weekends Hannah and the children escaped to Portland so she could get a break from the sadness of her life. Jentry hadn't met Toby yet. She'd heard good things, and she hoped this man would give her friend the life she deserved.

"Like I've always said, if you love him, we love him. I hope I get to meet him before I head home."

"For sure. In fact, I think Sally invited Sam and Toby up on Saturday to go to the beach with us on our last day. If only Donovan could come too," Hannah said.

Jentry smiled. She had worried unnecessarily her friends would judge Donovan for not being Mormon. It was a non-issue, and she loved them even more for accepting him.

She loved him so much and hoped Hannah would find the same kind of happiness and fulfillment in this relationship as she and Donovan had in theirs.

"Skip-Bo!" Sally shouted excitedly.

"This isn't like Uno, Turtle," Paige laughed. "You don't have to shout it out."

"Maybe I like to," Sally said. "It's so rare I beat you guys at any games. I've got to celebrate."

"One more round, and then let's get the kids in bed and hot tub," Hannah offered.

"Let's make this interesting. Last one out of cards puts all the kids to bed," Paige said.

"You're on!" said Sally.

Jentry smiled and shook her head. Her life was so different from that of her friends. More different than they even knew, considering they didn't know she was inactive and had a glass of wine almost every night. Still, they were her touchstone, and she loved them with all her heart. She'd do anything for any one of them. While she didn't practice Mormonism any longer, she was grateful for her baptism because that journey had brought her to BYU and the Commons Room at Deseret Towers, where she met the most amazing women she had ever known.

September 16, 2000

Hannah's boss, Silas Clark, had let Hannah have her wedding at the Old Rock Church free of charge. The weather had been perfect for an outdoor ceremony, and chairs had been set up the night before on the south lawn.

The guests were in their seats while Marissa, a cellist from church, played love songs from different movies in homage to where Toby and Hannah had met.

Hannah had chosen lavender and lemon as her colors. Heather was in a precious purple dress with a wreath of flowers on top of her dark curls. Seth was in a matching vest with his hair slicked down. Hannah had sent them downstairs with Grammy while she finished getting ready in the Bridal Suite with her friends.

"One more bobby pin, and I think we'll have this updo secure," Paige said, pinning Hannah's curls into place on top of her head and attaching her veil beneath them.

"You look so beautiful, Hannah," Sally said as she tied a ribbon around Hannah's bouquet of yellow roses, lilacs, and daffodils.

"Purse your lips, Love," Jentry ordered, applying the last bit of make-up to Hannah's face.

Her friends stepped back, and she walked to the full-length mirror and smiled. She had found a simple dress off the clearance rack at Leven's, and Sally had added sequin and crystal detail to the front, as well as made her a tulle skirt that tied around the waist with yellow and purple ribbon. Hannah felt like a princess and was so grateful to have her friends help her with another wedding. She was also grateful this one was under much better circumstances.

Esther poked her head into the room. "I think your groom is getting nervous. Are you ready yet?"

"Five minutes, Esther. Get everyone in their places," Sally said to her sister-in-law. "What else do we need?" Sally asked as she turned back to Hannah.

"I think this is it. Hard to believe I'm here again. And this soon," Hannah said with a nervous laugh. "Let's go get me married!"

The girls walked out onto the balcony off of the bridal suite, which overlooked the lawn. Jentry, Paige, and Sally hurried down the stairs to their seats. Sally cued the cellist to start playing Cannon in D. Julie had Heather and Seth waiting for Hannah at the bottom of the stairs. Hannah smiled at her children as she descended the stairs, and then together, they walked down the aisle.

Toby smiled at her with tears in his eyes as he took her hand and turned to face the Bishop. She was so grateful to have found him. She had always hoped for a love like this. He made her feel beautiful, smart, competent, and special. She was so excited to spend the rest of her life with him.

After the ceremony, tables were brought out, and the chairs moved around them. Her friends helped her mother and Esther bring out the food. Instead of a wedding cake, Hannah had decided on a cheesecake bar. There were several fruit toppings and syrups. Hannah, Toby, and the children stood in a receiving line for thirty minutes, accepting hugs and well wishes, and then hit the dance floor. This wedding was everything her first one wasn't, and it gave her hope for a wonderful future.

As the sky turned dark, the guests left, and Julie came to grab Heather and Seth off the dance floor so they could head home. They and their cousins had been dancing and running around nonstop for two hours, and Hannah knew they would sleep well for her mother.

"I need hugs from my favorite people," Hannah said, crouching down and wrapping them in her arms. "I'll miss you stink bugs. Be so good for Grammy. I'll be home before you know it."

Heather and Seth squeezed her tight and then gave Toby a hug as well.

"Congratulations on your matrimony," Heather said, pleased with the use of a new word. "Come on, Sethy. Time to follow Grammy and Pappy." Heather took her brother by the hand and followed Julie to the parking lot.

Toby turned to Hannah and pulled her close, a look of intensity in his eyes. "Does this mean it's time for us to retire to the bridal suite?"

"Are you sure you don't want to go to bed early before our drive tomorrow?"

"That's exactly what I want to do. In fact, is it too late for separate rooms?"

Hannah laughed as Toby pulled her tighter and kissed her neck. "Okay, Mr. Keller, follow me."

Hannah took his hand and headed into the Inn to the Bridal Suite on the second floor. Her boss not only let her use the facilities for her wedding free of charge, but he also let them have a night in the Bridal Suite on the house. The second the door was unlocked, Toby swept her up and carried her inside, laying her on the bed.

"I have been waiting so long to do this," he said, removing his glasses and unbuttoning his dress shirt.

Hannah giggled and suddenly felt shy. Toby knew she had been disfellowshipped for having sex after her divorce and didn't judge her for it. He had also had sex outside of marriage but not gone to a Bishop to confess like Hannah had. Toby had had more partners than her and been a bit of a player before they started dating. It made her a little insecure and uncomfortable when he would talk about past girlfriends, and she hated that about herself.

They had fooled around a little in the short time they had dated, but they hadn't had sex, and she was proud of that. She wanted this marriage to be different from the start.

Toby stood before her now, completely undressed. She sat up and pulled him towards her. "Promise to always look at me with that much love," she said.

"Always. You're my everything, Hannah."

"Then you better help me with this dress so you can make love to your wife, Mr. Keller." Hannah stood and turned around so Toby could help with the zipper. The dress fell to the ground and revealed her garments, not the sexiest underwear for a wedding night, so she quickly slipped them off.

"Wow," Toby said, then grabbed Hannah around the waist and laid her back on the bed, this time climbing on top of her.

He came fast enough they both laughed.

"That's what too much anticipation looks like," he said sheepishly.

"It's flattering," Hannah said. "And you have all weekend to work on your stamina. Let's get in the bathtub and go for round two after a nice soak."

"I love you, Hannah. I hope you know that," Toby said, kissing her on the nose.

"I do. And I love you, too. This has been the best summer, and I can't believe this is my life now." Hannah kissed her new husband passionately and then slipped out of bed to start the bath.

<h1 style="text-align:center">January 10, 2001</h1>

Paige opened the doors to the Whittier Center and headed upstairs to the small classroom where she had been attending a grief group for several years. It was held on the first and third Wednesday of each month. She didn't always attend, as things came up with the boys or school, but as the anniversary of Evan's accident approached, she knew she would need all the support she could get. It had been seven years. She wasn't lonely, per se, because she had her children, but it wasn't the same as having a romantic partner. There were so many family members close by. Her parents were in Providence. Hannah, Sally, and their families were in Millville. Lane lived back east with his wife, Wendy Beth, but they flew out at least twice a year. Her sisters were just over the mountains. She had teacher friends and church friends. Her life was full and filled with love. Yet a piece was still missing, though she wasn't ready to do anything about it yet.

The meeting had barely started when she entered the room and took a seat in the back row. She wasn't sure she would share tonight, but it was nice to not feel so alone.

"We have someone new with us tonight," she heard the group leader, Isela, share. "Would you like to introduce yourself?"

A tall man from the front row stood up and turned around to wave awkwardly at the group.

"Is there anything you'd like to share with us tonight? An introduction?"

"My name is Drake."

"Hi, Drake," the room rang out.

"Hi. Umm. My friend told me about this group, and I thought I would check it out."

"We're so glad you're here, Drake. Thank you for joining us."

Forty-five minutes later, Paige was moving to the front of the room to say hello to Drake Pennington.

"Paige," he smiled when he saw her approach and gave her a big hug.

"Hey, Drake. It was so nice to see you here tonight. Sam told me about Kendyl. I should have reached out."

"No, no, it's good. He's actually the one who recommended I come here and consider sharing my feelings," Drake said with a nervous laugh.

"I think you'll like it. I don't come to every meeting, but it's nice to know there are other people out there who know what I've been through."

"How long since you lost your husband?"

"It was seven years on the third. You?"

"It was a year on November second. It was hard to take the girls trick or treating. I was a wreck for a week."

"I guess I don't know how your wife died."

"She choked on Halloween candy."

"Oh my gosh!" Paige gasped.

"Just a freak accident. She thought she had grabbed something safe, but she had a peanut allergy, and it was a mess. I was at work. Issy was down for a nap. Our neighbor found her when she brought Ellie home from kindergarten."

"Oh, Drake." Hannah squeezed his hand. "Accidents are the worst. Evan had run to the store for formula and diapers and never came back."

"How old was your baby?"

"Babies. Twin boys. They were three weeks old. Here, I'll show you pictures. They turned seven last month." Paige pulled a small photo album out of her purse. "This is us Christmas morning. Ammon is on the right, and Jarom on the left," she said, smiling proudly.

"You have a beautiful family, Paige. They have your smile."

"Really? I look for Evan so much I don't always see myself. Oh, and don't forget my girl." She flipped to another photo of her cuddling Juniper, the black Australian Shepherd the boys had received for their fifth birthday.

"Aussies are the best. We had one growing up."

"How about you? How many children?"

"Two girls," Drake said, digging for his wallet. "Kendyl was a big Jane Austen fan and gave them names from her favorite books. Elinor, Ellie will be seven in March." Drake showed her a picture of two little girls dressed in ballet tutus. The oldest one, in blue, was a pretty little girl with red curls like her father.

"Elinor Dashwood, I presume?"

"You got it." They walked to the back of the room and sat down again. "Number two is Isabella. She's a spitfire. I don't know what I'm going to do with that one. We call her Issy. She'll be five in May. Spitting image of her mother."

"Then her mother must have been beautiful. Look at those eyes." Paige smiled at the photo of the brown-eyed girl in a pink tutu, her light brown hair in a disheveled bun. "I'm not placing Isabella in the Austen books I've read, but admittedly, I haven't read them all."

"There are two that I know of. In Emma and Northanger Abbey. I don't know if Kendyl loved either character, just the name. And, yes, Kendyl was beautiful."

"They are so adorable. How are they doing? My boys never had to register the loss of a parent the way your girls must have."

"It hasn't been easy, for sure. I worry about raising girls on my own. Ellie acts out some. Nothing serious. Issy cries a lot. I worry she won't remember Kendyl much longer. She was only three when Kendyl died." Drake sighed as he put his phone back in his pocket.

"You'll get through it. One day at a time. Sounds cheesy, but it's true," Paige smiled reassuringly at him.

She remembered Drake so fondly growing up. He was always at the Limbrey's house and looked out for her and Hannah once they got to high school. Of all Sam's friends, he had always been her favorite because he was so genuinely kind. Her heart hurt to know the pain he was going through.

"I left the boys home with leftovers, a movie, and a somewhat hyper puppy. I better get back. It was so nice running into you. Let me give you my number, and anytime, day or night, you need to talk or a shoulder to cry on, I'm here." She pulled a gum wrapper from her purse and quickly wrote her number down. "I mean it, Drake."

"Then don't be surprised when I call."

January 14, 2001

Hannah tucked Seth into bed with a song and back rub and then went downstairs to Heather's room. The old farmhouse had no hallways, each room leading to another. To get to Seth's room upstairs, you had to walk through Heather's room. Heather was fine with it for now, but Hannah knew within a few years, her daughter would require more privacy.

"What chapter are you on?" Hannah asked, sitting down on Heather's bed.

"The one where she breaks an egg on her head. That would be so gross!" Heather said, peeking at her mother over the top of Ramona Quimby – Age 8.

Hannah had saved most of her books growing up and loved sharing them with Heather and Seth. Some of them were almost falling apart from the number of times she had read them.

"I loved Ramona so much. Junie B. Jones reminds me of her. Did you know the author was from the Portland area?"

"No wonder I like her," said Heather.

"It's a school night. You can finish this chapter and then lights off, alright?"

"Alright, Momma."

Hannah placed a kiss on top of Heather's head and slipped out of the room. Toby would be home in an hour. He was doing overtime at Gossner's on the weekends. It made him extremely tired and somewhat snappy at the children. He had started back in school last September. He would graduate in May with a B.A. in Project Management. Marriage, children, school, and work were a lot for him all at once, and Hannah tried to offer him grace. When he was rested, he was so much fun, and she remembered why she had fallen in love with him. Dating was much easier than marriage, but they had had a good four months with only a few bumps. She was convinced once he graduated and got a real job, things would be better.

Hannah quickly picked up the living room and wiped the kitchen counters after soaking the dishes. There was time to write her portion of their group email and get it off to Jentry before Toby came home. She sat down at the computer in the corner of her bedroom and clicked the mouse to bring the screen to life. Several tabs were open, and she clicked on them to make sure it wasn't anything important before closing them.

Her heart dropped into her stomach. Tab after tab was pornographic. Her eyes widened as she took in the images. This wasn't some famous Playboy Bunny like Pamela Anderson, the images Luke had preferred. These were young women dressed like schoolgirls. They were wearing plaid skirts and ties, with their youthful breasts exposed. Some of the girls were bent over, showing their naked rear beneath the skirt. Hannah counted the open tabs. Twenty-two. Each one revealed a young-looking girl, likely still in their teens. She was disgusted and unsure of what to do when she heard Toby come through the front door.

"Is there any dinner left?" he asked from the kitchen. She could hear him rummaging in the fridge. "Hannah?"

"I'm in here," she heard herself say, sounding strained to her own ears.

Toby walked into the room and instantly froze. Hannah stared at him, a look of contempt on her face, waiting for him to explain himself.

He said nothing.

"I don't even know what to say, Toby."

"Maybe the kids looked that up," he stammered.

"The kids?" Hannah said incredulously. "My eight-year-old daughter or six-year-old son? Which one do you mean?"

"No. Sorry. It wasn't the kids. I just…. I just…. you caught me off guard."

"And your first instinct was to lie? To blame your porn addiction on my children? What the hell, Toby?"

"I've worked a long day, Hannah. I'm tired. Do we have to do this right now?"

"Umm. Yeah. Yeah, we have to talk about this right now. You knew, Toby. You knew Luke's porn addiction destroyed our marriage. I told you on our first date I wouldn't do it again. I wouldn't marry a porn addict again." Hannah started crying. "I can't believe you did this to me. You knew I didn't want this." Hannah put her hands over her face and sobbed.

Toby knelt down beside her. "Shh. Shh. Don't cry. It's okay. I'm sorry, Hannah. I didn't want to tell you. I loved you, and I wanted to be with you, and I knew if I told you that, you'd leave me. I thought once I was married, it would go away. Things were so stressful, though. School, work, the kids, even you. I needed a break."

"It's our fault? We were so stressful you had to look at teenage porn?" Hannah couldn't believe what she was hearing. This felt like a nightmare. A familiar recurring nightmare.

"It's not your fault exactly, and those aren't teenagers. I'm not a pedophile."

"They look like teenagers, it's the same thing." Hannah stood up and grabbed her coat out of the closet. "I need to get out of here." She slipped on her snow boots and went out the back door. It was freezing outside, with two feet of snow on the ground, but she didn't care.

She walked down the street, hands shoved deep in her pockets, crying and trying to figure out what had just happened to her life. They were happy! Yes, he'd yelled some, but she knew how hard it was to be perfectly patient with children all the time. They had done so many activities with the children, had date nights, went to game night every week at Sam and Sally's. Toby slow danced with her in grocery stores and was constantly grabbing her butt and telling her how beautiful she was. How could this man have kept this addiction from her, and what did she do now?

"Hannah," Toby said, coming alongside her.

Hannah let out a scream. The dark night and snow-packed street had muffled his approach.

"Sorry, I didn't mean to scare you. I didn't mean to...." He took her in his arms, and she sobbed. Her torturer was her comforter. "I didn't want to hurt you. I'll get help. I can stop. Please give me another chance."

Toby lifted her head off his chest and wiped her tears with the back of his hand. "I love you, Hannah. Please forgive me."

Hannah did what she had been taught to do as a young girl at church, what had been reinforced through studying the scriptures her whole life, and what she believed Christ would want her to do.

She forgave him.

Or at least she told herself she did.

July 12, 2001

The Limbrey-McLean cabin was filled to the gills. Sally had the idea of having their Bear Lake week in July so they could call it a thirtieth birthday party. Husbands were invited, and even Donovan had taken time off to spend a long weekend with them.

The group had arrived Wednesday afternoon, with the exception of Sam, who they expected any minute.

"Alright, kiddos, line up for breakfast," Sally ordered as she placed another waffle on a warming plate. Six children, ages three to nine, lined up obediently. Fourteen-month-old Sadie was already in a highchair eating bits of waffle, with Juniper happily cleaning up when she spilled.

Sally placed a waffle and slice of bacon on each plate and sent the children out to the deck to eat. Donovan and Jentry came in from a morning walk and started dishing up.

"These waffles smell amazing, Sally. Thank you," Donovan said.

"You've got to eat them with her homemade buttermilk syrup, Love. You'll never enjoy maple again." Jentry placed two waffles on her plate and grabbed extra bacon. "Eating for two, remember?" she smiled and then followed Donovan to the dining room table.

Jentry and Donovan had excitedly shared the news of their pregnancy the night they arrived as they sat around the fire talking after the children were in bed. She was ten weeks along and glowing. Sally was so excited for Jentry to have a baby. She was due in February, and Sally had already told her she would be in Portland to help when the baby arrived.

The loud honking of a truck startled Sally, and she turned around to see Sam pulling into the driveway. Sally stepped out onto the deck to greet him and stopped in her tracks. Behind his truck was a brand new, sparkling blue boat.

"Samuel Limbrey! What have you done?" Sally asked, a smile on her face. They had talked about wanting to get a new boat for the lake, but she didn't expect him to show up with one. He loved surprising her with things, and she laughed as he hopped out of the truck, grabbed her hand, and took her to the back of the boat.

By now, all the children, as well as the adults, were gathered around, looking at Sam's new purchase.

"Sorry I'm late to the party, but I had to add a little something to this girl before we could get her here." Sam pointed dramatically at the back of the boat. In large blue cursive letters were the words "SS Limbrey."

Sally laughed out loud. "For Sam and Sally?"

"SSSSS Limbrey was a little much. Plus, you tell me we aren't done having babies," Sam said with a grin.

"Do we get to go on the boat today, Uncle Sam?" Seth asked.

"We sure do. And I bought a big tube to pull you kids on."

"You better have life jackets," Hannah said, coming over to inspect the boat.

"We have all sorts and sizes of life jackets. How soon can we sail?"

The group finished up breakfast and went to their rooms to find swimsuits. Sally gathered sunblock and water, as well as some snacks, not sure how long they would be on the water.

"Do you like your boat, Sally Jane?" Sam asked, wrapping his arms around Sally from behind and kissing her on the neck.

"Almost as much as I like you."

"Remember the first time we met in person? Right in this kitchen. You were singing your heart out into a spoon with some green goo on your face. I knew right then I loved you."

"You did not," Sally laughed. "I barely made eye contact with you. I froze in your glorious presence."

"Alright. You got me. It was when you jumped off the cliffs at the ice cave. That's when I knew." Sam kissed Sally tenderly, and she melted into him.

"Gross," Hannah said teasingly as she came into the kitchen. "What can I do to help us get this show on the road?"

"Gather your group and follow us to North Beach," Sam said, tugging on his sister's braid.

The water was calm today, which isn't always a given at Bear Lake. Winds were known to whip the water into a frenzy, even building to over eight feet high waves in a bad storm. The group set up an awning on the east end of North Beach, spread a large blanket in the sand, and placed their towels and coolers on top. All fourteen of them climbed into the boat and went for a ride.

Sally sat next to Sam, holding Sadie close to her. Jentry, Donovan, and Paige sat at the front of the boat with the little boys while Hannah and Heather held Sariah and Sabrina in the back. Toby tried with no success to get Sabrina to come to him, but she clung close to Aunt Hannah, which made Sally smile. Her second daughter was as shy as she was at three.

After driving around for thirty minutes, Sam stopped and pulled the large tube down.

"Okay, the rules are there has to be an adult for every child, and everyone needs to have a life jacket on."

"Not adults, though, right?" Toby asked while jockeying to go first.

"Even the adults, Toby. We want to set a good example for the kids, right?" Sam said, passing Toby a life jacket.

Toby, Hannah, and her kids went first. Sam kept the boat at a nice, easy pace and gave them a ride for fifteen minutes before pulling them in to let others have a turn. Sally noticed he ignored Toby's signals to go faster. Sam loved an adrenaline rush as much as anyone she knew, but not at the expense of a child's safety, and she respected him for being careful.

Next, it was Paige, and the twins turn. Hannah went with them as the second adult.

When it was time for Sariah and Sabrina to have a turn, Sally passed Sadie over to Jentry and asked Hannah to come with again.

"You're really hogging the rides," Toby said in a low menacing voice as Hannah climbed over the boat, though not low enough that Sally didn't hear. She was appalled and instantly got a sick feeling in her stomach.

After all of the children had a turn, Sam asked if Donovan and Toby wanted a ride together.

"Only if you'll go faster," Toby said, already putting a life jacket back on.

"I'm happy sitting here with my wife," Donovan said, an arm around Jentry.

"Alright, Toby. It's all yours. Unless Hannah wants to join you."

"She's had enough rides. I'll go alone."

Sally watched Hannah's jaw tighten, but she didn't respond to what he had said. What was going on? Sally was seeing glimpses into behavior by Toby, which she found very concerning. Hannah noticed her staring and gave her a weak smile in return.

"Ready," Toby yelled from the tube.

Sam took off in a southerly direction, going as fast as he dared with such small children on board. He turned in circles, causing a large wake for Toby to jump. Toby motioned for Sam to go faster, but he kept the speed even, not wanting to make Jentry sick.

Sam made two large turns around the lake and then pulled Toby back into the boat.

"Man, this thing could go so much faster," he complained as he dried off.

"Well, we do have small children and a pregnant woman on board, Toby."

"Maybe you should all stay on shore next time, then."

"Excuse me?" Hannah said.

Sally watched as Toby stepped towards Hannah and whispered something angrily into her ear. She could see his neck veins bulging.

"Hey, Hannah," she said, standing up. "Would you hold Sadie so Sam and I can go for a ride?" Sally stepped in front of Toby and handed Sadie to Hannah.

"Donovan, you know how to drive a boat?" Sam asked.

"I do, Captain."

Sam turned the wheel over to Donovan and jumped in the water with a front flip. Sally followed, and they climbed onto the tube.

"Not too fast, Donovan. I get scared," Sally laughed. The boat lurched forward, and Sally turned to Sam with worry on her face.

"Something isn't right with Hannah and Toby."

July 14, 2001

"We've got to hurry if we're going to make it," Paige said to her friends as they filed into the kitchen. They had decided to do a sunrise hike on the Limber Pine trail for their birthday celebration.

They had told Donovan, Sam, and Toby to expect them back before breakfast and asked the children to sleep in as long as possible.

Three years ago, they had climbed this trail for Donovan and Jentry's wedding and headed west at the fork toward the namesake Limber pine. Today, they went east, armed with flashlights and headlamps.

"Do you promise there are no cougars on the trail right now?" Sally asked from the rear.

"I can't promise," said Paige, "but Juniper will let us know if she spots one. She'll start barking like crazy."

"That's not funny, Love," said Jentry.

"Juniper barks like crazy when she sees a bird," Sally added.

"I've never seen a cougar on this trail. It's not remote enough," Hannah said.

The eastern horizon started to glow as they made their way around to the far side of the trail. A wooden bench faced toward the lake, and Sally and Jentry sat on it while Paige and Hannah found boulders to sit on.

They watched in silence as the cloud-filled sky turned bright pink, peach, and orange as the sun made its ascent over the eastern mountains.

"I love sunrises," Hannah sighed. "There is something about them that speaks to my soul."

"They're really amazing," Paige agreed. "Alright, my friends, I thought for thirty, we could do a little activity like we did for twenty. Your friendships mean so much to me. We say it all the time, but again, you're all family to me, and I couldn't imagine my life without you. You're the best support system a girl could ask for. I thought we could go around and share a favorite memory of this little group in the last ten years."

"That's a great idea, Love."

"Thanks, Jentry. Who wants to go first?

"I will," Jentry said. "I haven't been back on this trail since the day I married my husband three years ago. Sharing that moment with the three of you made it even more special. Donovan was shocked when I told him the plan," Jentry laughed. "He was sure I would want a big showy wedding. Never did he ever dream it would be on a random trail in Utah. But I'm so glad it was. And I'm so grateful for how you have embraced Donovan. I love him with all my heart, and I want to thank you for letting him into your hearts, too." Jentry wiped a small tear from the corner of her eye with surprise. "What is this? Am I crying? I don't cry."

"Pregnancy hormones," Hannah said. "They've turned you soft."

"Be careful, Jentry," Sally said, "or you'll end up soft all over like me. I think I gain another permanent ten pounds with each baby. My baby weight gets harder and harder to lose. I'm thirty pounds heavier than I was when I had Saraih."

"It doesn't seem to stop your husband from wanting to ravish you, Love. Look at all your children, and he said yesterday they'll be more."

Sally slapped at Jentry's arm playfully. "My favorite times in the last ten years are every single time we're all together. Whether it's a quick Thanksgiving reunion, trips to Bear Lake, weddings, or even our group emails. I just love the way being together fills my cup. You all bring me so much happiness."

"Agreed," said Hannah. "I'm like Sally, I love being together. But I think for me, one of the most important times was when Sally and Paige came out to Oregon when I went through my divorce. Being at the beach with the three of you and feeling your love for me and my children got me through a really hard time."

"I know exactly how you feel, Hannah," said Paige, with a catch in her voice. "There are so many wonderful, happy, joyful, ridiculously goofy times I have spent with you three over the last ten years. But the one that stands out is when Evan died. I was so broken. His funeral was one of the hardest days of my life. Just sitting with me helped strengthen me. Then Hannah did her cheesy shake dance around the room," Paige said, laughing at the memory.

"Hey!" Hannah said, laughing too. "That stuff works! I still do the shakes when I have a hard day."

"Well, it worked that day, for sure. I can neither confirm nor deny if I've done it since then."

The sky was a robin egg blue now, the clouds white instead of pink.

"We better get back to the troops," Hannah said, standing up.

By the time they got back to the cabin, everyone was awake, and the men had made a cold cereal bar. Boxes and bags of cereal covered the island, and the children were trying some of everything.

"Oh, wonderful," Paige said dryly. "They'll be hopped up on sugar all morning."

"I love cold cereal. Pass me the Golden Grahams," Hannah said, grabbing a spoon and bowl.

"That sky doesn't look great all of a sudden," Sally said, looking out the north-facing windows.

The blue sky they observed from the trail was quickly being taken over by dark grey, ominous, looking clouds coming in fast from the northwest.

"Are we supposed to get rain today?" Sally asked.

"That will definitely change our plan for the day. Good thing we have board games and TV if a storm comes," Hannah said between bites.

"You three had me up before the crack of dawn. I'm going to take a hot shower and go back to bed. Wake me up in an hour. Maybe two." Jentry kissed Donovan and headed to their room.

The storm broke two hours later. Lightning lit up the sky, winds rocked the lake, and raindrops hit the metal roof with a sound that scared some of the children and sent Juniper hiding under a bunk bed.

Paige put a Disney movie on for the children in the loft and set up a puzzle table in the living room, which immediately drew Sam, Hannah, and Toby. Sally was occupied in the kitchen making cupcakes, and Donovan was reading in the corner. Paige decided to go wake Jentry and headed down the hall to the master bedrooms. She tapped lightly on Jentry's door and waited before opening it a crack.

"Jentry?" she whispered, not wanting to startle her friend. "Oh no," Paige said, her hand flying to her mouth.

Jentry sat on the bed, softly crying, the sheets underneath her red from blood.

Paige rushed to her side and put her arms around her friend. Jentry leaned into Paige's shoulder and let herself be comforted.

"Oh, honey. How long have you been sitting here?"

"I woke up thirty minutes ago," Jentry said, her voice drained of emotion. "I felt something wet between my legs and worried I had lost bladder control at first. Then I saw the blood."

"My dear friend, I'm so sorry. What can I do?"

"Will you go get Donovan for me? And help me clean up?"

"Of course. Let's get these clothes off of you and get you in the shower. I bet we have some pads in there." Paige helped Jentry out of her clothes, grabbed new underwear and one of the oversized tee shirts Jentry wore as pajamas, and led her into the bathroom. She started a warm shower for her and found a box of sanitary napkins under the sink. "I'll grab Donovan and strip the bed. I'll bring you some tea, too."

Jentry stepped into the shower, the water turning pink as it ran down the drain.

"I'll be right back with Donovan."

Paige walked back into the living room and got Donovan's attention. "Hey, Jen wants you for a second."

Donovan followed her down the hallway, where she explained Jentry was having another miscarriage. He went into the bathroom, and she heard Jentry start crying harder as he shut the door behind him.

Paige stripped the sheets off of the bed and sprayed them with stain remover before throwing them in the wash. She grabbed fresh sheets out of the closet and made the bed. Her heart hurt for the loss Jentry must be feeling right now. She and Donovan wanted a family of their own. They had struggled to get pregnant again after the first miscarriage, and now this. Paige started to cry for her friend and then quickly wiped the tears away.

She went into the kitchen and started making a cup of Peppermint tea.

"Is everything alright?" Sally asked as she spooned batter into the cupcake tin.

"No, Sal, it's not. I went to wake Jentry, and she's having another miscarriage. She's in the shower cleaning up. I'm making her a cup of tea, and I think she'll rest a little more. I'm not sure. I don't really know what to do for her."

"Oh, how terrible. Poor Jentry."

Paige saw Hannah looking at them and motioned her over.

"What's going on?" Hannah asked.

"Jentry is having another miscarriage," Paige explained.

"Oh, crap. That sucks. What can we do?"

"I'm not sure. I got her in the shower and changed the sheets. Donovan is with her now."

"She's probably so devastated," said Hannah.

"Yeah," said Paige, removing the tea bag from the mug and adding a little milk, the way Jentry liked her tea.

Donovan stuck his head around the corner. "She's asking for you guys."

Hannah, Paige, and Sally walked into the room to find Jentry sitting up in bed, watching the summer rain out the large picture window. Her long dark hair dripped onto her tee shirt, but she didn't appear to notice.

"Hey, sweetie," Paige said, setting the tea down on the nightstand.

Jentry turned to look at her friends. "I lost another baby," she said sadly.

"We heard, Jentry. We're so sorry," Sally said, sitting down on the edge of the bed and patting Jentry's legs beneath the down comforter.

"What can we do for you, Jentry? For you and Donovan?" Hannah asked.

"I don't know. The last one wasn't as far along and didn't have this much blood. I don't know if we need to see a doctor or not. Maybe we should go home early. I don't know. I don't want our sadness to ruin the weekend."

"Hey, none of that," Paige admonished. "If you need to go home, you can, but we're here to help and support you. You could never ruin our weekend."

"We'll do whatever you need, Jen," Hannah said.

"I need a hug," Jentry said, putting her arms out towards them.

They hugged and cried together while mourning the loss of Jentry's baby.

December 25, 2001

Hannah rolled over in bed and smiled at Toby. "Merry Christmas, Bubba," she said, kissing him on the cheek.

"Merry Christmas, Bunny," Toby said, rolling over and kissing her.

They had come up with new nicknames for each other a few months ago after watching the Schmoopie episode of Seinfeld. Things could be so strange with Toby. One minute, he could be badgering her, calling her a nag for asking for help, being impatient with the children, and an all-around jerk. The next minute, he was the most romantic, loving, adoring husband. It definitely kept Hannah on her toes.

He was graduated now and working as a shift lead at Gossner's. The money wasn't great, but the benefits were. He had settled down a little after finishing school. His temper tantrums were rarer, but when he blew, he blew. He had hurt her only once. And not even that bad. He had been looking for an old game and asked her about it. Where he was a bit of a hoarder, she liked to downsize and donate things to second-hand stores. She had taken a load a few days before, and in it was a dusty old Monopoly of Toby's she didn't realize was in Spanish and from his mission. He had grabbed her by the shoulder, screaming in her face, before picking her up and throwing her on the bed.

He was immediately so sorry. He brought flowers home the next day and the day after that. There wasn't another blow-up for weeks.

When Toby was tender, he was amazingly tender. There was so much good in her marriage that it was easy to overlook the hard times. He was more impatient with Seth than Heather. Her daughter had once commented that Toby seemed "Kiddish." When she asked Heather what she meant, she realized that her daughter thought Toby was immature. An interesting observation for a nine-year-old.

Things were good enough that when they celebrated their first anniversary, Toby told Hannah how much he would love to have children with her, and she had her IUD removed. Hannah was pregnant by November.

"How are you feeling this morning?"

"If I start with a cracker before I get out of bed, I bet I'll be great."

"How are you feeling without Heather and Seth? That has to be hard."

Hannah signed. Luke hadn't taken the children for Christmas since 1999. He lived in Colorado with his new wife and her children, and at times, it seemed he had forgotten about his own. There was still no child support or alimony. He called Heather and Seth on their birthdays but never sent a gift. He took them for two weeks in June the last few years. Heather and Seth liked his stepchildren and looked forward to seeing their dad. Hannah was so lonesome whenever they were away.

"I'm trying not to think about it. I hate being away from them. But I'm excited to have a second Christmas morning with them when they get back."

"This should be a fun Christmas still, with what we're giving your parents."

"It will. It will. I loved seeing your parent's reaction yesterday." Hannah kissed Toby again before heading into the bathroom to shower. She let out a scream and then giggled when he pulled back the curtain and got in with her. Where Luke was rarely interested in intimacy with her, Toby couldn't get enough of it. She told herself if she kept him satisfied, he would have no need to look at pornography. She had asked him about it once, a few months after she discovered it. The conversation hadn't gone over well, so she didn't ask about it again.

He held her hand on the drive to River Heights. Sam and Sally pulled up at the same time they did. Esther and Dustin had come down on Christmas Eve. The family enjoyed a delicious breakfast and then went into the living room to open gifts. The grandchildren opened their gifts first, so they could go play with their new things from Pappy and Grammy. Sariah and Sabrina helped Sadie and Jaken off to the playroom while the adults opened their gifts. Esther's newborn son, Griffin, was asleep in the swing, oblivious to all the noise and commotion.

"We decided to get everyone a gift we can do together as a family. I hope you'll like it." Julie slid an envelope to each of her children. Inside was a homemade gift card for a season pass to Lagoon, the amusement park in Farmington.

"This will be so fun! I can't wait to go with everyone!" said Sally excitedly. "The cousins are going to make such great memories."

"Dad and I are happy to push babies around in strollers and hang out in Kiddyland so you kids can go on the big rides a few times," Julie said. "We used to have so much fun taking you to Lagoon when you were younger.

"This is amazing. Thank you, Dad and Mom," Hannah said, smiling at her parents. "Alright, you're getting my gifts for you one at a time." Hannah pushed a flat object towards her parents. Her mother's reaction was exactly what she had hoped for when she saw the family picture Hannah had framed for her. Paige had taken their photo in October at Tony Grove Lake. The fall colors against the craggy mountains and alpine lake were spectacular and a great backdrop for their first family portrait. They were dressed in browns, yellows, and navy.

"Hannah, this is beautiful! Look at this, Bruce. You know, we really ought to get a new family photo. The family has grown a lot since the last one."

Hannah slid another gift towards her parents. This time, it was a photograph of Heather. She looked so beautiful. Her dark curls were to the middle of her back.

"Look at Miss Heather," Bruce said, "A beauty like her mother."

Next, Bruce and Julie opened up a photo of Seth. He was sitting cross-legged on a large boulder, and Paige had caught him mid-laugh. The photos were passed around the room.

"I can't believe how big they are, Hannah," said Esther. "I don't want my boys to grow that fast."

"You'll be shocked by how fast they grow," said Sally. "Oh, these are so darling. I need to schedule something with Paige for us."

"Oh, I have one more," Hannah said, slyly pulling a fifth present from her purse. This one was smaller. She passed it to her parents, who carefully unwrapped the small frame.

"Is this what I think it is?" Julie asked excitedly.

"If you think it's an ultrasound of my new baby, then yes," Hannah smiled.

"Congratulations, guys. That's really great," Sam said, patting Toby on the back.

"When are you due?" Julie asked.

"August. I'm only about a month along. We figured this would be such a fun way to tell you that we couldn't keep it to ourselves. I guess I'll be in Kiddyland with you this summer. Not sure how many rides I can go on at Lagoon."

"Are Heather and Seth excited?" asked Sally.

"They are. It's cliché, but Heather hopes for a sister, and Sethy hopes for a brother. I hope for an easy pregnancy and a healthy baby."

<u>March 15, 2002</u>

It's a girl!! It was the most incredible thing to see an ultrasound and find out the gender of your baby before they are born!!!

Heather is so excited to be getting a sister. Seth was sad at first, but Toby took him to get ice cream at The Bluebird, and that helped cheer him up.

Toby thinks because Heather and I share an initial, he and this daughter should share one, so we've been thinking of T names for her. The short list is Tessa, Taya, Tara, Tandie, and Taylor.

And guess who is having another baby girl in May? Sally! We're really excited to have babies so close together. However, our joy is tempered knowing Jentry hasn't been able to get pregnant again. Our hearts hurt for her so much.

Last week, Toby got promoted from Shift Lead to Team Lead at work. We're so excited. It's a good little raise. It should make up for the income we'll lose once this peanut is born. I got pregnant again on the condition I didn't have to work and could be home raising the baby. Toby agreed in the moment, but ever since, makes little remarks about how I could probably take the baby to work with me most of the time or work part-time. Nope. We had an agreement. Silas is really sad to lose me, and I'll miss everyone at The Old Rock. I'll work up until my birthday and then take a few weeks off to get everything ready. How we are going to fit five people in this little old house I do not know. We've been talking about trying to buy our own place.

We shall see.

March 30, 2002

"Hey, Supermom," Drake said as Paige answered the phone.

"Hey to you, Superdad."

"What are you and the boys up to?"

"Papa and Nana took them to Mesa for two weeks for the school break. They'll miss a week of school, but it's 6th grade. It doesn't count."

"Have you ever been without them that long?"

"No. And I'm trying not to freak out. I'm glad spring break is only a week. Being back at school will help distract me, and I'll take Juniper for lots of walks."

"I have another distraction idea, if you're up for it?"

"I'm committing to nothing until I've heard it," Paige said.

"The girls and I are trying to make Crystal Hot Springs a tradition. We went last year on the first Monday of the break. They asked if you guys wanted to come. Probably because they know your snacks will be better than mine."

"Don't kid yourself, Drake. You want my snacks too," she said almost flirtatiously, and then quickly covered her mouth with her hand, even though he couldn't see her.

"Your snacks, your sunblock, your water bottles. All of it," he laughed, not catching what Paige had let slip.

Drake had called her four days after bumping into her at the grief group. At first, he would want help processing his grief. Then, it became tips on raising little girls. Before long, they were talking almost every night. Never for too long because they were both so busy with children, but long enough that it made a positive impact on her day.

By March, she asked if she could bring him to game night. Sally and Hannah had looked at her with wide eyes. She'd assured them they were just friends. And anyway, six was a better number for a lot of the games they played.

In April, they decided to meet at the park with all the children. They chose Willow Park so they could walk through the small zoo as well. Paige was instantly enamored with Drake's little girls. When Issy put her little hand in Paige's as they walked around the zoo, her heart melted. Her boys thought Drake was fun and didn't mind having the girls around because they were used to all their girl cousins.

In August, Sam and Sally took their annual camping trip to City of Rocks, where they invited Paige and the boys, as well as Drake and the girls. It was the perfect combination, as Sam and Drake had been best friends since second grade. There were seven children and one dog to keep an eye on. It was chaotic and incredibly fun. Sam and Drake took the twins and Ellie rock climbing, while Sally and Paige took the younger four children for an easy walk among the rocks.

After that, Drake started joining most group activities, and every once in a while, Paige would catch herself looking at him and wondering what it would be like to go on a real date. As soon as those thoughts came, she would shake her head to loosen their grip. She was Evan's, and he was Kendyl's. They had each been married in a temple, sealed for time and all eternity. She still loved Evan. She knew Drake missed Kendyl in the same way.

This continued into the fall, and as group activities slowed down, Drake started inviting Paige and the boys over for dinner and a movie on most Sundays. He didn't mind Juniper tagging along, either. He said it let his girls have the fun of a pet without him getting stuck with the work of one. Paige would do the cooking, but Drake bought all the ingredients and did the cleanup.

"What do you say?" he asked. "It will be fun. The girls want to go in the evening this time for swimming in the dark. I guess I don't need your sunblock," he teased.

"I'm in," Paige agreed easily. "I haven't been to Crystal since I was in high school. Sounds fun."

"Great. I'll pick you up on Monday around five. Bring good snacks." He teased.

"See you then."

April 1, 2002

Always prepared and organized, Paige had packed a small cooler with Capri Suns, sliced apples, baby carrots, and no-bake cookies. She had showered and shaved, braided her hair, and was now trying to decide on a swimsuit. She had tried on three so far, which she realized was an excessive number of swimsuits for someone who lived in snow for half the year. She adjusted the final one and looked in the mirror. A one-piece navy and white striped suit with a rouching in the tummy area. She would be thirty-one this summer. She didn't exercise as much as she used to, but she kept in shape and ate well. She turned around to make sure the suit covered her completely in the back. The sound of the phone ringing made her jump and Juniper bark.

"Quiet, Junie," she scolded. "Hello?"

"Hey, Love," Jentry said across the line.

"Jentry! I love it when you call. It's always a fun surprise."

"I've been texting but couldn't reach you."

Paige held her phone away from her ear and saw several mixed texts. "My ringer must have been turned down. Sorry. How are you?"

"I'm good as ever. How are my favorite nephews?"

Paige laughed, knowing Jentry said this to each of them. "They're in Mesa with Papa and Nana for two whole weeks. They left Saturday. I'm dying without them."

"Enjoy the break. Get your nails done. Do something for you."

"Great advice. I'll do that. I haven't had my nails done in ages."

"So, I hear through the grapevine you and your *friend* are going somewhere special today."

"Oh my gosh. Who said something? It's nothing. We're taking his girls swimming. We're just friends. I keep telling everyone that."

"The lady doth protest too much, methinks," Jentry teased.

"Har Har. So funny."

"Seriously, Love, you have been friends for over a year. Friends who are constantly together. Friends whose children blend really well. Are you missing something that is staring you in the face?"

"Drake isn't like that. He doesn't see me that way. I'm just Widow Lindburg to him."

"Very interesting."

"What's very interesting?" Paige said, throwing a sundress over her suit and stuffing her towel in a bag.

"You didn't say you don't see him that way. Very telling."

Paige was about to protest when she heard a knock on the door. "He's here. I'll call you later."

The hot springs were surprisingly uncrowded for the first day of spring break. They found a spot in the grass on the north side of the pools to set up their towels. The setting sun cast a golden glow on everything it touched as it sank lower on the horizon.

"Help yourself to anything in the cooler, girls," Paige said, pulling out two water bottles. "You're welcome to juice pouches, or I brought you this," she said, tossing Drake the water.

"I do have a weakness for juice pouches."

"Let's get in, Dad," Ellie said, walking to the larger pool and sitting on the edge.

"Do they know how to swim?" Paige asked.

"Ellie does, and Issy is getting there, aren't you, Bug?" he said, tapping Issy on the nose. She smiled up at him from beneath her hair.

"Come here, Issy, sweetie. Let me get your hair out of your face before you get in the water."

Issy obediently walked over to Paige and sat down. Paige pulled a comb and some elastics out of her bag. Before long, Issy's hair was pulled up in two top knots. Paige looked up to find Drake smiling at her appreciatively.

"You've got to teach me how to do that. Let's get your wings on, Issy." He called to his daughter.

"Happy to help. I'll give you a tutorial someday."

They played games in the big pool, waiting for the sun to set. Sharks and minnows were favorites, eliciting screams from the girls each time Drake went under the water and swam toward them. Once the sky was dark, Ellie insisted it was time for the waterslide. The slides were two identical tubes that Paige had played on as a teenager. The smell of chemicals was thick inside the covered stairwell, and water dripped down the walls in spots. Dim lights lit the stairs as they made their way to the top.

"Me first!" Ellie shouted, jumping into the first tube.

Drake picked Issy up, but she reached for Paige. He raised an eyebrow at her and smiled before jumping onto the slide with a war cry.

Paige settled Issy in her lap. She held her arms tight around the little girl that, though almost six years old, was quite small for her age. Paige giggled and screamed as much as Issy did as they raced down the slide. She could hear Drake cackle as he exited the tube in front of them. She held Issy above her arms as they shot out of the tube.

Ellie was already out of the pool and ready to head back up the stairs.

"That was so fun!" Issy said, jumping up and down with excitement. "Let's do it again, Mommy," she said, grabbing Paige's hand and trying to pull her out of the pool.

Paige's eyes went wide, and she grasped for a response. She was equal parts touched beyond measure and horrified.

"That's not Mommy, Issy," Ellie said matter of fact. "That's Daddy's girlfriend," she explained before running up the stairs to the slide.

Paige and Drake stared at each other uncomfortably for a minute, with Issy still trying to pull Paige toward the end of the small pool. Then Paige picked the little girl up, gave her a kiss on the cheek, and, laughing, said, "What have you been saying to the girls about me, Drake Pennington?"

Drake smiled as he took a step towards her. He pulled her close, squishing Issy in the middle, and gave her a quick but tender kiss. "Something I should have said to you long before this."

He smiled at her with such affection she felt her heart melting. She wanted to wrap her arms around his neck and pull him close, but a persistent child was still begging for another ride down the slide.

"Come on, little Issy," Drake said, hoisting her easily into his arms. He winked at Paige and slapped her butt as she headed up the stairs in front of him.

April 6, 2002

Right now, I'm sitting in the brand-new Conference Center about one hundred feet away from President Gordan B. Hinkley. It was awesome when he walked in the room. This is my first time to see him in person. The last time I was in the presence of a prophet was April 1989 with President Ezra Taft Benson. It is such an incredible feeling to be in the same room as the prophet. I love President Hinckley so much. I know he is the Lord's chosen prophet. How grateful I am for my membership in The Church of Jesus Christ of Latter-Day Saints.

I drove down with Toby and my parents. Sally is watching Heather and Seth. I am praying Toby feels the spirit today and is inspired to try to live the Gospel better. He never wants to pray or read scriptures with me. He'll go to church but doesn't pay tithing or hold callings. It's heartbreaking. I want a worthy Priesthood holder as the head of my family so desperately. I asked him a few months ago if he would work on getting a temple recommend so we can be sealed before this baby is born. It isn't going to happen in time. Hopefully soon after, but he doesn't feel motivated. I told him it makes me feel like he doesn't love me enough to be sealed to me and that only made him mad.

The most beautiful choir is singing right now. President Packer gave such a lovely talk on children. He said "Children should not be ignored or neglected. They absolutely must not be abused or molested. Children must not be abandoned or estranged by divorce. Parents are responsible to provide for their children." It made me think of how Luke doesn't do enough for the children and how disappointed that must make the Lord.

August 5, 2002

"Thanks for being willing to go on a hike with me. I'm the size of a hippo, so I know I'm slowing you down," Hannah said to Paige as they started up the Jardine Juniper trailhead. Hannah had convinced Paige to take her on one small hike while Toby and the kids were at the annual Keller reunion. She had been trying to walk and go on small hikes throughout this pregnancy to avoid the weight gain she had with the first two.

"You are hardly the size of a hippo. In fact, I think you look healthier this time around. You're a beautiful preggers woman, no matter what you say."

"You only say that because you love me."

The Jardine Juniper trail went into a hollow at the base of Mount Jardine before winding up switchbacks that led to a viewing platform overlooking the oldest Juniper in the Rocky Mountains. The gnarled tree had been clinging to life on the side of the mountain for over fifteen hundred years. The eleven-mile round-trip trail was a popular destination year-round for hikes, mountain bikers, and cross-country skiers.

The trail had been a favorite of theirs in high school and was the trail Evan had proposed to Paige on. Hannah and Paige had both had their children on this trail multiple times. They were too young to hike the full eleven miles, but they knew the bottom half of the trail well.

Today, the plan was to turn around after the first mile. The incline wasn't steep enough to tax Hannah greatly, who was due in five days. She hadn't felt like she dared leave the valley and go with Toby and the kids to Island Park for a long weekend. But she felt like this easy hike with Paige would be one more step towards a smooth delivery.

"I know you swoon for your Pacific Northwest hikes, but you have to admit Northern Utah has so much beauty," Paige said, turning in a circle and taking in the views.

"You're comparing apples to oranges, which are both delicious, but one is better than the other."

"The orange," Paige said matter-of-factly.

"What? No. The apple. It's much more versatile."

They continued up the trail, jokingly arguing about fruit, before switching to baby names and birthing plans.

"I can't believe we're less than a week out and don't have an official name," Hannah complained. No one was as obsessed with baby names as Sally, but Hannah felt strongly you should have your name chosen before you went into labor.

"What's the hold-up again?" Paige asked, kicking a loose rock out of the middle of the path.

"Toby is on the fence about the first name and pushing for the middle name to be Ethel, after his great-grandmother, which I refuse to do."

"Tell him he gets to give her the last name and to mind his business on the rest," Paige said. "Evan was so great about letting me have final say on the boys' names."

"Evan was a gem," Hannah said, breathing heavily. "Drake is as well. I'm so happy you guys are together. Drake has always been the nicest...ahhhh!" Hannah screamed, clutching her belly as her uterus contracted. "What the hell? That was so...oh shit, oh shit!" A second contraction was followed by a flow of water. Hannah's eyes were wide with fear and pain.

"Hey, look at me," Paige said, "It's going to be okay. Let's get back down the trail. Breathe slow and stay calm."

"Paige, oh my gosh, I don't want to have my baby out here," Hannah said, trying her best to make it back down the trail safely.

"Think positive. Think about keeping your baby girl inside. And don't panic." Paige hooked Juniper back onto her leash and walked ahead of Hannah so the dog wouldn't accidentally trip her.

"Toby will kill me if I have this baby in the woods."

"He won't kill you. He's going to be too excited about getting her here. What are we naming her, Hannah?"

"What? I don't know. Toby and I can't agree." Hannah was trying to time the contractions while watching where she stepped so she didn't fall.

"You're the one doing all the work. What's her name?" Paige asked again, calmly.

"He really likes Taylor best, but I think Tandie is so...oww oww oww." Hannah paused through another contraction. "I like Tandie," she said, teary-eyed from the pain.

"Tandie. I love it. Okay, you focus on keeping Miss Tandie inside. We're almost back to the car."

Contractions were three minutes apart when they reached the gravel parking lot. Paige grabbed a blanket from her trunk and lay in the back seat. She helped Hannah lay down and then put Juniper upfront. She drove as quickly as she dared down the rocky dirt road before getting onto the highway.

Hannah started screaming in the backseat as another large contraction wracked her body.

"Two minutes since the last one," Paige said under her breath as she hurried through the winding canyon.

"Paige!" Hannah screamed, "Paige! She's crowning Paige. Oh my gosh. Help me!!"

Paige pulled the car off the road in front of the Wind Cave parking lot. There was no cell signal in the entire canyon. They were five miles from Logan and another five from Cache Valley Hospital.

Paige opened the back door of the car while hollering over her shoulder to some hikers coming off the trail. "We need help over here! We've got a baby coming and need an ambulance!"

A young college student volunteered to drive to Logan for help, while an older couple took Juniper away from the car so she wasn't in the way. A small crowd of hikers gathered at the sound of Hannah's screams of pain.

"Han, we've got to get your pants down because I think Tandie wants to be born here and now, and I'm ready to help. I've seen this in movies, and I've got you." Paige removed Hannah's clothing, talking soothingly to her.

Tears streamed down Hannah's face as she fought, to no avail, to keep her daughter inside. The body knows what to do in labor, and there is no stopping the inevitable.

"You're doing amazing, Hannah. Just keep breathing," Paige instructed, holding Hannah's hand.

"Paige, don't let her die."

"What? No, she's not..."

Hannah screamed again as the little head of her daughter crowned through the birth canal.

Paige had her hands ready to catch the baby when they heard the sirens heading their way. With another gush of fluid and blood, the baby's head was completely delivered.

"It's okay, Han. It's okay," Paige said through tears of her own as she cradled the baby's head in her hands. "You're both going to be okay. The paramedics are almost here."

The ambulance pulled up next to Paige's car just in time to completely deliver Tandie. The baby's first wail was met with cheers from the crowd of hikers. Hannah and the baby were lifted into the ambulance in what seemed like seconds later.

"Thank you, Paige," Hannah said through tears of gratitude and relief to her smiling cousin as the ambulance doors shut.

****

Paige knocked lightly on the hospital room door.

"Come in," Hannah said.

"Hey," Paige said, smiling. "How's our little girl?"

"She's so good. She's in NICU right now. They're making sure everything is okay, but my doctor said she is looking really good, considering."

"I'm so glad to hear that. Sorry I didn't get over here faster. I ran Juniper home and then showered real quick. Have you been able to get a hold of Toby?"

"My mom texted him as soon as she heard from you. 'Surprise! You have a baby now,'" Hannah said. "I don't know what kind of signal they have at some of those campgrounds. They were coming home tomorrow anyway, so I imagine he'll get the message before long."

"Where are your parents?"

"They left to grab me a change of clothes and make sure our place is ready for us to come home. They should be back in an hour or so."

"I talked to Sal. She said she and Sam are on their way. Jentry and Donovan are somewhere over the ocean, headed to Greece for a vacation. I'll keep trying her."

"You're the best. Thanks, Paige. In fact, I have taken your advice and given Tandie her full name. Toby will have to deal. It's already recorded in the paperwork. Tandie Alison Keller." Hannah said, taking Paige's hand.

"Alison?" Paige said. "You named her after me?"

"Absolutely! After all you did for us today, it was the least I could do.

The door opened, and a nurse rolled the hospital bassinet into the room. "Are you up for a feeding? This girl is hungry." The nurse placed the baby into Hannah's arms. "I'll be back in twenty minutes. We'll keep her in NICU until dinner, and then she can be with you. She's doing great."

Hannah looked lovingly at the dark-haired baby in her arms. "Do you want to hold her real quick?" she asked Paige, who was already washing her hands.

Paige took the baby carefully from Hannah and smiled through tears. "I have a namesake," she said with a laugh.

"I love you, Paige Alison. With all my heart. I'll never forget what you did for me today," Hannah said.

"I might need a new car now," Paige teased. "You destroyed my backseat. But having this little peanut share my middle name makes it all worth it. I love you, too, Han. And I love you, little Tandie Alison," Paige cooed.

May 7, 2005

The Minidoka Acequia Rupert Cemetery sat on a small hill five miles outside of Rupert town square. Sally had found cemeteries romantic since first reading Anne of the Island in ninth grade. She had been to some beautiful cemeteries, with carefully tended lawns and flower beds, sweeping views of mountains, rivers, and even oceans. This cemetery was plain, like the land surrounding it, but like all places of final rest, there was a peace that hung over it, even on someone's darkest day.

She sat in the front row with her siblings and father and listened as the ground was dedicated as the final resting place of her mother. She had her arm around her sister, Carrie, who cried openly, her head on Sally's shoulder. Their mother had been diagnosed with stage-four breast cancer five months ago. It had spread to her brain, liver, lungs, and lymph nodes. Even with aggressive treatment, she didn't live the nine to twelve months the doctors had given her.

It had never occurred to Sally she might lose her mother so young. She would be turning thirty-four this summer. Her mother had celebrated her sixty-first birthday in February. The world felt different without Ellen Johnson, who was still a part of it.

The family dropped yellow roses onto the grave before her father thanked everyone for coming and invited them back to the church for a luncheon.

The seven Johnson siblings milled around the cemetery, accepting condolences and hugs, as well as hearing happy memories shared of their mother. It was a surreal experience. Sally searched the area until her eyes fell upon her three best friends in the shade of a tree, entertaining her two youngest daughters. Five-year-old Sadie and three-year-old Salena were far too young to understand death, funerals, or what the loss of a mother and grandmother even meant. Nine-year-old Sariah and seven-year-old Sabrina, on the other hand, had been inconsolable for the last week.

Sally kissed her dad on the cheek and then walked back to her friends and babies.

"Thank you for helping with the girls today."

"It was no problem at all and the least we could do," Hannah said. "How are you doing?"

"Honestly? Going through the motions today. I shed my tears the night she passed. I can fall apart again after this once I'm home. I don't want to burden my dad with my grief."

"Aren't you the one always telling me not to fight all my feelings, Love?" Jentry asked.

Sally gave a small chuckle. "I am. Feelings are good. But there are places and times."

"I hope you feel safe to share them with us whenever you need. This is a big loss, Sally, and you're going to feel it for a long time. We're here to talk it out with you whenever you need."

"Thanks, Paige. Thanks, all of you. I love you guys so much. And my mom…" Sally's voice caught. "My mom loved you all so much, too. She was so grateful that you came into my life. She credits you three with helping me out of my turtle shell, and with finding the love of my life. She told me a few weeks ago she knew I would be okay because I had you in my life. Carrie doesn't have friends as cool as mine, so I promised to look out for her."

"Aww. Ellen was the best. She always made me feel so loved." Hannah hugged Sally with the arm that wasn't holding Salena.

"She was an incredible example. And an amazing homemaker. I use so many of her recipes," Paige said.

"Her jam. No jam compares," said Hannah.

"I think her rump roast recipe is why Donovan fell in love with me."

"Umm. I'm sure a rump is why he fell in love, but not a rump roast," Hannah teased.

"Little ears around!" Paige interjected, nodding at Sadie and Salena.

"Speaking of little ears, I think these little girls are hungry. Let's head to the church." Sally took Salena from Hannah, and the group made their way to the parking lot.

October 6, 2005

Jentry pulled the comforter up on the guest bed in the second bedroom and fluffed the pillows. Hannah and Heather were coming to Portland to celebrate Heather's thirteenth birthday. She had requested a Mommy-Daughter trip, and while Toby had been bothered in the beginning, he relented and agreed to watch the other children so they could go to Oregon. They would be flying in tomorrow morning. Heather wanted to go to the museum and then get lunch at The Old Spaghetti Factory. Jentry couldn't wait to spend time with them.

Jentry had kept her condo when she and Donovan married to have more room for her friends to visit. She kept her art studio in the third bedroom because it was easier than recreating it upstairs. She was glad she'd made that call now that one of the rooms in their place had been turned into a nursery.

After putting some fresh towels out in the bathrooms, she took the elevator up the five floors to her home. She slipped off her shoes, went directly into her room, and laid down, propping her feet on a pillow. After four miscarriages, all in the first three months, she had finally carried a baby into the second trimester. She was due on December third, and they had toyed with naming their daughter Noelle, but in the end, they chose Amia, a name meaning beloved.

Jentry had taken the first twelve weeks of the pregnancy easy. The museum had let her work fewer hours, and she rested often. Once they passed into the second trimester, they both started to get their hopes up that they would have a successful pregnancy.

Donovan had turned his home office into a nursery, moving his desk into the spare bedroom. They had chosen a soft blush pink color to paint the walls, and Jentry had painted a blue sky and clouds on the ceiling. She finally felt like she belonged to the same club as her friends.

Technically, she had been a mother first, having Elodie when she was in high school. She had been confused that she could get pregnant so easily as a teenager but struggle so much as an adult. A diagnosis of endometriosis after her second miscarriage had come as a surprise.

Jentry sent Hannah a quick text about how excited she was to see her and Heather and then went to the kitchen to get a drink.

"Girls, I'm home," Donovan said as he came through the door. He gave Jentry a hug and kiss and then lifted up her shirt and placed a kiss on her tiny baby bump. "How are you feeling?"

"You ask me every night," Jentry said, taking his coat and briefcase while he slipped off his shoes.

"Is it getting old?"

"Never. I like knowing you care. Dinner is in the oven and will be ready in about ten minutes. Hope you like warmed-up pizza. I was cleaning my old place today and went shopping for treats for Heather, so don't eat all the fruit snacks and nutty bars," she said over her shoulder as she headed into the kitchen to get Donovan a beer.

"I love how excited you get when any of your friends visit," Donovan said, kissing Jentry on the top of her head. "How is Princess Amia today?"

"Really calm, actually. I feel like she was kicking up a storm on Tuesday, and it has settled down considerably. It's a nice break for my bladder. I can't believe how tired this makes me. Don't get me wrong. I wouldn't trade it for the world. But there is a big difference between being pregnant as a teenager and at thirty-four."

"Tomorrow will be busy. Let's get you to bed early tonight. I'll draw you a bath after your gourmet dinner and then rub your feet as you fall asleep. How does that sound?"

"Like I've got the best husband in the whole world."

Donovan pulled Jentry into his arms and kissed her passionately. His mouth leaving her lips and traveling to her neck while his hands slipped under her hoodie and found her breasts.

"Donovan," Jentry sighed, "You say you're going to put me to bed early, and then you start something you know I'll want you to finish. Love."

"I can't help myself," he said, still nibbling on her neck. "You're too irresistible."

"Pause." Jentry walked to the stove, pulled the pizza out, and sat it on the counter. Then she took Donovan by the hand and led him to the bedroom. "I guess I can stay up a little later tonight."

October 7, 2005

Jentry rolled over and looked at the time on her phone. It was five o'clock in the morning. She lay there for several minutes with her hands on her belly, waiting for the familiar flutters of early morning kicks. Her first two pregnancies had ended before she felt movement. She had made it to thirteen weeks with her third and fourth pregnancies and felt the tiny little flutter of their baby moving inside her for a few days before miscarrying. It made the loss all the more painful. She was almost thirty-two weeks along with Amia and had enjoyed the flutters and kicks for over three months. After thirty minutes of feeling nothing, she nudged Donovan.

"What is it, Sweet?"

"The baby isn't kicking."

Donovan rolled over to face her, rubbing the sleep from his eyes. "What time is it?"

"It's five. She's always kicking this time of morning. She wakes me up two hours before I'm ready for weeks now. And I didn't think about it last night, but yesterday I slept until seven.

"It's probably fine. She must be on a new kicking schedule. Try to sleep for another two hours before we have to get ready for the airport. If you haven't felt a kick by mid-morning, we can call Dr. Ramboz."

"I get worried, Donovan."

"I know, I know. It's okay. Roll over and let me rub your back so you can sleep."

***

"Auntie Jentry!" Heather yelled when she saw Jentry and Donovan by the baggage claim.

"Heather, girl! Look how grown up you look. Beautiful too, like your momma," Jentry said. "How was the flight?" she asked, looking at Hannah as she hugged Heather.

"Short. Which was lovely. Thank you for letting us celebrate this girl becoming a teenager with you. We've definitely set a precedent. Poor Seth was so sad to miss a visit to his favorite city."

"You're always welcome. You could show up unannounced, and we'd make it work. Let's get your bags."

"We didn't check luggage, so we can just go," Hannah said, patting Jentry's stomach. "I knew you would be the most stylish pregnant woman on the planet. Tiny little round belly. Look at you. So sleek. I was in sweatpants every day by this point with all four of my kiddos."

"If I remember correctly, you liked sweatpants long before babies came along, Love. Anything you could exercise in."

"How are you feeling?" Hannah asked as they exited the airport and walked down the sidewalk towards Donovan's Jeep Cherokee.

"Well," Jentry sighed, "I haven't felt any kicking in a while. Donovan said I should call my doctor when we get back from the airport if I haven't felt anything by then."

"I'm sure it's nothing," Hannah said, but Jentry noticed the look of concern in her eyes.

After touring the Portland Art Museum and getting a behind-the-scenes look at what Jentry did in her curator position, the group headed to the waterfront for lunch at The Old Spaghetti Factory, a favorite of Heather and Seth's when they lived there. Heather stuffed herself with the browned butter and mizithra spaghetti and still had room to eat two scoops of spumoni ice cream.

Donovan dropped Jentry, Hannah, and Heather at Harrison Towers and ran into the office for a client call. It was a lovely fall day, so Jentry and Hannah sat by the Lovejoy fountain and visited while Heather waded her feet.

"How are things in Cache Valley?" Jentry asked while keeping her eyes on Heather.

"They're good. Sam and Sally have their hands full with four little girls. Sally is such a wonderful mother. She is so patient and nurturing. She never even trips up on the girls' names! Sariah is a good helper. She keeps Sabrina and Sadie entertained so Sally can focus on Salena, who is a little tornado."

"I would butcher those names if they all belonged to me. I worry about messing up every time I'm around them."

"It doesn't help they're all exact replicas of each other. They're the perfect mix of Sam and Sal and look like little cookie-cutter girls."

"How is her family doing?"

"Her dad and Carrie are struggling the most. But she says her older brothers are doing okay. She gets weepy sometimes, but mostly she's good."

"How are Paige and Drake?"

"Madly in love. They're somehow still in the honeymoon stage after two years of marriage. For someone who was so determined to never date again when she fell, she fell hard. So funny it was with someone she'd known her whole life. I always liked Drake best out of Sam's friends. And little Lottie is so adorable! She is a chubby, pink-faced cherub with the softest red fuzz for hair. She's a tiny little thing for her age. I think it was really cool of Paige to stick with the Jane Austen theme and name her baby Charlotte, so she had that in common with her sisters."

"How old is she again?"

"She'll be four months old on the twenty-fourth."

"I hope she and Amia will be good cousin friends someday. How are things with your family?"

"I'll have a teenager in three days, so I would feel old if I didn't have a two-year-old. Seth has gotten a little sassier lately. I'm not used to it. He was such a Momma's boy for so long. But he's still a good kid. Tandie is a firecracker. Heather was so much calmer as a little girl. She's going to give me a run for the money. And Tyson is the sweetest. It was hard to leave him behind for a week."

"You could have brought him. The more the merrier, Love."

"I thought about it. But I wanted Heather to have one-on-one time. I'm so distracted with the little children that I worry I'm neglecting her and Seth."

"And Toby?"

Hannah sighed. "Toby is Toby. One minute a prince, one minute a prick. He's been so hard on Seth lately. I don't understand what his deal is. He's always ranting on and on about how we don't show him enough respect. Maybe treat us respectfully, and we will. I don't know. Like I said, he can be a dream. I want my marriage to work, Jen. I want to be as happy as the rest of you. Sometimes I think I am. And sometimes not so much."

Jentry felt so sad for Hannah and so angry at Toby. How did she keep ending up with such pitiful men? She tried so hard to be a good wife and mother and her choice of men made it so difficult.

"I'm sorry, Hannah. I wish you weren't going through the exact same things again. Your husbands have never recognized the jewel they have in you."

"Well, I get beautiful children out of it, at least."

"Oh, I meant to call Dr. Ramboz. One sec, Love." Jentry picked up her cell phone and dialed his number.

"Hi Lydia, it's Jentry Dixon. Can I speak to Dr. Ramboz's nurse, please?... Yes, I can hold." Jentry smiled at Hannah apologetically. "Hi, Suzette. I haven't felt the baby move for some time, and Donovan thought I should call to ease my worry...Hmm. Today is Friday, so the last time would have been Wednesday morning...Really? Today?... Yeah, anything you have is fine...Oh. Okay. See you soon, then." She hung up the phone and rubbed her eyes.

"They want you to come in today?" Hannah asked, concerned.

"Yes. They say because of my history of multiple miscarriages, they want to do an ultrasound before the weekend." Jentry's voice cracked, and she started to cry.

"Hey," Hannah said consolingly as she moved to sit next to her friend, "Think positive. Calm vibes. What time is it?" She checked her watch. "Two o'clock. Let's get Donovan home and get you to the doctor. Heather and I can hang out. It's fine.

***

"Alright, Jentry, let's take a look at what's going on." Dr. Ramboz said as he dimmed the lights in the room and turned the ultrasound machine on. "You say it's been almost forty-eight hours since you've felt movement?"

"Around there. I hadn't paid perfect attention, but I knew it was Wednesday. It wasn't until this morning I realized I hadn't felt anything yesterday. I guess I was too busy getting ready for company to notice," Jentry said apologetically.

"Let's see what's going on," Dr. Ramboz said, moving the wand over Jentry's belly and studying his monitor.

Donovan stood behind him, holding Jentry's hand. Their eyes were locked on each other. Jentry held her breath, afraid of what she suddenly knew she was going to hear.

"Jenrty, Donovan. I'm so sorry. I'm not getting a heartbeat on this little one. I'll give you a moment and then come back to discuss our next options. I'm so sorry for your loss."

Jentry let out a primal scream as Dr. Ramboz left the room. Donovan pulled her into his arms as she sobbed.

"Nooooo!!!! Nooooo!!!! My baby. My baby. Amia. Nooooo!!!! God. No. No. This isn't happening." She buried her face in Donovan's chest and screamed at the top of her lungs.

"Let it out, Sweet. Let it out. It's okay," Donovan said, his voice husky with emotion.

"I killed our baby," Jentry cried, her hysterics calming but tears still falling heavily. "I should have noticed sooner. I should have come in sooner. Donovan. Oh My God."

"Jen, Jen, Jen, no. This isn't your fault." He stepped back and tipped her face up to his and looked her in the eyes. "This is fucking awful. But this is not your fault. These things... they just happen."

"I'm so sorry," she whispered.

"Please," Donovan's voice cracked, "please do not say that. I cannot have you blaming yourself for this, honey. It will undo me."

The door opened, and Dr. Ramboz stepped back into the room. Jentry laid back on the table and rolled to her side, facing the wall.

"Donovan, Jentry, these rooms aren't very soundproof, unfortunately. I want to assure you, dear, you are not to blame. Even if you had come in Wednesday night or Thursday morning we would likely be facing the same scenario. Mothers tend to blame themselves and slip into depression. I'll prescribe something temporary to help with that if needed."

Dr. Ramboz sat down on his stool and addressed Donovan as Jentry's back was still turned. "There are three options at this point. First, we wait for the body to naturally go into labor. This could take two to three weeks, and the baby will start to deteriorate in this time. Once active labor begins, Jentry would check into Labor and Delivery and deliver the baby vaginally with whatever assistance is necessary. There are times we can tell the cause of death, but it isn't guaranteed."

Jentry rolled onto her back and took Donovan's hand. He squeezed it and then brought it to his lips for a kiss.

Dr. Ramboz continued. "The second option is to induce labor. I would administer a pessary tablet or gel vaginally, but your labor would not start right away. It could take several hours. You would then go through the normal labor process. Holding the baby would be a stronger possibility with this option, as there wouldn't be the deterioration we find a few weeks down the road."

"I'm going to be sick." Jentry sat up, covering her mouth with her hand. Dr. Ramboz grabbed the garbage can next to him in time for her to vomit.

Donovan went to the small sink in the room, wet a paper towel, and wiped her mouth and chin. "I love you, Jen. We'll get through this," he said, his eyes red and teary.

"The third option," Dr. Ramboz continued, "is a procedure known as a D and E. Similar to the D and C you received with your last miscarriage. In this case, the cervix is dilated, and an evacuation tool is used to clean out the uterus. This is an out-patient procedure, where you are put under while it is performed. There would not be an option of seeing the baby in this case, as the procedure can damage the fetus in the process."

"Not that one," Jentry said with a sob.

"If we go with option two, how soon could an appointment be scheduled?" Donovan asked.

"I could administer the pessary tablet now. It takes a few hours before you start feeling contractions. You'd have time to go home and gather what you want to have on hand at the hospital. You could head in as soon as you start feeling contractions."

"You would throw off your weekend?" Jentry asked.

"Another Saturday will be here in seven days. My main objective is taking care of my mothers. Especially the ones who have lost their child. I don't tell all of my patients this, but my sister had a stillborn my first-year practicing. Her experience is what shaped how I approach my practice and my patients. I want you to take the lead on what we do next, and I will do everything in my power to help you through this dark moment."

"Thank you, Dr. Ramboz," Jentry said. "I think Donovan and I both want to start the induction."

Jentry had sent Hannah a simple text on their way home, so when they came in the door, the friends flew into each other's arms. Hannah was crying as hard as Jentry.

Heather stood back from her mother but reached out to pat her Aunt consolingly.

"I love you, Aunt Jentry. I'm so sorry about your baby."

"Thank you, Love," Jentry said while squeezing Heather's hand.

"Let's go back to our bedroom and talk about the next steps. Heather, help yourself to anything in the kitchen," Donovan directed Jentry and Hannah back to the master bedroom.

Jentry sat down on the edge of the bed, her hands on her belly, and continued to weep. "I can't stop crying," she sniffled.

"Of course, you can't, Jen," Hannah offered. "It's okay to feel all of this terrible grief." She wiped her own tears away.

"We've decided to induce labor now rather than waiting for her to go into labor in a few weeks." Donovan paced for a moment before sitting on the chaise lounge in front of the patio doors. "She was given something at the office to get things going, and contractions could start within the next couple of hours."

"I'm sorry, Hannah. You flew all this way for Heather's birthday weekend, and now..." the sentence hung in the air.

"There is nowhere I'd rather be than with you right now, my sweet friend. What can I do to help?"

"Jen and I talked on the way home. We'd like you to be at the hospital with us. I've already called my sister. You remember my niece, Kennedy, who used to watch the kids?"

"Of course. We love her."

"She's off at college, but her sister Magen is able to come over. She's seventeen and just as responsible as Kennedy."

"I trust you and your family, Donovan," Hannah said, grabbing his hand. "Heather understands what has happened. She said she doesn't care about the birthday weekend, only that we do what we can for our Jentry. She'll be fine with your niece."

"I'll let Emma know to send Magen over. We need to get some things packed and..." Donovan's voice grew husky with emotion. "I don't know all the things we need to do, Hannah."

Hannah stood and hugged Donovan. "You need a small bag for comfort items. Jen will be placed in a gown, but labor can last a long time. You'll want to be comfortably dressed, Donovan. Jentry shouldn't eat anything from now until the baby is delivered, but some hard candy is nice to have on hand to keep her mouth from getting dry. Jen will need fresh underwear for tomorrow. What she's wearing now will be fine to come home in."

Jentry wiped her tears and took some deep breaths. "Thank you, Hannah."

"On a more difficult note, you may want to bring a blanket to have her wrapped in, though I'm sure the hospital will have something. It's up to you, but you could take a picture with her if you choose, and I don't want you to forget about it at the moment."

"Will you do that for us, Hannah?" Jentry asked, taking her hand.

"Of course. I'll let Heather know what's happening and get some dinner figured out. I'll grab a bag for myself as well." Hannah started to walk out of the room and then paused. Turning back, she said, "This is the worst day you have faced thus far. And you've faced some hard days with miscarriages. Your grief and your sadness feel all-encompassing right now. Lean on the Savior, and lean on each other, and know this too shall pass. You will feel joy again. It doesn't feel like it right now, but you will."

<h1 align="center">October 8, 2005</h1>

Jentry's contractions had started two hours after they returned home. Amia Elizabeth Dixon was delivered at half past midnight, weighing one pound. Dark-haired and perfectly formed, she was wrapped in the pink crocheted blanket Sally had sent with Hannah and placed in her mother's arms.

"Sweet Amia," Jentry whispered. "I will love you forever." Jentry kissed the baby's soft head, which was covered with dark hair. Her skin was tinged blue, but otherwise, she looked like a perfect angel to Jentry.

Donovan and Jentry took turns holding their daughter and let Hannah take a few photos of the three of them, as well as just Amia.

Dr. Ramboz had been able to ascertain immediately a knot in the umbilical cord had tightened to the point of cutting off circulation to the baby, causing her premature death.

Donovan kissed Jentry on the top of her head. "I love you, Sweet. You can tell she would have had her mother's beauty."

At last, the nurse came to take the baby to prepare her for the mortician. Jentry became hysterical as the baby was taken from her arms and was given a sedative so she could sleep.

As she was being wheeled into a recovery room, with Donovan and Hannah following behind, she mumbled to the nurse, "Tell Dr. Ramboz I want my tubes tied," before falling asleep.

September 9, 2010

Oh my gosh. How in the world? I lost this journal when we bought a house in Providence a few years ago. I've been terrible at documenting my life lately. Maybe it's better in some ways, because my life has had a lot of trials and hardships the last few years. I really don't want to rehash or ever read about them again.

February 14, 2011

Happy Valentine's Day! This year I wanted to do more for the kids on this day. Sunday night after they went to bed I hearted the kitchen with over 80 construction paper hearts with little messages written on them in sharpie. Then I filled cute heart shaped boxes with chocolates and left them, along with a card, on everyone's dresser, including Toby's. For dinner we went to Rumbi Grill and for dessert I made Éclair cake. Sethy turns 17 next month and says he wants that instead of regular cake.

February 18, 2011

The weather has been crazy this week! It was 60 on Sunday and then snowed a foot on Wednesday. This has been the warmest, driest winter ever. Normally I wouldn't complain because I usually hate winter. But I went snow shoeing with my dad around Thanksgiving and loved it. So now I've wanted snow and there hasn't been any.

Tyson has been doing so good this week with going to school. It helps that I bribe him with candy bars. Yesterday when I picked him up he wanted to walk home by himself, which is so out of character for him. Tandie and I followed along in the van until he got closer to home. He was so cute. I put his name in the temple last week for his anxiety and I'm already seeing a difference.

April 3, 2011

Right now, I am at the Conference Center with Heather and Seth for the 4th session of the 181st General Conference. Toby stayed home with Tandie and Ty as church "isn't his thing" anymore. I love being here and being in the same room as the prophet. I love President Monson! Seth is struggling with his testimony and his friend's influence. I'm very concerned. He just turned 17 and he is off doing who knows what half of the time. I hope he will feel the Spirit today and decide who to follow.

I enjoyed the talks from the previous session and want to make many changes. President Monson talked about temples and said there should be a picture of a temple in every child's room. I think those might be their Easter gift.

President Monson just came in. I still wish I was brave enough to start singing We Thank Thee Oh God For A Prophet. Next time for sure!!

May 2, 2011

I had another dream about Morgan last night. It had been months since the last one. We were in the little shelter in the rain laughing and having a wonderful time and then he turned very serious and said, "Why do you keep choosing men who don't choose you?" I woke up crying. It's been two years since Toby cheated on me. I can't pass The Old Rock without thinking about it. How could he do that to me at the place we got married? At a landmark in the valley that I'm bound to pass or attend an event at for the rest of my life?

Toby got fired again last week. This is the second time in three years. Honestly, I think it's his personality as much as anything. Hopefully he finds something soon. There are six mouths to feed and a mortgage to pay.

He and Seth went at it again a few days ago. Toby knocked Seth into the wall and put a huge hole in the sheetrock. Seth ended up with a black eye. Toby says it was an accident, and he didn't mean to. That's what he said when he pushed Seth down the stairs years ago and broke his leg. It's always an accident, and never Toby's fault. My mother is constantly telling me to get a divorce. How could I leave him with two young children and two teenagers to care for on my own? I feel like I can protect the children better in this marriage. I don't have the means to leave. And it's not always awful. He can be so fun and loving to all of us.

I'm trying so hard to be happy, make the most of things and make my life work. Sometimes the darkness creeps in and takes over.

I absolutely love being a mother! Even on the hard days. But being a wife? Being married is not for the weak.

May 7, 2011

Paige laced up her new shoes and headed out the door for a run after tucking Lottie into bed. Drake and Issy were on the couch eating popcorn and watching Bob's Burgers together. The older kids were out with friends and not expected back for a few hours, so she decided to take some time for herself.

She was always on the go with five children. The twins, Ellie and Hannah's son, Seth, were wrapping up their junior year of high school. Once she and Drake had married, they bought a house on the bench in Providence. With Hannah in Providence and Sally in Millville, their children attended the same Middle School and High School. Sariah would be a sophomore this year, and her older cousins had promised to look out for her.

Paige had been called as the Young Women's President a few months ago. It kept her busy. There were fifteen young women in the ward, including Ellie and Issy. Paige loved being with the girls during class on Sunday and activities every Wednesday. Paige had thought Issy would be the more difficult teenager when the girls were little because she was stubborn and strong-willed. However, it turned out she used those traits for good. She took the teachings of the church to heart and Paige often overheard Issy telling Lottie Book of Mormon stories.

Ellie, on the other hand, had been pulling away for about a year. Going to church each week was a fight and she was frequently ditching Seminary. Paige was in constant prayer that Ellie would soften her heart and turn back into the little girl who loved the Savior and wanted to follow Him.

She had run two miles down the hill and was starting back towards home when the noise coming from a house she was passing caught her attention. She was positive she had heard chants of "Ellie." She turned around and walked back towards the house. Music blared from the backyard, mixed with the sound of voices. Paige crept towards the fence and cocked her ear towards the din.

"Ellie! Ellie! Ellie!" she heard a group of kids chant from around the pool deck. She stood on her tip toes and looked over the fence. At least twenty teenagers milled around, beer cans in hand. Standing on the diving board, chugging a can of beer, was her daughter. And next to her, cheering her on, was her cousin, Seth.

Paige had left her phone at the house, so she couldn't call Drake for help. She scanned the fence and saw a gate next to the house. She paused for a second, unsure if this was the right decision, then moved forward with the safety of her daughter in mind. She marched into the yard and made a beeline for Ellie. She saw her daughter's eyes go wide as she approached.

"You're coming home with me right now, young lady." Paige grabbed Ellie by the wrist and pulled her down from the diving board. She noticed Seth trying to make a retreat.

"Seth Russell, don't you try to hide from me. You better get home, too, because I'm calling your mother and reporting this. Tell your friends they're lucky I don't call the police."

It was a long walk home with Ellie sullen and unrepentant. Paige was shocked at her behavior and lack of remorse.

"Ellie, I'm just…just so disappointed. This behavior is not becoming a daughter of God."

"Oh please," Ellie said, rolling her eyes.

"I don't want to fight with you, Elinor, so please don't get sassy. We can discuss all of this with Dad when we get home, but tell me this: was this your first time drinking?"

"Yes."

"Did Seth give you the beer?"

"What? Are you trying to put this on Seth?"

"I know he's been giving Hannah a lot of trouble, and I want to make sure you're not getting dragged into it."

"Yeah, my cousin forced beer down my throat, and I had no say in it. Yep. Sounds just like him."

"This isn't funny, young lady. The Word of Wisdom is there for a reason."

"Don't start, Mom."

They walked up the rest of the hill in silence. When they returned to the house, Paige passed Drake on the couch with Issy and asked him to meet them in Ellie's bedroom.

After a heated discussion with Ellie, which ended in Drake grounding her for a week, Paige took a deep breath and dialed Hannah.

"Hello?" Hannah answered.

"Have you talked to Seth?" Paige said, getting right to the point.

"No, he's out. What's up?"

"What's up is that he took Ellie to a beer party. I caught him cheering her on as she chugged a Bud Light."

"Oh, Paige. Oh my gosh. I'm so sorry. I had no idea."

"No idea he drank, or no idea he encouraged my daughter to join him?"

"What? Paige. I understand you're mad, but blaming Seth, or by the sounds of it, me, isn't helpful."

"Well, Seth no doubt has access to liquor through Toby. I'm sure he's seeing it modeled all the time."

"Paige! What the hell? Is this what you think of my family?"

"You're the one constantly complaining about Toby leaving the church and starting to drink. You're the one who is stressed because Seth is rebellious. Now, your family's issues are impacting mine. I'm not trying to be mean. I'm trying to protect my daughter. If this is how Seth is going to act, then I think he needs to take a break from my kids."

"You can't be serious."

"I'm very serious, Hannah. This is very serious."

"I'm not saying it isn't. I'll talk to Seth. But I think you're being a little extreme and judgmental."

"I'm being a good mother. I'm protecting Ellie. Please don't make this about you."

"Gotcha. Have a good night, Paige," Hannah said tersely before hanging up.

Paige put her phone back in her pocket and rubbed her temples. This wasn't how she wanted things to be with her cousin, one of her best friends. But Hannah didn't have the same boundaries and rules that she did, and she was determined to protect her children and keep them on the straight and narrow path at all costs.

May 10, 2011

I had my septoplasty surgery yesterday. Did not sleep well. Woke up at 2 and slept fitfully until finally getting up at 4:15 for a hot shower before taking Tyson on the paper route. Couldn't take meds until after and felt awful. My nose and teeth just ached.

Went back to bed and then got up at ten to clean the house because Toby said I'm cutting into his job search time by taking so long to recover. Okey Dokey. He lost his job last month and I don't think he's been trying too hard to find another, but my recovering from surgery is a problem.

May 11, 2011

Spent most of the day in bed. Tandie keeps using the word pitiful to describe me.

Toby had a phone interview with Grandview Missouri. He said it went well. They'll fly him out if he gets a second interview. Watched some of The Muppet Show and old Flintstones cartoons in bed with Ty.

I talked to Silas about getting back on at Old Rock part-time while Toby finds something. Helping with housekeeping, anything. He said he'll call me next week.

What will our future hold? I absolutely hate uncertainty.

June 1, 2011

Cleaned the kitchen today. Toby went off on me because I had thrown away a message he wrote on a piece of garbage. Just a big douche about it. I get so tired of his tirades. He can be so condescending to me. This is his second or third time to yell at me this week. Then he wonders why I never want to have sex.

June 2, 2011

Felt pretty good this morning. Stuffy, but no pain really. Showered and got dressed and did my hair and makeup. Asked Toby if there was anything he wanted to say to me before the day got going. He stared at me a bit and then said, "Like what?" I said, "Like, I'm sorry." He said no and went back to what he was doing. Alrighty then. He has such a hard time saying sorry or admitting mistakes. He is so prideful! DRIVES ME INSANE!!

Just got into a big fight about our fight.

I HATE BEING MARRIED!!!

And if a shitty marriage isn't enough, Seth is really giving me a hard time lately. He is so defiant and angry all the time. Constantly making little snide remarks about me under his breath. It's heartbreaking.

Wonder where he gets it from?

June 14, 2011

Jentry's private art gallery, Dixon Designs, had been open for three years now. It was a small space tucked into the Pearl District of Downtown Portland. She and Donovan had sold their condos at Harrison Tower in exchange for a brand-new penthouse at Waterfront Pearl in 2008. Shortly after, she decided to pursue selling her own art full-time while also hosting up-and-coming artists from the city. She didn't need the money. They were sitting on millions in the bank, but she needed the distraction.

She had been in a depression for months after losing Amia. She couldn't get out of bed for weeks. Donovan suggested a trip to Utah to ease her spirits, and not even seeing her friends enticed her. Instead, she turned to her art. At first, her paintings were dark, ominous, and disturbing. Unlike anything she had painted before. With time and hours of therapy, they morphed back into the style she was known for: vibrant, colorful interpretations of landmarks in the Pacific Northwest. She sold a series of five paintings from that first year battling back from her loss, which she titled "A progression in grief." She donated the proceeds to the Endometriosis Foundation of America.

The ground floor of the space was the gallery, while upstairs was her office and her private studio. She was thinking of converting a corner of that space to teach art classes in the evenings. Her cell phone rang thirty minutes before she was going to lock up for the night.

"Hello?"

"Hey, Jentry, am I interrupting anything?" Sally asked.

"I would drop anything to talk to you, Sal? How are you?"

"I'm good. Life is good. Busy. The girls seem to be going in different directions at all times between dance, sports, and school. Sam jokes that we should paint my van yellow with a black and white taxi stripe down the middle."

"The girls would love that, wouldn't they?" Jentry laughed.

"I'll cut to the chase because Sadie is almost done with soccer practice. It's our fortieth birthday in July, which seems impossible. We're supposed to dig up the time capsule this year, but I got all of the dates for girls camp this summer, and I am booked within an inch of my life. I don't know how I'll juggle it all."

"Too bad you can't take all the girls with you."

"I know. Only Sariah and Sabrina are old enough."

Jentry heard the bell on the front door ring and turned to welcome whoever had walked into the gallery, but the sight of the young woman stopped her cold.

"Sal," she said in a hushed whisper. "Sal, it's her."

"Her who?"

"Sally, I think my daughter just walked into the gallery," Jentry said, trying hard to retain her composure. "I don't know what to do."

"Take a breath. It might not be her. Treat her like any other customer until you know for sure. Call me back as soon as you can. You've got this, Jentry. Love you."

Jentry put her phone in her pocket and tried to decide what to do. Standing twenty feet in front of her was the daughter she had given up for adoption twenty-two years ago. She was sure of it.

The girl stood staring at an Art Nouveau collection, her hands behind her back. Her long dark hair fell in silky waves past her shoulders. Her skin had the same olive tone as

Jentry's. The end of her nose turned up just slightly. It was like looking at her own profile.

The bell rang again, and a short Hispanic woman walked into the gallery. Jentry knew her in an instant. Sofia.

"Elodie, we've got twenty minutes until they can seat us," she called to the girl.

"Lovely. We have time to enjoy this gallery."

Jentry smiled softly at the sound of Elodie's voice. It was soft and lyrical. A higher pitch than her own. She felt frozen in place as she watched Elodie and Sofia interact.

As they turned to look at a different exhibit, Jentry saw the look of recognition in Sofia's eyes when she saw her across the room.

"Sofia," she said warmly.

"Jentry? I didn't realize…is this your gallery?"

"It is. Dixon is my married name." Jentry watched the girl turn from the paintings and approach her."

"Hi. I'm Elodie," she said, extending her hand.

Jentry took the girl's hand in hers, holding it for the first time. "I'm Jentry, an old friend of your mother's."

"This is a beautiful studio. I love the watercolor of Mount Hood. Great use of luminosity."

"Thank you," Jentry said, taken off guard by Elodie's knowledge of watercolor technique.

"Elodie fell in love with art in kindergarten," Sofia said, smiling proudly at her daughter. "She was a natural."

Jentry fought to keep her emotions in check. "Do you enjoy art still?"

"I dabble when I'm not studying or working. Nothing like the talent you have on display here," Elodie said graciously while also looking intently at Jentry.

Jentry was at a loss for words, so overwhelmed by a desire to pull Elodie into her arms. Could she see the resemblance between the two of them? Could she feel a biological pull towards her birth mother, Jentry wondered?

"Well, our reservation is ready. Such a surprise running into you after all these years," Sofia said guardedly. "I do hope life has been good to you, Jentry."

"You as well, Sofia. It was a pleasure to meet you, Elodie."

Sofia and Elodie walked out the door, and Jentry locked it behind them before pulling her phone out of her pocket.

"It was her," she started crying as soon as Sally answered the phone.

"Oh, honey. That must have been such a shock."

"Sofia came in right behind her. It was beautiful and heartbreaking watching them interact."

"Did they see you?"

"Yes. We talked. I shook her hand." At this, Jentry cried harder. "I had never touched her hand before. Never held her. The moment she was delivered, she was handed to David and Sofia."

"Did she know who you were?"

"No. She must have never heard of me before. She showed no recognition of my name. But Sal, she was my twin, my clone. She looked exactly like me. Long dark hair, dark eyes, olive skin. It was like looking back in time. Surely, she noticed the similarities."

"What will you do now?"

"There's nothing to do. Our paths didn't cross for twenty-two years, I doubt they'll cross again. She has a mother who loves her. They seemed so close. And she was healthy, happy, friendly and all of the good things. It's good." Jentry took a deep breath to slow her crying.

"What a good way to look at it, Jen."

"Thanks, Sally, for listening to me cry. I hate when I get emotional."

"It's good for you. Repeat after me. Feelings are normal. All feelings are okay."

Jentry chuckled. "I love you, Turtle."

June 16, 2011

The move to Washington had been a whirlwind. Toby had accepted a job as a project manager at Amazon at the end of May. He made more than he had been making before, but with the rise in the cost of living, they broke even.

They rented their home out within a week for three hundred more than their mortgage. They had found a townhouse to rent in Puyallup, across from a Mormon church building, which brought Hannah comfort. There was a nice trail across the street, and the children's new schools were within walking distance.

Seth had been furious about having to change schools his senior year. He was sullen and withdrawn, nothing like the little boy she had raised. It broke Hannah's heart to constantly be at odds with him. Motherhood was everything to her, and this change with Seth had her crying herself to sleep most nights.

It had also been gut-wrenching to say goodbye to Heather when they moved. She was now a freshman at BYU, easing into college with a summer semester and enjoying the fun and excitement of life on her own while she waited for her high school sweetheart, Noah, to return from his mission.

Hannah climbed on a stool to reach the cupboard over the fridge so she could unpack Christmas dishes. They had been in the house a week, and she had almost everything put away.

"I'm thirsty," Seth said, coming into the kitchen. "Do you have any soda?"

"I don't, sweetie. Only water and milk."

He sighed loudly. "There's never anything good to eat or drink here. I'm so tired of water and tuna casserole."

"You know, Seth," Hannah said, trying to keep her voice even, "You could consider getting a part-time job, and then you could buy all the soda you want."

"Whatever. I'm going to go walk that trail."

"Why don't you take your sister and brother? I bet they could use a nature break as well."

"Yeah, that sounds great. I'll go get them right now," he said as he walked out the door without a backward glance.

Hannah rubbed her temples and got a drink of water. Maybe she and the kids would take their own walk. She was tired of unpacking anyway. Toby wouldn't be home for a few hours. A break would be nice.

"Tandie, Tyson," she hollered up the stairs. "Let's go for a walk. Grab your shoes and scooters."

The kids obediently came down the stairs and grabbed their scooters from the garage.

"Should we go on the trail or to your new school?"

"Let's take the trail all the way to the park," said Tyson.

"Sounds good. Grab a hoodie in case it rains."

"Mom!" Tandie and Tyson said in unison.

"It's cloudy. This is the Pacific Northwest. There's a chance of rain almost every day," Hannah said as she laced up her shoes. "If it rains and you're cold, it's on you. Let's go, little bugs."

Hannah and the children crossed the main street in front of their community and headed for the Nathan Chapman Trail, which wound around South Hill Park. It reminded her of the Logan River Trail she frequented with the children, only instead of a river it was thick with pine trees and foliage.

Grey clouds hung low in the sky, something she was used to from the years she lived here with Luke. The kids raced back and forth on their scooters, hollering at each other, while Hannah kept an eye out for Seth, hoping she could get him to join their outing. As they approached the soccer field and playground on the far side of the park, the clouds parted, and what started as a drizzle quickly turned into an unusual downpour.

Screaming and laughing, they headed for the play structure and took cover under the landing by the slide.

"Who wishes they had a hoodie now?" Hannah asked her eight and nine-year-old children as she tickled them.

"Not me!" said Tandie, smiling. "You're soaked! A heavy shirt will make you colder on the way home."

"We might have to make some hot cocoa when we get back."

The children nodded their heads in agreement, and they watched the summer storm in silence for a moment.

"Do you two like it here so far?" asked Hannah.

"I miss my cousins and Grammy and Heather," said Tandie.

"I miss my friends and my old room. I don't like sharing with Seth. He's mean."

"He's mean?" Hannah knew Seth could be short-tempered with everyone lately, but he had always been such a good big brother to Tandie and Tyson. He had been eight when Tandie was born, and he was so excited to become a big brother. When did that change?

"He said if I touch his stuff, he'll punch me in the face," Tyson said, looking heartbroken.

"What?" Hannah asked, shocked.

"And he makes fun of me because, you know," Tyson paused and looked at Hannah pointedly.

Tyson had a problem with bedwetting and struggled to stay dry more than a few days at a time.

"I'm sorry, Ty. I'll talk to him."

"No! Don't! That will make him madder at me."

"Maybe we need to watch more Star Wars. Those movies used to always make Sethy happy," offered Tandie.

"If you think a Star Wars marathon could do the trick, I'll buy treats, and we'll use the Force to help Seth not be so grumpy anymore," Hannah said, smiling at her youngest two.

The rain started to let up, so they headed back to the trail and started for home. Tandie and Tyson rode through puddles, seeing who could make the biggest splash, while Hannah scanned the woods for a trace of Seth, to no avail.

Once home, she and the kids changed into dry clothes, and she made dinner. Tuna Casserole. A staple all of her children had once loved, but now she was sure would send Seth into another fit.

As if on cue, he walked in the door, and the first thing Hannah noticed was that he was completely dry.

"Where were you?"

"I went for a walk, I told you."

"No, we went for a walk and got rained on. Bad enough, we had to change clothes. You're completely dry. Where were you, Seth?"

"Jonah was out front, and we walked around the block and then went in his place for a snack. Okay."

Jonah was a boy Seth's age who lived across the street and had befriended him the first week they moved in. Hannah was glad he had someone he felt like hanging out with but was not happy about the dishonesty and defiance she was getting from him.

Hannah stepped out of the small kitchen and stood closer to Seth. "I need you to be honest with me, young man. Always. Honesty is incredibly hard to build back from once destroyed. I don't know what your issue is with me, but you are making your life harder by making me the enemy."

"Are you serious? You don't know what my issue is?"

"You won't talk to me, Sethy. You're shutting me out. No, I don't know."

"Hmm. I wonder if it's that you pulled us from our life to follow that asshole to another state."

"Seth!" Hannah said, eyes wide.

"That man has made your life miserable and made mine and Heather's life miserable, too. And you just take it. You take how he treats you, and you take how he treats us. You know what he was like to me as a kid. He might not hit me anymore, but that's because I'm bigger than his punk ass. I don't know why you stay with him. Or why you followed him to this rain-soaked forest. He makes you cry all the time. He treats you like a second-class citizen, and you just take it. You're a terrible example for your children." Seth looked at the bowl of food on the counter. "And I'm not eating your shit casserole for dinner ever again." He turned and stormed off to his room while Hannah sunk to the floor and cried.

After getting Tandie and Tyson ready for bed and settling in their room with a book, Hannah drew a bubble bath and grabbed her library copy of The Help. She was undressed and about to get in the tub when Toby walked into the bathroom.

He looked over her naked body with a smile and pulled her to him, nuzzling her neck.

"Toby," Hannah said, pushing him away. "Not right now. I'm about to get in the tub."

"Not right now? It's always not right now with you, Hannah. What's wrong with you? A normal woman would want to be with her husband. I'm so tired of you putting me off. Then you wonder why I look at porn."

"Toby, can we not tonight. I'm tired, and I've had a hard evening."

"You had a hard evening? I have to leave this house at six in the morning to catch the train into Seattle, and it's almost seven before I'm home each night. It's a long day for an ungrateful wife."

"I'm not ungrateful. I tell you all the time I appreciate how hard you work."

"You don't show it."

"Raising the children? Keeping the house clean? Making meals? Planning activities? That isn't showing it?"

"No. That's your job. You could show it by having sex with me more often and making me feel desirable."

"Oh, boy. The 1950's called." Hannah turned her back to him to step in the tub and felt her feet slip out from under her as he pulled her down by the hair. She hit the ground with a thump, whacking her head on the hard floor, and immediately started to cry.

Toby was instantly at her side, contrite and comforting, "I'm sorry! I'm sorry! I didn't mean to. You were just being so rude. I lost my temper."

Hannah rolled onto her side and curled into the fetal position. Toby hadn't laid a hand on her since the time he threw her on the bed. He usually only yelled at her. This was shocking and scary. It made her think of Seth's words earlier, and she cried harder. Less from the pain in her head, and more from the pain in her heart.

September 18, 2011

The sixteenth was our 11ᵗʰ anniversary. We celebrated Saturday since Toby had work on Friday. On Saturday, we took Tandie and Tyson to Olympic National Park. It was a fun adventure. Sol Duc Falls was gorgeous. After a few hikes we went to Frugals in Port Angeles. I wish Seth would have wanted to come. He and Toby fight all the time now. Toby used to be in his face and push him around a lot, but now that Seth is taller, it's yelling more than anything.

October 3, 2011

I haven't seen Toby since Friday morning. We're fighting again. We have such a love/hate relationship. No idea where he has been staying. Don't care either. It's more peaceful without him around.

February 4, 2012

Jentry and Donovan came up for a few days because he had some meetings in Seattle. They stayed at the Hyatt and the kids had fun swimming at the pool. We had such an awesome Saturday with them. We went to Pointe Defiance Park first. I love the park and those trails so much. We walked along Owen Beach and collected rocks. The sky was clear, and the temperature was 60. Next we went to Gig Harbor, a cute little harbor town. It was a chocolate art walk, so we got free chocolate at every store. We drove to Bremerton and took the ferry to Seattle. It was so great. Simply gorgeous! We live in such a cool place. Tandie and Ty had fun feeding the seagulls as they would fly alongside the Ferry. Even Seth was smiling and enjoying himself. Donovan has always been so good to him and was great at making sure Seth was included.

There was a passenger who was wearing a dog collar and leash. Ty was very concerned and curious about that.

The Seattle skyline was beautiful in the golden light of sunset as we came into the Port.

Living up here means more time with Jentry and makes my heart happy.

February 5, 2012

I left church in the middle of sacrament with Ty, who had a fever. He has had a fever on and off for a month. I made some yummy food for a Super Bowl party. Seth invited Jonah to watch with us.

February 11, 2012

Went to Mt. Rainier today. It was misty/rainy today and we never saw the big peak, but the drive and the park were so pretty. I look forward to hiking there this summer.

We had the Elders over for dinner. I was surprised Toby agreed. He goes to church for show a few times a month, but drinks and doesn't wear his garments anymore. I think he likes the social aspect of being Mormon but he for sure doesn't have a testimony.

March 4, 2012

Toby and I went to Seattle and had such a fun day yesterday. First we went to the Yukon Gold Rush Museum. Then we walked around the Pioneer Square area and did the Seattle Underground Tour. Very interesting. We had lunch at Taste Thai and then walked down to the waterfront. I love living by the water so much. We walked through Pike Place and then drove past U of W and across Lake Union before heading home. It was a very awesome day. I've been trying to have sex with him more often, so we don't fight as much. He can be so loving and charming when he's getting his way. Haha. Luke and I never had this much fun. It's a really cool place to live when you can go explore.

I talked to Heather earlier today. Noah has been home for a month, and they are having a lot of fun dating and getting to know each other again. She's head over heels. It's super cute.

March 11, 2012

Monday Tyson stayed home from school because he is struggling so much. His anxiety is through the roof. He is so homesick for Utah still. He also said the children aren't nice to him, and he has no friends. I have been toying with the idea of homeschooling for a few weeks, but Toby really doesn't support it.

May 19, 2012

I love our adventures here so much! Last Saturday we went to the Nisqually Wildlife Refuge, Yauger Park, and Percival Landing Park in Olympia, and hiking at McClane Creek in Capital State Forest. So fun! Seth thinks our outings are lame, so we don't force him, it just ends up a fight. But I wish he was seeing all the things we are.

Last Sunday was Mother's Day. Tandie and Ty brought me breakfast in bed. It was a bowl of Cream of Wheat with raspberries. Haha. They also had me go on a hunt for foot rub coupons. Tandie made me some cute pictures glued onto cardboard.

Seth worked right after church, so he took me out for Thai food on Tuesday. He finally got his shoplifting charge paid off. He's talking about joining the Army, which Luke is trying to talk him out of. Things are so weird with us. One minute he hates me, the next he wants to hang out. I'll take what I can get. I love my son with all my heart, but his choices make me sad.

Toby and the Littles and I went to Saturday Market. Very fun. We've had a beautiful two weeks of sun. We're making good friends in the ward and finding lots to do. I wish the children were all as happy as I am. I think Tandie is, but the boys still struggle.

May 23, 2012

"Good Morning, Beautiful," Sam said, kissing Sally on the shoulder. She stretched and turned over to face him.

"Good Morning, love of my life," Sally smiled at Sam, snuggling closer to him.

"Did you sleep well?"

"Like a dream. I think I was so excited about this adventure the last few days that I was wiped out by the time we went to bed. You?"

"This bed is a little lumpy, but I always sleep well with my Queen in my arms."

Sally and Sam had flown into Charlotte, North Carolina, yesterday evening and driven four hours to New Bern, the setting of The Notebook, Sally's favorite Nicholas Sparks novel. Sally had devoured his books the last several years and found his North Carolina settings charming and romantic. As their twentieth anniversary approached, Sam asked her how she would like to celebrate, and exploring North Carolina was at the top of her list.

After a delicious dinner of seafood at Persimmons, they had checked into the Courtyard New Bern and walked along Union Point Park, holding hands and talking about their plans for the next few days.

They had been married twenty years now, and Sally still remembered the thrill when Sam took her hand for the first time at the Paris Ice Cave. He still gave her butterflies.

Sam had treated her with love and respect from day one. He didn't care if she carried extra weight from each of the pregnancies. She was easily fifty pounds heavier than the day they rode four-wheelers in Bear Lake, but he made her feel as beautiful as he did the summer they fell in love.

They had a wonderful life together with their beautiful daughters. Sam made such a great girl dad. He was such a champion of everything the girls did and worked hard so they would have as many opportunities as possible. Sariah and Sabrina had been dancing since they were three. Sadie was their athlete, a star on the soccer field. Salena had tried dance, sports, and an instrument, trying to figure out what she was drawn to the most. Sally was so grateful to Sam for encouraging the girls to develop skills and talents.

"Sammy, I love you. Do I tell you enough?"

"That depends on if you think seventeen times a day is enough."

Sally laughed. "Do I show you enough? In words and actions?"

"Hmm. I guess you could show me in some very specific ways right now. You always look so sexy in the morning with your bedhead." Sam winked, and then rolled Sally on top of him.

"It's the least I can do to show you how much I love being your wife."

After a shower and breakfast at the hotel, they loaded their things into their rental car and headed for the Outer Banks. Rodanthe would be their next stop. Sam had reserved a room at the Inn at Rodanthe. They were going to ride horses, go parasailing, and relax on the beach.

"We've got almost three hours until we reach the hotel," Sally said, rummaging in her backpack. She pulled out a worn paperback copy of Nights of Rodanthe by Nicholas Sparks. "Settle in, my dear, you're about to hear the love story of Adrienne and Paul."

"I must really love you," Sam teased, placing a hand on Sally's thigh.

Sally smiled at him and placed a hand over his. "Happy twentieth anniversary, Sam. I love you with my whole heart. Thank you for bringing me here and tolerating my obsession with these books."

Sam squeezed her leg as she opened the book. "Chapter One. Three years earlier, on a warm November evening in 1999, Adrienne Willis had returned to the Inn and at first glance had thought it unchanged."

I don't even have words for the decisions Seth is making. He came home last night with a tattoo! I have spent his whole life teaching him his body is a temple, and he vandalized it with the Death Star! I'm so sad. Toby lost his shit over it. Screaming and yelling and threatening to kick him out. Seth threatened to move out as soon as he graduates to get away from Toby, which made him madder. That kid is going to be the death of me.

I've been reading the Doctrine & Covenants all the way through for the first time. I enjoyed it very much. I struggle lately with feeling like I'm not doing enough for my children. Seth's choices have destroyed my confidence in my abilities. He is so off track. His life is a hot mess and 100% opposite of everything I thought I had taught him. I feel so much guilt where he is concerned for so many reasons.

I just want to be better! I want to be MORE. I want the Lord to approve of my life and how I spend each day. I waste so much time on pointless things. Sometimes I feel like I have no 'wins' or 'successes' in my 40 years. I look at my life, my marriage, my children, my relationships, my callings, my health, etc. and I think "I can't get it right!" It's a shame sometimes I want exaltation so bad and believe the Gospel. I'm not serious when I say that of course, but life would be easier if I didn't believe there was a purpose to it. But how empty would that be? I'm so glad I know God lives, Jesus Christ lives, the Gospel has been restored, the Church of Jesus Christ of Latter-Day Saints is the Lord's one and only true church on the earth. One other thing I know is I am a daughter of God. He knows me and loves me. As flawed and weak as I am – God loves me. As much as I struggle with loving myself – my Father in Heaven loves me and believes in me...even when I don't believe in myself.

June 22, 2012

Sally kissed Sam on the cheek, cleared her breakfast, and headed to the front of the ship to stake out loungers for her and her friends. She and Jentry had come up with the idea of a family cruise rather than their usual vacation at Bear Lake or Cannon Beach. A Carnival ship seemed the perfect way to entertain children from ages seven to nineteen.

They had decided on one of the shorter cruises, with stops at Catalina Island and Ensenada, Mexico. Today was a day at sea, and after breakfast, all of the children had dispersed to various activities, with the younger ones planning on spending the entire day going down the water slides. Sam and the other husbands were playing basketball while she and her friends relaxed for a few hours.

She found four lounge chairs next to each other, facing the back of the ship, and spread towels across them while she waited for Hannah, Jentry, and Paige to find her.

Sally inhaled deeply and let the scent of the salty ocean air fill her lungs. She loved being with her friends and their families with all her heart. She had been so sad to see Hannah move away again last year. They talked on the phone a couple times a week, but it wasn't the same as seeing her in person. Her little girls had been thrilled to spend time on the cruise with Tandie. They missed her very much.

Sally was a quiet observer of people. She rarely spoke up about what she saw out of respect for the other person's privacy, but she had noticed some interesting things in the last few days.

Jentry had a sadness about her that she was fighting hard to cover. Sally was sure it was due to the loss of Amia and their inability to have a child of their own. Jentry had a wonderful marriage, was very financially secure, and was a successful artist, but Sally could tell something was missing. Should she suggest adoption?

Paige was struggling to relax. She had eyes on Ellie almost constantly. It had been a year since she had found her drinking, and she had confided to Sally the pressure she felt to make sure she raised Kendyl's girls well. Paige seemed suspicious of Seth and paranoid every time Ellie and Seth were in the same group, which was frequently, as they were the same age. Sally felt bad for Seth. Yes, he was giving Hannah some issues, but it would be hard to overcome them if everyone expected the worst from you.

Hannah's smile seemed forced at times. Especially when talk turned to marriage, or she witnessed sweet moments between the other couples. Sally was trying to be aware of not overdoing it with praising Sam, yet at the same time, she didn't want to punish him because Hannah's marriage wasn't what she had hoped for.

"There you are!" Hannah said brightly, sitting down next to Sally. She waved across the pool deck to Jentry and Paige, who made their way over.

"This is the life," said Paige, dressed in a gauzy pink coverup with an oversized straw hat. "Genius idea, you two. This ship is perfect for allowing family time and keeping the children safe and entertained. Lottie is in heaven following after the big girls."

"I can't believe how big she has gotten. Her little lisp is so precious, and I love those red curls," Hannah said.

"Seven years went by fast. She keeps me young, for sure."

"It's all gone by so fast. I remember holding Heather for the first time, and odds are she'll be married by this time next year."

"I wish she and Noah could have joined us for the cruise," Jentry said, sipping on Diet Coke. "I would have liked to interview him to see if he's worthy of our girl."

Hannah laughed. "Can you imagine if whoever our children are serious about had to be interviewed by each of us?"

"I think we start writing down questions now. Noah can be our practice person," Sally said with a laugh. "It's nice that you got to know him for years with them growing up together."

"It is. I'm lucky. He's seen her through a lot of good and bad times. As you all have seen me through good and bad." Hannah smiled warmly at her friends.

"Cheers to that, Love!" Jentry said, raising her soda can in a mock toast.

"Are you liking things in the PNW still?" Sally asked.

"I am so in love with where I live. It's so strange because Luke and I never did anything when we lived in Tacoma. This time, it is a whole new ball game. We go on an adventure almost every Saturday. Having older children and a little bit of extra cash helps."

"What they don't do is make it to Portland as often as they did when Heather and Seth were little, and I object," Jentry said.

"Forgive! Forgive! It's so much harder with children in school and sports."

"It sounds like you and Toby have a lot of fun together, then?" Sally pried.

"You betcha," Hannah answered with a touch of sarcasm to her voice. "When we aren't fighting, anyway."

"I'm sorry to hear that, Han, truthfully." Paige turned and looked at her cousin seriously. "Can I ask a hard question?"

"Can I stop you?" Hannah said. "Go ahead."

"Why do you stay? You've shared with us he has a bad temper with the kids and you. You've told us how critical he is of you. I mean, gosh, we hear it half the time when we're all together. He's left the church and isn't helping you raise your children the way you want to. I can't imagine alcohol makes his temper better. Why not leave?"

"It's so much more complicated, Paige. For one, I saw what divorce did to Heather and Seth. I don't want to put Tandie and Tyson through it too. For two, I don't have a degree. I don't have a great way of supporting myself if I do leave. Third, I feel like I can do more for my children in my marriage than as a single mother working outside of the home. And last, as crazy as it sounds, I love him. I mean, I hate him too," Hannah laughed dryly. "It's fifty-fifty. When he's in a good mood and being nice to us, it feels like all the bad stuff is in my head."

"I want more than fifty-fifty for you, Hannah," Paige said.

"I want more than that, too. Really. But this is what I know. It's what I knew with Luke, and it's what I know with Toby, and I'm fine. Really." Hannah was silent a moment. "We got in a big fight a week ago. He was so angry at me. I could see the veins in his forehead throbbing and bulging as he screamed at me. I had been out with the children and grabbed a burger without calling Toby to see if he was hungry, too. He was livid. He yelled at me about how selfish I am. Sometimes, I wonder if I'm the real problem. Two marriages, and I'm the common denominator, you know? Maybe I really am selfish and just don't realize it."

Sally's eyes started to water, picturing her beloved Hannah being screamed at. Sam had never raised his voice at her, never once called her a name or said anything unkind. "It's not you, Sweetie. I promise." Sally took Hannah's hand and gave it a squeeze.

"Thanks, Sal. On that depressing note, I'm going to go get some ice cream. I'll be right back." Hannah headed to the buffet area of the ship while Jentry, Paige, and Sally tried their best to change the mood and get back into vacation mode.

The day flew by. The smaller children came and went, checking in with their mothers and asking about meals, while the teenagers seemed to keep themselves occupied all day. The group met for dinner in the formal dining room and then decided to shower and meet back up for a movie on the pool deck. They sent the younger children off to save seats and met them right as Disney's Tangled started playing.

Sally and Sam sat with their arms around each other, her head resting on his chest, with the girls around them. In front of them, Donovan and Jentry snuggled under a large towel to keep warm from the ocean breeze.

Drake held Lottie on his lap while Paige sat with an arm around Issy. Sally noticed her looking around every so often, no doubt in search of Ellie.

Hannah showed up a few minutes late, and it was obvious to Sally she had been crying. Her eyes were red-rimmed and glossy. She walked past Sally to get next to Tandie and Tyson.

"Where's Toby?" Sally whispered as she passed.

"Drunk in a casino," Hannah said curtly before sitting down next to her children.

Sally was a sucker for Disney cartoons, and Tangled was a favorite, so before long, she was immersed in the movie experience. However, halfway through the movie, she noticed Jarom come and whisper into his mother's ears and caught the upset look on Paige's face. She watched as Paige loudly whispered to Hannah to join her, and the two of them followed Jarom from the pool deck back toward the state rooms.

Sally kissed Sam on the cheek, tapped Jentry on the shoulder, and the two of them followed their friends.

"I cannot believe you let this happen again," Paige said to Hannah.

"Let it? I can't believe you think I have any control over any of this. It must be nice to have perfect children."

Hannah and Paige walked briskly in front of them. Sally looked at Jentry, wondering what was going on. Jentry shrugged as they kept following.

They had chosen interior state rooms, the larger families needing two. The twins and Ellie shared a room across the hall from their parents and the younger girls.

Paige gave two knocks on the door, which was immediately opened by Ammon. They all walked inside and found Seth and Ellie sitting on the bed in a cloud of skunk-scented smoke. The two were so high it had been easy for Ammon to keep them there while Jarom grabbed their mother.

"Seth!" Hannah said, aghast, tears coming to her eyes. "What are you doing?"

"What does it look like he's doing, Hannah? He's giving my daughter drugs. Ellie, get in the shower right now. Seth, get out of this room, and I don't want you anywhere near my children for the rest of this trip."

"Whoa, whoa, Paige, Love. Take a breath," Jentry interjected.

"Take a breath? That delinquent has corrupted my daughter again!"

"Hey, don't talk about my son that way, Paige. He's not a delinquent. He's just struggling."

"There you go. Hannah and her excuses. Let's give awful behavior a pass because they're going through a hard time," Paige said sarcastically, using air quotes.

"Paige," Hannah started to cry and angrily wiped at her eyes. "This sucks. I'm sorry. But please don't take this out on me." Turning to Seth, she added, "Get up, young man. We're going back to our room."

"You should probably stay there the rest of the trip and keep him from doing anything stupid with any of the other children."

"You're not the boss of my mom, Aunt Paige."

"Excuse me?" Paige said, turning to Seth. "You will not talk to me like that. Get out of my room."

"Paige," Sally reached out and placed a hand on her friend's shoulder. Paige turned, knocking it off. "Not now, Sally."

Seth climbed off the bed and put his arm around his tearful mother. "C'mon, Mom. You don't need that bitch making you feel bad because of me."

"What did you say?" Paige asked

"Sethy, please don't make it worse. Let's just go. Paige, I'm sorry. I'll talk to him. I didn't mean for this to happen."

"You never mean for things to happen, Hannah, but they do. Over and over to you, because you have no backbone. You let your husbands and your kids walk all over you. Your life is what you've made it, and your children are what you've allowed them to be."

Sally's eyes went wide at the shock of what Paige was saying. She could understand why Paige was upset, of course. But felt like she was being unusually cruel to Hannah.

"Take her back to her room," Jentry whispered to Sally. "I'll help out here."

Sally followed Hannah and Seth down the hall towards their room.

"I'm sorry, Mom. I didn't mean to get you in trouble with Aunt Paige."

"Seth, she is the least of my worries. I worry about you, and your choices, and how they'll impact your future. Please be smarter. I know you have it in you."

"Aunt Hannah!" Ellie hollered as she ran down the hallway and into Hannah's arms, with Paige following after her.

"I'm sorry, Aunt Hannah. I love you."

Hannah took Ellie's face in her hands and kissed her on the cheek. "I love you, Ellie. No matter what. Promise me you'll make better choices, okay?"

"I promise." Ellie turned and ran back to Paige, who they could hear lecturing her on the way back to their room.

"Get in the shower, okay Seth? And then bed. Sleep this off."

"Are you going to tell Toby?"

"I don't have a death wish. No. Let's keep this between us."

Seth went into the bathroom, and Hannah sat on the bed, placed her hands over her face, and cried.

Sally sat next to her and pulled her into a hug.

"We ruined the cruise,"

"You did not! This is one tiny portion of it. It's a bugger, but we had a great time until this."

"Paige was so mean. I don't understand it. It's like she thinks I gave Seth marijuana and told him to smoke it with Ellie."

"She'll calm down by morning. Paige has put a lot of pressure on herself to raise those girls well after the death of their mother. It was the same with the twins. She got lucky with Ammon and Jarom, who were so easy from day one. Ellie has a rebellious spirit, and Paige and Drake don't know what to do with it. I think she snapped, and you and Seth were in the crosshairs. I know it hurt. It hurt me to hear it. But Paige loves you. Try so hard not to take it personally."

Hannah wiped her eyes and nose on the edge of her shirt and sighed deeply. "I'll try."

"The movie is probably finishing up. I'll grab Tandie and Ty and get them a snack with my girls. The kids were talking about playing some night games on the ship. Sam and I will supervise. You and Seth go to bed."

"If you bump into Toby, tell him Seth and I have a headache. Please don't tell him about this. And ask Jentry and Paige not to say anything either."

"I'll spread the word. I love you, Hannah. You're a good mother who loves the Lord and loves her children. I see your efforts."

Sally hugged Hannah again and then let herself out of the room. She wondered how everyone would interact tomorrow. She said a quick prayer for Seth, Ellie, and their parents and headed off to find Sam.

September 20, 2012

On the 16th Toby and I celebrated twelve years of marriage. We went camping on Mt. Rainer and tried to hike to Spray Park, but I fell and sprained my ankle! I was so upset. It hurt so bad, and I was so disappointed. Toby made me a crutch out of a branch. We ended up lying by Mowich Lake for a few hours with my foot propped.

Seth had moved in with Luke out in Colorado right after the cruise. He lasted two months and came back. He says he wants to get off drugs and get a fresh start. He has been drug and alcohol free since September first. Twenty days is still a victory. I hope he can stick with it. He still smokes, and stinks so bad. I make him go across the street. He's funny and inappropriate and has the mouth of a sailor. He has great ambitions but needs a job so he can go to college and make them happen.

A couple weeks ago Seth met with the bishop and asked to have his name removed from the church records. I'm heartsick over it. He doesn't believe in God, Christ or religion. He says such horrible things about them and their "non-existence." My only hope is that when he dies one of us can do all his work for him again.

October 3, 2012

Noah and Heather are engaged!!! I can't believe my baby is going to be a wife by this time next year.

Noah's family is from Cache Valley, and that's where most of our family is as well, so they'll get married in Logan. She and Noah are coming here for Thanksgiving, and I can't wait to see them and see her ring in person. She is thinking about a June wedding, so we'll have to plan as much as we can while she's here.

Tyson has started wrestling. He's had two meets and is fantastic. He has practice three nights a week, which is crazy busy. He gets whiney on Thursday because he also has choir practice with Tandie. They'll be singing in a Children's Choir for a Community Christmas Concert.

November 25, 2012

We had a lovely Thanksgiving weekend. Noah and Heather flew in Tuesday night. They fly back to Utah tomorrow. They are so cute together and he looks at her with so much love and respect. I'm kind of envious.

I organized a Turkey Trot on the Chapman Trail in the morning with friends. It was grey out, but dry, so a lot of fun.

We ate our meal at 1:00 on Thursday. I worried about being able to do it in my tiny kitchen, but I pulled it off. Made turkey, mashed potatoes, sauerkraut, stuffing, rolls, pumpkin pie, and raisin pie. Toby and all the kids went to see Skyfall, the new James Bond movie at 7:00. I stayed home to clean everything up.

Friday morning Heather and I went for a walk on the trail and just talked and talked. It was wonderful. I'm sure lucky to have such an amazing daughter and friend. We made some plans for the wedding. I'll go out to Utah for a long weekend in April to get stuff arranged and then we'll be back in June for the big day.

I called family and friends Friday to ask about their holiday. Paige didn't pick up. I don't understand why she is punishing me for Seth's mistakes. I asked Sally about it, and she tried to say Paige is super busy with the kids and her calling, but I don't buy it. We haven't talked since the cruise. What is that? Five months? We have never gone this long without talking. I'm still heartsick over the things she said to me, but I miss her so much.

December 26, 2012

Paige and Drake sat side by side on the couch, eating leftover pie and watching Holiday Inn with Bing Crosby. They had enjoyed the holidays and having everyone home before Ammon and Jarom left for their missions in the next few months.

Drake noticed Paige's phone light up for the fourth time in the last hour. "Are you going to get that?" he asked her, kindly.

"I don't know what to say to her, Drake. We haven't talked since the cruise. It feels so awkward now."

"I know you love Hannah with all your heart, and I know you regret saying what you did to her, even if you're too stubborn to admit it right now."

"I do regret it, honey! I was awful. At the same time, I don't feel like what I said wasn't true. I don't want things to be off between us. But I don't know how to get things back to how they were."

"My guess is if Hannah didn't want you back in her life, she wouldn't have called every day since Thanksgiving. We can pause the movie. Go talk to her."

Paige kissed Drake, grabbed her phone, and headed to their bedroom. Then, she dialed Hannah.

"Oh my gosh. I thought you'd never answer!" Hannah said, sounding emotional on the other end.

"You know how to wear a girl down," Paige said with a slight laugh.

"Paige, I...I don't even know where to start. I just know I miss you. I miss us and our friendship."

"I do, too, Han. I'm sorry for all those things I said. I really am."

"It was an awful moment, and we reacted. It was ugly, and I want it to be behind us."

"Can you forgive me, then? I was really mean."

"You were a total witch! It was awful. I cried myself to sleep for days," Hannah said.

"When I married Drake, I wrote a letter to Kendyl, which I keep in a box for the girls with other photos and mementos of her. I told her I would be the best mother to her girls and love them like she would have.

I promised to raise righteous daughters of God, and when Ellie started pulling away, I felt like I was failing Drake, Kendyl, Ellie, and the Savior. It was a lot. I shouldn't have put all of that on you and Seth. She was a big girl who could have said no."

"I bet there is so much pressure raising children who have lost a parent, and I think you've done a wonderful job. You were amazing on your own with the twins, and you're even better with Drake and the girls. I really respect you, Paige. You can handle so much with grace and style."

"You're a good mom, too, Hannah. I know you've had it hard, and you're doing your best to survive. Let's pretend the last night on the cruise never happened and go back to being besties."

Paige heard Hannah start crying on the other line, which made her start to tear up.

"I love you so much, Paige Alison. I don't want to ever fight like this again. I'm so glad you called me back. I'll be in Utah in April to do some wedding planning. Can we please go on a hike together? Just you and me. Get back to where we were?"

"Absolutely. I love you, Han."

"I love you, Paige."

February 5, 2013

The snow hadn't stopped since they left Cache Valley. Getting through Sardine Canyon had been treacherous, and UDOT was closing it as they came through into Brigham City.

Doug and Krisit had flown in for the mission farewell talks at church, as well as a brunch Paige had hosted on Sunday for friends and family. The boys had spoken so well, sharing their testimonies and their excitement to go out and spread the Gospel.

Ammon had been called to the Denmark Copenhagen Mission. Jarom would be serving in the Baltic Mission, covering Estonia, Latvia, and Lithuania. Both of them were thrilled to visit new parts of the world, learn new languages, and teach others about Jesus Christ.

It would be the first time the twins had ever been separated. They would be able to write each other letters, but they wouldn't see each other for two years. There had been tears last night at family prayer, as Drake prayed for them to be strengthened while they were apart.

They had stopped for breakfast at Denny's. The twins were sitting at a table with their three sets of grandparents. Drake's parents had loved them like they were their own when she and Drake married, and she was grateful to them for welcoming her and the boys into their family.

She and Drake sat at a table with the girls. She had her platinum hair pulled back into a low ponytail and had left her face makeup-free, knowing she would only cry it all off today. She nibbled on her French toast while watching her sons visit and laugh at the table next to her.

Drake leaned over and kissed her on the cheek. "You doing okay, P?"

She turned to him and smiled. "I am. It's hard, but it's a beautiful hard, you know? This is what I've worked for since they were born. I did my best to raise righteous young men, and now, here they are about to enter the MTC. It's a dream come true. And my heart feels like it is going to beat right out of my chest."

"You're doing really good, Mom," piped up Issy. "I thought you'd be a wreck."

Paige laughed. "We'll see how I do on the ride home."

They finished their breakfast, paid the bill, and headed to the restaurant lobby to say goodbye to their grandparents. Only the boy's immediate family was allowed to pull up to the MTC.

Jenny McLean pulled her grandsons to her and started weeping. "Oh, my sweet twins. I'm so proud of you. You're going to make such wonderful missionaries."

Grandpa Doug and Grandma Kristi hugged them next. "Your father would be so proud," Doug said, emotion in his voice. "Grandma and I are so proud."

After hugs and tears, the twins climbed back into the Yukon with their family.

"How are you boys doing?" Drake asked over his shoulder as he pulled out of the restaurant and headed for the Missionary Training Center.

"It's so hard seeing all our grandparents cry," Jarom offered. "It was so nice of them to drive down here in all this snow to support us."

"They love you very much," Paige said, smiling back at the boys. She reached back and patted each of them on the knee. They looked so handsome in their dark suits, with their matching haircuts and ties.

They turned into the drive of the MTC and stopped under the covered driveway to unload the boys' suitcases. A senior couple came out to assist and welcome them.

Paige placed a hand on each of their cheeks and smiled through tears. "My little men. I'll miss you with my whole heart, but I am so proud of you for making this choice. You have the most amazing hearts, and the people of Denmark and the Baltic will love you."

Ammon wrapped his arms around his mother. "You're the best mom. I love you."

"Me too. Thank you for getting us to this point. You did a wonderful job teaching us the Gospel, Mom. Hopefully, our example will mean something to Ellie." Jarom whispered. "I'll be praying for her."

After a hug from Drake and their three sisters, the boys headed into the MTC, waving at their family as they walked through the doors.

July 1, 2013

My girl is married! It was the most magical and busy week! Noah and Heather were married in the Logan Temple. They had their reception at the American West Heritage Center and had a fun pioneer theme. It turned out super cute. They are going on a cruise for their honeymoon and then they'll be back in school at BYU.

She was a little funny in the temple before the sealing. More uptight and anxious than I've ever seen her. She hated having her dress covered by temple clothing. Made it easy for me not to be weepy. Haha.

They'll be living in a tiny one-bedroom apartment in Provo while they finish school. Small, dark, but cheap.

I'm so proud of her for getting a degree and having the kind of grades to earn scholarships. One of my biggest regrets is not getting an education.

Seth got really mad at me for posting a Happy Father's Day "to the father of my four children" on Instagram. I know Toby isn't Heather and Seth's bio dad, but Luke is barely in the picture. He and his friend, Jonah, have a place in Tacoma, and I haven't seen him since the wedding.

September 3, 2013

Tandie is now a 6th grader and Ty is in 5th. They are growing way too fast! SLOW DOWN! There are only three other Mormon kids at their school. I thought it would be fun to read some books on other religions, so they had an idea of what other people believe.

we checked out some kid's books on Christianity, Buddhism, Judaism, Islam, Sikhism, and Baha'i. It was really interesting to see how many things were similar across the board, and how many were different. I've been thinking a lot about it lately and how strange it is that everyone thinks they have the truth. Everyone can't be right, can they? And if there really is only one way back to Heaven, why doesn't Heavenly Father do more to unite all the faiths?

September 20, 2013

I am really struggling lately with confusion, anger, frustration, and depression. I feel like everything I've built my life around and everything I thought about myself is unraveling.

My husband tricked me into drinking vodka, thinks Joseph Smith was a pedophile, and has stopped going to church, even for show.

Tyson won't go to church anymore, and says if his dad gets to stay home, he should be able to. Toby doesn't support me in getting the kids there at all.

Tandie is struggling with her faith. She confided to me the other night she doesn't say her prayers anymore because she doesn't believe God is listening.

Seth is delusional and hates me for something that didn't even happen. Tandie and Ty think drugs have made him crazy. He didn't last long at staying clean in 2012. He lives in some altered reality where he is a huge victim. He doesn't want anything to do with me and I doubt that will ever change.

I feel like nothing I did good as a mother counted. I feel like all my mistakes, flaws, faults, and poor choices have shaped my family.

I feel powerless to help or change anyone. I feel like I'm losing my faith.

I haven't been to the temple in over a month. What's the point? I went every week and put my family's name on the prayer roll. To what end? I can think of no blessings which came from attending the temple.

So, what do I do? Do I abandon the faith I've built my life around? I've had too many experiences I can't deny. Too many prayers answered. But why is so much going wrong? Am I not faithful enough? Am I not obedient enough? I know I'm not. Would it matter? If I was 100% who I am supposed to be would that change who my family has become?

October 4, 2013

I don't even know where to start with this week. Toby and I got in a huge fight a few days ago. I was ready for a divorce, but we were able to make a truce. He admitted to looking at porn that day, which usually proceeds a big blow-out.

On Saturday my mom called and told me she thinks I should get a divorce and she can't stand Toby. We talked a lot about it, but the reality is I can't do that to Tandie and Tyson.

Turns out Toby had been listening around the corner. He told the kids I wanted a divorce and I had to assure them that wasn't true. I sent them off to their rooms and we talked and talked. In the end we decided to stay together for the kids, but as roommates and not really married people. I told him I want to try and have a friendship, but I won't be intimate with a porn addict, abuser who won't seek professional help.

we both blame each other for so much and justify our actions. I don't know if we'll recover enough to have a "real" marriage. Then as I went to bed Seth texted me telling me off out of nowhere. He's so angry about his childhood and feels like I didn't protect him. It breaks my heart.

I just laid in bed sobbing. I'm losing my children and my marriage just died. I think Tandie and Tyson are doomed having the genetics of two crazy loser parents. I feel like I'm failing at life. I don't think I'm who I thought I was. I thought I was strong and hopeful and positive, forgiving and loving. I thought I could handle any trial and come out stronger. But I feel like I'm dying inside. Like any goodness in me has been beaten out with this last year. I feel like all I do is harm those I love. I don't know how to move forward with light and hope in my heart.

I haven't talked to my friends or any family in weeks. It's too depressing to think about their perfect lives while mine is just one struggle after another.

October 14, 2013

Tyson had a terrible skateboarding accident. He crashed and smashed his face into a cement barricade. He is really cut up and his lips are so swollen. Poor kid.

Things are weird with Toby, obviously. I think about all our good times a lot. I do love him. He's the father of my children. But I don't see things working out in the long term. Too much hurt, too many differences. I don't think either of us are humble enough to forgive, see our faults, or change. This marriage will end someday. Maybe not for ten years, but in spite of the good times and the love we feel, I don't see it lasting once the kids leave home.

At the same time, I wonder if I'm being melodramatic and blowing things out of proportion. Am I looking at my life through the lens of depression? I just feel so lost. I feel like Satan has been trying to destroy me and mine for decades and I finally feel defeated. I don't feel strong enough to fight. And I'm fighting on my own. My husband is not fighting with me. Seth, Tandie and Tyson are not fighting with me.

I have to find the strength to keep going. I can't give up. I have to raise Tandie and Tyson better than I did Heather and Seth. If I give up they don't stand a chance.

I'm full of grief and regret. I feel weak and flawed.

I only see what's wrong in my life right now. I feel so alone.

November 1, 2013

After straightening an already perfectly clean home and setting out a plate of meats, cheeses, and fruits, Jentry changed her outfit for the third time. She had gone from dressy to casual to business casual. She slid on pinstriped black slacks and pulled a white turtleneck sweater carefully over her head so she wouldn't smudge her makeup or add static to her dark waves.

"You look beautiful, Sweet," Donovan said, coming up from behind and wrapping his arms around her.

She smiled at him in the mirror. He was fifty-three and more salt than pepper. His eyes still crinkled when he smiled, though now with a few more lines than when they had met seventeen years ago. She still found him incredibly sexy.

"I'm overthinking this, aren't I, Love?" she said, turning and wrapping her arms around his waist.

"Just a little," he said, kissing the top of her head.

"I'm still so stunned she called and wants to meet. What if it goes poorly? I don't want to ruin anything."

"You are the consummate hostess. You'll do fine. Breathe. And smile. No one can resist your smile." Donovan kissed Jentry lightly and then again more passionately.

She melted into him, letting his mouth and hands take her mind off of the stress of the moment. "Mmmm," she purred. "I'm going to have to put on more lipstick." She reapplied her signature red lip stain and walked back into the living room.

The doorbell rang as she lit a vanilla candle for ambiance. She flashed a nervous smile at Donovan and opened the front door.

"Elodie. Hello, please come..." Her voice caught. Standing in front of her was the daughter she had given up for adoption as a teenager, who stood on the landing with a baby stroller.

Jentry stared at the baby and then back at Elodie, surprise clearly on her face, before stepping aside so they could enter. "Please come in and make yourself comfortable."

It had been over two years since Elodie and her mother, Sofia, had happened into Jentry's gallery. She had held no hope their paths would cross again, so she was stunned when Elodie called her two days ago asking if they could meet.

The young woman unlatched the carrier from the stroller and walked into Donovan and Jentry's penthouse waterfront condo. The fall sky was grey, but bright orange, yellow, and red leaves broke up the gloom. Elodie sat on one of the overstuffed chairs while Jentry sat next to Donovan on the sofa.

"Donovan, this is Elodie Mulder. Elodie, this is my husband, Donovan."

"Pleased to meet you," Elodie smiled warmly. "I'm sure you're both wondering what I'm doing here. I guess I'll... whew. This is so strange. I guess I'll just talk."

Jentry nodded encouragingly and tried to remember to breathe.

"When I came into your gallery that day, it was not lost on me how much we looked alike or how guarded my mother was. They had always told me I was adopted and answered any questions I had, which weren't many, honestly. I grew up in a loving home, I had a lot of extended family and good friends, and it wasn't until I was sixteen or seventeen that I wanted to know more about where I came from."

Elodie smiled at Jentry and continued. "My mother told me my Auntie Lucia knew a young girl who needed to give up a baby. She explained the young girl had no family support in keeping the child and had actually been encouraged to abort the pregnancy."

A tear slid down Jentry's cheek as she wondered how different things might have been those many years ago if anyone other than Lucia had been on her side.

"That must have been so difficult. Thank you for choosing to give me life and for placing me with David and Sofia."

Jentry could only nod and felt Donovan squeeze her hand.

"That was all I needed back then. I didn't need a name or need to know what happened to that young girl, until around the time I turned twenty. I asked my mother if she had kept in contact with you or knew where you were. She said they had sent photos of me the first year, but you had written them and said it was too painful to watch me grow up from afar and it would be easier for you to move on without me in your life. She wouldn't tell me your name to protect your privacy."

"I'm so sorry, Elodie," Jentry said, the pitch of her voice high and emotional.

"Please, don't apologize for anything. You did what you had to do." Elodie turned to Donovan, "May I please have a drink of water?"

"Of course, my dear." Donovan quickly went to the kitchen, filled a glass with ice water, and returned.

"Thank you," Elodie said, taking a drink, and then continued her story. "After the gallery, we went to dinner and talked about everything but what I had just seen, my birth mother. I didn't want to push my questions on my mother yet. She seemed shocked as well. So, we finished our day together, and then I went home and looked you up online. I found the website for your gallery and read all about your art. You're incredibly talented. I love the paintings you do of local landmarks. I bought a small print off of your website of Haystack Rock. I have it framed in my room. I found your Instagram account and looked at all the photos of you for hours on end. I look exactly like you. Even our noses."

"I was on the phone with my friend when you came into the gallery. I knew who you were instantly."

"I saw photos of a wonderful life with a happy marriage and what looks to be some really wonderful friends."

"Hannah, Paige, and Sally. We met in college and have been best friends ever since. And Donovan is my world," Jentry said as she looked lovingly at her husband.

"I noticed you had many photos of nieces and nephews but no children."

Jentry looked at Donovan and smiled sadly. "I was unable to have more children. I have a very bad case of endometriosis. We had four miscarriages and then a stillbirth. A daughter, Amia."

"I'm so sorry. I hope I wasn't out of line to ask about it."

"Not at all. I want to be completely transparent with you. You can ask me about anything. Please, continue your story," Jentry said.

Elodie took a deep breath. "Well, I was content to know who you were from afar until I became a mother. When I held my child for the first time, I thought of you, how brave you were as a young girl, and how difficult it must have been to place me for adoption."

As if on cue, a small squeak of a cry burst out from the carrier. Elodie pulled back the pink polka-dotted blanket, unbuckled the squirming child, and pulled a tiny, dark-haired infant into her arms.

Jentry placed a quivering hand over her mouth as she looked at her daughter and granddaughter across the room.

"This is Gianna," Elodie said proudly.

"She's beautiful, Elodie," Donovan said, wrapping an arm around Jentry, who was openly crying.

"I'm so…I'm so sorry, Elodie, Love. I don't…mean to be…such a mess. I never thought…I would see you…again, and then to see your…daughter…it's…everything to me," Jentry said through her tears.

"Would you like to hold her?" Elodie asked, her voice catching. She placed the little bundle into Jentry's arms.

Jentry stared in amazement and wonder at her beautiful granddaughter. "She's so tiny. How old is she?"

"Only two months. She's a little thing, isn't she?" Elodie sat on the ottoman in front of Jentry and Donovan.

"May I, may I please take a photograph of her?" Jentry asked timidly.

"Of course. I've got my phone right here."

Jentry held up the baby, a smile spread across her face as tears continued to fall. "Thank you. May I have a photo with you, Elodie?"

"Of course, I was hoping we could."

Elodie traded spots with Donovan, who took several photos of the three generations.

"Donovan, will you grab the photo by my bed and the box?"

Donovan returned with a framed photo of a dark-haired, pink-cheeked baby sitting on a blanket in the park. "Jentry keeps this by her bed."

Elodie's eyes went wide with recognition of her ten-month-old self.

Jentry nodded at the box. "I've written to you on your birthday every year. My whole life story is in that box, as well as all the hopes and dreams I had for your life. I didn't think I would ever be able to give it to you."

"Thank you, truly," Elodie said.

"Look at you, little Love," Jentry cooed at Gianna, who had wrapped a tiny hand around her pinky. "Donovan, can you believe how beautiful she is?"

"I can, Sweet. She has wonderful genetics."

Jentry looked up at Elodie. "Do David and Sofia know you're here?"

"They do. We had a wonderful conversation about the blessings of adoption and how we were meant to be a family while at the same time feeling you can never have enough people to love in this life. I'd like to be part of your life, Jentry. And Donovan," Elodie added. "And I would like for you to be in Gianna's life."

Jentry kissed Gianna on the cheek and reached out and grabbed Elodie's hand. "I would like that very much."

<u>March 16, 2014</u>

Today is Seth's 20th birthday. He hasn't spoken to me since September. I can't stop crying. I miss him with my whole heart and worry about him so much. He still talks to Heather, and she reports that he has a new job and a new girlfriend. I left a card with $100 on his doorstep early this morning.

I pray for his happiness. I pray he finds peace in regard to his past and present. I pray his heart is softened to us, and I pray our hearts are softened toward him. I pray when the time comes to reconcile I will be able to forgive and move on.

Now if only I believed prayer really worked. It doesn't feel like it lately.

Toby took me to the Space Needle over the weekend and wrote me a poem again. He hasn't done that since we were dating. He asked me to give him another chance at being a husband, and not just a roommate. It would be amazing if we could make this work.

Last weekend I went to Portland and got to meet Jentry's daughter and granddaughter!!! I can't remember if I mentioned they were reunited. It's the most beautiful story. Jen hosted a dinner for Elodie, her boyfriend Jack, baby Gianna, and Elodie's parents, Sofia, and David. It is so amazing to see how the Mulder's welcomed Donovan and Jentry into their family. Elodie is the SPITTING IMAGE of Jen in her twenties. It's crazy! She is so sweet and wanted to hear all my stories about Jentry. Gianna is the sweetest little baby. So cute and precious. Jentry is obsessed with her.

May 16, 2014

Jentry opened the door with a smile from ear to ear. "You're here! I'm so excited for this weekend. Thank you for making it happen."

"We have been waiting for this invite," said Sally, hugging Jentry.

Calendars had finally aligned so everyone could visit Cannon Beach for a quick weekend getaway to meet Elodie. Hannah had picked Paige and Sally up at the airport this morning and headed straight to the coast.

"I need a hug, and then I need to pee. I drank too much water on the drive over," said Paige, hugging Jentry quickly and then hurrying off.

"Everyone is so excited, Jen. And they're so jealous of me for getting to meet them first, which never happens with my life," Hannah said, laughing.

"They're out on the deck," Jentry said, leading everyone outside.

Elodie was pushing Gianna in a baby swing Donovan had hung from one of the rafters. The little girl was squealing and kicking her feet with excitement.

Jentry grabbed Elodie by the hand and gave it a squeeze. "Everyone, this is Elodie and Elodie, these are my dearest friends."

"She remembers me!" Hannah said, hugging her.

"Hi, I'm Sally, and I'm a hugger, too, if that's okay?" Sally didn't wait for Elodie to answer before pulling her in for a hug. "Oh, my goodness. I'm crying," Sally said. "It's so wonderful to meet you, sweetheart."

"Thank you, Sally."

"I'm Paige," Paige said, offering a hug as well. "Wow. Hannah and Jentry were not exaggerating. It's like I've stepped back in time and come face to face with Jen in college."

"Imagine bumping into her and seeing your own face," Elodie said, smiling.

"And this peanut is my Gianna," Jentry said, taking the baby out of the swing and giving her a kiss. "Look at this face. Isn't she perfect?"

"She's so little and cute. And look at all her hair! Do you want to come to Aunt Sally?" Sally reached her hands out toward the baby, who turned and burrowed her face on Jentry's shoulder.

"Oh no, she's a shy girl, isn't she?" Jentry cooed to the baby.

"How old is she, Elodie?" Paige asked.

"She's eight months."

"She'll be walking before you know it. Can you imagine how much childproofing Jen will have to do with all her fancy, expensive, artsy fartsy décor?" Hannah teased.

"You can hire people to do that, Love. Alright, let's eat. I picked up some Pizza a Feta a bit ago."

The group moved to the dining room, where Jentry had several pizza options, as well as soda. She held Gianna on her lap, kissing her frequently.

"Jen, I just love seeing you with Gianna," Sally said. "Elodie, thank you for letting Jentry be a part of your life. We watched her struggle through her miscarriages and then lose Amia in such a tragic way. It broke our hearts knowing Jentry had so much love to give. I'm so grateful you found each other. You know, I was on the phone with her the day you walked into the gallery?"

"You were?"

"Yes. She told me her daughter had just walked in. It was a miracle."

"It was," Elodie said, smiling at Jentry. "But initially, it was the shock of my life seeing someone with my face."

"So, Elodie, what's something that has surprised you about Jentry?" Paige asked.

"Hmm. Well, other than the number of high heels she owns, I would say for someone who looks like her, dresses like her, and lives like her, she is very down to earth and relatable."

"Right? I was so intimidated by her when we first met. She seemed so fancy, and I was a farm girl. It turned out we had so much in common, which surprises me still," Sally laughed and winked at Jentry. "Have you found things you two have in common? Other than being doppelgangers?"

"Art. Though I can't touch her skill level."

"Not yet," Jentry interrupted.

"She's giving me lessons. I was always drawn to art. My mom had drawings all over the fridge when I was growing up. Art was my favorite class in school. So, it was unbelievable to learn my birth mother was a famous artist."

"She used to give our children art lessons when we'd all come to Cannon Beach," Hannah said. "There would always be one afternoon dedicated to an art class. They loved it."

"Oh, I thought of another question," said Sally. "I promise we'll stop grilling you soon."

"Keep them coming. It's how we'll get to know each other," Elodie said.

"Did you know your middle name was after your birth mother?" Sally asked.

"Not at first. It was when I was a teenager and starting to ask more questions that my mom told me."

"Elodie Elizabeth has such a nice ring to it, doesn't it?" Jentry said. "Makes me glad I didn't have a horrible middle name like Maude or Bertha."

"I have a question for you guys, and then I need to feed Miss Gianna. One of the first things I noticed about Jentry was she would throw the word love into her sentences. Good Morning, Love," Elodie imitated, causing everyone to laugh. "She says she's always talked like that, and I wonder if it's true."

"Oh, here we go," said Jentry.

"One hundred percent not true," said Hannah. "We're having an activity a few weeks into school with our church group. A group of guys and girls from the ward would get together once a week. Anyway, this one night we're playing this charades, impersonations, improv game. I don't even know what the rules were."

"It was a free for all," Paige interjected.

"So, it's Sally's turn, and she gets a piece of paper that has Jentry's name on it. So, she starts trying to walk really sophisticated, like she was on a runaway. People are shouting out guesses and so Sal says, in this highbrow accent, "What in the world is fry sauce, Love? Portlanders do not dip their food.""

"It was the most preposterous impersonation. Yes, I had never heard of fry sauce, but we have ketchup. I'm not a snob," Jentry teased.

"Everyone knew who I meant immediately. I was so shy back then. Having all the attention directed at me was nerve-wracking, and I was grasping for something to say. I don't know what I was thinking with the accent."

"But it took!" Paige added. "To be funny, Jen starts using love all the time, and it just stuck. It became a part of her, and it's who she is now."

"We all tried to have a catchphrase after that. Paige's was Cheese Chicas whenever she would take a photo. It still shows up every once in a while. Sally tried to do well. I'll be hog-tied," Hannah said, laughing so hard she could barely get it out.

Sally was laughing so hard tears were streaming down her cheeks. "I barely understood what a catchphrase was. I said it four times, and then Jentry told me if I said it again, the only people who would date me were pig farmers."

"Oh wow," Elodie said, laughing along with everyone else. "That's amazing. I'm going to go feed Gianna. She gets too distracted if we're around people. I'll be back." Elodie took Gianna from Jentry and headed to one of the bedrooms.

"Jentry, she's so wonderful," Sally gushed.

"She is, isn't she? I love her so much. And the baby? Don't even get me started. Between you three, Donovan, and now Elodie and Gianna, and the Mulders, I feel like the Universe has given me more than I deserve."

July 4, 2014

Happy 43rd Birthday to me!!! Sethy texted me first thing in the morning and wished me a Happy Birthday. I cried so many happy tears. We're going to meet for dinner tomorrow at Dirty Oscar Annex. My heart wants to burst with happiness.

August 27, 2014

The kids started school on the 23rd. Tandie is a 7th grader at Ballou, and Ty is a 6th grader at Fircrest. Time goes by so quickly!

I have recently discovered podcasts and I'm really enjoying them. I was listening to one the other day about how our thoughts control our feelings. The woman said feelings are vibrations in our body caused by our thoughts. She gave an example of two women at church. One feels the spirit and one doesn't, based on their thoughts that morning and their individual frame of mind.

My question is, if feelings are vibrations in our body based on our thoughts, and we feel the spirit based on our thoughts – how do we know if we are really feeling it, or if we are telling ourselves we are supposed to?

September 23, 2014

I've read different accusations about the church over the years. By themselves they're easy enough to explain away or dismiss. To be confronted with a list, with annotations and links to sources, mainly LDS, confirming accusations and problems with church history and doctrine, has left my testimony shaken and my worldview turned upside down.

I don't even remember how I came across it, but I found the CES Letter by Jeremy Runnells online. It's about a hundred pages, detailing item after item that doesn't match what we've been taught. Some of the things I had heard before and some of them were shockingly unfamiliar. There is so much. Lies upon lies. To say my shelf broke is an understatement. By the time I finished reading I no longer believed in my religion.

I am feeling a mix of sadness, confusion, betrayal, anger, loss, and fear. I built my whole life on something I don't think is true anymore. What now? What do I trust now? What do I base my life on? How do I raise my children? What credibility will I have with them?

How do I tell Heather? And my parents, siblings, and friends?

And when?

September 25, 2014

I have spent so much time talking this out with Toby the last week or two. How did he go through this on his own? I was so judgy! I cried and cried. It is the biggest loss of my life. I gave everything I had to that church. The time spent in callings, the money donated to tithing. I want my time and money back! I based so many of my life decisions around the principles and doctrines of a fraudulent church. It's just so upsetting and heartbreaking.

We have told Tandie and Tyson because there will be a noticeable difference – not going to church for one. They have taken it decently well. We've told them they can believe however they want, and if they still want to go to church, we can. I'm sure their world feels rocked too, even though they weren't "all in" for the last few years. They knew I was. I hope I haven't lost all credibility.

I hope figuring out who I am outside of Mormonism and what I want to model my life after will be a grand adventure.

If the church is a fabrication I lose nothing walking away.

If the church is "true" I believe in a God who loves all His children and is full of mercy and compassion. This won't send me to Hell.

Assuming there is a Hell.

September 28, 2014

I laid in bed and cried all morning. This wasn't my first Sunday to ever skip church, but it was the first one knowing I'll never be back. My heart is split in two. I don't know who I am without my belief in Mormonism, but my testimony is destroyed.

I've spent my entire adult life trying so hard to please a God that turned out to be a fairy tale. So many of my decisions were based on trying to please him. My parenting, good and bad, was centered around trying to teach children a Gospel I now think is a fraud. Is anything I believe true?

I feel so untethered. So gutted.

October 6, 2014

Last Sunday Toby, Tandie, Tyson and I attended Lighthouse Christian Center. The people were super welcoming. I felt a little like I was cheating on my church. Everything is SO different.

<u>November 2, 2014</u>

I'm still attending Lighthouse. I have started going to a Women's Bible Study and I LOVE Jesus Music. Or Worship music, if you want to call it that. I love the sermons too. The pastors are so engaging.

I put a Bible app on my phone. I thought I knew the Bible – and I thought I knew Jesus...but I didn't. Sometimes I get a little down feeling like I've lost 40 years worshipping the wrong God. All that time! All that money! I'm a Baby Christian trying to wrap my mind around Grace.

I have read Unveiling Grace by Lynn Wilder, a former BYU Professor who is now a Biblical Christian. Very interesting. Their family all left the church. I love them because their message is so loving, whereas CES Letter had some snark.

Last week I decided to bite the bullet and tell the people in my life I have left the church.

My heart hurt for Heather, who in a moment became the only Mormon in the family. She wondered why I went looking for negative things and holds out hope I'll return.

Seth told me he was proud of me for having the courage to leave.

My parents took it better than I expected. Dad was really calm and kind. He suggested I not go fully public yet. My guess is he hopes this will pass. Mom is worried about what the relatives will say, as usual. I asked them not to tell Sam and Esther until I get a chance to at Thanksgiving. Mom does keep sending me articles about staying in the faith. I understand where she's coming from, and also hate it. Haha.

November 26, 2014

Toby had insisted they spend Thanksgiving day with his family. Admittedly, when they lived in Utah, they spent much more time with Hannah's family and friends. Her side planned things in advance, and it was a lot of fun. The Keller's were wonderfully nice people, but there was a lack of organization and communication that could drive her crazy.

They had flown in last night. Heather and Noah picked them up at the airport and drove them to Cache Valley. They were staying with Noah's family but spending as much free time as possible with her. Marriage looked good on Heather. She was happy and bubbly and had only praise for her husband.

They had a tradition of seeing a matinee on Thanksgiving and decided to go on Wednesday since a movie wasn't in the plans at the Keller's. Toby took Seth and Noah to see Interstellar, while Heather took Tandie and Tyson to see Penguins of Madagascar.

Hannah had decided to use this two-hour window to talk to her friends about leaving the church. She was ready to rip off the band-aid.

She met Sam, Sally, Drake, and Paige for lunch at The Bluebird, a vintage Logan restaurant. The strawberry chicken was one of her favorite dishes, along with the homemade rolls.

"Thanks for fitting this in, guys," she said. "I'm sure you're all busy with holiday plans."

"It would be easier if you skipped the in-laws, Sis. We don't get to see you enough as it is."

"I know. I tried. Toby was adamant his family had a turn. Are you running up to Rupert Friday?"

"Of course," Sally said. "It's a must. The girls love it as much as I do."

"What about you guys?" Hannah asked Paige and Drake.

"Another holiday without the boys, which is tough, but we're making the most of it. Drake's parents have reserved a few rooms in Ogden Friday night, and we're taking the kids to Fat Cats. Ellie works, but Issy and Lottie are really excited."

"That will be amazing. Would you ever try the surfing thing they have?"

"Not on your life," Paige said with a laugh.

"I wish we had more time with you, Hannah. The four of us have started doing a temple session every Tuesday night. It would have been so nice if you could have joined us." Sally said.

Here we go, thought Hannah, taking a deep breath. "About that. There's something I wanted to talk to you guys about in person." She paused and took a drink of water, feeling like her mouth had gone dry.

"Go ahead, Han," Sam said encouragingly.

"There isn't a super easy way to say this, and I want to keep it simple, so, umm, I've left the church. It's been a few months, and it was really sad at first, devastating, actually, but I'm doing really well now." She looked at their faces, trying to gauge their reactions.

"That's…that's a shock, Sis. I didn't see that one coming," Sam said. "I'm here if you want to talk or if you need resources to help you find your way back."

Sam had been the bishop of their ward for two years, and his response was about what Hannah expected. She had zero interest in finding her way back but smiled politely at the offer.

Sally reached her hand across the table and squeezed Hannah's. "I love you, Hannah. No matter where you sit on Sunday. I believe in the church with my whole heart, and I'm sad you have lost your way, but it doesn't change our friendship."

"Thanks, Sal. That means a lot to me." Hannah ignored the 'lost your way' comment, knowing Sally meant no harm, and turned and looked at Paige expectantly.

Paige sat for a moment, looking at her hands in her lap. "I assume you brought us to a public spot to try to control our reaction?" Paige said tersely.

"What? No. I just thought lunch would be nice."

"Nice? A nice lunch doesn't involve you telling us you've given up on everything you believe in. I'm stunned, Hannah. This is not the cousin I know."

"You're right, Paige. It's not the me you know. It's a new me, on a new path, and I'm trying to be honest with you about it so we can have a productive conversation."

"You know what, Hannah? I don't know anyone who has left the church and gone on to have a meaningful and purposeful life. You're selling yourself short. Throwing away your salvation and that of your family for what?"

"Paige," Sally tried to interrupt.

Paige put a hand up towards Sally and kept talking. "You have been backsliding on your resolve and covenants for years, and it's been heartbreaking to watch. You've had no rules or standards for your marriage or your children."

"Paige, stop," Hannah said, leaning across the table. "You have no idea how hard I've worked for my family.

Just because we aren't perfect, like you apparently are, doesn't mean I haven't been trying."

"So why give up now? Did Toby finally wear you down? Do you drink with him now? And who knows what else to keep him happy?"

"Hey," Sam said defensively.

"Nice, Paige. Nice. Real classy. Keep it coming. Let me have it."

"P, sweetie, maybe you better take a breath," Drake said, putting an arm around Paige, who immediately shrugged it off.

"My boys are on the other side of the world, sacrificing so much to bring the truth to others. A truth you have had your whole life, and now you're throwing it away? You've been poisoned, Hannah. By Toby, by Seth, by whatever dark path you have gone down which has led you here."

"This has nothing to do with Toby, Paige. Do you honestly think I would walk away from everything I knew for him? If that was the case, I would have done it years ago. I think I'm strong enough to follow my own path."

"You aren't strong at all, Hannah. You're weak. You're a little puppy dog following after your loser husband, and I've lost all respect for you."

Hannah heard Sally gasp but couldn't look at her or Sam. She took twenty dollars out of her purse and threw it on the table. This wasn't the first time Paige had verbally attacked and insulted her, but this time, she wouldn't be begging for Paige's forgiveness and affection.

"You know what, Paige? Fuck you. I'm so damn sick and tired of how judgmental and cruel you are about my life and my family." Hannah turned and walked out of the restaurant without looking back. She walked down the street and got into her mother's car before falling apart.

December 17, 2014

One week until Christmas Eve.

I haven't felt much like writing since Thanksgiving. I'm still so livid at Paige, who was an absolute jerk to me about leaving the church. I'm so tired of her self-righteousness.

I saw Esther the day after Thanksgiving and told her. She cried, and said she'd keep me in her prayers, but she didn't call me a poisoned puppy dog, so that's a win.

I called Jentry last week to talk to her about it and she confessed she hasn't been an active member since she moved back to Portland in her twenties! I had suspicions, but I wasn't sure. She didn't have the whole faith crisis like me. She just lost interest. She apologized for not telling us, but said she'd been afraid of the reaction. Based on what a bitch Paige was, I don't blame her. We decided it was best if she didn't "come out" right now to the group, because we didn't want Paige thinking I influenced her or something stupid.

I've been meeting with my Lighthouse Christian Center Mentor. She is such a nice lady. Last week we met at a Christian bookstore and spoke for an hour with one of the owners, who is a Paster. I have so many questions. I'm trying to sort what the Bible says against what the Mormon Church says. Is there truth in anything I was taught my whole life? Turns out some of the bigger things I believed in were made up by Jospeh Smith.

One really amazing thing to come out of this faith transition is that I have a newfound love and appreciation for myself. Years and years of shame and guilt have melted away. I don't feel like I fall short on everything anymore.

Toby was fired from Amazon. This is his third firing and I'm so over it. Apparently there were three women who complained about him being inappropriate with them. I'm not surprised. He has no boundaries and is way too friendly. Heather and Seth used to talk all the time about how they would see him creep on girls. Some of Heather's friends wouldn't come to our house because of it. So that's fun. A year ago, Sam pulled me aside and said his girls didn't want hugs from Uncle Toby anymore. So embarrassing. Anyway, he is looking for a new job at the worst time of year.

January 2, 2015

We had a quiet New Year's with Toby, Tandie, Ty and me. I made a bunch of appetizers and desserts, and we had a Harry Potter marathon.

Seth called me this morning and was very excited because he was one-year meth free. No drugs at all. He has worked really hard to get clean. Well, I mean, he still drinks and vapes, but not like he used to. I'm proud of him. It's hard to believe he once went a whole year without talking to me. We're very close now. He doesn't think much of Toby, and has a lot of anger there, but he is respectful to him out of love for me. Next week he's starting the EMT program at Pierce College. He's trying to decide between being a paramedic or a firefighter. I think that will be a great career for him.

January 7, 2015

Toby got a job with Starbucks. He'll be working at the warehouse in Kent, so he has a long commute still. But it's more money, which is a miracle. I've been working as a day shift lead at the Starbucks by our house for about five months, so that's kind of funny. I'm part-time right now, but the kids are old enough I'm going to try to go to full-time soon. I want some extra spending money. Toby can be so controlling with the money he makes.

July 19, 2015

The green of spring was fading to the browns of summer in Cache Valley, with the last bits of snow clinging to the Wellsville Mountains. The sky was dotted with clouds, which reminded Sally of cotton balls. The slightest breeze rustled the trees in her backyard, taking the edge off the warm evening. Family and friends milled around the backyard, enjoying cupcakes and visiting. Sally's heart was so full of love and gratitude for the support being shown to Sariah.

"Are we ready?" Sam asked, coming up behind her.

"Yes. Where's Sariah?"

Sam scanned the yard. "Talking to Paige, Heather, and Aunt Jenny." Sam got Sariah's attention and motioned her over.

"Ready?" he asked, hugging their oldest daughter.

"Yes," Sariah said, with a huge smile on her face.

"Hey, everybody," Sam said loudly, getting the large group's attention. "We want to thank all of you for coming out here tonight. Some of you have driven hours to hear this, and it means a lot to Sally and me, and I know it means a lot to Sariah." Sam paused as his voice caught. "Being a father of four girls has made me such an emotional man," he joked. "We're so proud of Sariah for making this choice and for the example she is setting for her sisters. Now, I'll stop talking and turn the time over to her."

"Hi everyone!" Sariah said, smiling at so many of their loved ones. "Like my dad said, thanks for coming out tonight. I'm really excited to share this moment with you."

Sariah opened the envelope in her hand, pulled out a crisp piece of paper, and began to read.

"Dear Sister Limbrey, You are hereby called to serve as a missionary for The Church of Jesus Christ of Latter-Day Saints. You are assigned to labor in the South Carolina Columbia mission." Sariah paused as the crowd clapped and cheered, and then continued. "It is anticipated that you will serve for a period of eighteen months. You should report to the Provo Missionary Training Center on Tuesday, September 2, 2015."

Sariah mingled and visited with family and friends for another hour, receiving many tips for making the most of her mission. It made Sally smile to see her oldest daughter so happy about her call and excited to serve the Lord.

"Congratulations, Cousin!" Heather said, hugging Sariah. "Is it both Carolina's you love, Aunt Sally?"

"North Carolina is where we went for our anniversary, but I've always wanted to go to Charleston."

"Wouldn't the coast be a dreamy place to serve," Sariah said. "Thanks for coming up for this. That was really nice of you and Noah. You look so cute with your little tummy."

"That's nice of you to say. It's growing, for sure. And Provo isn't too far a drive. It's always nice to see everyone."

"Sally, how are our children older than we were when we met?" Paige said, coming alongside Heather and giving her a side hug. "Time is flying by! Heather is married. We have two returned missionaries, and one about to go out."

"Don't forget Aunt Jentry is a grandma now," Sariah said with a smile.

"You don't need to remind me. Mom can't wait to be a Nana," Heather laughed. "She wanted me to wait until I graduated. We'll cut it close. He'll be born a month before I finish my degree."

"Good girl. Get your degree. Oh dear. I've got to stop Lottie from eating another cupcake," Paige said, hurrying towards her ten-year-old daughter, who had a cupcake in each hand and frosting all over her face."

"I don't blame Lottie. These are so delicious, Aunt Sally. As usual. How will you survive without your mother's cooking in the mission field, Sariah?"

"I know. I don't know what I'll miss more, my family or home cooked meals. Mom's been giving me some lessons on quick and easy things to cook for two."

"I might need in on those. Too bad I'm in Provo and can't run up for lessons."

"Congratulations, Sister Limbrey!" Jarom said, hugging Sally first. "Let me know what I can do to help you prepare the next few weeks."

"Absolutely. Thanks, Jarom."

The twins had been home from their missions for almost five months. Sally knew their testimonies and stories had helped encourage Sariah to put in her mission papers, which made her love them even more.

"Hey, you guys," Ammon called to them, motioning them toward the opposite side of the yard. "Mom wants to get a picture with all the cousins that are here."

"Of course she does," Jarom laughed. "I give her credit for documenting our life so well."

"Her one regret is not getting to follow you around Europe, photographing every day of your missions," Sally said as they made their way toward Paige and the growing group of cousins. They were only missing Heather's three siblings.

She smiled, thinking of all the photos Paige took of them in college. Her favorite being the one of her and Sam at Hug Point at the end of their road trip. It was framed on her dresser, next to one of the four of them in front of Haystack

Rock the first day they had arrived in Cannon Beach. What a life she had lived since that summer.

"Scootch in. Heather, I can't see you behind Ammon."

"You're just trying to make me feel good." Heather laughed, stepping forward.

"Alright everyone, on three. One. Two. Three."

"Cheese Chicas!" the group rang out, causing Paige and Sally to laugh.

November 20, 2015

The drive from Puyallup to Provo was almost fourteen hours. Hannah remembered how easily she and her friends had road-tripped at twenty, but now it felt like way too long of a drive to do by herself. Instead, Jentry drove up to Washington, and the two of them flew to Salt Lake.

They rented a car and headed to Provo, arriving at Utah Valley Hospital an hour after Heather had been induced. They had visited with Heather and Noah for a while before contractions started. The plan had been for Hannah to be present for the birth, but after two hours of pushing, Heather had been whisked off to emergency C-section surgery.

Hannah sat cross-legged in the waiting room, her foot bouncing with nervous energy, worrying about her daughter and grandson. She had texted her mother and Sally as Heather was being taken to the OR and expected them to arrive shortly.

"Do you need another coffee, Love?" Jentry asked.

"This is terrible coffee. I think I'm a Starbucks snob."

"That's fair. Water?"

"The only thing I need is to know they're alright."

"She'll be fine. She's tough, like you, who birthed a baby on a trail."

"I'm going to go ask the nurses if they've heard anything yet." Hannah walked down the hall to the Labor and Delivery nurse's station. "Hi there, sorry to bother you. I'm Heather Smythe's mother. She was having a C-section, and I'm wondering if you know how things are going?"

427

The nurse smiled at her kindly. "Let me check." Looking at the computer, she said, "It looks like they are back in their recovery room. Let me go see if they're ready for visitors."

"Thank you." Hannah quickly walked back to the waiting room to get Jentry, and they were waiting at the nurses' station when she returned with Noah.

"Hey," Noah said, giving Hannah a hug.

"Are they okay?" Hannah asked.

"Come see for yourself," Noah smiled, leading Hannah and Jentry down the hall. They walked into the room to find Heather sitting up in bed, her dark curls still tucked up in a surgical cap, holding a crying, but very healthy, baby boy.

"Momma, Aunt Jentry, come meet our little guy," Heather said, beaming.

Hannah and Jentry washed their hands and then came around the sides of the hospital bed.

"Oh, Heather," Hannah said, tears spilling down her cheeks. "He's beautiful." Hannah bent down and hugged Heather, kissing her on top of her head as she removed the cap.

"Does this handsome man have a name?" Jentry asked.

"Liam Henry," Noah answered proudly.

"May I?" Hannah asked, putting her arms out towards her grandson.

"Of course," Heather smiled.

Hannah carefully took the bundle from Heather's arms and held him close. "My heart feels like it's going to explode," she said. "I love you, little Liam. Welcome to our crazy family."

***

Julie and Sally had arrived at the hospital with balloons and flowers. Everyone took turns holding Liam before handing him back to his parents and leaving so they could get some sleep. Hannah had promised to be back in the morning so Noah could have a break.

Now she, Jentry, and Sally were soaking in the hotel hot tub and catching up on life, while Julie had headed back to Cache Valley.

"Is it a little crazy I'm jealous you two are grandmothers already?" Sally asked.

"I am not a grandmother," corrected Jentry.

"She's too hip and stylish for that name," Hannah joked.

"Well, what does Gianna call you?"

"Gigi," Jentry said. "We struggled to come up with something. Sofia was already Grandma, and Jack's mother was Nanny. So, we waited to see what Gianna would say. She made a sound, which was probably an attempt at Jentry, but it sounded more like Gigi."

"How darling," smiled Sally.

"Heather told me I would be Nana a few months ago, because it rhymes with Hannah."

"It's so interesting to me grandparents have so many fancy names nowadays. When I was young, I had Grandma Johnson and Grandma Heggie. Straightforward."

"I like the individuality of how folks do it now," said Hannah.

"I wonder who will become a grandmother next? Ammon and Jarom will likely be the next married. Sariah won't be home from her mission until January 2017. I'm sure the boys will beat her to the punch."

"How is Sariah?" Jentry asked.

"So good. Her letters are such a treat. The members there are taking such good care of her and her companion. Lots of home cooked southern food. She was saying in her last letter she had okra last week and was surprised at how much she liked it."

"Okra," Hannah sighed. "Morgan and I talked about comfort food that day in the rain, and he loved okra."

"There's a blast from the past. I haven't heard his name since that summer. I wonder what happened to him?" Jentry said.

"I wish I knew. Would you think I was the worst if I told you I dream about him all the time?"

"You do?" asked Sally. "Like daydream or real dream."

"Real dream. For the last, what, twenty-four years?"

"Do tell, Love."

"It's always the same. We're in the shelter, laughing and talking and having the best time. Then a husband appears in the door."

"Which husband?" Sally asked.

"Whichever one I was married to at the time. The husband appears, and I have to choose between them. Never have I ever chosen my dear hubby. Is that terrible?"

"Considering your options, Love, it sounds about right."

Sally's phone buzzed on the towel behind her. "It's Paige. She wonders how Heather and the baby are." Sally looked at Hannah expectantly.

"Why isn't she asking Hannah?"

"Jentry, you know we haven't talked in a year. She's not suddenly going to talk to me today."

"Maybe this is her cry to be included," Jentry said.

"I doubt it. Whatever her feelings are about me, she loves Heather, and that's great. They're welcome to a relationship. I just don't want one."

"Really? I don't believe that," Sally said. "I think you're both being stubborn. There's no way you don't each miss the other. Imagine how much more fun it would be if Paige was here with us."

"I don't know. Jentry might get in trouble for rocking her bikini." Hannah winked at Jentry.

"Can I tell her about Heather and the baby, at least?" Sally asked.

"Of course. Anything she wants to know about them."

"This is a year missed, Han. I think you two will regret this someday," Jentry said. "I hope one of you comes to your senses sooner than later."

February 10, 2016

Religiously I'm in a weird place. I haven't attended Lighthouse in a few months. At first it was because we were out of town, but truthfully, there were teachings that didn't add up to me anymore. Some were beautiful, and some seem to come from a very vengeful god.

I recently read a book about goddess worship by early Israelites. It casts so much doubt on the historicity of the Old Testament that I am losing faith in God and Jesus. I feel untethered and lost again. But the story of Christianity isn't making sense to me anymore.

February 28, 2016

I finished The Age of Reason by Thomas Paine, one of the founding fathers who was a Deist. It did to the Bible and Christianity what the CES Letter did to Mormonism for me. He suggests there is a God, which is evident through creation and nature, but that God doesn't intervene, inspire scriptures, or speak to prophets. It was fascinating thinking and written in the 1700's.

He said all you need to know about God can be witnessed in nature. That really appeals to me.

March 16, 2016

Happy 22nd Birthday to Seth Lucas! We had some rough years, but we're so good now, and I'm so grateful for it. He has grown in so many ways and is such an awesome young man. He and his girlfriend, Willa, came over for dinner. I made fish tacos and better-than-sex cake. They've been dating for about nine months. She is the manager at the Tacoma Boys in Puyallup, and they met when he asked her for a wine recommendation for me. So cute! She is two years older than him, has the most beautiful strawberry blonde hair, and big green eyes. She wears all these really fun and funky glasses and is so cool and sweet. She's wonderful to Tandie and Tyson as well.

I'm so glad Heather and Seth have found such awesome people to be with.

April 9, 2016

I've lost all my great pens. As well as my belief in God and Religion. I've felt so sad and adrift. Now what?

I've begged my grandmothers to come to me for months. They did love me. If they could come to me, they would. And I am left believing they don't come because they no longer exist. I feel more disconnected from my parents, siblings, and friends than ever. There is no feeling or connection to God/Jesus left in my heart. I "know" nothing anymore. I talk about this with Heather constantly. She and Noah have also lost their belief in Mormonism but seem open to God and a life after this.

What will be the foundation of my life now? What is the purpose? The point? If there is no longer a mansion in heaven and _all_ the blessings waiting for me _there_, then how do I reframe the last forty-five years to not be such a bitter disappointment and make the most of my life? Because apparently this is it. This is all I get and then I'm just done.

I'm not built to have no belief in my life, but I can't force something that is so shattered.

So, I'm trying to see if I can find something meaningful in what was likely the beliefs and rituals of my Norse and Scottish ancestors – Pagan practices focused on celebrating the earth and seasons. Those are real, tangible, factual. The Wheel of the Year is something I want to incorporate into my life this year. But don't tell my mother or Paige!

People took my leaving Mormonism hard. There is no way in hell I'm telling anyone outside of my children I'm Atheist.

May 1, 2016

Helped Seth and Willa move into an apartment in Graham last week. He's been assigned to the Graham Fire and Rescue Station 96 and wanted to be close. Seth purposefully moved when Toby was at work. He told me Willa has complained about feeling like Toby ogles her. Nice. It's so embarrassing.

I usually try to put my head down and ignore the most annoying things about Toby. I never ask about porn anymore. His temper has settled down a lot since Seth moved out of the house. He doesn't lose it on his bio kids like he did my big ones. So, I focus on the good times. And there are good times. Toby can be so much fun. We have a lot of great adventures together. There's no trust, and I cry during sex a lot thinking about how he cheated on me, but other than that, we're good. Haha.

June 12, 2016

Toby and I are doing really well. I read an interesting article about improving your marriage. It talked about making your greetings special when you've been apart. When he gets home from work we dance around the living room and talk about our day. It reminds me of the romantic man I fell in love with.

I'm full-time at Starbucks now and one of the assistant managers. I work from 6 to 3 Monday to Friday, which is nice. I've but in an application for the manager position. I'm the oldest person on the staff, and I have management experience, so I'm hopeful. It would mean a different schedule more than likely, but we'll see. Fingers crossed.

We've been taking the kids hiking as much as possible on the weekends. Seth and Willa join us when they can. We all went to Little Mashel Falls last weekend. So gorgeous!

June 24, 2016

I got it!!!! I'm so excited. This is like a $20,000 raise. It's life changing. Toby says I've got to help more with bills. He'll cover the mortgage, cars, insurance, etc. I've got to cover food, household supplies, birthdays and Christmas, and half of vacations. Sure, dude. Whatever.

Tandie and Ty have been so supportive with me working. They keep the house clean, help with meals, and get along. Best kids ever. Tandie will turn 14 this summer, and Ty will be 13.

August 21, 2016

Ammon Lindberg was introduced to Marlee Jensen during the last month of his mission. She was a sister missionary who was serving in his district in Denmark and, by strange coincidence, lived on the same street as his grandparents in Mesa, Arizona. They had been on the same flight back to Utah and smiled at each other whenever they passed on the plane. Ammon gave her his phone number as they were waiting at baggage claim with their families, and the romance had taken off from there.

Paige had been thrilled the first time he brought Marlee home to meet the family. Ammon was living at home and attending USU, while Marlee was at school in Salt Lake, attending the University of Utah. They made the long-distance relationship work. A year after returning from their missions, they were engaged. Last week, her family had traveled to Mesa to see them married in the Gilbert temple.

Today was the open house for the couple, held at The Logan House in historic downtown Logan. Paige mingled with the guests while making sure the donut bar was stalked.

Paige was so happy today, seeing Ammon married to a wonderful woman, and hoped Jarom and Ellie would find love soon. Her five children were the light of her life, and she was so proud of the family she and Drake had formed when they married and blended their children together.

"We're getting low on milk," Jentry said, brushing past Paige and heading into the serving area.

Paige was grateful for the help she had received from Jentry and Sally in preparing for the evening. Their friendship was so important to her, now more than ever, as she and

Hannah were still estranged. Paige had been in shock when Hannah had said such a vile and crude thing to her at the restaurant. Honestly, it proved her point. People needed the Gospel to be the best version of themselves. Her heart hurt thinking of all Hannah had rejected, knowing how deeply she had believed in the church at one point. She may not be on speaking terms with Hannah, but she still put her name on the temple prayer list whenever she attended, in hopes she would come back to the church.

"Can I have this dance, sexy lady?" Drake said, coming up from behind, and pulling Paige into his arms. She laughed as he twirled her out and back into a dip. He brought her back up and kissed her tenderly. "Do you feel bad about upstaging the bride today?" he asked her, a grin on his face.

"I'm hardly upstaging Marlee. She looks like a princess today. So beautiful."

"You, my dearest wife, look like a queen." Drake twirled Paige around the dance floor until the song finished. "My old roommate, Aaron, just arrived. I'll be back." Drake kissed her again and hurried off.

Paige was walking towards the bride and groom to see if they needed anything, when she stopped in her tracks. Hannah was in line, hugging Ammon and being introduced to Marlee. Noah, Heather, and the baby were with her, as were Tandie and Tyson. Paige's heart dropped into her chest.

"You look like you've seen a ghost," Sally said, approaching Paige. She turned around to look in the same direction. "Oh, I didn't know Hannah was going to swing by."

"You knew she was in town?" Paige asked.

"Yes, for Bruce and Julie's anniversary. Then Tandie is staying with Salena for a week."

"Oh," Paige said, eyes still on Hannah. She watched as Hannah hugged Ammon one more time, then turned towards the gift table. She pulled an envelope out of her purse, set it on the table, and left, leaving her children behind, no doubt to visit with family.

Right before Hannah walked through the gate, she turned and caught Paige's eye. Her expression didn't change. It wasn't angry. It wasn't sad and longing for reconnection either. It was blank, and in a second more, she was gone.

"Excuse me," Paige said, stepping away from Sally. She quickly found the bathroom, locked the door behind her, and cried.

October 10, 2016

My hands and heart are shaking as I write this. Today as I was leaving work I got a Facebook message from a stranger telling me Toby was on a dating site saying he was divorced. It was devastating. She sent me screenshots of his profile, which is a photo I took of him at Mt Rainier! She sent me the text from him about the date he'd set up with her. She had done some research and found him on Facebook listing he was married to me. She called him out on it and sent me those screenshots as well. He tried to back pedal and say he was in a loveless marriage and was trying to see what was out there before he left me. She thought I had a right to know.

I thought we were trying to work things out. Things aren't perfect. It's been a rollercoaster. We have been fighting more this month, but overall, I thought we were doing okay. To learn he is actively trying to cheat on me again completely guts me. It makes me wonder if he has cheated on me more than I realize.

I think in my past efforts to be Christlike and forgiving, I have trained Toby, and Luke before him, to treat me like shit. There was never a consequence for their actions.

I've been looking back at my journal tonight and I came across an entry from years ago that said "I'm miserable, but this is a commandment. It will bring me closer to God to stay and fight for my marriage."

Well guess what...it didn't. God didn't help my marriage, because God isn't there. At least not the version I believed in. I went and walked around Bradley Lake before I went home. I think I went around it three or four times thinking about what I should do.

I came to the conclusion I'm going to do what I should have done years ago. The first time he cheated. The first time he laid a hand on one of my kids. I'm going to leave his sorry, lying, cheating angry ass and make a new and improved life for myself. No idea how. But that's tomorrow's problem. I'm not letting him know I heard from that woman – who, btw is almost twenty years younger than me! She told him she wouldn't tell me if he took his profile down. He's been acting weird for the last few days, and now I know why.

I'm going to get a gameplan, and then I'm going to tell that piece of shit to hit the road.

October 20, 2016

When Hannah Limbrey set her mind to something, she was a force to be reckoned with. It had been ten days since she had learned of Toby's Plenty of Fish account and decided to end her marriage. It was an easy decision to stay in Puyallup. She had a good job, and Tandie and Tyson were doing well in school. Seth and Willa would be a support to her as well. At first she had looked into renting a home, but upon realizing she was entitled to half the equity of their Utah house, she decided to look into purchasing a place of her own. A mortgage would be cheaper than rent in this current economy. She contacted a mortgage agent and a realtor to see what her options were.

She researched how to do an uncontested divorce in Washington in hopes Toby could be persuaded to give her what she wanted. The fees were minimal, and if things went smoothly, the divorce could be final by February.

She called her parents to see if they were willing to offer any assistance. They naturally wanted her to return home but understood she had a good job. They said they would loan her $5000 once she officially filed.

Next, she spoke to Heather and Seth to make sure they were aware of the situation. Heather worried about the impact on Tandie and Tyson, as well as the financial burden on Hannah, but offered support in whatever way was needed. Seth offered to help her move when the time came and threatened to hurt Toby if he gave her a hard time at all.

She sent Jentry and Sally a text with a quick recap. They also offered to help in any way possible.

The hardest piece so far was a conversation with Tandie and Tyson this afternoon as they made no-bake cookies. They had heard their parents fight plenty of times and had admitted they could hear her cry in the bathtub on more than one occasion. She asked how they would feel if she ever wanted to strike out on her own. They both had said they wanted her to be happy.

Hannah was waiting at the train station when Toby got off the Sounder. He looked surprised to see her and more surprised when she told him to get in her car, because they were going for a little drive.

"I'm about to forward you some texts," Hannah said, with the car still in park. "Look these over, and then we can discuss what's going to happen next." She hit send on the screenshots of his dating profile and pulled away from the station.

Toby opened what she had sent him and then swore under his breath.

"That's one word to describe this, for sure," she said, amazingly calm. "So, I'm done. Let's start there so you aren't wondering. This marriage is over."

"Hannah, I can explain," Toby tried interrupting.

"Oh, I bet you could," Hannah laughed. "You've always been great at explaining away your bad choices and making everything look like our fault. I don't need your explanation, Toby. It won't change a damn thing. I have said I was done with this marriage more times than I can count. I don't know if there was a year where I didn't wonder if we'd make our next anniversary because you're such an asshole. My heart has always softened, and I've always been willing to try again. I have forgiven and forgiven and forgiven again. But not this time. This time, I'm done, and I have more hope and excitement for my future than I have in a long time."

"So, this is all going to go how you want? Is that what you think?"

"Bingo!" Hannah said in a sing-song voice. "I have spent the last ten days planning my exit. I have all my ducks in a row, all my plans made. We can do this the hard way if you want. We can go to court, and drag things out, and make things awkward and difficult for the children, and I can tell your family what a piece of shit you are. Or, and this is the one I suggest you go with, you can cooperate with me. We can file an uncontested divorce for cheap, be done with each other in ninety days, and move on with our lives. We can co-parent in a happy and positive way and cause as little collateral damage to Tandie and Tyson as possible. How does that sound, Buddy?"

"You can lose the condescending tone, Hannah. It isn't necessary."

"I'll take whatever tone I want. So, we're going to keep living together while we craft the divorce, get our finances in order, and I find a place to live. You're going to move into the bonus room."

"Like hell I am. I pay the rent. You can move into the bonus room. And what finances do we have to get in order?" Toby asked, genuinely curious.

"Well, for starters, figuring out alimony and child support."

"Alimony? What have you ever done to deserve alimony?"

Hannah took a breath so she wouldn't reach over and throat-punch him. "Put up with you for sixteen years. It's the law. I'm entitled to it, look it up."

"Well, that's all you're getting. The house in Utah is in my name only, and this lease is in my name only. So is your car. So good luck surviving on your own."

"Oh, bad news, Tobester. Washington and Utah are both community property states. I get fifty percent of everything you own, whether or not I'm on the title or loan. That means the equity of the house, your 401K, meager as it is since you keep getting fired, vehicles, savings, etcetera. Google it."

"Son of a bitch," Toby said, punching the dash of the car.

"That's funny. That's exactly what I said when I got the messages about your dating profile."

"Okay. So, you're wanting money and what else," Toby said, somewhat resigned.

"I want what is legally mine. I want a parenting plan that puts Tandie and Tyson first. I want to do this without fighting and being ugly to each other. I want somewhere to live until I can get my own place."

Hannah paused, softening her approach. "This can be a positive thing, Toby. We didn't make great marriage partners, and you know it. But there were times when we were really good friends, and I think we can still have a friendship if we do this right."

"I want what's best for the kids too. Do they know?"

"Heather and Seth do. Tandie and Tyson might suspect. I think they'll be okay if we can be grownups. The more respectful and cooperative we are, the safer they'll feel."

"I'm sorry, Hannah. I don't know if it means anything at this point, but I am sorry."

"Thanks for saying that. It doesn't mean anything to me now, but it was nice of you to say."

"So, if the marriage is over, can I date now?"

"Really, Toby? Well, being married didn't stop you, so knock yourself out."

"Oh, you just had to say that," Toby said angrily.

"Actually, tell me one thing. I know you cheated years ago at The Old Rock, and I know you just tried to hook up with this girl. Tell me how many other times you've been unfaithful to me."

"I don't know what good that will do," Toby said defensively.

"That's what I thought," Hannah said, realizing his answer meant there were more times than he wanted to admit to.

445

January 7, 2017

"Hello?" Willa called as she opened the front door.

Hannah carefully set her paintbrush down and headed into the living room. "Hello, my dear. You're up and about early."

It was eight o'clock in the morning. Hannah had been awake since six o'clock finishing up the painting on her house. The previous owners had painted the walls beige, which made the small house feel dark to her. When she got the keys on Tuesday, she had deep cleaned the house, shampooed the carpets, and started repainting every wall. It was exhausting and exhilarating at the same time.

"I knew you would be up and busy with furniture coming today. I grabbed you some doughnuts and a coffee."

"That is so thoughtful, Willa. Thank you."

"I need a tour," Willa said, passing the doughnuts and coffee to Hannah. "I'm sorry I didn't get over here sooner."

"You're a busy girl. It's all good. Well, you can see the front door opens right into the living room. I love the vaulted ceiling and fireplace."

It had been important to Hannah that she find somewhere to live that kept Tandie and Tyson in the same schools and made it easy for them to go back and forth between their parents. She told her realtor she needed to find a home within her budget and in the South Hill area. Toby had agreed to let her live in the bonus room through the end of the year. It was incredibly awkward, especially when he immediately started dating and even brought a girlfriend over.

She found the perfect home right after Thanksgiving, but the homeowners weren't moving out until after Christmas. That gave Hannah time to pack and organize, so she waited for the year to end before she took ownership of the house.

It was located on 148th Street, a mile and a half southeast of Toby's home. The one-story, three-bedroom home was next to a large, forested area, which meant she only had a neighbor on one side. The yard was small, which would be much easier for her to maintain.

"I love vaulted ceilings. They make the space seem much bigger," Willa said, following her into the kitchen. "And the white walls really open it up."

"Look at this gorgeous kitchen. It's so much bigger than my last one."

"Oh, this is lovely. I love the dark wood."

The kitchen and dining room also had a vaulted ceiling, as well as a sliding door leading to the patio and backyard.

"Back here, we have the three bedrooms, two baths, and laundry. It's not huge, but it's perfect. Large enough to have family dinners, small enough to afford," Hannah said with a laugh.

"I'm really happy for you, Hannah. And I'm so glad you are finally on your own. I can't imagine having to live with your ex-husband for any length of time."

"That wasn't my favorite, for sure."

"The place looks great. You have it so clean, and I think it was smart to do mostly white with some pops of color."

Hannah had painted one wall in the kitchen a fern green, bringing the outdoors inside. She had let the children choose a color for an accent wall in their bedrooms. Tandie chose a golden yellow, and Ty chose navy. For her room and bathroom, she embraced being a woman on her own, and painted the entire thing a pale pink. It made her so happy she couldn't stop smiling whenever she went into the room.

She had been sleeping on a foam mattress for a few nights while Tandie and Tyson stayed at Toby's. Today, she would get her furniture from Toby's, and what she was picking up from The Old Cannery. The equity in the Utah house had been enough to make a downpayment on this place and have ten thousand left over for savings. Jentry had insisted on buying her new furniture for the living room and her bedroom, claiming she enjoyed shopping and needed a reason to design a space.

Seth had taken the day off, and was going to use his truck, as well as have a few firefighter friends help get her moved in. Hannah had promised pizza at the end of the day.

Toby had agreed to take Tandie and Tyson out for the day, so the move wasn't awkward for them. She would finish getting everything set up this evening and have it ready when they came home tonight.

"I've got to get to work. I'll be back after my shift to help," Willa said, hugging Hannah goodbye.

"You were really wonderful to stop by. I'm going to enjoy my doughnut right now. I'll see you later."

Hannah shut the door behind her and headed to the kitchen. She warmed the doughnut for a few seconds and was enjoying the first bite when the phone rang.

"Hello?"

"Happy moving day!" Sally said on the other line.

"Sal! Hey! Thank you. I am so excited I can't stand it. I've got a lot of my boxes in here, but it's pretty empty."

"The pictures on Instagram look amazing. I love the pink bedroom."

"Seth and Ty gave me a hard time about it, but I don't care."

"I wish we could be there to help."

"Seth and his friends have it covered, but thank you. And besides, you got your daughter back two days ago. How is she adjusting?"

"Well, Sariah got spoiled with heat on a mission to the South. She has returned to three feet of snow. She's thrilled to be reunited with her sisters. Salena hasn't left her side."

"Tell her Auntie Hannah loves her, and if she wants to get away from snow, she can always come here."

"I will. How are Tandie and Tyson doing now you're out of the house?"

"I worry they put on brave faces to make me feel better. Tandie has mentioned she's worried about what they'll eat at Toby's since he doesn't cook. She also worries he's going to expect her to be the maid, since he was that way with me. I think he'll try to be the Disney dad at first, lots of fun, easygoing. But he's so focused on dating and women and sowing oats, I imagine entertaining the kids won't be his first priority for long. We'll see."

"That's really hard, Hannah. I'm sorry. I'm sorry you have to start over a second time."

"Think of it as I get to start over because I was finally strong enough to leave."

"I like that better," Sally said. "Have you heard from Jentry or Paige this week?"

"Sally, you know I haven't heard from Paige in over two years. She's not going to suddenly call me about my life now."

Sally sighed. "A friend can hope. You've each had so many things happen since your falling out. You've become a Nana, gotten a divorce, and bought a house. Ammon has gotten married, Jarom is engaged, Ellie moved to Arizona, Issy has started college, and Paige and Lottie went to Disneyland."

"Well, maybe if she hadn't said such horrible things to me, things would be different. At least I still have you and Jen."

"I wish it was like it used to be. I'm sorry. I always will."

"I always will, too, Sally. But I'm not going to let people treat me poorly anymore. If Paige wants to apologize, we can see."

"You know she thinks you owe her the apology because of the F word."

"Oh, please. Of course, she does."

"On a better note, I had Noah, Heather, and Liam for dinner last Sunday. Liam is so precious and sweet, and Heather is such a good little mother."

"Aww, Sally, that was so nice of you to do for them."

"You'd do the same if my girls lived near you and I was away."

"Absolutely, I would."

"I love you, Hannah. Have fun moving in and getting settled today. Send me pictures once you have it put together."

"Will do. Sal, thanks for calling. I love you, Turtle."

March 13, 2017

Tandie got her braces off today. She looks so beautiful! She knows how to work her curls way better than I did at fourteen. She has been wanting to go to the YMCA and swim whenever Toby or I can take her, because she wants to try out for the Rogers swim team next month.

I've started running again. It's hard to believe I was ever a runner, because it is painful to go more than a mile now. But my goal is to be able to do a 5K in May. I've lost ten pounds since the beginning of the year. Turns out I wasn't overeating from depression — I was overeating from hating being married. Lol.

March 14, 2017

I have the best son-in-law on the planet!!!!! Noah and Heather called me tonight. They didn't want to say anything and get my hopes up, but back when he graduated in December, he told Heather as much as he loved Utah and living close to his family, he thought the kids and I would need them more. How sweet is that? So, he's been applying for jobs from Olympia to Seattle, and he's been hired as an interpreter for the Pierce County District Court. I can't believe it. He had served his mission in Japan and taken Chinese in high school. He decided to major in Japanese with a minor in Chinese. There are a lot of Asian-Americans in this area, so he had multiple offers. His job starts April tenth. They're renting a place at Aldera apartments until they're able to look into buying. They'll be here by the fifth of April. CRAZY!!! I'll get to see my Liam Boy grow up.

How is my life this wonderful? The me crying in the fetal position in the closet all these years could never have imagined being so happy.

May 26, 2017

"Skip Bo!" Sally shouted, laughing.

"It doesn't matter how many times we tell her that isn't necessary; she's still going to do it," Paige said, throwing down her hand of cards.

"You have a gift, Love. Is that three turns in a row?"

"Four," Sally gloated.

"You need to take your talent to the casinos," Elodie said.

"I quit. Sally is unbeatable. Who's hungry?" Jentry asked, pushing back her chair from the table and going into the kitchen for a snack.

"I'n hungwy, Gigi," Gianna piped up from the corner of the room, where she had been coloring.

"Let's get you some fruit snacks, Fancy Face," Jentry said to her three-year-old granddaughter.

Paige had called a few weeks ago to see what Jentry's Memorial Weekend plans were. So many of the children were either married, in college, or busy with friends. Hanging out with parents on this particular holiday was no longer a draw. Jentry happily offered the beach house to whoever could make it.

Drake, Paige, and Lottie flew in from Utah, along with Sam, Sally, Sadie, and Salena. They rented a large passenger van and arrived in Cannon Beach last night. Elodie, her longtime boyfriend, Jack, and Giana had driven up earlier today. The men were currently golfing at Seaside. Sadie, Salena, and Lottie, at sixteen, fifteen, and twelve, were deemed old enough to walk to Hug Point with a picnic and book like they knew Aunt Jentry had done at their age.

Jentry loved filling the beach house with friends and family. It had been so cold and empty in her childhood, and now it was filled with so many memories of love and laughter.

"What time is it?" asked Paige, checking her phone. "Four o'clock. The guys should be back any minute.

"Our reservation is in thirty minutes. We could probably get the girls and head over." Jentry had placed the reservation at Pacific Coast as soon as she could. A table for twelve at this time of year was not easy to come by.

As if on cue, the girls were spotted walking up the beach, almost to Jentry's. "Let's get everybody loaded up. I'll text Donovan and let him know to meet us there."

The group started gathering what they needed and heading out to the cars. Jentry was locking the door when her phone rang. She could see on the caller ID it was Hannah. Not wanting her to hear everyone in the driveway, she quickly stepped back inside.

"Hey, Han!" she said, answering the call.

"Hey, Lady! I'm so glad I caught you. I know you usually spend Memorial Day at the beach, and I wondered if you would like a little company? Toby will have Tandie and Tyson, and Seth has to work, but the rest of have some time off. We were trying to think of which direction to head, and Heather suggested a visit to you."

"Oh, Han," Jentry said, trying to figure out how to be diplomatic. "That is such an amazing offer, and I would usually take you up on it, but this weekend won't work."

"No worries at all. This is super late notice. We'll probably head to North Cascade and spend the day at Diablo Lake. It's been on Noah's bucket list."

"I'm really sorry, Hannah. Can we pick another weekend?"

"Hey, Jen, you coming? We're all loaded?" Paige asked, stepping back into the house."

"Be right there," Jentry hollered back.

"Was that Paige?" Hannah asked, sounding a little hurt.

"Yes," Jentry said, being honest. The rift between Hannah and Paige had put her and Sally in an awkward position. They didn't want to take sides, and both Hannah and Paige had emphatically told them they didn't have to choose one over the other. However, the practicality of that wasn't always possible.

"Oh, gotcha."

"She and Sally are both here, with their husbands and some of the kids. Elodie too. We're heading out for dinner. I wish you were here too, Hannah. You know I do."

"I do," Hannah agreed. "You know I get it, right? It's complicated to juggle the different friendships. I understand."

"It shouldn't be so complicated, Love. You should be here too. But you both are so damn stubborn. It's infuriating sometimes, honestly. I want to shake the both of you. Or lock you in a room together to figure your shit out."

"You'd have to catch us both in the same location first," Hannah said. "Go to dinner. No hard feelings. I love you."

"I love you too, you stubborn idiot."

"Hey!" Hannah said, laughing. "No need for name calling. Bye, Jen."

<u>June 2, 2017</u>

<u>Today is the 17th anniversary of meeting Toby. I tripped over him at the Hollywood Video. He was so friendly and romantic in the beginning. We were married fifteen weeks later. I had such high hopes for Happily Ever After. Instead, out of the gate I wondered if we'd make our next anniversary. Almost every year! There were so many wonderful times, so many times I loved him so much. And then so many lows, where I would cry to Heavenly Father about how much I hated him. I pushed through, making the most of things, forgiving abuse and infidelity, looking for the good, and trying to make a loving home for my children for over sixteen years. And in the end, I think...</u>

<u>I was going to say it was all for nothing and we're all so damaged now. But I'm not going to. Yes, there are deep hurts inside Heather and Seth and me. I couldn't have stayed until Tandie and Ty were out of high school and now they are children of divorce too.</u>

<u>But I did what I thought I had to do and was able to give my children more in those circumstances than I would have as a single mother of four.</u>

<u>Now, I'm a better mother on my own. A stronger, happier woman.</u>

<u>I'm ready to put it all behind me and move on.</u>

<u>The last few months on my own have been amazing. There is a lot of financial pressure, for sure! And I hate when Tandie and Ty are at his house instead of mine.</u>

I absolutely love my little home. I am so proud of myself for being able to purchase my own place. It is so nice, pretty, and clean. There is such a wonderful peaceful energy here and it feels so nice inside.

Having Heather and Seth living close and having Liam in my life is just a dream. Everyone is living their best life and gets along with each other.

I'm so excited about this new chapter of my life. It's a simple little life, without a lot of frills, but it's all mine, and I get to spend the rest of my life feeling safe and secure, and loving on my children, family, and friends.

June 3, 2017

Hannah's morning run on the Chapman Trail had been six miles, the longest she had done this year. She loved putting her music on and running around the forested trails. Heather would often meet her and walk a lap or two, pushing Liam in the stroller. It was a wonderful way to start the weekend.

She had run into her store for a meeting with the assistant, Breckon, and the new shift lead, Kobe, and then come home to clean the house. The first Saturday of every month was dinner and game night with all the kids, a tradition Hannah had started when Noah and Heather moved back.

It was Tandie and Tyson's week at Toby's house. Their parenting plan was fifty-fifty custody, so they spent a week with each parent, switching on Sunday afternoons.

She put a pan of chicken enchiladas in the oven and then hopped in the shower. She had two hours until the children came over, and she hoped to read on the back porch in the swing before they got there.

She stepped out of the shower, wrapped a pink towel around herself, moisturized her face, and put curl enhancer in her hair. She opened the bathroom door and screamed.

Toby was sitting on the chair in the corner of her room.

"What the hell, Toby? You scared me to death." Hannah held her towel tightly, glaring at her ex-husband.

"You are determined to ruin my life," Toby said.

Hannah noticed the bottle of whiskey in his hand, and the slur of his speech.

"First of all, how did you get inside my house? Second, you better not be driving under the influence, and third, get out."

"Your back door was unlocked. You're too trusting." Toby stood and walked towards her. "Lily broke up with me today. We were supposed to have dinner tonight, but she called to say she doesn't want to see me anymore. Can you guess why?"

Hannah knew exactly why. Lily and Toby had been dating for a few months. She had a fifteen-year-old daughter, who had confided to Tandie that Toby made her uncomfortable. Tandie told Lily she should talk to Hannah. Last night, Lily and Hannah had met for coffee, and Hannah had answered all of Lily's questions about Toby truthfully. Unfortunately for Toby, the answers weren't flattering.

"Lily wanted to know your history, and I answered honestly."

"You had no right, Hannah," Toby screamed, inches from her face, the smell of alcohol strong on his breath.

"Lily had every right to know who she was dating and to have all the information to protect herself and her daughter. I didn't protect my children from you, Toby. I should have put an end to so many things. But I didn't. I made excuses for you when you hurt my children. Not just physically but emotionally. You're an abuser. You're also a predator. When we divorced, so many women and young girls came out of the woodwork with stories about how uncomfortable you had made them. You commented on the breast size of the Greene girl to her dad, for hell's sake. Woman after woman with stories of feeling like you were a creeper. Heather telling me how her friends didn't want to come to our house, because of how inappropriate you were. Tandie making comments about feeling like you were obsessed with her best friend in sixth grade. It's disgusting, Toby. I remember the porn I found on our computer. If those girls weren't teenagers, they sure as hell looked like it."

"You are such a bitch, Hannah. So judgmental. I've never touched a young girl."

"That is unequivocally not true. You had our babysitter on our bed tickling her. You used to tickle all of Heather and Tandie's friends. You'd practically force their friends to let you lift them in the air, with your hands all over them. Tandie told me you kissed her friend on the forehead a month ago. I've told her not to have friends at your house. It's not safe now that I'm not there to buffer. Other men don't do what you do. At least other men who aren't perverts and predators. You have no sense of boundaries or propriety. I looked the other way for too damn long, trying to keep our marriage together. That's on me. I have to live with the shame and guilt of that. But I won't stay silent now. I will educate the people in your life to make sure they know to be careful around you."

"You're blowing things out of proportion. You want to make me out to be evil to make yourself feel better."

"Toby, I would give anything to not feel this way. To not see what I see. You need help. Tandie and Tyson deserve better than having a dad other people think is a creeper. Get help, Toby. Go see someone."

"You're trying to turn Tandie and Ty against me the way you turned Heather and Seth. The sacrifices I made for you and your ungrateful children! Now I'm the villain, and it's the Saint Hannah show. I'm sick of it." Toby had backed Hannah up against the wall.

Hannah stared at him defiantly, clutching her towel tighter around her body. She was not going to cower in front of him again. Not going to cry and beg him to settle down or show her kindness.

"Sick of it," Toby said again, with a snarl. "And sick of you."

Hannah's head whipped back into the wall as Toby backhanded her across the cheek. The towel dropped to the floor as she brought her hand up to her jaw. Her face stung, and the back of her head hurt.

"Get out of my house, you pathetic piece of shit."

Toby turned to retreat, and Hannah made the mistake of picking up a shoe and throwing it at him. It hit him on the back of the head, and he snapped. He turned around and ran at her. He slammed her naked body to the ground, knocking the wind out of her. He stood over her, repeatedly kicking her in the gut and chest.

She couldn't catch her breath to scream. Blow after blow sent waves of pain through her body.

"You're a fucking bitch!"

Hannah tried to curl up into the fetal position to protect herself. Finally, she recovered enough to scream. She rolled onto her stomach, trying to crawl to the bathroom to escape Toby.

"You better keep your filthy mouth shut about me. Stay out of my life," he screamed, with one final kick to the side of her face.

The pain radiated through her body, and she couldn't move. She lay on her stomach, watching Toby stagger away, tears streaming down her face. "I hate you," she choked out in a sob. She tensed as she saw Toby turn around and come back towards her.

Kneeling down next to her, he leaned in close and whispered in her ear, "Enjoy your next run, Hannah." He stood up and, with all his strength, stomped on her left foot.

The sounds of crunching bone mingled with her scream. Hannah heard the back door slam as he left. She tried to move, to get to her phone and call for help, but the effort caused too much pain. She felt dizzy and nauseous. She could hear the timer of the oven start beeping and knew her children would find her soon. She lay there on the carpet, whimpering in pain, until she heard the front door open.

"Mom?" Heather called. "The timer is going off on the oven. Noah, will you get that? I'll go find her."

Hannah heard her daughter's footsteps coming down the hallway and into her room.

"Mom? Oh my gosh, Mom, Momma. Noah!!!" Heather pulled a blanket off the bed and covered Hannah's bruised and bleeding body. "Momma, what happened?"

"Toby."

Noah came into the room, Liam on his hip, and quickly sat the baby down on the bed. "Hannah, it's okay. We're going to get help. Heather, call 911. I'll call Seth."

"Momma, oh my gosh," Heather cried, stroking Hannah's hair. "What did he do?" Heather fumbled for her cell phone and dialed 911. "Hi," she said, her voice shaky, "My mother has been attacked. I think she needs an ambulance. She's really hurt."

Noah reached Seth as he and Willa pulled into the driveway. Seth came running into the bedroom.

"Mom, holy shit. Heather, what happened?"

"I don't know," Heather cried, still on the phone with 911. "I found her on the floor, she was naked, and she's hurt. She said Toby did this." Heather paused, listening to the operator. "Toby Keller. He's her ex-husband. She can barely talk, but she said he did this to her."

"Willa, get my bag out of the truck. Mom, I want to try to take your vitals, okay? Everything is going to be okay. We're here."

"The kids," Hannah said hoarsely. "Get them...from him...protect...them."

"I'm on it," Noah said as he ran out of the room to get Tandie and Tyson from Toby's house.

Willa returned with Seth's spare medical bag. He carefully rolled Hannah over, propping her head on a pillow. "The ambulance will be here soon, Mom. It's okay."

"She looks so scared," Heather whispered to Seth. She took Hannah's hand in hers. "I love you, Momma."

Hannah let Seth listen to her heart and take her blood pressure. The sound of a siren could be heard coming down the street.

"Can we put a gown on her?" Heather asked her brother. "She's not going to want to be found naked."

"Carefully."

Heather hopped up, grabbed a nightgown out of Hannah's dresser, and carefully slipped it over her head as the paramedics entered the house.

Within minutes, Hannah was on the gurney and being lifted into the ambulance.

"Heather, you've got to call 911 back and report Toby. That bastard is getting arrested tonight."

"Okay," Heather said, wiping the tears from her face.

"Text me once Noah has the kids."

"Okay. Which hospital are they taking her to?"

"Good Sam," Seth said, climbing into the back of the ambulance with Hannah.

<h1 style="text-align:center">June 4, 2017</h1>

Hannah stirred and slowly opened her eyes. She was in a hospital room, an IV drip in her right arm. She felt groggy and thirsty. The lights in the room were dimmed, though the window blinds were open, revealing an overcast sky.

"Hey, look, who's awake?" Seth said from a chair next to the bed. He gently nudged his older sister, who had fallen asleep with her head on his shoulder on the padded bench under the window in the corner.

"Hi, Mom," Heather said, coming around the bed. She and Seth each gently took one of Hannah's hands.

"I had to be hospitalized?" Hannah asked, her voice dry and scratchy.

"Your foot was obviously broken. As the doctors were casting it, you fainted. Upon exam, they found your spleen had ruptured, and they got you into the OR for a splenectomy. You've got two cracked ribs, a lot of bruising, and a badly cut lip, but you're going to be okay, Mom," Seth explained. "Your vitals are good. You're such a fighter." Seth bent down and kissed her on the forehead.

Hannah started to cry and squeezed her oldest two children's hands. "I'm so sorry."

"What? No. Mom, you have nothing to be sorry about," Heather said.

"I didn't protect you. I let him hurt you. Physically. Emotionally. When Toby was kicking me, I was so scared, and it hurt so bad, and I thought about how I didn't stop him from hurting you. I shouldn't have stayed. I'm so, so sorry."

"We all have things we wish we could go back and change, Mom," Seth said. "We all cause people hurt and wish we could undo it. Do I wish things had been different? Yeah. But we got through it."

"We love you, Momma. We know you love us. We know you fought for us in the way you thought was best. Sure, we're all wounded, but we're all warriors too." Heather squeezed her mother's hand as she wiped a tear away.

"I will never forgive myself for not protecting you. For defending that man. I don't deserve your forgiveness, but thank you. Your grace and compassion mean so much," Hannah said, with a catch in her voice. She turned and looked around the room. "Where are Tandie and Ty? Are they okay?" she asked, concern in her voice.

"Noah picked them up at their house, and they were fine. Toby wasn't there. They're at your house with Noah and Willa right now. We told them they could see you when you woke up."

"They must be so confused and upset."

"They're worried about you. They understood we had to call the police. It's going to be a rough road for them, emotionally. Toby wasn't as angry and abusive after they came along. He had settled down in a lot of ways, so they don't have a memory of him being physical with anyone. It's a shock to them, but they're smart kids. They've picked up on more than we realized, and they want their dad to get help," Heather said. "Seth and I will do whatever we need to help in any way. Noah and Willa, too. We're so glad we live here now and can help out."

"Toby has been arrested. He's being held without bail for aggravated assault and unlawful entry. Heather and I have been talking, Mom." Seth paused and looked at his sister, who nodded. "We're within the statute of limitations to press charges for child abuse. We don't have a lot of physical evidence now, but I know you put things in your journal. We confided in friends and family as well, so there is a paper trail, so to speak. Heather and I are going to submit a witness statement to the prosecutor and see if we can press charges for what he did to us as kids. More than anything, we hope it gives more credence to your case."

"My sweet Heather and Sethy. How I love you," Hannah said, tears running down her face. "You're so brave. So strong."

"Hey, you're awake," Jentry said, coming into the room with two coffees and handing them to Heather and Seth. "Oh, Hannah. Everyone is so glad you're okay." Jentry carefully hugged Hannah.

"You're here. I thought you and Donovan were headed to Cabo this week?"

"We were. Seth called me on my way to the airport, and we changed our plans immediately. Donovan is picking your parent's up from Sea-Tac as we speak."

"Seth, thank you for letting her know," Hannah said, smiling at her son while squeezing Jentry's hand.

"Seth has been so freaking amazing. You should be so proud of him. He's had a clear head and knew exactly what to do and who to call. Who knew my little brother would be my rock?" Heather smiled at Seth.

"I am proud of him. I'm proud of both of you. All of you. I have always thought I had the most amazing children."

Heather pulled her phone out of her pocket when she heard it buzz. "That's Grammy. They just got to the hospital. She's been worried sick. I'll go downstairs and help all of them find the room. Be right back." Heather kissed her mother on the cheek before leaving.

"I'm going to call Willa, and let her know to bring the kids up if you're feeling strong enough for more company."

"Yes, please. I need all my babies here."

Seth stepped out of the room, leaving Jentry and Hannah alone.

"Thank you for being here, Jen."

"A hospital room with you is way better than Cabo any day," Jentry said with a wink. "How do you really feel, Love?"

"Like shit. I hurt all over," Hannah said. "I think I need an epidural to block all the pain," she joked.

"I'll let the nurse know you need more painkillers, but first, Sally said to call her as soon as you woke up. Let's get her on the phone," Jentry said, putting her phone on speaker mode.

"Jentry, is she awake?" Sally asked as soon as she answered the phone. "I've been so worried."

"Hey, Sally Jane. It's good to hear your voice," Hannah said, smiling through her pain.

PART THREE

June 23, 2018

She was relieved the summer rain was a light drizzle. Ever since hydroplaning during her first pregnancy on the I-15, Hannah had been nervous driving at high speeds when there was water on the roadway. She had the wipers set to intermittent, and that was enough to keep her vision clear. The radio played in the background, and she sang along occasionally, but mostly, she was lost in her own thoughts.

Her mind drifted back to the summer of 1991. They were turning twenty and had decided to celebrate with a two-week road trip. They were on the cusp of their adult lives and naïve enough to think everything would turn out roses. She took a deep breath, feeling the familiar bitterness start to constrict her chest. Wishes had come true for Sally and close for the others. Her? Not so much.

She flashed back to their last night in Portland, hiking into Forest Park at night to bury their time capsule. Rain like this one had started ten minutes into their hike. Hannah scoffed, thinking of each young and hopeful face caught in the glaring beams of light, casting a wish into the night each of them sincerely thought would come true. What fools they had been! They had written out their dreams of Happily Ever After as though they stood a chance. Instead, life had knocked the shit out of them. Some more than others.

Hannah still couldn't believe she'd agreed to meet everyone in Portland this weekend. She had been surprised when Sally called, as they hadn't talked in a few months, through no fault of Sally's. She hadn't been in a headspace to be social.

"Hannah?" Sally had asked, sounding a little nervous.

"Yeah, Sal? Hey. How are you doing? It's been a minute. I've been…distracted."

"How are you and the kids doing?"

"We're surviving the best we can."

"It must be so hard. I tried calling you on the year anniversary of…you know…" Sally hesitated.

"Of Toby sending me to the hospital and getting arrested?" Hannah offered.

"Yeah. I think about you guys all the time and hate what you've been through."

"We're used to crap over here. What can I do for you, Sally?" Hannah asked, wanting to get off the phone and into her nightly bath.

"I hate to ask this with everything that's going on, but I'd really like us to open the time capsule this month."

"Are you serious? This month? It's already the fourteenth. I have a job, Sal. Kids to take care of."

"I know. I know. I wouldn't ask if it wasn't important. Jentry and Paige have already said yes. They can do it the twenty-fourth."

Hannah took a deep breath and tried to control the tone of her voice. The last few years weren't Sally's fault. She didn't need to push more people away. She couldn't imagine being face-to-face with Paige again, but Sally sounded desperate.

"Paige and I are flying in on the twenty-first. We're going to the coast for a night first. You're welcome to join us."

"No thanks," Hannah replied, biting back the "on a cold day in hell" that wanted to come out. "I'll just meet up for the capsule."

"OK," Sally said, sounding disappointed. "Jentry said we can all stay with her. Up to you."

"Yeah, I'll reach out to her and discuss it. Maybe I'll get a place. I don't know."

"Thank you so much, Hannah. You have no idea what this means to me."

She wasn't in a good place, and reading her ridiculous rainbow and unicorn rantings from all those years ago wasn't going to help. She took a swig of her coffee, now cold, and looked at the GPS map on her dashboard. Twenty more miles.

She turned the music up, singing along to distract herself from her thoughts. She knew she was in a dark place and frankly got on her own nerves with her self-pitying moroseness. The last year had been so difficult. Running had been out of the question as her foot healed, and even now, she had pain when walking long distances. Life without her spleen meant she was at an increased risk of infection, which made her paranoid working with the public. Her doctor had her taking a low-dose antibiotic, as well as supplements, to help with immune support. She'd missed several weeks of work recovering, which meant a loss of income. She couldn't rely on child support and alimony any longer, as Toby was in jail.

More specifically, prison. His court case had dragged on and on. She lost count of how many court appearances and continuances they had to deal with until he was finally sentenced. He had been delusional and narcissistic enough, in the beginning, to try to claim self-defense because Hannah had thrown a shoe at him. He was pushing for a trial until Heather and Seth were able to get him charged with child abuse. Eight months after he was arrested, he pleaded no contest, like a coward, to felony charges of aggravated assault, child abuse, and unlawful entry. He was sentenced to five years in prison.

Tandie and Tyson were struggling emotionally from all they had been through the last year. Tandie tried too hard to be the caretaker of her mother, while Ty sunk into a depression. It was more than Hannah could handle some days. She was grateful she had Heather and Seth to shoulder the burden. She felt a constant bitterness in her chest, angry at the hand she had been dealt. She felt like a fool for thinking life would suddenly be roses after her divorce. Now she was strapped for cash, struggling to make ends meet, dealing with heartbroken children, and waking up every night in a panic, thinking Toby was in her room.

As she crossed the Broadway Bridge and turned onto Naito Parkway in Downtown Portland, she took a deep breath, rolled her shoulders, and popped her neck. Maybe this could be a new beginning. Maybe being reunited with her friends and going through this damn time capsule would be the jumpstart she needed to get her life back on track. Maybe it wasn't too late for her to have Happily Ever After.

"Who the hell are you kidding, Han? Your shot is over," she said to herself as she pulled into the parking lot at Waterfront Pearl.

Hannah took the elevator up to the penthouse with an anxious knot in her stomach. She had been pushing her friends away for the last year. Seeing their happy lives on Instagram, while hers was harder than ever, was too much to take. A post of Sally's a few months ago with all of them at Bear Lake pushed her over the edge. She unfollowed each of them and deleted her social media.

Jentry and Sally tried to call and text, and if she replied, it was short. She didn't think she could ever forgive Paige for not reaching out when she was in the hospital. Their lives had gone on without her, and she was heartbroken.

She squared her shoulders as she walked down the hall, ran her fingers through her short hair, and knocked on the door. She quickly applied some lip balm and smoothed her shirt.

"I was hoping it was you," Jentry smiled as she opened the door. The women hugged. "I'm so glad you're going to stay here. I've missed your visits. I've got a room ready for you, Love. Can I help with your bags?"

"This is it. I packed light."

"The others are on the patio. Donovan picked up some sushi for us and then retreated to his office. Are you hungry?"

"I've only had coffee and a KitKat since lunch. I'm very hungry. And thirsty for an adult beverage. Is that allowed around Sister Pennington? I have something red in my car," Hannah asked sarcastically.

"Anything you want is allowed in my home, Love. I would just caution you against poking the bear on the first night." Jentry pointed down the hall. "You're in the room you always sleep in. They're across the hall. Wash up and meet us on the patio."

"Thanks, Jen." Hannah smiled and then slipped into the bathroom to freshen up. Although it was late June, the evening air was brisk. She put on her favorite hoodie and some fuzzy socks and headed to the living room. She could hear the laughter wafting in from the patio before she turned the corner and saw everyone. The lights of the city danced off the Willamette River, and music could be heard from the patio below them.

She took a deep breath. "Hey," Hannah said softly as she stepped outside.

Sally shot out of her chair and raced over to her sister-in-law, wrapping her arms around her. "I'm so glad you came, Hannah. Truly. Gosh. It feels like I haven't seen you in forever."

"You haven't," Hannah half smiled.

"You cut your hair," Sally reached up and touched Hannah's short bob.

Hannah ran her fingers through her blonde curls. "Emotional breakdown moment. But it's grown on me."

"I like it," Paige said from across the table.

Hannah nodded towards her but didn't say anything.

"Eat! Eat!" Jentry ordered. "There are plenty of rolls. Wasabi and soy sauce are here," she motioned to the center of the table, "and soda is in the fridge."

Hannah grabbed a Fresca out of Jentry's perfectly ordered fridge and put a few sushi slices on a plate.

"How was the drive?" Sally asked.

"Good. It took me under three hours with traffic. But it gave me time to think. And cry."

"That's good," Sally responded awkwardly.

The conversation between the others picked right back up. Before long they were laughing again, sharing stories about husbands, children, and grandchildren. Hannah tried to covertly study them. Jentry was as stunning as ever, her dark hair still worn long and in a sleek ponytail. She was dressed smartly, and it was obvious she inhabited a very different world than Hannah. Paige was wearing her platinum hair off the shoulders with bangs. Hannah wondered when she had changed her hairstyle. She could see faint smile lines at the corners of her mouth and eyes. Paige's eyes sparkled as much as they ever had. Sally had let her brown hair go silver when the first strands started appearing several years ago. She wore it to her shoulders, with some curls in it. Hannah noticed that Sally had lost some weight since she last saw her and noticed a hint of dark circles under her eyes.

"Would that be alright, Hannah?"

Hearing her name, she returned to the conversation. "What's that?"

It was Paige who had spoken. "Would it be alright if you and I talk?"

All three of them were looking at her. "Did I seriously come here for an ambush? An intervention? What are we calling this?" Hannah asked, temper rising.

"It's not like that, Hannah. I promise. Paige was hoping to talk to you before we do the capsule," Sally said, patting Hannah on the hand like a child.

"Oh, we need kumbaya feelings tomorrow. I see. So, Paige and I have to, what, work through years of issues? In a night?" Hannah took a breath. "Look. I'm sorry. I don't want to be like this. I kind of hate who I am right now, but it has been a year of hell for me and my family, and I'm not in a great place. I don't know if I'm ready to hash things out with you, Paige. You said some horrible things to me about leaving the church. Saying you lost all respect for me and calling me a poisoned puppy dog was really low. But worse, Paige, worse, you took your friendship away when I needed it the most." Hannah wiped a tear from her face. "I needed you. The last year has been…there aren't even words for how awful it's been," she whispered.

"Look, Han," Paige tried to interrupt.

"I needed you!" Hannah screamed. "One thing after another was going down in my life, and I was drowning. You were too self-righteous and high and mighty to care."

"I was too self-righteous?" Paige gaped. "You're kidding, right? You left the church and started acting like you were the only one with any kind of common sense and the rest of us are a bunch of duped idiots. You refer to the church as a cult."

"Have you looked up the definition of a cult?" Hannah asked sarcastically.

"Real funny. This is exactly what I am talking about. You're a hypocrite. You want us to accept your new beliefs or non-beliefs, or whatever, but you look down your nose at us."

"No, I don't. I hate your church, but I don't hate my Mormon family and friends. You've been programmed to believe a certain thing, like people all over the world in a thousand other religions, and you're doing your best to live what you believe. I don't hate you for that. Nor do I think I'm better than you. In the beginning? Sure. I thought I needed to save all the Mormons from hell. Now I don't believe in hell, so I don't really care. But you don't know that because you haven't asked. You haven't reached out at all. About anything." Her voice caught, and a tear escaped.

Paige was silent for a few minutes. "Do you remember being on the phone with me the night Evan died?" she asked quietly.

"Of course I do."

"In those first few weeks after his death, I clung to my belief in this church. In the Restored Gospel of Jesus Christ. I clung to priesthood blessings and promises. I clung to my temple marriage. I have raised my twins on the belief they will get to meet their dad someday, and the girls will be reunited with their mother. So, how do you think I feel when you mock my beliefs? When you suggest my life is a lie?"

Hannah continued to cry, staring at the ground now. "Paige I never said anything unkind about your church to you. To any of you."

"No, not to our faces. But it was all over your social media. Little digs. It was obvious what you were saying with your little quotes and anti-religion innuendos."

Hannah looked up, eyes wide. "I'm not allowed an opinion? I didn't personally attack anyone, but you and other family members have treated me and my kids like pariahs. The proverbial Black Sheep. I'm in therapy once a week trying to deal with how abandoned I feel by half my family and friends because I can think for myself, to say nothing of the therapy needed to deal with the Toby situation."

"There it is." Paige pointed at Hannah, "You can think for yourself, implying we can't."

"Fine. Because I think differently than the rest of you guys."

"This does not feel productive," Sally interrupted.

"I think the time for productivity passed years ago," Jentry interjected calmly. "Still, we have got to hash this out. Our friendships and love for each other have gotten us through so much, Loves. Evan's death. My infertility. Hannah's divorces. Her…life." Jentry looked at Hannah apologetically and received a grin in return. "There's more coming. Don't think there isn't."

"I can't take anymore. Truly. Full up on hardships," Hannah laughed, almost maniacally.

"Could you take feeling not so alone?" Jentry asked.

"Always."

Jentry turned to Paige and Sally. "I'm also no longer going to church."

"Since when?" asked Sally.

"Oh, I don't know, since I moved back to Portland after you all got married? I had doubts, but I wanted to believe, I think. But I couldn't make the pieces fit anymore. I wasn't living as an active member when I met Donovan, and it was easy to adapt to his lifestyle. When Hannah left, I read some of the things she had and came to the same conclusions she did."

"Why wouldn't you tell us?" Paige asked.

"Honestly, there were times I suspected you all knew. Times I thought about sharing, but it never felt right. For so long, I didn't know what I believed exactly, so why have a conversation about it? Then, once I officially disconnected from the church, I had seen what happened with you and

Hannah, and I didn't want that to happen to any more of us."

"You didn't trust me?" Paige asked incredulously.

"Doesn't mean I didn't love you deeply. If anything, it meant I loved you too much to risk losing you. So, I kept it to myself. It was much easier living here."

"So, you went through this alone?" Sally asked.

"I wasn't alone. I had Donovan. And I was never in long enough for it to devastate me the way it did Hannah."

"Jentry hid who she was because she couldn't trust my reaction?" Paige shook her head, almost talking to herself. "Wow. Talk about a wakeup call." Paige paused for a few moments. "Hannah, I'm sorry. I took it personally when you left. It threatened my worldview. I've always trusted your gut instincts, and I didn't want this one to be right. So, I pushed you away. I said horrible things. And you're right. You've been to hell and back, and where was I? Nursing my wounds, instead of treating yours." Paige put her face in her hands and cried. "I am truly sorry, and I hope you can forgive me."

"Paige, I've missed you, damnit. I hated that I missed you. I laid in the hospital crying because I hadn't heard from you. It hurt so bad. All because of some dumb church. We lost four years." Hannah walked around the table as Paige stood up from her chair. The two cousins threw their arms around each other. "I've missed you so much. I was too mad and proud to reach out first. Gosh. Why do we keep doing this? I was such a bitch."

"At least you can admit it," Paige laughed, squeezing Hannah tighter, who laughed as well.

"I've missed all of you so much. I was in such a dark place, and I retreated when I needed you guys most. I hope you can forgive me."

"And Jen," Paige said, reaching over and taking Jentry's hand. "I am so sorry I was ever the kind of person who made you think you had to hide something about yourself. Forgive me?"

"Always, Loves." Jentry joined Hannah and Paige in a group hug.

"Now I feel left out," said Sally, standing and joining them.

The four friends hugged and cried and laughed.

"There, Sally, did you get your kumbaya moment?" Jentry asked.

"Well, we didn't sing. Do we need to sing to make it official?" Hannah asked, making her way back to her seat while humming the song.

"This is a good start," Sally said. "It was so important to me that we all reconcile and remember the love we had for each other when we buried that box almost thirty years ago. Those girls were going to be together through thick and thin. I'm sorry we ever got off track, and for anything I may have said to cause any of you pain. Ever! But I need those girls from 1991. I need the women you have become and the strength you've built to get you through your trials. I need you now more than ever. That's why I needed us to come back with such little notice."

Paige took Sally's trembling hand. "Sally, what's going on?"

Sally smiled at her friends as she squared her shoulders. "I have stage-four breast cancer."

***

The women had moved inside and were seated around Jentry's living room. Sally asked for a blanket and settled into the comfortable sectional. Concern and worry were etched on each woman's face.

"As you know, my mom died of breast cancer in 2005. She was sixty-one. She got behind on her mammograms and didn't go in until she noticed a lesion on the side of

478

her breast. It took her so fast. Five months from diagnosis to death. I've tried to be very diligent. I missed one mammogram because I was distracted with Sariah coming home from her mission, and then delayed again when she got married last fall, and those might have been the ones to save me." Sally shook her head, looking into her glass of water.

"I had been feeling very tired and had body aches. I thought it was perimenopause. I finally went in for my mammogram and my doctor called me a few days later. He explained I would need to meet with an oncologist and got us in right away."

"Oh, Sally," Hannah whispered. "Those words must have been so scary. When did you find all of this out?"

"Around Mother's Day. Sam and I met with Dr. Duke, an oncologist at Logan Regional. She told us it had metastasized and gave me anywhere from six months to a year to live, with heavy treatment. I wanted to get all the information I could before I told you. And I wanted Hannah and Paige on speaking terms," Sally said as she tucked her silver hair behind her ears. "I told Sam I had to dig up the time capsule. That summer was everything to me, and I couldn't die without going back into Forest Park with my best friends."

"Have you told the girls?" Jentry asked.

"Last week. It was awful. Salena laid her head in my lap and sobbed. Sariah is four months pregnant and worries I won't be here for the baby. Sabrina and Sadie were silent. Just stunned. Telling the girls was worse than learning I was dying."

"Sally! Don't say that!" Paige said with alarm. "You don't know the outcome for sure. You've got to think positively."

Sally grabbed Paige's hand and laid her head on her shoulder. She smiled across the room at Hannah and Jentry. "I am dying. But not tonight. Not before we open our time capsule."

"When will you start treatment, and how can we best support you, Sally?" Jentry asked, leaning forward.

Sally let out a big sigh. "We're not going to attempt treatment. We're working with my health team to manage my pain and make me as comfortable as possible."

"What?!" Hannah almost yelled. "What are you talking about?"

"I saw what treatment did to my mother. She whittled away. The treatment bought her a little more time, very little, but it also stole her quality of life. That's not how I want to spend my remaining time on this earth. Sam and I talked about this long before I got sick. We knew if I ever got terminal breast cancer, I wouldn't follow my mother's route as long as the girls were older. Salena turned sixteen last month. I hate to leave her so young. I hate to leave all of them, but I don't want them to see me waste away like my mother did, only to buy a few more months."

"But still," Hannah said, her chin quivering. "They need their mother as long as possible. They love you so much."

"They do," Sally smiled softly. "But they have so many people in their lives who can step into a motherly role for me. Carrie, my brothers' wives, but most importantly, the three of you. You know you're their favorite Aunties. That is how you can support me. Love my girls. Look after them." Sally's voice broke. "Love my grandchildren."

Hannah and Jentry moved across the room to sit at Sally's feet. Hannah placed her head in Sally's lap and wept.

"How is Sam? He must be devastated. My poor brother. He's so in love with you, Sally. I don't know how he'll function."

"I was a little surprised he let me come here, to be honest," Sally said. "He's hardly let me out of his sight. We told Jen ahead of time. I needed her to understand why we all had to come up. She promised him she'd look out for me."

"Always," Jentry replied, patting Sally's leg. "What happens next?"

"We're going to take the family on a cruise to Greece. I've always wanted to see the Mediterranean, and what better way to convalesce? Sariah isn't due until winter and cleared it with her doctor. Everyone has arranged time off from work or school, like champs. My sweet son-in-law has said he'll do whatever is needed to make sure Sariah is with her sisters and me as much as possible over the next few months. Or weeks. We don't really know how long I'll live without chemo."

"When is the cruise?" Jentry asked.

"The first week of July."

"Sounds lovely, Sal. Plan on me being in Cache Valley when you get back for as long as you need."

"I can't ask that of you, Jen," Sally said, wiping another tear from her face.

"You didn't, Love. But you're not just one of my best friends, Sally. You're like a sister to me. I'll be there. For however long you need."

"My heart is so full, my dear, dear friends. Thank you for giving me this weekend."

June 24, 2018

Hannah awoke at six-thirty in the morning, and after some light stretching, she put some music on her phone and started her Tai Chi practice. Her therapist had recommended that she meditate daily to calm her mind, but she struggled to keep focused. With Tai Chi, her focus on breathing and movements kept her mind clear, allowing her a blissful, quiet start to each day.

She heard a light knock on the door and, without pausing, called for the person to enter.

Paige stuck her head in the room. "What's this?" she asked, shutting the door behind her.

Without turning around or stopping her movements, Hannah answered, "My attempt at Qigong. I'm not well versed in it, but I enjoy what I'm able to do. Calms my mind." Hannah stepped back into a lunge position, bringing her arms together at her feet and then raising them up to the sky before circling back down to her feet.

"What music is this? It sounds slightly familiar."

"It's the soundtrack to Avatar: The Last Airbender. The cartoon the kids were all into forever ago. Spotify has everything."

"Oh my gosh! The twins loved that show," Paige said as Hannah moved into another position. "Hey, when you're done, could we maybe go for a walk?"

Hannah finally turned and looked at her. "Give me five minutes."

"Thanks, Han."

Paige was admiring a watercolor painting of Multnomah Falls when Hannah came around the corner a few minutes later.

"You were fast. Thanks." They rode down the elevator, out the front doors, and hopped onto the Willamette River Trail. Hannah's phone said it was already sixty degrees. Perfect temperature for a morning walk.

"I did a lot of thinking last night," Paige began, jumping right into it. "I was surprised when Jentry said she didn't tell us about leaving the church because she didn't trust my reaction. I mean, it's just not how I saw myself, you know? I thought back to our road trip and the night Jentry told us about her baby. She could trust me then. She could confide in me then. You all could. When did I become someone who couldn't be trusted? Who put her beliefs above her friendships? I mean, I really believe what I believe, Hannah. I believe in the Restored Gospel and everything it entails. But when did I become so 'holier than thou'?"

Hannah sighed. "Is this rhetorical? Or are you just talking out loud?"

"No, sincerely. What happened to me? What happened to us? We were there for each other through so much. Evan's death. Raising the boys alone for so long. Falling in love with Drake. And your stuff! A hard first marriage, an even harder second marriage. When did things change?"

"When I left the church. You said it last night. It threatened your worldview. You want to believe the church is true because you want to believe you'll see Evan again, that the boys will see him. I get it."

"But I didn't need to let it come between us. Hate the sin, love the sinner kind of thing."

"OK, first," Hannah interrupted. "That is a super offensive, condescending phrase. Think it all you want, but please never say it out loud again. I mean, what if I said hate Mormonism, love the Mormons? You wouldn't like it. Second, you weren't the only one who let it come between us. I wasn't easy. I thought a lot about the last few years all night too. I've felt superior, and I've assumed the worst in a lot of interactions. So much was going wrong in my life, and I think rather than looking inward, I looked for people to blame. Like I said, I'm in therapy and I am trying to work on it. Though, I have bigger concerns after the last year. Way harder things are going on in my life. Still. I'm working on letting shit go and trying to show up in relationships how I want to, regardless of past hurts."

Paige stopped and grabbed Hannah's hands. "I'm sick we ever fell out, Han. Now, with Sally, I think about all the time we've all lost and how much more we're going to lose, and I feel like I could start crying and never stop."

"We can start fresh. A do-over. I ask my kids for those all of the time. I tell them, 'This isn't the kind of mom I want to be. Let me do that over.' We can do the same thing." Hannah squeezed Paige's hands. "Paige, will you please allow me a do-over. This isn't the kind of cousin and friend I want to be."

Paige threw her arms around Hannah and held her tight. "Only if we both get one," she whispered through tears.

Hannah showered after the walk with Paige and then decided to run out for a coffee. She enjoyed a hot coffee no matter the time of year. She had discovered coffee and pastries at Lovejoy Bakers two years ago, and decided to go for another short walk, this time strolling more slowly and taking in the sights. She stepped into the busy coffee shop and got in line.

"Hi," Hannah said distractedly when she got to the counter. "Large lavender white mocha and a croissant."

"Name?" the young barista asked.

"Hannah." She dug out her wallet, paid for her drink and dropped a dollar in the tip jar before finding an empty table by the window. She watched the clouds float by and thought of Sally and Sam, and her nieces. They were about to lose the greatest woman in the world, and her heart hurt thinking of their pain.

She heard one of the baristas call out a few names, including hers, bringing her back to the present. She walked to the counter and reached for a cup at the same time as the man in front of her.

"Whoops," she said with a laugh. "Is that one mine or yours?" she asked, looking to see what name was written on the side of the paper cup.

"If your name is Morgan too, we're in trouble," said a deep voice from her past.

Hannah looked up, and her jaw dropped. "Morgan?"

The man looked at her, and the light of recognition lit up his eyes in seconds. "Hannah Limbrey of Utah?" he said with a deep laugh.

"Wow." Hannah shook her head, "Of all the coffee shops in all the world."

"Do you have a table? Do you have time for a visit?"

Hannah grabbed her drink, nodded to where her croissant was, and walked in that direction in a daze. What were the odds? She was glad she had fixed her hair and put some mascara on before leaving the house.

Morgan West sat down across from Hannah with a huge smile on his face. "So, your ankle healed?"

"It did." She didn't mention the break she had suffered last summer. "And you finished your ride?"

"We did. It was a great time. We haven't been able to keep it up every year with age and families, but we get together for some type of ride regularly."

"That's great. Do you live around here?"

"I listed my house last week. I work at Legacy Good Samaritan up the hill, but I'm transferring to Virginia Mason in Seattle next month. Are you still in Utah? On another road trip?"

"I can't believe you remember so much," Hannah laughed. "No, I'm in Puyallup, Washington. Not quite on a road trip. Not like the last one. I've come down for the weekend. All of us are here, actually. The others are back at Jentry's. I just ran out for coffee."

"I sure enjoyed meeting you and your friends. Would you believe your phone number got destroyed in the rain? I truly did mean to call," Morgan said, looking at Hannah seriously.

"I would have liked that. Who knows what could have come of it?" Hannah said. "I'm sure you met someone and lived a wonderful life, so perhaps it was meant to be."

"I was married almost twenty years. We had two children, who I think are rock stars. We grew apart and divorced six years ago. We've been able to stay friendly for the kids' sake."

"Impressive. I'm always amazed by people who can have positive divorces. I have two under my belt, and I don't have the kindest feelings about either ex."

"I'm sorry to hear that, Hannah. Sort of," Morgan winked.

Hannah took a sip of her coffee to try to hide her blush.

"I like to visit Pike Place every once in a while. Who knows. Maybe in another 30 years, we'll bump into each other again. Better odds if we're both going to be in Washington."

"Oh no, no. Nay, nay. That won't work at all. This is like catching lightening in a bottle twice. Happening across a beautiful and beguiling woman like you? I can't wait another thirty years. Have dinner with me. My shift ends at nine o'clock tonight. I know it's late, but I think it will be enjoyable."

"Morgan, that is the most lovely offer. Truly," Hannah hesitated.

"But?"

"Last night, we learned Sally has stage-four breast cancer. We're up here to open this time capsule we buried in Forest Park thirty years ago. I don't know if I dare leave my friends right now."

"I'm so sorry about Sally. Such a difficult diagnosis."

Morgan reached over and placed his hand on top of Hannah's. "I understand if tonight is not the night. Would you be willing to give me your number again? This time, I'll put it somewhere safe," he said, patting the cell phone in his breast pocket.

"Absolutely."

***

"You are not going to believe what just happened!" Hannah screamed as she walked back into Jentry's. She found her friends on the back deck enjoying a late brunch.

"You won the lottery?" Paige asked.

"Better!"

"Whoa. Better than the lottery? Is this our Hannah?" Paige pinched Hannah's arm.

"Ow! Yes, better!"

"Well, sit down, Love, and tell us."

"I ran down to Lovejoy Bakers, and I ran into Morgan! Sprained ankle, Morgan. Gorgeous chocolate brown, green-eyed Morgan. Morgan, who is as fine and fit now as he was thirty years ago," Hannah said excitedly.

"That's incredible. I knew it wasn't too late for you to find happiness," Sally said, as though she had orchestrated the whole thing.

"He asked me out tonight. Wanted to take me to a late dinner when he gets off work, but I told him we're here for Sal."

"What?" Sally said indignantly. "Don't you dare miss this opportunity because of me! Please say you got his number."

"I did," Hannah said, popping a grape in her mouth.

"Call him back right now and tell him you'll meet him for dinner. And then I want every detail."

"You better kiss on the first date, so Sally has something to look forward to," Paige teased.

A huge grin spread across Hannah's face. She bit her lip as she pictured meeting Morgan for dinner. She was surprised to find her stomach filled with butterflies. "Okay, okay," she said, picking up her phone.

It rang three times before he answered. Jentry, Paige, and Sally watched her expectantly.

"Morgan? It's Hannah. Can I say yes to dinner after all?"

***

The walk to the hidden time capsule proved too tiring for Sally. The women were quick to insist she rest, so she and Hannah returned to the car while Jentry and Paige dug up the plastic box and brought it back. Jentry pulled a blanket out from the trunk and laid it on the soft ground. They sat down around the box while Jentry pried the lid off.

"I was nervous to do this," piped up Hannah. "On the drive over, I kept thinking about the last few decades of my life and how disappointing they've been. I'm nervous to read what I wrote and be faced with how different things turned out."

"I don't think anyone is living the exact life they imagined. Things go off course for everyone, but you see what you focus on, that's for sure," Paige said.

"Well, my next therapy appointment will be much more about focusing on the good and leaving the past in the past. Maybe by sixty, I can figure out how to do it," Hannah laughed, then abruptly stopped.

"It's okay," Sally said, smiling at Hannah. "You're allowed to talk about your future. In fact, it makes me happy to see you contemplating the possibility of a happy one. It's never too late for a happy ending."

"OK," Jentry interrupted. "Let's read what we wrote." Jentry pulled a rusted can of Diet Coke and dried-up watercolors from the container, along with a yellowed envelope. She carefully pulled the paper out and read it."

"Future Jentry,

I've been sitting here for thirty minutes trying to think about what I predict for my future. I'm certain of two things I really want. To own an art gallery, and to be best friends with these girls forever.

I might have to open an art studio in Utah so I can stay close to my friends. However, being back in my city makes me homesick. Perhaps I'll convince them to move here.

I'm not sure I see myself married. If I do decide to tie the knot, may he be equal to the task! He must adore my friends, like Diet Coke, read, and have an accent. And love art.

I hope future Jentry is still taking road trips with her friends every July."

"Does Donovan adore us? Or tolerate us?" Hannah asked, teasingly.

"We haven't had a trip every year, but we've come close," Paige said. "Dixon Designs is amazing, and you are such a talented artist. You called it, Jentry. Nice."

"Do you know what strikes me?" Jentry asked. "I didn't seem to want to be a mother when I wrote this. Then, when I was ready for children, my body couldn't make them."

Sally patted Jentry on the back. "No one could have been a better Auntie than you. You've been amazing to all of our children."

"Definitely the cool aunt," Hannah added.

"And now you have Elodie and Gianna in your life. It happened late but probably made you appreciate it all the more," said Paige.

"It did. The biggest plot twist of my life was being reunited with her, and I'll love David and Sofia forever for supporting it."

"Okay, my turn." Paige leaned over the box and pulled out a canister of film and her letter. "Who would have predicted, for the most part, that camera film would become obsolete? Alright. What did young Paige have to say?"

"Predictions for my future…

100% I'm going to have the most wonderful life with my amazing husband, Evan, and live happily ever after! We'll have a lovely home and lovely babies. Probably four. We'll live in Mesa, where it's WARM! Though I haven't broken it to the girls yet. No more snow for me!

I know most women stay home and raise the babies. I'm fine with that, but I'm also fine working once my children are in school. So, I predict I'll have a little part-time job as a photographer. I'm happy to get my degree in History, but let's be real, I'll likely never use it.

Are my predictions and future too ordinary? Should I have bigger goals? Oh well. I'm sure whatever my future holds will be amazing, and I'll love it. As long as Evan is by my side, everything will be perfect. We'll make goals together and accomplish them one by one.

I also predict that Hannah, Jentry, and Sally will be in my life forever. I love them so!"

Paige wiped a tear from her cheek. "Oh, Evan," she sighed. "How I loved him. And I love Drake just as much, which I would never have thought possible. What a loss Evan's death was. My degree came in useful as it supported the boys and me until I remarried. It's funny, thinking Drake and I grew up together and had no romantic feelings. Ever. And then one day, he was my best friend and one of the great loves of my life."

"You're very lucky," Hannah said. "To have known such a wonderful love twice. To be loved and adored. Treated like a queen by two men. Don't take it for granted, okay? I had wanted true love so desperately and instead had my heart broken by each husband. At least Luke disappeared from our lives. Toby...well, there aren't words for the damage he's caused."

"It's not too late for you to be loved like that, Hannah," Sally smiled. "You do have a hot date tonight," she said in a sing-song voice.

"Sally Jane! How the tables have turned. I remember when it was me teasing you about Sam at City of Rocks," Hannah said. "Okay, let's get this over with." Hannah pulled out the headband and Nike key chain she had placed inside the box all those decades ago and gave a rueful laugh. "Well, running is something I didn't keep up on."

"You were trying again until your foot was broken," Sally said consolingly.

"Here goes nothing," Hannah said, opening her letter.

"Hannah Limbrey Life Goals!

- *Run a marathon each year.*
- *Graduate in English and write the Great American Novel.*
- *Travel. Life of Leisure.*
- *Learn how to cook and quilt like Grandma Mary.*
- *Be worthy to marry in the Temple.*

- *Have a Christ-centered family.*
- *Read the Book of Mormon cover to cover every year.*
- *Always and no matter what be best friends with Jentry, Paige, and Sally.*
- *We all need to live on the same street. For real!"*

Hannah covered her face with her hands and cried. "I haven't done any of them," she wailed from beneath her hands. "I can't run anymore. I didn't graduate. I never wrote a book. Life of leisure? Ha! What a joke. I don't cook like Grandma, and I've never made a quilt. I wasn't temple-worthy either time! All the church stuff. But worst of all," she said, coming up for air, "Worst of all, I didn't stay best friends with all of you no matter what." Hannah broke into contagious sobbing, and soon, all of the women were crying.

"Listen to me," Sally said sternly. "It is not too late for you. Screw this list. Make a new one."

Hannah's eyes went wide, and she started laughing. "Did my little Turtle just say screw?"

Paige and Jentry laughed as well.

"I did," Sally smiled. "Make a new list, Hannah. You have so much time left. My time is almost up. Yours isn't. Reclaim your life, Han. Please. For me. For me, go out and make these last decades the best of your life. Do all the living I can't. All of you."

The tears returned. Hannah crawled across the blanket to hug her sister-in-law and friend. "I will, Sally. I'll do better. I'll write a new list right away. I promise."

"I believe in your future happiness, Hannah. I need you to believe in it, too," Sally said and then kissed Hannah on her forehead.

"Alright, pass the bucket over here." Sally lifted out the little onesie and smiled. "It's so tiny! Oh, my goodness. I love baby clothes. Alright, what did Sally have to say?" She opened her letter.

"Dear Future Sally,

Hello from 1991. Jentry is having us write down predictions for our future and save it in a time capsule.

I don't know if this is a prediction as much as a great hope, but I want Sam Limbrey to love me. It probably seems foolish to think it could ever be more than pen pals. But he sent me this letter last week, which gave me hope. He's kind, and funny, and has such a great testimony. He would make such a wonderful husband. Plus, Hannah would be my sister!

I want to be a wife and mother. I love geology and enjoy studying and keeping my mind sharp, but at the end of the day, I want a house full of children. I grew up with six siblings. My mother was the best homemaker. We had a gospel-centered home, and she and my father taught us how to work hard and love hard. That's what I want. A life like I had. Simple. Family Centered. Christ Centered. With lots and lots of children. At least seven. I wish I still had the list of 100 names I made at 13. I can't remember them all. I do know I would want meaningful names. I guess we'll see how many of these make it...Asher, Benjamin, Caleb, Daniel, Ezra, Isaac, and Jeremiah. Or Sariah, Abigail, Bethany, Dinah, Esther, Leah, and Mary.

I want to know the Gospel inside and out so I can teach it to my children. It's everything to me! I love belonging to God's true church! I can't wait to raise up a righteous family and be with them forever.

I hope it's with Sam. But if it's with someone else, I'm sure they'll be wonderful.

And I want these friends in my life forever. Meeting them has been one of the greatest blessings of my life. I love them with all my heart."

The girls cheered.

"Sally got her wish almost exactly," Jentry said, smiling.

"I did. I truly did. Just not for as long as I had hoped." Sally tucked her hair behind her ears and looked at each of her friends. "Life is so precious. Whether your life is everything you ever wanted or filled with disappointments and regrets. Cherish every day, my sweet friends. The mundane. The laundry. The errands. The extra weight. The wrinkles," she laughed. "Make the most of every moment. I have something for each of you. Jen, will you grab those items from the car?"

Jentry stood up and walked back to her Tesla, opening the trunk. She pulled out three gallon-sized glass jars, each with a colored ribbon around the top.

"What are these?" Hannah asked, examining her jar.

"These are Joy Jars," Sally said with a smile. "Every night, I want you to write down something wonderful from each day before you go to bed. On my birthday each year, I want you to read all your notes for the year. Think of me as you celebrate the little successes of your lives and know I'm cheering you on from the other side."

"This is a beautiful idea, Sal. Thank you," Paige said almost reverently.

"Promise me. It's my dying wish," Sally said solemnly.

"We promise," Hannah, Jentry, and Paige said simultaneously.

"There is one other thing. I have a letter for each of you. Read it after I'm gone." Sally opened the purse next to her and took out three pink envelopes. "I had this realization over the last few weeks. I have spent my whole life imagining it's the Savior who has been with me each day, who has helped me through trials, encouraged me when low, picked up the slack, and He has, for sure. However, when I looked back at the last thirty years, the biggest constant was you three women. Husbands and religious beliefs are great," Sally smiled, wiping a tear, "but it's our girlfriends who do the heavy lifting. Not a day has gone by since 1989 that I have not talked to at least one of you. You have been there at all of the most important times of my life. I hope you feel the same about me. I hope when you look back, you see all of us helping you too."

Sally saw Hannah and Paige give each other a meaningful look. "If there have been slip-ups and missed opportunities, it's okay. The majority of our lives have been intertwined with love, happiness, and support. You three..." Sally's voice caught, and she paused before continuing. "You three have been my dearest friends, and it's been an honor to walk through life with you. Take good care of each other when I'm gone."

EPILOGUE

Wisps of clouds covered the sky, and a warm breeze blew from the south. Seagulls could be heard squawking overhead as the waves crashed against the shore. The smell of salt water filled the air.

Hannah, Jentry, and Paige sat on a blanket outside the caves at Hug Point. After Sally's funeral, they had committed to meeting at the coast every summer on her birthday to read from their Joy Jars and remember their friend.

"It's strange not having her here," Jentry said, staring at the ocean.

"She's here," Hannah answered. "I may not believe in a lot or even know what I believe. But I believe with all my heart Sally Jane is standing right over there with her feet in the water, watching us with a big smile on her face." Hannah pictured Sally as she looked back in 1991, the night Sam met them on the beach. Sally never did comprehend how beautiful she was.

"Are we reading all of these notes to each other?" Paige asked, eyeing their jars.

"Why not, Loves? We've got all day." Jentry reached into her jar and pulled out a random note. "Witnessed Sariah give birth to baby Sally-Grace."

"I'll never forget the look on Sam's face when he heard her name for the first time. I'm so sad Sally didn't get to meet her granddaughter," Hannah said.

"I felt like that when Evan died, so sad he would miss watching the boys grow. But like I did, her girls will tell their babies so many stories about Grammy Sally. She'll be a beloved legend to them in no time." Paige reached into her jar. "Hiked Naomi Peak with Hannah. That hike was so hard. I had no idea it was so steep. Was it that steep when we were younger?"

"It was a killer. I hated watching all those young people run up and down it like it was nothing." Hannah pulled out a piece of paper and unrolled it. "I think Sally made me pick this one," she laughed. "Kissed Morgan."

They took turns reading from their jars until the sun started to make its descent over the Pacific Ocean. They reminisced on times spent with Sally and the different ways she had made them feel loved over the years.

"Remember how timid Sally was around me in the beginning?" Jentry asked, smiling at the memory. "I miss her so much it hurts."

"It does, it's fresh. She's almost been gone a year," Paige said. "Right now, thinking of her brings tears and a pain in the chest. Someday, I promise you, we'll be able to think about Sally and all the good times, and the pain will turn into peace."

"Any regrets on our tattoos, Paige?" Hannah asked, looking at the matching ink they had on their wrists.

"I bet you thought Sally and I wouldn't go through with it."

"Nothing shocked me more, Love," said Jentry, running a finger over the cursive letters.

Hannah had the idea the morning after they opened the time capsule. She gave Sally a piece of paper and told her what to write. They took it into a tattoo parlor, and by lunch, each of them had the same tattoo, in Sally's handwriting, on their left wrists.

"Sam about killed me, but I stand by it, and so did Sal," Hannah said with a grin.

"It was a perfect end to a difficult and beautiful weekend. A great way to honor our friendship and what we've been through together," said Paige, choking up.

Jentry traced the letters on her wrist in Sally's beautiful penmanship.

She smiled and wiped a tear as she said, "Companions Forever."

AFTERWARD

They say 'write what you know.' Those that know me well will recognize large parts of my life throughout this novel. In fact, a majority of Hannah's journal entries are taken directly from my own journals.

I was in my mid-thirties when I first had the idea of writing the story of a road trip adventure for four college-aged best friends. In the original version, the novel would follow the friends through several decades and show how their religion would support them through the joys and sorrows of life. There wasn't a lot of writing time as I was raising five children, and by my mid-forties, I had not even completed Part One.

Which was a good thing, as, like Hannah, I also lost my faith in my religion in my forties. What was I going to do with this story now? With these Mormon characters? The story was ignored for a few years as I tried to figure out a workaround and went through a second divorce.

In 2020, I decided that the overarching theme would be that it is *your friends* who help you through the joys and sorrows of life. That has certainly been the case for me, especially as I started over again at age 50. I have the most amazing group of friends, local and spread across the country. I was inspired by them as I wrote of the love between Hannah, Jentry, Paige and Sally.

Writing about Mormon characters as someone who no longer believes in that faith was an interesting exercise. I wanted to be true to my experience in and out of Mormonism and reflect the earnestness of the wonderful people that I know and love. Most of my family and friends are active members of The Church of Jesus Christ of Latter-Day Saints, and I respect how hard they work to live what they believe.

I hope the chapters that deal with Hannah losing her faith do not bring anyone discomfort or offense.

At the beginning of 2024, I had written eighty pages of this story, and it had taken me fifteen years. I made a goal to complete it by the end of the year and wrote my final sentence on June 4, 2024, six months ahead of schedule. I was encouraged daily by my daughter, Rachel, also an author. The feedback from friends who read portions of the story was so helpful, and I appreciate the enthusiasm they showed for this story.

I have dropped the names of several friends and relatives throughout this book, and I hope it makes you smile when you see your name.

BOOK CLUB QUESTIONS

1.   This is a story about four best friends who met in college. Have you kept in touch with friends from high school and college? What do you most value in a friendship?

2.   Which character did you relate to the most? Whose storyline did you find the most interesting?

3.   This book weaves Hannah's journal entries throughout the story. Did you enjoy that glimpse into her life? Are you a journal keeper? Many of Hannah's journal entries came from the author's own life. Would you be willing to make your journal entries public? Why or why not?

4.   This story deals with many themes, including adoption, adultery, cancer, divorce, domestic violence, drug use, faith crisis, infertility, and death. Have any of these issues impacted you or someone you love? Did you feel like the portrayal of these issues was realistic? Why or why not?

5.   In her forties, Hannah goes through a faith crisis. This leads to alienation with Paige, and it is hinted that other family members treat her differently. Have you ever gone through a faith crisis? Did you feel like anyone in your life treated you differently? Has someone you love left your faith? How did that impact your relationship with them?

6.   Jentry kept secrets from her friends. First, she took two years to tell them about Elodie. Then, she hid that she no longer practiced Mormonism for several decades. Do you think that was dishonest? Can you have a deep, authentic relationship without telling someone everything about your life? Are there things you keep